ATTAC

Far above, in the main saloon, the regular evening dance was in full swing. The ship's orchestra crashed into silence, there was a patter of applause, and Clio Marsden, radiant belle of the voyage, led her partner out into the promenade and up to one of the observation plates.

"We can't see the Earth any more!" she exclaimed. "Which way do you turn this, Mr. Costigan?"

"Like this." Conway Costigan, the young first officer of the liner, turned the dials. "There — this plate is looking back, or down, at Tellus; this other one is looking ahead."

Earth was a brilliantly shining crescent far beneath the flying vessel. Above her, ruddy Mars and silvery Jupiter blazed in splendor against a background of utterly indescribable blackness — a background thickly besprinkled with dimensionless points of dazzling brilliance which were the stars.

"Isn't it wonderful!" breathed the girl. "Of course, I suppose that it's old stuff to you, but I — a ground-gripper, you know, and I could look at it forever, I think. That's why I want to come out here after every dance. You know, I . . ."

Her voice broke off with a strange, rasping catch, as she seized his arm in a frantic clutch and as quickly went limp. He stared at her and understood instantly the message written in her eyes — eyes now enlarged, staring hard, brilliant, and full of soul-searing terror as she slumped down, helpless but for his support. In the act of exhaling as he was, lungs almost entirely empty, yet he held his breath until he had seized the microscope from his belt and had snapped it to "Emergency."

"Control room!" he gasped. Every speaker throughout the great cruiser blared out the warning as he forced his already evacuated lungs to absolute emptiness. *"Vee-Two Gas! Get tight!"*

Also included is "Masters of Space," a second classic tale by E.E. "Doc" Smith and E. Everett Evans!

KED IN SPACE!

TRIPLANETARY

E. E. "DOC" SMITH

Includes the bonus story "Masters of Space"
by E.E. "Doc" Smith & E. Everett Evans

COSMOS BOOKS

TRIPLANETARY

Published by
Dorchester Publishing Co., Inc.
200 Madison Ave.
New York, NY 10016
in collaboration with Wildside Press LLC

ISBN-10: 0-8439-5949-5
ISBN-13: 978-0-8439-5949-9

Printed in the United States of America.

CONTENTS

TRIPLANETARY

CHAPTER I

Pirates of Space

Apparently motionless to her passengers and crew, the Interplanetary liner *Hyperion* bored serenely onward through space at normal acceleration. In the railed-off sanctum in one corner of the control room a bell tinkled, a smothered whirr was heard, and Captain Bradley frowned as he studied the brief message upon the tape of the recorder — a message flashed to his desk from the operator's panel. He beckoned, and the second officer, whose watch it now was, read aloud:

"Reports of scout patrols still negative."

"Still negative." The officer scowled. "They've already searched beyond the widest possible location of the wreckage, too. Two unexplained disappearances inside a month — first the *Dione*, then the *Rhea* — and not a plate nor a lifeboat recovered. Looks bad, sir. One might be an accident; two might possibly be a coincidence. . . ." His voice died away. What might that coincidence mean?

"But at three it would get to be a habit," the captain finished the thought. "And whatever happened, happened quick. Neither of them had time to say a word — their location recorders simply went dead. But of course they didn't have our detector screens nor our armament. According to the observatories we're in clear ether, but I wouldn't trust them from Tellus to Luna. You have given the new orders, of course?"

"Yes, sir. Detectors full out, all three courses of defensive screen on the trips, projectors manned, suits on the hooks. Every object detected in the outer space to be investigated immediately — if vessels, they are to be warned to stay beyond extreme range. Anything entering the fourth zone is to be rayed."

"Right — we are going through!"

"But no known type of vessel could have made away with them without detection," the second officer argued. "I wonder if there isn't something in those wild rumors we've been hearing lately?"

"Bah! Of course not!" snorted the captain. "Pirates in ships faster than light — fifth order rays — nullification of gravity — mass without inertia — ridiculous! Proved impossible, over and over again. No, sir, if pirates are operating in space — and it looks very much like it — they won't get far against a good big battery full of kilowatt-hours behind three courses of heavy screen, and a good solid set of multiplex rays. Properly used, they're good enough for anybody. Pirates, Neptunians, angels, or devils — in ships or on sunbeams — if they tackle the *Hyperion* we'll burn them out of the ether!"

Leaving the captain's desk, the watch officer resumed his tour of duty. The six great lookout plates into which the alert observers peered were blank, their far-flung ultra-sensitive detector screens encountering no obstacle — the ether was empty for thousands upon thousands of kilometers. The signal lamps upon the pilot's panel were dark, its warning bells were silent. A brilliant point of white in the center of the pilot's closely ruled micrometer grating, exactly upon the cross-hairs of his directors, showed that the immense vessel was precisely upon the calculated course, as laid down by the automatic integrating course-plotters. Everything was quiet and in order.

"All's well, sir," he reported briefly to Captain Bradley — but all was not well.

Danger — more serious far in that it was not external — was even then, all unsuspected, gnawing at the great ship's vitals. In a locked and shielded compartment, deep down in the interior of the liner, was the great air purifier. Now a man leaned against the primary duct — the aorta through which flowed the stream of pure air supplying the entire vessel. This man, grotesque in full panoply of space armor, leaned against the duct, and as he leaned a drill bit deeper and deeper into the steel wall of the pipe. Soon it broke through, and the slight rush of air was stopped by the insertion of a tightly fitting rubber tube. The tube terminated in a heavy rubber balloon, which surrounded a frail glass bulb. The man stood tense, one hand holding before his silica-and-steel helmeted head a large pocket chronometer, the other lightly grasping the balloon. A sneering grin was upon his face as he awaited the exact second of action — the carefully pre-determined instant when his right hand, closing, would shatter the fragile flask and force its contents into the primary air stream of the *Hyperion*!

Far above, in the main saloon, the regular evening dance was in full swing. The ship's orchestra crashed into silence, there was a patter of applause, and Clio Marsden, radiant belle of the voyage, led her partner out into the promenade and up to one of the observation plates.

"We can't see the Earth any more!" she exclaimed. "Which way do you turn this, Mr. Costigan?"

"Like this." Conway Costigan, the young first officer of the liner, turned the dials. "There — this plate is looking back, or down, at Tellus; this other one is looking ahead."

Earth was a brilliantly shining crescent far beneath the flying vessel. Above her, ruddy Mars and silvery Jupiter blazed in splendor against a background of utterly indescribable blackness — a background thickly besprinkled with dimensionless points of dazzling brilliance which were the stars.

"Isn't it wonderful!" breathed the girl. "Of course, I suppose that it's old stuff to you, but I — a ground-gripper, you know, and I could look at it forever, I think. That's why I want to come out here after every dance. You know, I . . ."

Her voice broke off with a strange, rasping catch, as she seized his arm in a frantic clutch and as quickly went limp.

He stared at her and understood instantly the message written in her eyes — eyes now enlarged, staring hard, brilliant, and full of soul-searing terror as she slumped down, helpless but for his support. In the act of exhaling as he was, lungs almost entirely empty, yet he held his breath until he had seized the microscope from his belt and had snapped it to "Emergency."

"Control room!" he gasped. Every speaker throughout the great cruiser blared out the warning as he forced his already evacuated lungs to absolute emptiness. *"Vee-Two Gas! Get tight!"*

Writhing and twisting in his fierce struggle to keep his lungs from gulping in a draft of that noxious atmosphere, and with the unconscious form of the girl draped limply over his left arm, Costigan leaped toward the portal of the rearest lifeboat. Orchestra instruments crashed to the floor and dancing couples fell and sprawled inertly while the tortured First Officer swung the door of the lifeboat open and dashed across the tiny room to the air-valves. Throwing them wide open, he put his mouth to the orifice and let his laboring lungs gasp their eager fill of the cold blast roaring from the tanks. Then, air-hunger partially assuaged, he again held his breath, broke open the emergency locker, donned one of the space-suits always kept there, and opened its valves wide in order to flush out of his uniform any lingering trace of the lethal gas.

He then leaped back to his companion. Shutting off the air, he released a stream of pure oxygen, held her face in it, and made shift to force some of it into her lungs by compressing and releasing her chest against his own body. Soon she drew a spasmodic breath, choking and coughing, and he again changed the gaseous stream to one of pure air, speaking urgently as she showed signs of returning consciousness. Now, it was Clio Marsden's life.

"Stand up!" he snapped. "Hang onto this brace and keep your face in this air-stream until I get a suit around you! Got me?"

She nodded weakly, and, assured that she could now hold herself at the valve, it was the work of only a minute to encase her in one of the protective coverings. Then, as she sat upon a bench, recovering her strength, he flipped on the lifeboat's visiphone projector and shot its invisible beam up into the control room, where he saw space-armored figures furiously busy at the panels.

"Dirty work at the cross-roads!" he blazed to his captain, man to man — formality disregarded, as it so often was in the Triplanetary service. "There's skulduggery afoot somewhere in our primary air! Maybe that's the way they got those other two ships — pirates! Might have been a timed bomb — don't see how anybody could have stowed away down there through the inspections, and nobody but Franklin can neutralize the shield of the air-room — but I'm going to look around, anyway. Then I'll join you fellows up there."

"What was it?" the shaken girl asked. "I think that I remember your saying 'Vee-Two gas.' That's forbidden! Anyway, I owe you my life, Conway, and I'll never forget it — never. Thanks — but the others — how about all the rest of us?"

"It was Vee-Two, and it is forbidden," Costigan replied grimly, eyes fast upon the flashing plate, whose point of projection was now deep in the bowels of the vessel. "The penalty for using it or having it is death on sight. Gangsters and pirates use it, since they have nothing to lose, being on the death list already. As for your life, I haven't saved it yet — you may wish I'd let it ride before we get done. The others are too far gone for oxygen — couldn't have brought even you around a few seconds later, quick as I got to you. But there's a sure antidote — we all carry it in a lock-box in our armor — and we all know how to use it, because crooks all use Vee-Two and so we're always expecting it. But since the air will be pure again in half an hour we'll be able to revive the others easily enough if we can get by with whatever is going to happen next. There's the bird that did it, right in the air-room! It's the chief engineer's suit, but that isn't Franklin that's in it. Some passenger — disguised — slugged the chief — took his suit and projectors — hole in duct — *p-s-s-t!* All washed out! Maybe that's all he was scheduled to do to us in this performance, but he'll do nothing else in this life!"

"Don't go down there!" protested the girl. "His armor is *so* much better than that emergency suit you are wearing, and he's got Mr. Franklin's Lewiston, besides!"

"Don't be an idiot!" he snapped. "We can't have a live pirate aboard — we're going to be altogether too busy with outsiders directly. Don't worry, I'm not going to give him a break. I'm taking a Standish and I'll rub him out like a blot. Stay right here until I come back after you," he commanded, and the heavy, vacuum insulated door of the lifeboat clanged shut behind him as he leaped out into the promenade.

Straight across the saloon he made his way, paying no attention to the inert forms scattered here and there. Going up to a blank wall, he manipulated an almost invisible dial set flush with its surface, swung a heavy door aside, and lifted out the Standish — a fearsome weapon. Squat, huge, and heavy, it resembled somewhat an overgrown machine rifle, but one possessing a thick, short telescope, with several opaque condensing lenses and parabolic reflectors. Laboring under the weight of the thing, he strode along corridors and clambered heavily down short stairways. Finally he came to the purifier room, and grinned savagely as he saw the greenish haze of light obscuring the door and walls — the shield was still in place; the pirate was still inside, still flooding with the terrible Vee-Two the *Hyperion's* primary air.

He set his peculiar weapon down, unfolded its three massive legs, crouched down behind it and threw in a switch. Dull red beams of frightful intensity shot from the reflectors and sparks, almost of lightning proportions, leaped from the shielding screen under their impact. Roaring and snapping, the conflict went on for seconds; then, under the superior force of the Standish, the greenish radiance gave way. Behind it the metal of the door ran the gamut of color — red, yellow, blinding whiter — then literally exploded; molten, vaporized, burned away. Through the aperture thus made Costigan could plainly see the pirate in the space-armor of the chief engineer — an armor which was proof against rifle fire and which could reflect and neutralize for some little time even the terrific beam Costigan was employing. Nor was the pirate unarmed — a vicious flare of incandescence leaped from his Lewiston, to spend its force in spitting, crackling pyrotechnics against the ether-wall of the squat and monstrous Standish. But Costigan's infernal machine did not rely only upon vibratory destruction. At almost the first flash of the pirate's weapon the officer touched a trigger; there was a double report, ear-shattering in that narrowly confined space; and the pirate's body literally flew into mist as a half-kilogram shell tore through his armor and exploded. Costigan shut off his beam, and, with not the slightest softening of one hard lineament, stared around the air-room; making sure that no serious damage had been done to the vital machinery of the air-purifier — the very lungs of the great space-ship.

Dismounting the Standish, he lugged it back up to the main saloon, replaced it in its safe and again set the combination lock. Thence to the lifeboat, where Clio cried out in relief as she saw that he was unhurt.

"Oh, Conway, I've been so afraid something would happen to you!" she exclaimed, as he led her rapidly upward toward the control room. "Of course you. . . ." she paused.

"Sure," he replied, laconically. "Nothing to it. How do you feel — about back to normal?"

"All right, I think, except for being scared to death and just about out of control. I don't suppose that I'll be good for anything, but whatever I can do, count me in on."

"Fine — you may be needed, at that. Everybody's out, apparently, except those who, like me, had a warning and could hold their breath until they got to their suits."

"But how did you know what it was? You can't see it, nor smell it, nor anything."

"You inhaled a second before I did, and I saw your eyes. I've been in it before — and when you see a man get a jolt of that stuff just once, you never forget it. The engineers down below got it first, of course — it must have wiped them out. Then we got it in the saloon. Your passing out warned me, and luckily I had enough breath left to give the word. Quite a few of the fellows up above should have had time to get away — we'll see 'em all in the control room."

"I suppose that was why you revived me — in payment for so kindly warning you of the gas attack?" The girl laughed; shaky, but game.

"Something like that, probably," he answered, lightly. "Here we are — now we'll soon find out what's going to happen next."

In the control room they saw at least a dozen armored figures; not now rushing about, but seated at their instruments, tense and ready. Fortunate it was that Costigan — veteran of space as he was, though young in years — had been down in the saloon; fortunate that he had been familiar with that horrible outlawed gas; fortunate that he had had the presence of mind enough and sheer physical stamina enough to send his warning without allowing one paralyzing trace to enter his own lungs. Captain Bradley, the men on watch, and several other officers in their quarters or in the wardrooms — space-hardened veterans all — had obeyed instantly and without question the amplifiers' gasped command to "get tight." Exhaling or inhaling, their air-passages had snapped as that dread "Vee-Two" was heard, and they had literally jumped into their armored suits of space — flushing them out with volume after volume of unquestionable air; holding their breath to the last possible second, until their straining lungs could endure no more.

Costigan waved the girl to a vacant bench, cautiously changed into his own armor from the emergency suit he had been wearing, and approached the captain.

"Anything in sight, sir?" he asked, saluting. "They should have started something before this."

"They've started, but we can't locate them. We tried to send out a general sector alarm, but that had hardly started when they blanketed our wave. Look at that!"

Following the captain's eyes, Costigan stared at the high powered set of the ship's operator. Upon the plate, instead of a moving, living, three-dimensional picture, there was a flashing glare of blinding white light; from the speaker, instead of intelligible speech, was issuing a roaring, crackling stream of noise.

"It's impossible!" Bradley burst out, violently. "There's not a gram of metal inside the fourth zone — within a hundred thousand kilometers — and yet they must be close to send such a wave as that. But the Second thinks not — what do you think, Costigan?" The bluff commander, reactionary and of the old school as was his breed, was furious — baffled, raging inwardly to come to grips with the invisible and undetectable foe. Face to face with the inexplicable, however, he listened to the younger men with unusual tolerance.

"It's not only possible; it's quite evident that they've got something we haven't." Costigan's voice was bitter. "But why shouldn't they have? Service ships never get anything until it's been experimented with for years, but pirates and such always get the new stuff as soon as it's discovered. The only good thing I can see is that we got part of a message away, and the scouts can trace that interference out there. But the pirates know that, too — it won't be long now," he concluded, grimly.

He spoke truly. Before another word was spoken the outer screen flared white under a beam of terrific power, and simultaneously there appeared upon one of the lookout plates a vivid picture of the pirate vessel — a huge, black globe of steel, now emitting flaring offensive beams of force. Her invisibility lost, now that she had gone into action, she lay revealed in the middle of the first zone — at point-blank range.

Instantly the powerful weapons of the *Hyperion* were brought to bear, and in the blast of full-driven beams the stranger's screens flamed incandescent. Heavy guns, under the recoil of whose fierce salvos, the frame of the giant globe trembled and shuddered, shot out their tons of high-explosive shell. But the pirate commander had known accurately the strength of the liner, and knew that her armament was impotent against the forces at his command. His screens were invulnerable, the giant shells were exploded harmlessly in mid-space, miles from their objective. And suddenly a frightened pencil of flame stabbed brilliantly from the black hulk of the enemy. Through the empty ether it tore, through the mighty defensive screens, through the tough metal of the outer and inner walls. Every ether-defence of the *Hyperion* vanished, and her acceleration dropped to a quarter of its normal value.

"Right through the battery room!" Bradley groaned. "We're on the emergency drive now. Our rays are done for, and we can't seem to put a shell anywhere near her with our guns!"

But ineffective as the guns were, they were silenced forever as a frightful beam of destruction stabbed relentlessly through the control room, whiffing out of existence the pilot, gunnery, and lookout panels and the men before them. The air rushed into space, and the suits of the three survivors bulged out into drumhead tightness as the pressure in the room decreased.

Costigan pushed the captain lightly toward a wall, then seized the girl and leaped in the same direction.

"Let's get out of here, quick!" he cried, the miniature radio instruments of the helmets automatically taking up the duty of transmitting speech as the sound disks refused to function. "They can't see us — our ether wall is still up and their spy-sprays can't get through it from the outside, you know. They're working from blue-prints, and they'll probably take your desk next," and even as they bounded toward the door, now become the outer seal of an airlock, the annihilating ray tore through the space which they had just quitted in their flight.

Through the airlock, down through several levels of passengers' quarters they hurried, and into a lifeboat, whose one doorway commanded the full length of the third lounge — an ideal spot, either for defense or for escape outward by means of the miniature cruiser. As they entered their retreat they felt their weight begin to increase. More and more force was applied to the helpless liner, until it was moving at normal acceleration.

"What do you make of that, Costigan?" asked the captain. "Tractor beams?"

"Apparently. They've got something, all right. They're taking us somewhere, fast. I'll go get a couple of Standishes, and another suit of armor — we'd better dig in," and soon the small room became a veritable fortress, housing as it did, those two formidable engines of destruction. Then the first officer made another and longer trip, returning with a complete suit of triplanetary space armor, exactly like those worn by the two men, but considerably smaller.

"Just as an added factor of safety, you'd better put this on, Clio — those emergency suits aren't good for much in a battle. I don't suppose that you ever fired a Standish, did you?"

"No, but I can soon learn how to do it," she replied, pluckily.

"Two is all that can work here at once, but you should know how to take hold in case one of us goes out. And while you're changing suits you'd better put on some stuff I've got here — Service special phones and detectors. Stick this little disk onto your chest with this bit of tape; low down, out of sight. Just under your wishbone is the best place. Take off your wrist-watch and wear this one *continuously* — never take it off for a second. Put on these pearls, and wear them all the time, too. Take this capsule and hide it against your skin, some place where it can't be found except by the most rigid search. Swallow it in an emergency — it goes down easily and works just as well inside as outside. It is the most important thing of all — you can get along with it alone if you lose everything else, but without that capsule the whole system's shot to pieces. With that outfit, if we should get separated, you can talk to us — we're both wearing 'em, although somewhat different forms. You don't need to talk loud — just a mutter will be enough. They're handy little outfits, almost impossible to find, and capable of a lot of things."

"Thanks, Conway — I'll remember that, too," Clio replied, as she turned toward the tiny locker to follow his instructions. "But won't the scouts and patrols be catching us pretty quick? The operator sent a warning."

"Afraid the ether's empty, as far as we're concerned. They could neutralize our detector screens, and the scouts' detectors are the same as ours."

Captain Bradley had stood by in silent astonishment during this conversation. His eyes had bulged slightly at Costigan's "we're both wearing 'em," but he had held his peace and as the girl disappeared a look of dawning comprehension came over his face.

"Oh, I see, sir," he said, respectfully — far more respectfully than he had ever before addressed a mere first officer. "Meaning that we both *will be* wearing them shortly, I assume. 'Service Specials' — but you didn't specify exactly *what* Service, did you?"

"Now that you mention it, I don't believe that I did," Costigan grinned.

"That explains several things about you — particularly your recognition of Vee-Two and your uncanny control and speed of reaction. But aren't you. . . ."

"No," Costigan interrupted, positively. "This situation is apt to get altogether too serious to overlook any bets. If we get away, I'll take them away from her and she'll never know that they aren't routine equipment in the Triplanetary Service. As for you, I know that you can and do keep your mouth shut. That's why I'm hanging this junk on you — I had a lot of stuff in my kit, but I flashed it all with the Standish, except what I brought in here for us three. Whether you think so or not, we're in a real jam — our chance of getting away is mightly close to zero. Now that I've gone this far, I might as well tell you that I don't believe these birds are pirates at all, in the ordinary sense of the word. And it may be possible that they're after me, but I don't think so — we've covered up too. . . ."

He broke off as the girl came back, now to all appearances a small Triplanetary officer, and the three settled down to a long and eventless wait. Hour after hour they flew through the ether, but finally there was a lurching swing and an abrupt increase in their acceleration. After a short consultation Captain Bradley turned on the visiray set and, with the beam at its minimum power, peered cautiously downward, in the direction opposite to that in which he knew the pirate vessel must be. All three stared into the plate, seeing only an infinity of emptiness, marked only by the infinitely remote and coldly brilliant stars. While they stared into space a vast area of the heavens was blotted out and they saw, faintly illuminated by a peculiar blue luminescence, a vast ball — a sphere so large and so close that they seemed to be dropping downward toward it as though it were a world! They came to a stop — paused, weightless — a vast door slid smoothly aside — they were drawn *upward* through an airlock and floated quietly in the air above a small, but brightly-lighted and orderly city of metallic buildings! Gently the *Hyperion* was lowered, to come to rest in the embracing arms of a regulation landing cradle.

"Well, wherever it is, we're here," remarked Captain Bradley, grimly.

"And now the fireworks start," assented Costigan, with a questioning glance at the girl.

"Don't mind me," she answered his unspoken question. "I don't believe in surrendering, either."

"Right," and both men squatted down behind the etherwalls of their terrific weapons; the girl prone behind them.

They had not long to wait. A group of human beings — men and to all appearance Americans — appeared unarmed in the little lounge. As soon as they were well inside the room, Bradley and Costigan released upon them without compunction the full power of their frightful projectors. From the reflectors, through the doorway, there tore a concentrated double beam of pure destruction — but that beam did not reach its goal. Yards from the men it met a screen of impenetrable density. Instantly the gunners pressed their triggers and a stream of high-explosive shells issued from the roaring weapons. But shells, also, were futile. They struck the shield and vanished — vanished without exploding and without leaving a trace to show that they had ever existed.

Costigan sprang to his feet, but before he could launch his intended attack a vast tunnel appeared beside him — an annihilating ray had swept through the entire width of the liner, cutting instantly a smooth cylinder of emptiness. Air rushed in to fill the vacuum, and the three visitors felt themselves seized by invisible forces and drawn into the tunnel. Through it they floated, up to and over the buildings, finally slanting downward toward the door of a great high-powered structure. Doors opened before them and closed behind them, until at last they stood upright in a room which was evidently the office of a busy executive. They faced a desk which, in addition to the usual equipment of the business man, carried a bewilderingly complete switchboard and instrument panel.

Seated impassively at the desk there was a gray man. Not only was he dressed entirely in gray, but his heavy hair was gray, his eyes were gray, and even his tanned skin seemed to give the impression of grayness in disguise. His overwhelming personality radiated an aura of grayness — not the gentle gray of the dove, but the resistless, driving gray of the super-dreadnaught; the hard, inflexible, brittle gray of the fracture of high-carbon steel.

"Captain Bradley, First Officer Costigan, Miss Marsden," the man spoke quietly, but crisply. "I had not intended you two men to live so long. That is a detail, however, which we will pass by for the moment. You may remove your suits."

Neither officer moved, but both stared back at the speaker unflinchingly.

"I am not accustomed to repeating instructions," the man at the desk continued; voice still low and level, but instinct with deadly menace. "You may choose between removing those suits and dying in them, here and now."

Costigan moved over to Clio and slowly took off her armor. Then, after a flashing exchange of glances and a muttered word, the two officers threw off their suits simultaneously and fired at the same instant; Bradley with his Lewiston, Costigan with a heavy automatic pistol whose bullets were explosive shells of tremendous power. But the man in gray, surrounded by an impenetrable wall of force, only smiled at the fusillade, tolerantly and maddeningly. Costigan leaped fiercely, only to be hurled backward as he struck that unyielding, invisible wall. A vicious beam snapped him back into place, the weapons were snatched away, and all three captives were held in their former positions.

"I permitted that, as a demonstration of futility," the gray man said, his hard voice becoming harder, "but I will permit no more foolishness. Now I will introduce myself. I am known as Roger. You probably have heard nothing of me yet but you will — if you live. Whether or not you two live depends solely upon yourselves. Being something of a student of men, I fear that you will both die shortly. Able and resourceful as you have just shown yourselves to be, you could be valuable to me, but you probably will not — in which case you shall, of course, cease to exist. That, however, in its proper time — you shall be of some slight service to me in the process of being eliminated. In your case, Miss Marsden, I find myself undecided between two courses of action; each highly desirable, but unfortunately mutually exclusive. Your father will be glad to ransom you at an exceedingly high figure, but, in spite of that fact, I may decide to keep you for — well, let us say for certain purposes."

"Yes?" Clio rose magnificently to the occasion. Fear forgotten, her courageous spirit flashed from her clear, young eyes and emanated from her slender, rounded young body, erect in defiance. "Since I am a captive, you can of course do anything you please with me up to a certain point — but no further, believe me!"

With no sign of having heard her outburst Roger pressed a button and a tall, comely woman, appeared — a woman of indefinite age and of uncertain nationality.

"Show Miss Marsden to her apartment," he directed, and as the two women went out a man came in.

"The cargo is unloaded, sir," the newcomer reported. "The two men and the five women indicated have been taken to the hospital," was the report of the man.

"Very well, dispose of the others in the usual fashion." The minion went out, and Roger continued, emotionlessly:

"Collectively, the other passengers may be worth a million or so, but it would not be worth while to waste time upon them."

"What are you, anyway?" blazed Costigan, helpless but enraged beyond caution. "I have heard of mad scientists who tried to destroy the Earth, and of equally mad geniuses who thought themselves Napoleons capable of conquering even the Solar System. Whichever you are, you should know that you can't get away with it."

"I am neither. I am, however, a scientist, and I direct many other scientists. I am not mad. You have undoubtedly noticed several peculiar features of this place?"

"Yes, particularly the artificial gravity, which has always been considered impossible, and those screens. An ordinary ether-wall is opaque in one direction, and doesn't bar matter — yours are transparent both ways and something more than impenetrable to matter. How do you do it?"

"You could not understand them if I explained them to you, and they are merely two of our smaller developments. I have no serious designs upon the Earth nor upon the Solar System, nor have I any desire to rule over, or to control the destinies of masses of futile and brainless men. I have, however, certain ends of my own in view. To accomplish my plans I require hundreds of millions in gold, other hundreds of millions in platinum and noble metal, and some five kilograms of the bromide of radium — all of which I shall take from the planets of this Solar System before I leave it. I shall take them in spite of the puerile efforts of the fleets of your Triplanetary League.

"This structure, floating in a planetary orbit, was designed by me and built under my direction. It is protected from meteorites by certain forces of my devising. It is undetectable and invisible — your detectors do not touch it and light-waves are bent around it without loss or distortion. I am discussing these points at such length so that you may realize exactly your position. As I have intimated, you can be of assistance to me if you will."

"Now just what could you offer any *man* to make him join your outfit?" demanded Costigan, venomously.

"Many things." Roger's cold tone betrayed no emotion, no recognition of Costigan's open and bitter contempt. "I have under me many men, bound to me by many ties. Needs, wants, longings and desires differ from man to man, and I can satisfy practically any of them. Personally, I take delight in the society of young and beautiful women, and many men have that same taste; but there are other urges which I have found quite efficient. Greed, thirst for fame, longing for power, and so on, including many qualities usually regarded as 'noble.' And what I promise, I deliver. I demand only loyalty to me, and that only in certain things and for a relatively short period. In all else, my men do as they please. In conclusion, I can use you two conveniently, but I do not need you. Therefore you may choose now between my service and — the alternative."

"Exactly what is the alternative?"

"We will not go into that. Suffice it to say that it has to do with a minor research, which is not progressing satisfactorily. It will result in your extinction, and perhaps I should mention that that extinction will not be particularly pleasant."

Bradley roared, "I say *no*, you —" He intended to give an unexpurgated classification, but was rudely interrupted.

"Hold on a minute!" snapped Costigan. "How about Miss Marsden?"

"She has nothing to do with this discussion," returned Roger, icily. "I do not bargain — in fact, I believe that I shall keep her for a time. She has it in mind to destroy herself, if I do not allow her to be ransomed, but she will find that door closed to her until I permit it to open."

"In that case, I string along with the Chief — take what he started to say about you and run it clear across the board for me!" barked Costigan.

"Very well. That decision was to be expected from men of your type." The gray man touched two buttons and two of his creatures entered the room. "Put these men into separate cells on the second level," he ordered. "Search them to the skin: all their weapons may not have been in their armor. Seal the doors and mount special guards, tuned to me here."

Imprisoned they were, and carefully searched; but they bore no arms, and nothing had been said or thought of communicators. Even if such instruments could be concealed, Roger would detect their use instantly. At least, so would have run his thought had the subject entered his mind. But even Roger had no inkling of the possibility of Costigan's "Service Special" phones, detectors and spy-ray — instruments of minute size and of infinitesimal power, but yet instruments which, working as they were, below the level of the ether, were effective at great distances and caused no vibrations in the ether by which their use could be detected. And what could be more innocent than the regulation, personal equipment of every officer of space? The heavy goggles, the wrist-watch and its supplementary pocket chronometer, the flash-lamp, the automatic lighter, the sender, the money-belt?

All these items of equipment were examined with due care; but the cleverest minds of Triplanetary's Secret Service had designated those communicators to pass any ordinary search, however careful, and when Costigan and Bradley were finally locked into the designated cells, they still possessed their ultra-instruments.

CHAPTER II

In Roger's Planetoid

In the hall Clio glanced around her wildly, her bosom heaving, eyes darting here and there, seeking even the narrowest avenue of escape. Before she could act, however, her body was clamped inflexibly, as though in a vise, and she struggled, motionless.

"It is useless to attempt to escape, or to do anything except what Roger wishes," the guide informed her somberly, snapping off the instrument in her hand and thus restoring to the thoroughly cowed girl her freedom of motion.

"His lightest wish is law," she continued as they walked down a long corridor. "The sooner you realize that you must do exactly as he pleases, in all things, the easier your life will be."

"But I wouldn't *want* to keep on living!" Clio declared, with a flash of spirit. "And I can *always* die, you know."

"You will find that you cannot," the passionless creature returned, monotonously. "If you do not yield, you will long and pray for death, but you will not die unless Roger wills it. I was like you once. I also struggled, and I became what I am now — whatever it is. Here is your apartment. You will stay here until Roger gives further orders concerning you."

The living automaton opened a door and stood silent and impassive, while Clio, staring at her in unutterable horror, shrank past her and into the sumptuously furnished suite. The door closed soundlessly and utter silence descended as a pall. Not an ordinary silence, but the indescribable perfection of the absolute, complete absence of all sound. In that silence Clio stood motionless. Tense and rigid, hopeless, despairing, she stood there in that magnificent room, fighting an almost overwhelming impulse to scream. Suddenly she heard the cold voice of Roger, speaking from the empty air.

"You are over-wrought, Miss Marsden. You can be of no use to yourself or to me in that condition. I command you to rest; and, to insure that rest, you may pull that cord, which will establish about this room an ether wall: a wall cutting off even this my voice. . . ."

The voice ceased as she pulled the cord savagely and threw herself upon a divan in a torrent of gasping, strangling, but rebellious sobs. Then again came a voice, but not to her ears. Deep within her, pervading every bone and muscle, it made itself felt rather than heard.

"Clio?" it asked. "Don't talk yet. . . ."

"Conway!" she gasped in relief, every fiber of her being thrilled into new hope at the deep, well-remembered voice of Conway Costigan.

"Keep still!" he snapped. "Don't act so happy! He may have a spy-ray on you. He can't hear me, but he may be able to hear you. When he was talking to you you must have noticed a sort of rough, sandpapery feeling under that necklace I gave you? Since he's got an ether-wall around you the beads are dead now. If you feel anything like that under the wrist-watch, breathe deeply, twice. If you don't feel anything there, it's safe for you to talk, as loud as you please.

"I don't feel a thing, Conway!" she rejoiced. Tears forgotten, she was her old, buoyant self again. "So that wall *is* real, after all? I only about half believed it."

"Don't trust it too much, because he can cut it off from the outside any time he wants to. Remember what I told you: that necklace will warn you of any spy-ray in the ether, and the watch will detect anything below the level of the ether. It's dead now, of course, since our three phones are direct-connected; I'm in touch with Bradley, too. Don't be too scared; we've got a lot better chance that I thought we had."

"What? You don't mean it!"

"Absolutely. I'm beginning to think that maybe we've got something he doesn't know exists — our ultra-wave. Of course I wasn't surprised when his searchers failed to find our instruments, but it never occurred to me that I might have a clear field to use them in! I can't quite believe it yet, but I haven't been able to find any indication that he can even detect the bands we are using. I'm going to look around over there with my spy-ray . . . I'm looking at you now — feel it?"

"Yes, the watch feels that way, now."

"Fine! Not a sign of interference over here, either. I can't find a trace of ultra-wave — anything below ether-level, you know — anywhere in the whole place. He's got so much stuff that we've never heard of that I supposed of course he'd have ultra-wave, too; but if he hasn't, that gives us the edge. Well, Bradley and I've got a lot of work to do. . . . Wait a minute, I just had a thought. I'll be back in about a second."

There was a brief pause, then the soundless, but clear voice went on:

"Good hunting! That woman that gave you the blue willies isn't alive — she's full of the prettiest machinery and communicators you ever saw!"

"Oh, Conway!" and the girl's voice broke in an engulfing wave of thanksgiving and relief. "It was so unutterably horrible, thinking of what must have happened to her and to others like her!"

"He's running a colossal bluff, I think. He's good, all right, but he lacks quite a lot of being omnipotent. But don't get too cocky, either. Plenty has happened to plenty of women here, and men too — and plenty may happen to us unless we put out a few jets. Keep a stiff upper lip, and if you want us, yell. 'Bye!"

The silent voice ceased, the watch upon Clio's wrist again became an unobtrusive timepiece, and Costigan, in his solitary cell far below her tower room, turned his peculiarly goggled eyes toward other scenes. In his pockets his hands manipulated tiny controls, and through the lenses of those goggles Costigan's keen and highly-trained eyes studied every concealed detail of mechanism of the great globe, the while he planned what must be done. Finally, he took off the goggles and spoke in a low voice to Bradley, confined in another windowless room across the hall.

"I think I've got dope enough, Captain. I've found out where he put our armor and guns, and I've located all the main leads, controls, and generators. There are no ether-walls around us here, but every door is shielded, and there are guards outside our doors — one to each of us. They're robots, not men. That makes it harder, since they're undoubtedly connected direct to Roger's desk, and will give an alarm at the first hint of abnormal performance. We can't do a thing until he leaves his desk. See that black panel, a little below the cord-switch to the right of your door? That's the conduit cover. When I give you the word, tear that off and you'll see one red wire in the cable. It feeds the shield-generator of your door. Break that wire and join me out in the hall. Sorry I had only one of these ultra-wave spies, but once we're together it won't be so bad. Here's what I thought we could do," and he went over in detail the only course of action which his surveys had shown to be possible.

"There, he's left his desk!" Costigan exclaimed after the conversation had continued for almost an hour. "Now as soon as we find out where he's going, we'll start something . . . he's going to see Clio, the swine! This changes things, Bradley!" His hard voice was a curse.

"Somewhat!" blazed the captain. "I know how you two have been getting on all during the cruise. I'm with you, but what can we do?"

"We'll do something," Costigan declared grimly. "If he makes a pass at her I'll get him if I have to blow this whole sphere out of space, with us in it!"

"Don't do that, Conway." Clio's low voice, trembling but determined, was felt by both men and both gasped audibly:

they had forgotten that there were three instruments in the circuit. "If there's a chance for you to get away and do anything about fighting him, don't mind me. Maybe he only wants to talk about the ransom, anyway."

"He wouldn't talk ransom to *you* — he's going to talk something else entirely," Costigan gritted; then his voice changed suddenly. "But say, maybe it's just as well this way. They didn't find our specials when they searched us, you know, and we're going to do plenty of damage right soon now. Roger probably isn't a fast worker — more the cat-and-mouse type, I'd say — and after we get started he'll have something on his mind besides you. Think you can stall him off and keep him interested for about fifteen minutes?"

"I'm sure I can — I'll do *anything* to help us, or you, get away from this horrible. . . ." Her voice ceased as Roger broke the ether-wall of her apartment and walked toward the divan upon which she crouched in wide-eyed, helpless, trembling terror.

"Get ready, Bradley!" Costigan directed tersely. "He's left Clio's ether-wall off, so that any abnormal signals would be relayed to him from his desk — he knows that there's no chance of anyone disturbing him in *that* room. But I'm holding my beam on that switch — it's as good a conductor as metal — so that the wall is on, full strength. No matter what we do now, he can't get a warning. I'll have to hold the beam exactly on the switch, though, so you'll have to do the dirty work. Tear out that red wire and kill those two guards. You know how to kill a robot, don't you?"

"Yes — break his eye-lenses and his eardrums and he'll stop whatever he's doing and send out distress calls. . . . Got 'em both. Now what?"

"Open my door — the shield switch is to the right."

Costigan's door flew open and the Triplanetary captain leaped into the room.

"Now for our armor!" he cried.

"Not yet!" snapped Costigan. He was standing rigid, goggled eyes staring immovably at a spot upon the ceiling. "I can't move a millimeter until you've closed Clio's ether-wall switch. If I take this ray off it for a second we're sunk. Five floors up, straight ahead down a corridor — fourth door on right. When you're at the switch you'll feel my ray on your watch. Snap it up!"

"Right!" and the captain leaped away at a pace to be equaled by few men of half his years.

Soon he was back, and after Costigan had tested the ether-wall of the "bridal suite" to make sure that no warning signal from his desk or his servants could reach Roger within it, the two officers hurried away toward the room in which their discarded space-armor had been stored.

"Too bad they don't wear uniforms," panted Bradley, short of breath from the many flights of stairs. "Might have helped some as disguise."

"I doubt it — with so many robots around, they've probably got signals that we couldn't understand, anyway. If we meet anybody it'll mean a battle. Hold it!" Peering through walls with his spy-ray, Costigan had seen two men approaching, blocking an intersecting corridor into which they must turn. "Two of 'em, a man and a robot — the robot's on your side. We'll wait here, right at the corner — when they round it, take 'em!" And Costigan put away his goggles in readiness for strife.

All unsuspecting, the two pirates came into view, and as they appeared the two officers struck. Costigan, on the inside, drove a short, hard right low into the human pirate's abdomen. The fiercely driven fist sank to the wrist into the soft tissues and the stricken man collapsed. But even as the blow landed, Costigan had seen that there was a third enemy, following close behind the two he had been watching, a pirate who was even then training a ray projector upon him. Reacting automatically, Costigan swung his unconscious opponent around in front of him, so that it was into that insensible body that the vicious ray tore, and not into his own. Crouching down into the smallest possible compass, he straightened his powerful body with the lashing force of a mighty steel spring, hurling the corpse straight at the flaming mouth of the projector. The weapon crashed to the floor and dead pirate and living went down in a heap. Upon that heap Costigan hurled himself, feeling for the enemy's throat. But the pirate had wriggled clear, and countered with a gouging thrust that would have torn out the eyes of a slower man, following it up instantly with a savage kick for the groin. No automaton this, geared and set to perform certain fixed duties with mechanical precision, but a lithe, strong man in hard training, fighting with every foul trick known to his murderous ilk.

But Costigan was no tyro in the art of dirty fighting. Few indeed are the maiming tricks of foul combat unknown to even the rank and file of the highly efficient Secret Service of the Triplanetary League; and Costigan, a Sector Chief of that unknown organization, knew them all. Not for pleasure, sportsmanship, nor million-dollar purses do those secret agents use Nature's weapons. They come to grips only when it cannot possibly be avoided, but when they are forced to fight in that fashion they go into it with but one grim purpose — to kill, and to kill in the shortest possible space of time. Thus it was that Costigan's opening soon came. The pirate launched a particularly vicious kick, the dreaded "coup de sabot," which Costigan avoided by a lightning shift. It was a slight shift, barely enough to make the kicker miss, and two powerful hands closed upon that flying foot in midair like the sprung jaws of a bear-trap. Closed and twisted viciously, in the same fleeting instant. There was a shriek, smothered as a heavy boot crashed to its carefully pre-determined mark: the pirate was out, definitely and permanently.

The struggle had lasted scarcely ten seconds, coming to its close just as Bradley finished blinding and deafening the robot. Costigan picked up the projector, again donned his spy-ray goggles, and the two hurried on.

"Nice work, Chief — it must be a gift to rough-house the way you do," Bradley exclaimed. "That's why you took the live one?"

"Practice helps some, too! I've been in brawls before, and I'm a lot younger and maybe some faster than you are," Costigan explained briefly, penetrant gaze rigidly to the fore as they ran along one corridor after another.

Several more guards, both living and mechanical, were encountered on the way, but they were not permitted to offer any opposition. Costigan saw them first. In the furious beam of the projector of the dead pirate they were riven into noth-ingness, and the two officers sped on to the room which Costigan had located from afar. The three suits of Triplanet-ary space armor had been sealed into a cabinet whose doors Costigan literally blew off with a blast of force, rather than consume time in tracing the power leads.

"I feel like something now!" Costigan, once more encased in his own armor, heaved a great sigh of relief. "Rough-and-tumble's all right with one or two, but that gen-erator room is full of grief, and we won't have any too much stuff as it is. We've got to take Clio's suit along — we'll carry it down to the door of the power room, drop it there, and pick it up after we've wrecked the works."

Contemptuous now of possible guards, the armored pair strode toward the room which housed the pulsating heart of the immense fortress of space. Guards were encountered, and captains — officers who signaled frantically to their chief, since he alone could unleash the frightful forces at his command, and who profanely wondered at his unwonted silence — but the enemy beams were impotent against the mighty ether-walls of that armor; and the pirates, without armor in the security of their own planet as they were, van-ished utterly in the ravening beams of the twin Lewistons. As they paused before the door of the power room, both men felt Clio's voice raised in her first and last appeal, an appeal wrung from her against her will by the extremity of her posi-tion.

"Conway! Hurry! Oh, hurry! I can't last much longer — good-bye, dear!" In the horror-filled tones both men read clearly the girl's dire extremity. Each saw plainly a happy, care-free young Earth girl, upon her first trip into space, locked inside an ether-wall with an over-brained, under-conscienced human machine — a super-intelligent but lecherous and unmoral mechanism of flesh and blood, acknowledging no authority, ruled by nothing save his own scientific drivings and the almost equally powerful urges of his desires and passions! She had fought with every resource at her command. She had wept and pleaded, she had stormed and raged, she had feigned submission and had played for time — and her torment had not touched in the slightest degree the merciless and gloating brain of the being who called himself Roger. Now his tantalizing, ruthless cat-play was done, the horrible gray-brown face was close to hers — she wailed her final despairing message to Costigan and attacked that hideous face with the fury of a tigress.

Costigan bit off a bitter imprecation. "Hold him just a second longer, sweetheart!" he cried, and the power room door vanished.

Through the great room the two Lewistons swept at full aperture and at maximum power, two rapidly opening fans of death and destruction. Here and there a guard, more rapid than his fellows, trained a futile projector — a projector whose magazine exploded at the touch of that frightful field of force, liberating instantaneously its thousands upon thousands of kilowatt-hours of stored-up energy. Through the delicately adjusted, complex mechanisms the destroying beams tore. At their touch armatures burned out, high-tension leads volatilized in crashing, high-voltage sparks, masses of metal smoked and burned in the path of vast forces now seeking the easiest path to neutralization, delicate instruments blew up, copper ran in streams like water. As the last machine subsided into a semi-molten mass of metal the two wreckers, each grasping a brace, felt themselves become weightless and knew that they had accomplished the first part of their program.

Costigan leaped for the outer door. His the task to go to Clio's aid. . . . Bradley would follow more slowly, bringing the girl's armor and taking care of any possible pursuit. As he sailed through the air he spoke.

"Coming, Clio! All right, girl?" Questioningly, half fearfully.

"All right, Conway." Her voice was almost unrecognizable, broken in retching agony. "When everything went crazy he . . . found out that the ether-wall was up . . . forgot all about me. He shut it off . . . and seemed to go crazy, too . . . he is floundering around like a wild man now. . . . I'm trying to keep . . . him from . . . going down-stairs."

"Good girl — keep him busy one minute more — he's getting all the warnings at once and wants to get back to his board. But what's the matter with you? Did he . . . hurt you, after all?"

"Oh, no; not that. But I'm sick — horribly sick. I'm falling. . . . I'm so dizzy I can scarcely see . . . my head is breaking up into little pieces . . . I just *know* I'm going to die, Conway! Oh . . . oh!"

"Oh, is *that* all!" In his sheer relief that they had been in time, Costigan did not think of sympathizing with Clio's very real present distress of mind and body. "I forgot that you're a ground-gripper — that's just a little touch of space-sickness. It'll wear off directly. . . . All right, I'm coming! Let go of him and get as far away from him as you can!"

He was now in the street. Perhaps two hundred feet distant and a hundred feet above him was the tower room in which were Clio and Roger. He sprang directly toward its large window, and as he floated "upward" he corrected his course and accelerated his pace by firing backward at various angles with his heavy service pistol, uncaring that at the point of impact of each of those shells a small blast of destruction erupted. He missed the window a trifle, but that did not matter — his flaming Lewiston opened a way for him, partly through the window, partly through the wall. As he soared through the opening he trained projector and pistol upon Roger, now almost to the door, noticing as he did so that Clio was clinging convulsively to a lamp-bracket upon the wall. Door and wall vanished in the Lewiston's terrific beam, but the pirate stood unharmed. Neither ravening ray nor explosive shell could harm him — he had snapped on the protective shield whose generator was always upon his person.

But Roger, while not exactly a ground-gripper, did not know how to handle himself without weight; whereas Costigan, given six walls against which to push, was even more efficient in weightless combat than when handicapped by the force of gravitation. Keeping his projector upon the pirate, he seized the first club to hand — a long, slender pedestal of metal — and launched himself past the pirate chief. With all the momentum of his mass and velocity and all the power of his mighty right arm he swung the bar at the pirate's head. That fiercely driven mass of metal should have taken Roger's head from his shoulders, but it did not. That shield of force was utterly rigid and impenetrable; the only effect of the frightful blow was to set him spinning, end over end, like the flying baton of an acrobatic drum-major. As the spinning form crashed against the opposite wall of the room, Bradley floated in, carrying Clio's armor. Without a word the captain loosened the helpless girl's grip upon the bracket and encased her in the suit. Then, supporting her at the window, he held his Lewiston upon the captive's head while Costigan propelled him toward the opening. Both men knew that Roger's shield of force must be threatened every instant — that if he were allowed to release it he probably would bring to bear a hand-weapon even superior to their own.

Braced against the wall, Costigan sighted along Roger's body toward the most distant point of the lofty dome of the artificial planet and gave him a gentle push. Then, each grasping Clio by an arm, the two officers shoved mightily with their feet and the three armored forms darted away toward their only hope of escape — an emergency boat which could be launched through the shell of the great globe. To attempt to reach the *Hyperion* and to escape in one of her lifeboats would have been useless; they could not have forced the great gates of the main air-locks and no other exits existed. As they sailed onward through the air, Costigan keeping the slowly-floating form of Roger enveloped in his beam, Clio began to recover.

"Suppose they get their gravity fixed?" she asked, apprehensively. "And they're raying us and shooting at us!"

"They may have fixed it already. They undoubtedly have spare parts and duplicate generators, but if they turn it on the fall will kill Roger too, and he wouldn't like that. They'll have to get him down with an airship, and they know that we'll get them as fast as they come up. They can't hurt us with hand-weapons, and before they can bring up any heavy stuff they'll be afraid to use it, because we'll be too close to their shell.

"I wish we could have brought Roger along," he continued, savagely, to Bradley. "But you were right, of course — it'd be altogether too much like a rabbit capturing a wildcat. My Lewiston's about done right now, and there can't be much left of yours — what he'd do to us would be a sin and a shame."

Now at the great wall, the two men heaved mightily upon a lever, the gate of the emergency port swung slowly open, and they entered the miniature cruiser of the void. Costigan, familiar with the mechanism of the craft from careful study from his prison cell, manipulated the controls. Through gate after massive gate they went, until finally they were out in open space, shooting toward distant Tellus at the maximum acceleration of which their small craft was capable.

Costigan cut the other two phones out of circuit and spoke, his attention fixed upon some extremely distant point.

"Samms!" he called, sharply. "Costigan. We're out . . . all right . . . yes . . . sure . . . absolutely . . . you tell 'em, Sammy; I've got company here."

Through the sound-disks of their helmets the girl and the captain had heard Costigan's share of the conversation. Bradley stared at his erstwhile first officer in amazement, and even Clio had often heard that mighty, half-mythical name. Surely that bewildering young man must rank high, to speak so familiarly to Virgil Samms, the all-powerful head of the space-pervading Secret Service of the Triplanetary League!

"You've turned in a general call-out," Bradley stated, rather than asked.

"Long ago — I've been in touch right along," Costigan answered. "Now that they know what to look for and know that ether-wave detectors are useless, they can find it. Every vessel in seven sectors, clear down to the scout patrols, is concentrating on this point, and the call is out for all battleships and cruisers afloat. There are enough operatives out there with ultra-waves to locate that globe, and once they spot it they'll point it out to all the other vessels."

"But how about the other prisoners?" asked the girl. "They'll all be killed, won't they?"

"Hard telling," Costigan shrugged. "Depends on how things turn out. We lack a lot of being safe ourselves yet, and it's my personal opinion that there's going to be a real war."

"What's worrying me mostly is our own chance," Bradley assented. "They will chase us, of course."

"Sure, and they'll have more speed than we have. Depends on how far away the nearest Triplanetary vessels are. Anyway, we've done everything we can do — it's in the laps of the gods now."

Silence fell, and Costigan cut in Clio's phone and came over to the seat upon which she was reclining, white and stricken — worn out by the horrible and terrifying ordeals of the last few hours. As he seated himself beside her she blushed vividly, but her deep blue eyes met his gray ones steadily.

"Clio, I . . . we . . . you . . . that is," he flushed hotly and stopped. This secret agent, whose clear, keen brain no physical danger could cloud; who had proved over and over again that he was never at a loss in any emergency, however desperate — this quick-witted officer floundered in embarrassment like any schoolboy, but continued, doggedly: "I'm afraid that I gave myself away back there, but. . . ."

"We gave ourselves away, you mean," she filled in the pause. "I did my share, but I won't hold you to it if you don't want — but I *know* that you love me, Conway!"

"*Love* you!" The man groaned, his face lined and hard, his whole body rigid. "That doesn't half tell it, Clio. You don't need to hold me — I'm held for life. There never was a woman who meant anything to me before, and there never will be another. You're the only woman that ever existed. It isn't that. Can't you see that it's impossible?"

"Of course I can't — it isn't impossible, at all." She released her finger shields, four hands met and tightly clasped; and her low voice thrilled with feeling as she went on: "You love me and I love you. That is all that matters."

"I wish it were," Costigan returned bitterly, "but you don't know what you'd be letting yourself in for. It's who and what you are and who and what I am that's eating me. You, Clio Marsden, Curtis Marsden's daughter. Nineteen years old. You think you've been places and done things. You haven't. You haven't seen or done anything — you don't know what it's all about. And who am I to love a girl like you? A homeless space-flea who hasn't been on any planet three weeks in three years. A hard-boiled egg. A trouble-shooter and a brawler by instinct and training. A sp. . . ." He bit off the word and went on quickly: "Why, you don't know me at all, and there's a lot of me that you never *will* know — that I can't let you know! You'd better lay off me, girl, while you can. It'll be best for you, believe me."

"But I can't Conway, and neither can you," the girl answered softly, a glorious light in her eyes. "It's too late for that. On the ship it was just another of those things, but since then we've come really to know each other, and we're sunk. The situation is out of control, and we both know it — and neither of us would change it if we could, and you know that, too. I don't know very much, I admit, but I do know what you thought you'd have to keep from me, and I admire you all the more for it. We all honor the Service, Conway dearest — it is only you men who have made and are keeping the Three Planets fit places to live in — and I know that Virgil Samms' chief lieutenant would have to be a man in four thousand million. . . ."

"What makes you think that?" he demanded sharply.

"You told me so yourself, indirectly. Who else in the known Universe could possibly call him 'Sammy'? You are hard, of course, but you must be so — and I never did like soft men, anyway. And you brawl in a good cause. You are very much a *man*, my Conway; a real, *real* man, and I love you! Now, if they catch us, all right — we'll die together, at least!" she finished, passionately.

"You're right, sweetheart, of course," he admitted. "I don't believe that I *could* really let you let me go, even though I know you ought to," and their hands locked together even more firmly than before. "If we ever get out of this jam I'm going to kiss you, but this is no time to be taking off your helmet. In fact, I'm taking too many chances with you in keeping your finger shields off. Snap 'em on, Clio mine; the pirates ought to be getting fairly close by this time."

Hands released and armor again tight, Costigan went over to join Bradley at the control board.

"How're they coming, Captain?" he asked.

"Not so good. Quite a ways off yet. At least an hour, I'd say, before a cruiser can get within range."

"I'll see if I can locate any of the pirates chasing up. If I do, it'll be by accident; this little spy-ray isn't good for much except close work. I'm afraid the first warning we'll have will be when they take hold of us with a beam or spear us with a ray. Probably a beam, though; this is one of their emergency lifeboats and they wouldn't want to destroy it unless they have to. Also, I imagine that Roger wants us alive pretty badly. He has unfinished business with all three of us, and I can well believe that his 'not particularly pleasant extinction' will be even less so after the way we rooked him."

"I want you to do me a favor, Conway." Clio's face was white with horror at the thought of facing again that unspeakable creature of gray. "Give me a gun or something, please. I don't want him to touch me again while I'm alive."

"He won't," Costigan assured her, narrow of eye and grim of jaw. He was, as she had said, hard. "But you don't want a gun. You might get nervous and use it too soon. I'll take care of you at the last possible moment, because if he gets hold of us we won't stand a chance of getting away again."

For minutes there was silence, Costigan surveying the ether in all directions with his ultra-wave device. Suddenly he laughed, deeply and with real enjoyment, and the others stared at him in surprise.

"No, I'm not crazy," he told them. "This is really funny; it had never occurred to me that all these pirate ships are invisible to any ether wave as long as they're using power. I can see them, of course, with this sub-ether spy, but they can't see us! I knew that they should have overtaken us before this. I've finally found them. They've passed us, and are now tacking around, waiting for us to cut off our power for a minute so that they can see us! They're heading right into the Fleet — they think they're safe, of course, but what a surprise they've got coming to them!"

But it was not only the pirates who were to be surprised. Long before the pirate ship had come within extreme visibility range of the Triplanetary Fleet, it lost its invisibility and was starkly outlined upon the lookout plates of the three fugitives. For a few seconds the pirate craft seemed unchanged, then it began to glow redly, with a red that seemed to become darker as it grew stronger. Then the sharp outlines blurred, puffs of air burst outward, and the metal of the hull became a viscous, fluid-like something, flowing away in a long, red streamer into seemingly empty space. Costigan turned his ultra-gaze into that space and saw that it was actually far from empty. There lay a vast something, formless and indefinite even to his sub-ethereal vision; a something into which the viscid stream of transformed metal plunged. Plunged, and vanished.

Powerful interference blanketed his ultra-wave and howled throughout his body; but in the hope that some part of his message might get through he called Samms, and calmly and clearly he narrated everything that had just happened. He continued his crisp report, neglecting not the smallest detail, while their tiny craft was drawn inexorably toward a redly impermeable veil; continued it until their lifeboat, still intact, shot through that veil and he found himself unable to move. He was conscious, he was breathing normally, his heart was beating; but not a voluntary muscle would obey his will.

CHAPTER III

Fleet Against Planetoid

One of the newest and fleetest of the Law Enforcement Vessels of the Triplanetary League, the heavy cruiser *Chicago*, of the North American Division of the Tellurian Contingent, plunged stolidly through interplanetary vacuum. For five long weeks she had patrolled her allotted volume of space. In another week she would report back to the city whose name she bore, where her space-weary crew, worn by their long "trick" in the awesomely oppressive depths of the limitless void, would enjoy to the full their fortnight of refreshing planetary leave.

She was performing certain routine tasks — charting meteorites, watching for derelicts and other obstructions to navigation, checking in constantly with all scheduled space-ships in case of need, and so on — but primarily she was a warship. She was a mighty engine of destruction, hunting for the unauthorized vessels of whatever power or planet it was, that had not only defied the Triplanetary League, but were evidently attempting to overthrow it; attempting to plunge the Three Planets back into the ghastly sink of bloodshed and destruction from which they had so recently emerged. Every space-ship within range of her powerful detectors was represented by two brilliant, slowly moving points of light; one upon a great micrometer screen, the other in the "tank" — the immense, three-dimensional, minutely cubed model of the entire Solar System.

A brilliantly intense red light flared upon a panel and a bell clanged brazenly the furious signals of the sector alarm.

Simultaneously a speaker roared forth its message of a ship in dire peril.

"Sector alarm! N. A. T. *Hyperion* gassed with Vee-Two. Nothing detectable in space, but. . . ."

The half-uttered message was drowned out in a crackling roar of meaningless noise, the orderly signals of the bell became a hideous clamor, and the two points of light which had marked the location of the liner disappeared in widely spreading flashes of the same high-powered interference. Observers, navigators, and control officers were alike dumfounded. Even the captain, in the shell-proof, shock-proof, and doubly ray-proof retreat of his conning compartment, was equally at a loss. No ship or thing could *possibly* be close enough to be sending out interfering waves of such tremendous power — yet there they were!

"Maximum acceleration, straight for the point where the *Hyperion* was when her tracers went out," the captain ordered, and through the fringe of that widespread interference he drove a solid beam, reporting concisely to G. H. Q. Almost instantly the emergency call-out came roaring in — every vessel of the Sector, of whatever class or tonnage, was to concentrate upon the point in space where the ill-fated liner had last been known to be.

Hour after hour the great globe drove on at maximum acceleration, captain and every control officer alert and at high tension. But in the Quartermaster's Department, deep down below the generator rooms, no thought was given to such minor matters as the disappearance of a *Hyperion*. The inventory did not balance, and two Q. M. privates were trying, profanely, and without much success, to find the discrepancy.

"Charged cells for model DF Lewistons, none requisitioned, on hand eighteen thous. . . ." The droning voice broke off short in the middle of a word and the private stood rigid, in the act of reaching for another slip, every faculty concentrated upon something, imperceptible to his companion.

"Come on, Cleve — snap it up!" the second commanded,

but was silenced by a vicious wave of the listener's hand.

"What!" the rigid one exclaimed. "Reveal ourselves! Why, it's . . . Oh, all right. . . . Oh, that's it. . . . Uh-huh. . . . I see. . . . Yes, I've got it solid. Maybe I'll see you again some time. If not, so long!"

The inventory sheets fell unheeded from his hand, and his fellow private stared after him in amazement as he strode over to the desk of the officer in charge. That officer also stared as the hitherto easy-going and gold-bricking Cleve saluted briskly, showed him something flat in the palm of his left hand, and spoke.

"I've just got some of the funniest orders ever put out, Lieutenant" — his voice was low and intense — "but they came from 'way, 'way up. I'm to join the brass hats in the Center. You'll know about it directly, I imagine. Cover me up as much as you can, will you?" And he was gone.

Unchallenged he made his way to the control room, and his curt "urgent report for the Captain" admitted him there without question. But when he approached the sacred precincts of the Captain's own and inviolate room, he was stopped in no uncertain fashion by no less a personage than the Officer of the Day.

" . . . and report yourself under arrest immediately!" the O. D. concluded his brief but pointed speech.

"You were right in stopping me, of course," the intruder conceded, unmoved. "I wanted to get in there without giving everything away, if possible, but it seems that I can't. Well, I've been ordered by Virgil Samms to report to the Captain, at once. See this? Touch it!" He held out a flat, insulated disk, cover thrown back to reveal a tiny golden meteor, at the sight of which the officer's truculent manner altered markedly.

"I've heard of them, of course, but I never saw one before," and the officer touched the shining symbol lightly with his finger, jerking backward involuntarily as there shot through his whole body a thrilling surge of power, shouting into his very bones an unpronounceable syllable — the password of the Secret Service. "Genuine or not, it gets you to the

Captain. He'll know, and if it's a fake you'll be breathing space in five minutes."

Projector at the ready, the Officer of the Day followed Cleve into the Holy of Holies. There the grizzled four-striper touched the golden meteor lightly, then drove his piercing gaze deep into the unflinching eyes of the younger man. But that captain had won his high rank neither by accident nor by "pull" — he understood at once.

"It *must* be an emergency," he growled, half-audibly, still staring at his lowly Q. M. clerk, "to make Samms uncover his whole organization." He turned and curtly dismissed the wondering O. D. Then: "All right! Out with it!"

"Serious enough so that every one of us afloat has just received orders to reveal himself to his commanding officer and to anyone else, if necessary to reach that officer at once — orders never before issued. The enemy have been located. They have built a base, and have ships better than our best. Base and ships cannot be seen nor detected by any ether wave. However, the Service has been experimenting for years with a new type of communicator beam; and, while pretty crude yet, it was given to us when the *Dione* went out without leaving a trace. One of our men was in the *Hyperion*, managed to stay alive, and has been sending data. I am instructed to attach my new phone set to one of the universal plates in your conning room, and to see what I can find."

"Go to it!" The captain waved his hand and the operative bent to his task.

"Commanders of all vessels of the Fleet!" The Headquarters speaker, receiver sealed upon the wave-length of the Admiral of the Fleet, broke the long silence. "All vessels, in sectors L to R, inclusive, will interlock location signals. Some of you have received, or will receive shortly, certain communications from sources which need not be mentioned. Those commanders will at once send out red K4 screens. Vessels so marked will act as temporary flagships. Unmarked vessels will proceed at maximum to the nearest flagship, grouping about it in regulation squadron cone in order of arrival. Squadrons most distant from objective point designated by flagship observers will proceed toward it at maximum; squadrons nearest it will decelerate or reverse velocity — that point must not be approached until full Fleet formation has been accomplished. Heavy and Light Cruisers of all other sectors inside the orbit of Mars . . ." the orders went on, directing the mobilization of the stupendous forces of the League, so that they would be in readiness in the highly improbable event of the failure of the massed power of seven sectors to reduce the pirate base.

In those seven sectors perhaps a dozen vessels threw out enormous spherical screens of intense red light, and as they did so their tracer points upon all the interlocked lookout plates also became ringed about with red. Toward those crimson markers the pilots of the unmarked vessels directed their courses at their utmost power; and while the white lights upon the lookout plates moved slowly toward and clustered about the red ones — the ultra-instruments of the Secret Service operatives were probing into space, sweeping the neighborhood of the computed position of the pirate's stronghold.

But the object sought was so far away that the small spy-ray sets of the Secret Service men, intended as they were for close-range work, were unable to make contact with the invisible planetoid for which they were seeking. In the captain's sanctum of the *Chicago*, the operative studied his plate for only a minute or two, then shut off his power and fell into a brown study, from which he was rudely aroused.

"Aren't you even going to *try* to find them?" demanded the captain.

"No," Cleve returned shortly. "No use — not half enough power or control. I'm trying to think . . . maybe . . . say, Captain, will you please have the Chief Electrician and a couple of radio men come in here?"

They came, and for hours, while the other ultra-wave men searched the apparently empty ether with their ineffective beams, the three technical experts and the erstwhile

Quartermaster's clerk labored upon a huge and complex ultra-wave projector — the three blindly and with doubtful questions; the one with sure knowledge at least of what he was trying to do. Finally the thing was done, the crude but efficient graduated circles were set, and the tubes glowed redly as their solidly massed output was driving into a tight beam of ultra-vibration. "There it is, sir," Cleve reported, after some ten minutes of delicate manipulation, and the vast structure of the miniature world flashed into being upon his plate. "You may notify the fleet — co-ordinates H 11.62, RA 124-31-16, and Dx about 173.2."

The report made and the assistants out of the room, the captain turned to the observer and saluted gravely.

"We have always known, sir, that the Service had *men*; but I had no idea that any one man could possibly do, on the spur of the moment, what you have just done — unless that man happened to be Lyman Cleveland."

"Oh, it doesn't . . ." the observer began, but broke off, muttering unintelligibly at intervals; then swung the visiray beam toward the Earth. Soon a face appeared upon the plate, the keen but careworn face of Virgil Samms!

"Hello, Lyman." His voice came clearly from the speaker, and the Captain gasped — his ultra-wave observer and sometime clerk was Lyman Cleveland himself, probably the greatest living expert in beam transmission! "I knew that you'd do something, if it could be done. How about it — can the others install similar sets on their ships? I'm betting that they can't."

"Probably not," Cleveland frowned in thought. "This is a patchwork affair, made of gunny-sacks and hay-wire. I'm holding it together by main strength and awkwardness, and even at that it's apt to go to pieces any minute."

"Can you rig it up for photography?"

"I think so. Just a minute — yes, I can. Why?"

"Because there's something going on out there that neither we nor the so-called pirates know anything about. The Admiralty seems to think that it's the Jovians again, but we don't see how it can be — if it is, they have developed a lot of stuff that none of our agents has even suspected," and he recounted briefly what Costigan had reported to him, concluding: "Then there was a burst of interference — on the *ultra-band*, mind you — and I've heard nothing from him since. Therefore I want you to stay out of the battle entirely. Stay as far away from it as you can and still get good pictures of everything that happens. I will see that orders are issued to the *Chicago* to that effect."

"But listen. . . ."

"Those are orders!" snapped Samms. "It is of the utmost importance that we know every detail of what is going to happen. The answer is pictures. The only possibility of obtaining pictures is that machine you have just developed. If the fleet wins, nothing will be lost. If the fleet loses — and I am not half as confident of success as the Admiral is — the *Chicago* doesn't carry enough power to decide the issue, and we will have the pictures to study, which is all-important. Besides, we've probably lost Conway Costigan to-day, and we don't want to lose *you*, too."

Cleveland remained silent, pondering this startling news, but the grizzled Captain, veteran of the Fourth Jovian War that he was, was not convinced.

"We'll blow them out of space, Mr. Samms!" he declared.

"You just think you will, Captain. I have suggested, as forcibly as possible, that the general attack be withheld until after a thorough investigation is made, but the Admiralty will not listen. They see the advisability of withdrawing a camera ship, but that is as far as they will go."

"And that's plenty far enough!" growled the *Chicago's* commander, as the beam snapped off. "Mr. Cleveland, I don't like the idea of running away under fire, and I won't do it without direct orders from the Admiral."

"Of course you won't — that's why you are going. . . ."

He was interrupted by a voice from the Headquarters speaker. The captain stepped up to the plate and, upon being recognized, he received the exact orders which had been requested by the Chief of the Secret Service — now not as secret as it had been heretofore.

Thus it was that the *Chicago* reversed her acceleration, cut off her red screen, and fell rapidly behind, while the vessels following her in their loose cone formation shot away toward another crimson-flaring leader. Farther and farther back she dropped, back to the limiting range of the ultra-cameras upon which Cleveland and his highly trained assistants were furiously and unremittingly at work. And during all this time the forces of the seven sectors had been concentrating. The pilot vessels, with their flaming red screens, each followed by a cone of space-ships, drew closer and closer together, approaching the *Fearless* — the British superdreadnaught which was to be the flagship of the Fleet — the mightiest and heaviest space-ship which had yet lifted her stupendous mass into the ether.

Now, systematically and precisely, the great Cone of Battle was coming into being; a formation developed during the Jovian Wars while the forces of the Three Planets were fighting in space for their very civilizations' existence, and one never used since the last space-fleets of Jupiter's murderous hordes had been wiped out.

The mouth of that enormous hollow cone was a ring of scout patrols, the smallest and most agile vessels of the fleet. Behind them came a somewhat smaller ring of light cruisers, then rings of heavy cruisers and of light battleships, and finally of heavy battleships. At the apex of the cone, protected by all the other vessels of the formation and in best position to direct the battle, was the flagship. In this formation every vessel was free to use her every weapon, with a minimum of danger to her sister ships; and yet, when the gigantic main projectors were operated along the axis of the formation, from the entire vast circle of the cone's mouth there flamed a cylindrical field of force of such intolerable intensity that in it no conceivable substance could endure for a moment!

The artificial planet of metal was now close enough so that it was visible to the ultra-vision of the Secret Service men, so plainly visible that the warships of the pirates were seen issuing from the enormous air-locks. As each vessel shot out into space it sped straight for the approaching fleet without waiting to go into any formation — gray Roger believed his structures invisible to Triplanetary eyes, thought that the presence of the fleet was the result of mathematical calculations, and was convinced that his mighty vessels of the void would destroy even that vast fleet without themselves becoming known. He was wrong. The foremost globes were allowed actually to enter the mouth of that conical trap before an offensive move was made. Then the vice-admiral in command of the fleet touched a button, and simultaneously every generator in every Triplanetary vessel burst into furious activity. Instantly the hollow volume of the immense cone became a coruscating hell of resistless energy, an inferno which, with the velocity of light, extended itself into a far-reaching cylinder of rapacious destruction. Ether-waves they were, it is true, but vibrations driven with such fierce intensity that the screens of deflection surrounding the pirate vessels could not handle even a fraction of their awful power. Invisibility lost, their defensive screens flared briefly; but even the enormous force backing Roger's inventions, greater far than that of any single Triplanetary vessel, could not hold off the incredible violence of the massed attack of the hundreds of mighty vessels composing the Fleet. Their defensive screens flared briefly, then went down; their great spherical hulls first glowing red, then shining white, then in a brief moment exploding into flying masses of red hot, molten, and gaseous metal.

A full two-thirds of Roger's force was caught in that raging, incandescent beam; caught and obliterated: but the remainder did not retreat to the planetoid. Darting out around the edge of the cone at a stupendous acceleration, they attacked its flanks and the engagement became general. But now, since enough beams were kept upon each ship of the enemy so that invisibility could not be restored, each Triplanetary war vessel could attack with full efficiency. Magnesium flares and star-shells illuminated space for a thousand miles, and from every unit of both fleets was being hurled every item of solid, explosive, and vibratory destruction known to the highly scientific warfare of that age. Offensive beams, rods and daggers of frightful power struck and were neutralized by defensive screens equally capable; the long range and furious dodging made ordinary solid or high-explosive projectiles useless; and both sides were filling all space with such a volume of blanketing frequencies that such radio-dirigible torpedoes as were launched could not be controlled, but darted madly and erratically hither and thither, finally to be exploded harmlessly in mid-space by the touch of some fiercely insistent, probing beam of force.

Individually, however, the pirate vessels were far more powerful than those of the fleet, and that superiority soon began to make itself felt. The power of the smaller ships began to fail as their accumulators became discharged under the awful drain of the battle, and vessel after vessel of the Triplanetary fleet was hurled into nothingness by the concentrated blasts of the pirates' rays. But the Triplanetary forces had one great advantage. In furious haste the Secret Service men had been altering the controls of the radio-dirigible torpedoes, so that they would respond to ultra-wave control; and, few in number though they were, each was highly effective.

A hard-eyed observer, face almost against his plate and both hands and both feet manipulating controls, hurled the first torpedo. Propelling rockets viciously aflame, it twisted and looped around the incandescent rods of destruction so thickly and starkly outlined, under perfect control; unaffected by the hideous distortion of all ether-borne signals. Through a pirate screen it went, and under the terrific blast of its detonation one entire panel of the stricken battleship vanished, crumpled and broken. It should have been out, cold — but, to the amazement of the observers, it kept on fighting with scarcely lessened power! Three more of the frightful space-bombs had to be exploded in it — it had to be reduced to junk — before its terrible rays went out; Not a man in that great fleet had even an inkling of the truth; that those great vessels, those terrible engines of destruction, did not contain a single living creature: that they were manned and fought by automatons; robots controlled by keen-eyed, space-hardened veterans inside the planetoid so distant by means of tight, interference-proof communicator beams!

But they were to receive an inkling of it. As ship after ship of the pirate fleet was blown to pieces, Roger realized that his navy was beaten, and forthwith all his surviving vessels darted toward the apex of the cone, where the heaviest battleships were stationed. There each hurled itself upon a Triplanetary warship, crashing to its own destruction, but in that destruction insuring the loss of one of the heaviest vessels of the enemy. Thus passed the *Fearless*, and twenty of the finest space-ships of the fleet as well. But the ranking officer assumed command, the war-cone was re-formed, and, yawning maw to the fore, the great formation shot toward the pirate stronghold, now near at hand. It again launched its stupendous cylinder of annihilation, but even as the mighty defensive screens of the planetoid flared into incandescently furious defense, the battle was interrupted and pirates and Triplanetarians learned alike that they were not alone in the ether.

Space became suffused with a redly impenetrable opacity, and through that indescribable pall there came reaching huge arms of force incredible; writhing, coruscating beams of power which glowed a baleful, although almost imperceptible, red. A vessel of unheard-of armament and power, hailing from a distant solar system of the Galaxy, had come to rest in that space. For months her commander had been investigating sun after sun in quest of one precious substance. Now his detectors had found it; and, feeling neither fear of Triplanetarian weapons nor reluctance to sacrifice those thousands of Triplanetarian lives, he was about to take it!

CHAPTER IV

Within the Red Veil

Nevia, the home planet of the marauding space-ship, would have appeared peculiar indeed to Terrestrial senses. High in the deep red heavens a fervent blue sun poured down its flood of brilliant purplish light upon a world of water. Not a cloud was to be seen in that flaming sky, and through that dustless atmosphere the eye could see the horizon — a horizon three times as distant as the one to which we are accustomed — with a distinctness and clarity impossible in our Terra's dust-filled air. As that mighty sun dropped below the horizon the sky would fill suddenly with clouds and rain would fall violently and steadily until midnight. Then the clouds would vanish as suddenly as they had come into being, the torrential downpour would cease, and, through that huge world's wonderfully transparent, gaseous envelope, the full glory of the firmament would be revealed. Not the firmament as we know it — for that hot blue sun and Nevia, her one planet-child, were many light-years distant from Old Sol and his numerous brood — but a strange and glorious firmament containing not one constellation familiar to Earthly eyes.

Out of the vacuum of space a fish-shaped vessel of the void — the vessel that was shortly to attack so boldly both the massed fleet of Triplanetary and Roger's planetoid — plunged into the rarefied outer atmosphere, and crimson beams of force tore shriekingly the thin air as it braked its terrific speed. A third of the circumference of Nevia's mighty globe was traversed before the velocity of the craft could be reduced sufficiently to make a landing possible. Then, approaching the twilight zone, the vessel dived vertically downward, and it became evident that Nevia was neither entirely aqueous nor devoid of intelligent life. For the blunt nose of the space-ship was pointing toward what was evidently a half-submerged city, a city whose buildings were flat-topped, hexagonal towers, exactly alike in size, shape, color, and material. These buildings were arranged as the cells of a honeycomb would be if each cell were separated from its neighbors by a relatively narrow channel of water, and all were built of the same white metal. Many bridges and more tubes extended through the air from building to building, and the watery "streets" teemed with surface craft, and with submarines.

The pilot, stationed immediately below the conical prow of the space-ship, peered intently through the thick windows of crystal-clear metal which afforded unobstructed vision in every direction except vertically upward and behind him. His four huge and contractile eyes were active, each operating independently in sending its own message to his peculiar but capable brain. One was watching the instruments, the others scanned narrowly the immense, swelling curve of the ship's belly, the water upon which his vessel was to land, and the floating dock to which it was to be moored. Four hands — if hands they could be called — manipulated levers and wheels with infinite delicacy of touch, and with scarcely a splash the immense mass of the Nevian sky-wanderer struck the water and glided to a stop within a foot of its exact berth.

Four mooring bars dropped neatly into their sockets and the captain-pilot, after locking his controls in neutral, released his safety straps and leaped lightly from his padded bench to the floor. Scuttling across the floor and down a runway upon his four short, powerful, heavily scaled legs, he slipped smoothly into the water and flashed away, far below the surface. For Nevians are true amphibians. Their blood is cold; they use with equal comfort and efficiency gills and lungs for breathing; their scaly bodies are equally at home in the water or in the air; their broad, flat feet serve equally well for running about upon a solid surface or for driving their stream-lined bodies through the water at a pace few of our fishes can equal.

Through the water the Nevian commander darted along, steering his course accurately by means of his short, vaned tail. Through an opening in a wall he sped and along a submarine hallway, emerging upon a broad ramp. He scurried up the incline and into an elevator which lifted him to the top floor of the hexagon, directly into the office of the Secretary of Commerce of all Nevia.

"Welcome, Captain Nerado!" The Secretary waved a tentacular arm and the visitor sprang lightly upon a softly cushioned bench, where he lay at ease, facing the official across his low, flat "desk." "We congratulate you upon the success of your final trial flight. We received all your reports, even while you were traveling with many times the velocity of light. With the last difficulties overcome, you are now ready to start?"

"We are ready," the captain-scientist replied, soberly. "Mechanically, the ship is as nearly perfect as our finest minds can make her. She is stocked for two years. All the iron-bearing suns within reach have been plotted. Everything is ready except the iron. Of course the Council refused to allow us any of the national supply — how much were you able to purchase for us in the market?"

"Nearly ten pounds. . . ."

"Ten pounds! Why, the securities we left with you could not have bought two pounds, even at the price then prevailing!"

"No, but you have friends. Many of us believe in you, and have dipped into our own resources. You and your fellow scientists of the expedition have each contributed his entire personal fortune; why should not some of the rest of us also contribute, as private citizens?"

"Wonderful — we thank you. Ten pounds!" The captain's great triangular eyes glowed with an intense violet light. "A full year of cruising. But . . . what if, after all, we should be wrong?"

"In that case you shall have consumed ten pounds of irreplaceable metal." The Secretary was unmoved. "That is the viewpoint of the Council and of almost everyone else. It is not the waste of treasure they object to; it is the fact that ten pounds of iron will be forever lost."

"A high price truly," the Columbus of Nevia assented, "And after all, I may be wrong."

"You probably are — of course you are wrong," his host made a startling answer. "It is practically certain — it is almost a demonstrable mathematical fact — that no other sun within hundreds of thousands of light-years of our own has a planet. In all probability Nevia is the only planet in the entire Universe. We are the only intelligent life in the Universe. But there is one chance in numberless millions that, somewhere with the cruising range of your newly perfected space-ship, there may be an iron-bearing planet upon which you can effect a landing, and it is upon that infinitesimal chance that some of us are staking a portion of our wealth. We expect no return whatever, but if you *should* by some miracle happen to find stores of iron somewhere in space, what then? Deep seas being made shallow, civilization extending itself over the globe, science advancing by leaps and bounds, Nevia becoming populated as she should be peopled — that, my friend, is a chance well worth taking!"

The Secretary called in a group of guards, who escorted the small package of priceless metal to the space-ship, and before the massive door was sealed the friends bade each other farewell.

" . . . I will keep in touch with you on the ultra-wave," the Captain concluded. "After all, I do not blame the Council for refusing to allow the other ship to go with us. Ten pounds of iron will be a fearful loss to the world. If we *should* find iron, however, see to it that the other vessel loses no time in following us."

"No fear of that! If you find iron all space will be full of vessels, as soon as they can possibly be built — good-bye!"

The last opening was sealed and Nerado shot the great vessel into the air. Up and up, out beyond the last tenuous trace of atmosphere, on and on through space it flew with ever-increasing velocity until Nevia's gigantic blue sun had been left so far behind that it became a splendid blue-white star. Then, projectors cut off to save the precious iron whose disintegration furnished them power, for week after week Captain Nerado and his venturesome crew of scientists drifted idly through the illimitable void. Sun after sun, as visible in their ultra-instruments as though the flying vessel were moving slower than light, they studied without finding a single planet.

Three months passed. Nerado had already applied the slight power which was to swing the vessel around in an immense circle, back toward his native world. In that course he was rapidly approaching a sun, an ordinary G-type dwarf, whose spectrum revealed a blaze of lines of the precious element for which he was searching. Now at close observing range — he had long since abandoned his former eager habit of studying a sun as soon as it showed the tiniest perceptible disk in his most powerful telescope — he turned on his powerful visiray beam without enthusiasm, swung it upon that very commonplace sun, and shrieked aloud in exultation. Not only one planet had that yellowish luminary — it had six, seven, eight; yes, possibly nine or ten; and several of those planets were themselves apparently centers of attraction around which were circling other tiny worlds! Nerado thrilled with joy as he applied a full retarding force, and every creature aboard that great vessel had to peer into a plate or through a telescope, before he could believe that planets other than Nevia did in reality exist!

Velocity checked to the merest crawl, as space-speed goes, and with electro-magnetic detector screens full out, the Nevian vessel crept toward our sun. Finally the detectors encountered an obstacle, a conductive substance which the patterns showed conclusively to be practically pure iron. Iron — an enormous mass of it — floating alone out in space! Without waiting to investigate the nature, appearance, or structure of the precious mass, Nerado ordered power into the converters and drove an enormous softening field of force upon the object — a force of such a nature that it would condense the metallic iron into an allotropic modification of much smaller bulk; a red, viscous, extremely dense and heavy liquid which could be stored conveniently in his tanks.

No sooner had the precious fluid been stored away than the detectors again broke into an uproar. In one direction was an enormous mass of iron, scarcely detectable; in another a great number of smaller masses; in a third an isolated mass, comparatively small in size. Space seemed to be full of iron, and Nerado drove his most powerful beam toward distant Nevia and sent an exultant message.

"We have found iron — easily obtained and in unthinkable quantity — not in fractions of milligrams, but in millions upon unmeasured millions of tons! Send our sister ship here as once!"

"Nerado!" The captain was called to one of the observation plates as soon as he had opened his key. "I have been investigating the mass of iron now nearest us, the small one. It is an artificial structure, a small space-boat, and there are three creatures in it — monstrosities certainly, but they must possess some intelligence or they could not be navigating space."

"What? Impossible!" exclaimed the chief explorer. "Probably, then, the other was — but no matter, we had to have the iron. Bring the boat in without converting it, so that we may study at our leisure both the beings and their mechanisms," and Nerado swung his own visiray beam into the emergency boat, seeing there the armored figures of Clio Marsden and the two Triplanetary officers.

"They are indeed intelligent," Nerado commented, as he detected and silenced Costigan's ultra-beam communicator. "Not, however, as intelligent as I had supposed," he went on, after studying the peculiar creatures and their tiny space-ship more in detail. "They have immense stores of iron, yet use it for nothing other than building material. They apparently have a rudimentary knowledge of ultra-waves, but do not use them intelligently — they cannot neutralize even these ordinary forces we are now employing. They are of course more intelligent than the lower ganoids, or even than some of the higher fishes, but by no stretch of the imagination can they be compared to us. I am quite relieved — I was afraid that in my haste I might slay members of a highly developed race."

The helpless boat, all her forces neutralized, was brought up close to the immense flying fish. There flaming knives of force sliced her neatly into sections and the three rigid armored figures, after being bereft of their external weapons, were brought through the air-locks and into the control room, while the pieces of their boat were stored away for future study. The Nevian scientists first analyzed the air inside the space-suits of the Terrestrials, then removed without ado the protective covering of the captives.

Costigan — fully conscious through it all and now able to move a little, since the peculiar temporary paralysis was wearing off — braced himself for he knew not what shock, but it was needless; their grotesque captors were not torturers. The air, while somewhat less dense than Earth's and of a peculiar odor, was eminently breathable, and even though the vessel was motionless in space, an almost-normal gravitation gave them a large fraction of their usual weight. The space suits were removed with care, and after the three had been relieved of their pistols and other articles which the Nevians thought might prove to be weapons, the strange paralysis was lifted entirely. The Earthly clothing puzzled the captors immensely, but so strenuous were the objections raised to its removal, but they did not press the point, but fell back to study their find in detail.

Then faced each other the representatives of the civilizations of two widely separated solar systems. The Nevians studied the human beings with interest and curiosity blended largely with loathing and repulsion; the three Terrestrials regarded the unmoving, expressionless "faces" — if those coned heads could be said to possess such things — with horror and disgust, as well as with other emotions, each according to his type and training. For to human eyes the Nevian is a fearful thing. Even to-day there are few Terrestrials — or Solarians for that matter — who can look at a Nevian, eye to eye, without feeling a creeping of the skin and experiencing a "gone" sensation in the pit of the stomach. The horny, wrinkled, drought-resisting Martian, whom we all know and rather like, is a hideous being indeed. The bat-eyed, colorless, hairless, practically skinless Venerian is worse. But they both are, after all, remote cousins of Terra's humanity, and we get along with them quite well whenever we are compelled to visit Mars or Venus. But the Nevians —

The horizontal, flat, fish body is not so bad, even supported as it is by four, short, powerful, scaly, flat-footed legs; and terminating as it does in the weird, four-vaned tail. The neck, even, is endurable, although it is long and flexible, heavily scaled, and is carried in whatever eye-wringing loops, knots, or angles the owner considers most convenient or ornamental at the time. Even the smell of a Nevian — a malodorous reek of over-ripe fish — does in time become tolerable, especially if sufficiently disguised with creosote, which purely Terrestrial chemical is the most highly prized perfume of Nevia. But the head! It is that member that makes the Nevian so appalling to Earthly eyes, for it is a thing utterly foreign to all Solarian history or experience. As most Tellurians already know, it is fundamentally a massive cone, covered with scales, based spearhead-like upon the neck. Four great sea-green, triangular eyes are spaced equidistant from each other about half way up the cone. The pupils are contractile at will, like the eyes of the cat, permitting the Nevian to see equally well in any ordinary extreme of light or darkness. Immediately below each eye springs out a long, jointless, boneless, tentacular arm; an arm which at its extremity divides into eight delicate and sensitive, but very strong, fingers. Below each arm is a mouth: a beaked, needle-tusked orifice of dire potentialities. Finally, under the overhanging edge of the cone-shaped head are the delicately frilled organs which serve either as gills or as nostrils and lungs, as may be desired. To other Nevians the eyes and other features are highly expressive, but to us they appear utterly cold and unmoving. Terrestrial senses can detect no changes of expression in a Nevian's "face." Such were the frightful beings at whom the three prisoners stared with sinking hearts.

But if we human beings have always considered Nevians grotesque and repulsive, the feeling has always been mutual. For those "monstrous" beings are a highly intelligent and extremely sensitive race, and our — to us — trim and graceful human forms seems to them the very quintessence of malformation and hideousness.

"Good Heavens, Conway!" Clio exclaimed, shrinking against Costigan as his left arm flashed around her. "What monstrosities! And they can't talk — not one of them has made a sound — suppose they can be deaf and dumb?"

But at the same time Nerado was addressing his fellows.

"What hideous, deformed creatures they are! Truly a low form of life, even though they do possess some intelligence. They cannot talk, and have made no signs of having heard our words to them — do you suppose that they communicate by sight? That those weird contortions of their peculiarly placed organs serve as speech?"

Thus both sides, neither realizing that the other had spoken. For the Nevian voice is pitched so high that the lowest note audible to them is far above our limit of hearing. The shrillest note of a Terrestrial piccolo is to them so profoundly low that it cannot be heard.

"We have much to do." Nerado turned away from the captives. "We must postpone further study of the specimens until we have taken aboard a full cargo of the iron which is so plentiful here."

"What shall we do with them, sir?" asked one of the Nevian officers. "Lock them in one of the storage rooms?"

"No. They might die there, and we must by all means keep them in good condition, to be studied most carefully by the fellows of the College of Science. What a commotion there will be when we bring in this group of strange creatures, living proof that there are other suns possessing planets; planets which are supporting organic and intelligent life! You may put them in three communicating rooms, say in the fourth section — they will undoubtedly require light and exercise. Lock all exits, of course, but it would be best to leave the doors between the rooms unlocked, so that they can be together or apart, as they choose. Since the smallest one, the female, stays so close to the larger male, it may be that they are mates. But since we know nothing of their habits or customs, it will be best to give them all possible freedom compatible with safety."

Nerado turned back to his instruments and three of the frightful crew came up to the human beings. One walked away, waving a couple of arms in an unmistakable signal that the prisoners were to follow him. The three obediently set out after him, the other two guards falling behind.

"Now's our best chance!" Costigan muttered, as they passed through a low doorway and entered a narrow corridor. "Watch that one ahead of you, Clio — hold him for a second if you can. Bradley, you and I'll take the two behind us — now!"

Costigan stopped and whirled. Seizing a cable-like arm, he pulled the outlandish head down, the while the full power of his mighty right leg drove a heavy service boot into the place where scaly neck and head joined. The Nevian fell, and instantly Costigan leaped at the leader, ahead of the girl. Leaped; but dropped to the floor, again paralyzed. For the Nevian leader had been alert, his four eyes covering the entire circle of vision, and he had acted rapidly. Not in time to stop Costigan's first Berserk attack — the First Officer's reactions were practically instantaneous, and he moved like chain lightning — but in time to retain command of the situation. Another Nevian appeared and, while the stricken guard was recovering, all four arms wrapped tightly around his convulsively looping, knotting neck, the three helpless Terrestrials were lifted into the air and carried bodily into the quarters to which Nerado had assigned them. Not until they had been placed upon cushions in the middle room and the heavy metal doors had been locked upon them did they again find themselves able to use arms or legs.

"Well, that's another round we lose," Costigan commented, cheerfully. "A guy can't mix it very well when he can neither kick, strike, nor bite. I expected those lizards to rough me up, but they didn't."

"They don't want to hurt us. They want to take us home with them, wherever that is, as curiosities, like wild animals or something," decided the girl, shrewdly. "They're pretty bad, of course, but I like them a lot better than I do Roger and his robots, anyway."

"I think you have the right idea, Miss Marsden," Bradley rumbled. "That's it, exactly. I feel like a bear in a cage. I should think you'd feel worse than ever. What chance has an animal of escaping from a menagerie?"

"These animals, lots. I'm feeling better and better all the time," Clio answered, and her serene bearing bore out her words. "You two got us out of that horrible place of Roger's, and I'm pretty sure that you will get us away from here, somehow or other. They may think we're stupid animals, but before you two and the Secret Service get done with them they'll have another think coming."

"That's the old fight, Clio!" cheered Costigan. "I haven't got it figured out as close as you have, but I see you, eye to eye. These four-legged fish carry considerably heavier stuff than Roger did, I'm thinking; but they'll be up against something themselves pretty quick, that is NO light-weight, believe me!"

"Do you *know* something, or are you just whistling in the dark?" Bradley demanded.

"I know a little; not much. The Science Service has been working on a new ship for a long time; a ship to travel so much faster than light that it can go anywhere in the Galaxy and back in a month or so. New sub-ether drive, new power, new armament, new everything. Only bad thing about it is that it doesn't work so good yet — it's fuller of 'bugs' than a Venerian's kitchen. It has blown up five times that I know of, and has killed twenty-nine men. But when they get it licked they'll *have something!*"

"When, or if?" asked Bradley, pessimistically.

"I said *when!*" snapped Costigan, his voice cutting like a knife. "When that gang goes after anything they get it, and when they get it it stays. . . ." He broke off abruptly and his voice lost its edge. "Sorry. Didn't mean to get high, but I think we'll have help, if we can keep our heads up a while. And it looks good — these are first-class cages they've given us. All the comforts of home, even to lookout plates. Let's see what's going on, shall we?"

After some experimenting with the unfamiliar controls Costigan learned how to operate the Nevian visiray, and upon the plate they saw the Cone of Battle hurling itself toward Roger's planetoid. They saw the pirate fleet rush out to do battle with Triplanetary's massed forces, and with bated breath they watched every maneuver of that epic battle to its savagely sacrificial end. And that same battle was being watched, also with intense interest, by the Nevians.

"It is indeed a blood-thirsty combat," mused Nerado at his observation plate. "And it is peculiar — or rather, probably only to be expected from a race of such a low stage of development — that they employ only ether-borne forces. Warfare seems universal among primitive types — indeed, it is not so long ago that our own cities, few in number though they are, ceased fighting each other and combined against the semi-civilized fishes of the greater deeps."

He fell silent, and for many minutes watched the furious battle between the two navies of the void. That conflict ended, he watched the Triplanetary fleet reform its battle cone and rush upon the planetoid.

"Destruction, always destruction," he sighed, adjusting

his power switches. "Since they are bent upon mutual destruction I can see no purpose in refraining from destroying all of them. We need the iron, and they are a useless race."

He launched his softening, converting field of dull red energy. Vast as that field was, it could not encompass the whole of the fleet, but half of the lip of the gigantic cone soon disappeared, its component vessels subsiding into a sluggishly flowing stream of allotropic iron. Instantly the fleet abandoned the attack upon the planetoid and swung its cone around, to bring the flame-erupting axis to bear upon the inchoate something dimly perceptible to the ultra-vision of the Secret Service observers. Furiously the gigantic composite beam of the massed fleet was hurled, nor was it alone.

For Roger in his floating citadel had realized at once that something untoward was happening; something altogether beyond even his knowledge and experience. He could not see anything — space was apparently empty — but he took his rays off the battleships and directed his every force just beyond the point in space where that red stream of transformed metal was disappearing. Then, for the first time in Triplanetary history, the forces of law and order joined hands with those of piracy and banditry against a common foe. Rods, beams, planes, and stilettoes of unbearable energy the doomed fleet launched, in addition to its main beam of annihilation, and Roger also hurled out into space every weapon at his command. Bombs, high-explosive shells, and deadly radio-dirigible torpedoes — all alike disappeared ineffective in that redly murky veil of nothingness. And the fleet was being melted. In quick succession the vessels flamed red, shrank together, gave out their air, and merged their component iron into the intensely red, sullenly viscous stream which was flowing through the impenetrable veil upon which Triplanetarians and pirates alike were directing their every possible weapon of offense.

The last vessel of the Triplanetary armada converted and the resulting metal stored away in their capacious reservoirs, the Nevians turned their attention upon the stronghold of the pirates. There ensued a battle royal. For this vast planetoid was no feeble warship, depending solely upon the limited power available in its accumulators. It was the product of a really mighty brain, a brain re-enforced by the many perverted but powerful intellects which Roger had won over to his cause. It was powered by the incalculable force of cosmic radiation, powered to drive its unimaginable mass through space, against any possible attractions, for an indefinite number of years. It was armed and equipped to meet any emergency which Roger's coldly analytical mind had been able to foresee.

The fact that the scientists of the Secret Service had discovered ultra-waves as yet unknown to him was unfortunate. That Service was itself unfortunate — impenetrable as it was, and incorruptible. He could learn nothing whatever about it. He had heard vague rumors of certain experiments — but even if they should discover something it would be too late to do them any good. Even without invisibility he would have no trouble in annihilating the massed Grand Fleet of the Triplanetary League. He would very shortly collect his tribute and disappear. And this new enemy, himself invisible and armed with heretofore unknown weapons of dire power, who was apparently unaffected by his beams — even he would discover that Roger the Great was no puny opponent. He would analyze those unknown forces, regenerate them, and hurl them back upon their senders.

Thinking thus, the man of gray sat coldly motionless at his great multi-shielded desk, whose top was now swung up to become a board of massed and tiered instruments and controls. He shut off his offensive beams and surrounded the entire planetoid with the peculiarly rigid and substantial shield which had so easily warded off Costigan's fiercest attacks. And that shield was more effective than even its designer had supposed — gray Roger had builded even better than he knew. For the voracious and all-powerful converting beam of the Nevians, below the level of the ether though it was, struck that perfectly transparent wall and rebounded, defeated and futile. Struck and rebounded, then struck and clung hungrily, licking out over that impermeable surface in darting tongues of red flame as the surprised Nerado doubled and then quadrupled his power. Fiercer and fiercer drove in the Nevian flood of force until the whole immense globe of the planetoid was one scintillant ball of scarlet energy, but still the pirates' shield remained intact — at what awful drain of resource, Roger alone knew.

"Here is the analysis of his screen, sir." A Nevian computer handed his chief a sheet of metal, upon which were engraved rows of symbols.

"Ah, a sixth-phase polycyclic. A screen of that type was scarcely to have been expected from such a low form of life," Nerado commented, and rapidly adjusted the many dials and switches before him.

As he did so the character of the clinging mantle of force changed. From red it flamed quickly through the spectrum, became unbearably violet, then disappeared; and as it disappeared the shielding wall began to give way. It did not cave in abruptly, but softened locally, sagging into a peculiar grouping of valleys and ridges — contesting stubbornly every inch of position lost. And gray Roger knew that the planetoid was doomed. His supposedly impregnable screen was failing in spite of its utmost measure of energy, and, that defense down, the citadel would not last a minute. Therefore he summoned a chosen few of his motley crew of renegade scientists and issued brief instructions. For minutes a host of robots toiled mightily, then a portion of the shield bulged out, extended into a tube beyond the attacking layers of force, and from it there erupted a beam of violence incredible. A beam behind which was every volt and ampere that the gigantic generators and accumulators of the planetoid could yield. A beam that tore screamingly through the ether; that by the very vehemence of its incalculable energy tore a hole through the redly impenetrable Nevian field and hurled itself upon the inner screen of the fish-shaped cruiser in frenzied incandescence. And was there, or was there not, a lesser eruption upon the other side — an almost imperceptible flash, as though something had shot from the doomed planetoid out into space?

Nerado's looped neck straightened convulsively as his tortured drivers whined and shrieked at the terrific overload; but Roger's effort was far too intense to be long maintained. Even before his accumulators failed, generator after generator burned out, the defensive screen collapsed, and the red converter beam attacked voraciously the unresisting metal of those prodigious walls. Soon there was a terrific explosion as the pent-up air of the planetoid broke through its weakening container, and the sluggish river of allotropic iron flowed in an ever larger stream, ever faster.

"It is well that we had an unlimited supply of iron." Nerado tied a knot in his neck and spoke in huge relief. "With but the seven pounds remaining of our original supply, I fear that it would have been difficult to parry that last thrust."

"Difficult?" asked the second in command. "We would now be swimming in space. But what shall I do with this iron? Our reservoirs will not hold it all."

"Seal up one or two of the lower storage compartments, to make room for this lot. Immediately it is loaded, we return to Nevia. There we shall install reservoirs in all the spare space, and come back here for more."

The last drop of the precious liquid secured, the vessel moved away, sluggishly now because of its prodigious load. In their quarters in the fourth section the three Terrestrials, who had watched with strained attention the downfall and absorption of the planetoid, stared at each other with drawn faces. Clio broke the silence.

"Oh, Conway, this is ghastly! It's . . . it's just simply perfectly horrible!" she gasped, then recovered a measure of her customary spirit as she stared in surprise at Costigan's face. For it was thoughtful, his eyes were bright and keen — no trace of fear or disorganization was visible in any line of his hard young face.

"It's not so good," he admitted frankly. "I wish I wasn't such a dumb cluck — if Lyman Cleveland or Ford Rodebush were here they could help a lot, but I don't know enough about any of their stuff to flag a hand-car. I can't even interpret that funny flash — if it really was a flash — that we saw."

"Why bother about one little flash, after all that really did happen?" asked Clio, curiously.

"You think Roger launched something? He couldn't have — I didn't see a thing," Bradley argued.

"I don't know what to think. I've never seen anything material sent out so fast that I couldn't trace it with an ultra-wave — but on the other hand, Roger's got a lot of stuff that I never saw anywhere else. However, I don't see that it has anything to do with the fix we're in right now — but at that, we might be worse off. We're still breathing air, you notice, and if they don't blanket my wave I can still talk."

He put both hands in his pockets and spoke.

"Samms? Costigan. Put me on a recorder, quick — I probably haven't got much time," and for ten minutes he talked, concisely and as rapidly as he could utter words, reporting clearly and exactly everything that had transpired. Suddenly he broke off, writhing in agony. Frantically he tore his shirt open and hurled a tiny object across the room.

"Wow!" he exclaimed. "They may be deaf, but they can certainly detect an ultra-wave, and the interference they can set up on it is enough to pulverize your bones. No, I'm not hurt," he reassured the anxious girl, now at his side, "but it's a good thing I had you out of circuit — it would have jolted you loose from six or seven of your back teeth."

"Have you any idea where they're taking us?" she asked, soberly.

"No," he answered flatly, looking deep into her steadfast eyes. "No use lying to you — if I know you at all you'd rather take it standing up. That talk of Jovians or Neptunians is the bunk — nothing like that ever grew in our Solarian system. All the signs say that we're going for a long, long ride!"

CHAPTER V

Nevian Strife

The Nevian space-ship was hurtling upon its way. Space-navigators both, the two Terrestrial officers soon discovered that it was even then moving with a velocity far above that of light and that it must be accelerating at a stupendous rate, even though to them it seemed stationary — they could feel only a gravitational force somewhat less than that of their native Earth.

Bradley, seasoned old campaigner that he was, had retired promptly as soon as he had completed a series of observations, and was sleeping soundly upon a pile of cushions in the first of the three inter-connecting rooms. In the middle room, which was to be Clio's, Costigan was standing very close to the girl, but was not touching her. His body was rigid, his face was tense and drawn.

"You are wrong, Conway; all wrong," Clio was saying, very seriously. "I know how you feel, but it's false chivalry."

"That isn't it, at all," he insisted, stubbornly. "It isn't only that I've got you out here in space, in danger and alone, that's stopping me. I know you and I know myself well enough to know that what we start now we'll go through with for life. It doesn't make any difference, that way, whether I start making love to you now or whether I wait until we're back on Tellus — I've been telling you for half an hour that for your own good you'd better pass me up entirely. I've got enough horsepower to keep away from you if you tell me to — not otherwise."

"I know it, both ways, dear, but. . . ."

"But nothing!" he interrupted. "Can't you get it into your skull what you'll be letting yourself in for if you marry me? Assume that we get back, which isn't sure, by any means. But even if we do, some day — and maybe soon, too, you can't tell — somebody is going to collect fifty grams of radium for my head."

"Fifty grams — and everybody knows that Samms himself is rated at only sixty? I *knew* that you were somebody, Conway!" Clio exclaimed, undeterred. "But at that, something tells me that any pirate will earn even that much reward several times over before he collects it. Don't be silly, dear heart — good-night."

She tipped her head back, holding up to him her red, sweetly curved, smiling lips, and his eager arms, hitherto kept away from her by sheer force of will, swept around her in almost fierce intensity. As his hot lips met hers, her arms crept up around his neck and they stood, clasped together in the motionless ecstasy of love's first embrace.

"Girl, girl, how I love you!" Costigan's voice was husky, his usually hard eyes were glowing with a tender light. "That settles that. I'll really *live* now, anyway, while. . . ."

"Stop it!" she commanded, sharply. "You're going to live until you die of old age — see if you don't. You'll simply *have* to, Conway!"

"That's so, too — no percentage in dying now. All the pirates between Tellus and Andromeda couldn't take me after this — I've got too much to live for. Well, good-night, sweetheart, I'd better beat it — you need some sleep."

The lovers' parting was not as simple and straightforward a procedure as Costigan's speech would indicate, but finally he did seek his own room and relaxed upon a pile of cushions, his stern visage transformed. Instead of the low metal ceiling he saw a beautiful, oval, tanned young face, framed in a golden-blonde corona of hair. His gaze sank into the depths of loyal, honest, dark-blue eyes; and looking deeper and deeper into those blue wells he fell asleep. Upon his face, too set and grim by far for a man of his years — the lives of Sector Chiefs of the T. S. S. are never easy, nor as a rule are they long — there lingered as he slept that newly acquired softness of expression, the reflection of his transcendent happiness.

For eight hours he slept soundly, as was his wont; then, also according to his habit and training, he came wide awake, with no intermediate stage of napping.

"Clio?" he whispered. "Awake, girl?"

"Awake!" Her voice came through the ultra-phone, relief in every syllable. "Good heavens, I thought you were going to sleep until we got to wherever it is that we're going! Come on in, you two — I don't see how you can possibly sleep, just as though you were home in bed."

"You've got to learn to sleep anywhere if you expect to keep in. . . ." Costigan broke off as he opened the door and saw Clio's wan face. She had evidently spent a sleepless and wracking eight hours. "Good Lord, Clio, why didn't you call me?"

"Oh, I'm all right, except for being a little jittery. No need of asking how *you* feel, is there?"

"No — I feel hungry," he answered cheerfully. "I'm going to see what we can do about it — or say, guess I'll see whether they're still interfering on Samms' wave."

He took out a small, insulated case and touched the contact stud lightly with his fingers. His arm jerked away powerfully.

"Still at it," he gave the necessary explanation. "They don't seem to want us to talk outside, but his interference is as good as my talking — they can trace it, of course. Now I'll see what I can find out about our breakfast."

He stepped over to the plate and shot its projector beam forward into the control room, where he saw Nerado lying, doglike, at his instrument panel. As Costigan's beam entered the room a blue light flashed on and the Nevian turned an eye and an arm toward his own small observation plate. Knowing that they were now in visual communication, Costigan beckoned an invitation and pointed to his mouth in what he hoped was the universal sign of hunger. The Nevian waved an arm and fingered controls, and as he did so a wide section of the floor of Clio's room slid aside. The opening thus made revealed a table which rose upon its low pedestal, a table equipped with three softly cushioned benches and spread with a glittering array of silver and glassware. Bowls and platters of dazzlingly white metal, narrow-waisted goblets of sheerest crystal; all were hexagonal, beautifully and intricately carved or etched in apparently conventional marine designs. And the table utensils of this strange race were peculiar indeed. There were tearing forceps of sixteen needle-sharp curved teeth; there were flexible spatulas; there were deep and shallow ladles with flexible edges; there were many other peculiarly curved instruments at whose uses the Terrestrials could no even guess; all having delicately fashioned handles to fit the long, slender fingers of the Nevians.

But if the table and its appointments were surprising to the Terrestrials, revealing as they did a degree of culture which none of them had expected to find in a race of beings so monstrous, the food was even more surprising, although in another sense. For the wonderful crystal goblets were filled with a grayish-green slime of a nauseous and overpowering odor, the smaller bowls were full of living sea spiders and other such delicacies; and each large platter contained a fish fully a foot long, raw and whole, garnished tastefully with red, purple, and green strands of seaweed!

Clio looked once, then gasped, shutting her eyes and turning away from the table, but Costigan flipped the three fish into a platter and set it aside before he turned back to the visiplate.

"They'll go good fried," he remarked to Bradley, signaling vigorously to Nerado that the meal was not acceptable and that he wanted to talk to him, *in person*. Finally he made himself clear, the table sank down out of sight, and the Nevian commander cautiously entered the room.

At Costigan's insistence, he came up to the plate, leaving

near the door three guards armed with projectors in instant readiness. The operative then shot the beam into the galley of the pirate's lifeboat, suggesting that they should be allowed to live there. For some time the argument of arms and fingers raged — though not exactly a fluent conversation, both sides managed to convey their meanings quite clearly. Nerado would not allow the Terrestrials to visit their own ship — he was taking no chances — but after a thorough ultra-ray inspection he did finally order some of his men to bring into the middle room the electric range and a supply of Terrestrial food. Soon the Nevian fish were sizzling in a pan and the appetizing odors of coffee and of browning biscuit permeated the room. But at the first appearance of those odors the Nevians departed hastily, content to watch the remainder of the curious and repulsive procedure in their visiray plates.

Breakfast over and everything made tidy and shipshape, Costigan turned to Clio.

"Look here, girl; you've got to learn how to sleep. You're all in. Your eyes look like you'd been on a Martian picnic and you didn't eat half enough breakfast. You've got to sleep and eat to keep fit. We don't want you passing out on us, so I'll put out this light, and you'll lie down here and sleep until noon."

"Oh, no; don't bother. I'll sleep to-night. I'm quite. . . ."

"You'll sleep now," he informed her, levelly. "I never thought of you being nervous, with Bradley and me on each side of you. We're both right here now, though, and we'll stay here. We'll watch over you like a couple of old hens with one chick between them. Come on; lie down and go bye-bye."

Clio laughed at the simile, but lay down obediently. Costigan sat upon the edge of the great divan, holding her hand, and they chatted idly. The silences grew longer, Clio's remarks became fewer, and soon her long-lashed lids fell and her deep, regular breathing showed that she was sound asleep. The man stared at her, his very heart in his eyes. So young, so beautiful, so lovely — and *how* he did love her! He was not formally religious, but his every thought was a sincere prayer. If he could only get her out of this mess . . . he wasn't fit to live on the same planet with her, but . . . just give him one chance, just one!

But Costigan had been laboring for days under a terrific strain, and had been going very short on sleep. Half hypnotized by his own mixed emotions and by his staring at the smooth curves of Clio's cheek, his own eyes closed and, still holding her hand, he sank down into the soft cushions beside her and into oblivion.

Thus sleeping hand-in-hand like two children Bradley found them, and a tender, fatherly expression came over his face as he looked down at them.

"Nice little girl, Clio," he mused, "and when they made Costigan they broke the mould. They'll do — about as fine a couple of kids as old Tellus ever produced. I could do with some more sleep myself." He yawned prodigiously, lay down at Clio's left, and almost instantly was himself asleep.

Hours later, both men were awakened by a merry peal of laughter. Clio was sitting up, regarding them with sparkling eyes. She was refreshed, buoyant, ravenously hungry and highly amused. Costigan was amazed and annoyed at what he considered a failure in a self-appointed task; Bradley was calm and matter-of-fact.

"Thanks for being such a nice bodyguard, you two," Clio laughed again, but sobered quickly. "I slept wonderfully well, but I wonder if I can sleep to-night without making you hold my hand all night?"

"Oh, he doesn't mind doing that," Bradley commented.

"Mind it!" Costigan exclaimed, and his eyes and his tone spoke volumes that his tongue left unsaid.

They prepared and ate another meal, one to which Clio did full justice; and, rested and refreshed, had begun to discuss possibilities of escape when Nerado and his three armed guards entered the room. The Nevian scientist placed a box upon a table and began to make adjustments upon its panels, eyeing the Terrestrials attentively after each setting. After a time a staccato burst of articulate speech issued from the box, and Costigan saw a great light.

"You've got it — hold it!" he exclaimed, waving his arms excitedly. "You see, Clio, their voices are pitched either higher or lower than ours — probably higher — and they've built an audio-frequency changer. He's nobody's fool, that fish!"

Nerado heard Costigan's voice; there was no doubt of that. His long neck looped and angled in Nevian gratification, and, although neither side could understand the other, both knew that intelligent speech and hearing were attributes common to the two races. This fact altered markedly the relations between captors and captives. The Nevians admitted among themselves that the strange bipeds might be quite intelligent, after all; and the Terrestrials at once became more hopeful.

"It isn't so bad, if they can talk," Costigan summed up the situation. "We might as well take it easy and make the best of it, particularly since we haven't been able to figure out any possible way of getting away from them. They can talk and hear, and we can learn their language in time. Maybe we can make some kind of a deal with them to take us back to our own system, if we can't make a break."

The Nevians being as eager as the Terrestrials to establish communication, Nerado kept the newly devised frequency-changer in constant use. There is no need of describing at length the details of that interchange of languages. Suffice it to say that starting at the very bottom they learned as babies learn, but with the great advantage over babies of possessing fully developed and capable brains. And while the human beings were learning the tongue of Nevia, several of the amphibians (and incidentally Clio Marsden) were learning Triplanetarian; the two officers knowing well that it would be much easier for the Nevians to learn the logically-built common language of the Three Planets than to master the senseless intricacies of English.

In a few weeks the two parties were able to understand

each other after a fashion, by using a weird mixture of both languages. As soon as a few ideas had been exchanged, the Nevian scientists built transformers small enough to be worn collar-like by the Terrestrials, and the captives were allowed to roam at will throughout the great vessel; only the compartment in which was stored the dismembered pirate lifeboats being sealed to them. Thus it was that they were not left long in doubt, when another fish-shaped cruiser of the world was revealed upon their lookout plates in the awful emptiness of interstellar space.

"That is our sister-ship, going to your Solarian system for a cargo of the iron which is so plentiful there," Nerado explained to his involuntary guests.

"I hope the gang has got the bugs worked out of our super-ship," Costigan muttered savagely to his companions as Nerado turned away. "If they have, that outfit will get something more than a load of iron when they get there!"

More weeks passed; weeks during which a blue-white star separated itself from the infinitely distant firmament and began to show a perceptible disk. Larger and larger it grew, becoming bluer and bluer as the flying space-ship approached it, until finally Nevia could be seen, apparently close beside her parent orb.

Heavily laden though the vessel was, such was her power that she was soon dropping vertically toward a large lagoon in the middle of the Nevian city. That bit of open water was strangely devoid of life, for this was to be no ordinary landing. Under the terrific power of the beams braking the descent of that unimaginable load of allotropic iron the water seethed and boiled; and instead of floating gracefully upon the surface of the sea, this time the huge ship of space sank like a plummet to the bottom. Having accomplished this delicate feat of docking the vessel safely in the immense cradle prepared for her, Nerado turned to the Terrestrials, who, now under guard, had been brought before him.

"While our cargo of iron is being discharged, I am to take you three Tellurians to the College of Science, where you are to undergo a thorough physical and psychological examination. Follow me."

"Wait a minute!" protested Costigan, with a quick and furtive wink at his companions. "Do you expect us to go *through water*, and at this frightful depth?"

"Certainly," replied the Nevian, in surprise. "You are air-breathers, of course, but you must be able to swim a little, and this slight depth — but little more than thirty of your meters — will not trouble you."

"You are wrong, twice," declared the Terrestrial, convincingly. "If by 'swimming' you mean propelling yourself in or through the water, we know nothing of it. In water over our heads we drown helplessly in a minute or two, and the pressure at this depth would kill us instantly."

"Well, I could take a lifeboat, of course, but that. . . ." The Nevian Captain began, doubtfully, but broke off at the sound of a staccato call from his signal panel.

"Captain Nerado, attention!"

"Nerado," he acknowledged into a microphone.

"The Third City is being attacked by the fishes of the greater deeps. They have developed new and powerful mobile fortresses mounting unheard-of weapons and the city reports that it cannot long withstand their attack. The inhabitants are asking for all possible help. Your vessel not only has vast stores of iron, but also mounts weapons of power. You are requested to proceed to their aid at the earliest possible moment."

Nerado snapped out orders and the liquid iron fell in streams from wide-open ports, forming a vast, red pool in the bottom of the dock. In a short time the great vessel was in equilibrium with the water she displaced, and as soon as she had attained a slight buoyancy the ports snapped shut and Nerado threw on the power.

"Go back to your own quarters and stay there until I send for you," the Nevian directed, and as the Terrestrials obeyed the curt orders the fish-shaped cruiser of space tore herself from the water and flashed up into the crimson sky.

"What a barefaced liar!" Bradley exclaimed. The three, transformers cut off, were back in the middle room of their suite. "You can outswim an otter, and I happen to know that you came up out of the old DZ83 from a depth of. . . ."

"Maybe I did exaggerate a trifle," Costigan interrupted him, "but the more helpless he thinks we are the better for us. And we want to stay out of any of their cities as long as we can, because they may be hard places to escape from. I've got a couple of ideas, but they aren't ripe enough to pick yet. . . . Wow! how this bird's been traveling! We're there already! If he hits the water going like this, he'll split himself, sure!"

With undiminished velocity they were flashing downward in a long slant toward the beleaguered Third City, and from the flying vessel there was launched toward the city's central lagoon a torpedo. No missile this, but a capsule containing a full ton of allotropic iron, which would be of more use to the Nevian defenders than millions of men. For the Third City was sore pressed indeed. Around it was one unbroken ring of boiling, exploding water — water billowing upward with searing, blinding bursts of superheated steam, or being hurled bodily in all directions in solid masses by the cataclysmic forces being released by the embattled fishes of the greater deeps. Her outer defenses were already down, and even as the Terrestrials stared in amazement another of the immense hexagonal buildings burst into fragments; its upper structure flying wildly into scrap metal, its lower half subsiding drunkenly below the surface of the boiling sea.

The three Terrestrials involuntarily seized whatever supports were at hand as the Nevian space-ship struck the water with undiminished speed, but the precaution was needless — Nerado knew thoroughly his vessel, its strength and its capabilities. There was a mighty splash, but that was all. The artificial gravity was unchanged by the impact; to the passengers the vessel was still motionless and on even keel as, now a submarine, she snapped around like a very fish and attacked the rear of the nearest fortress.

For fortresses they were; vast structures of green metal, plowing forward implacably upon immense caterpillar treads. And as they crawled they destroyed, and Costigan, exploring the strange submarine with his visiray beam, watched and marveled. For the fortresses were full of water; water artificially cooled and aerated, entirely separate from the boiling flood through which they moved. They were manned by fish some five feet in length. Fish with huge, goggling eyes; fish plentifully equipped with long, armlike tentacles; fish poised before control panels or darting about intent upon their various duties. Fish with intelligent brains, waging desperate war upon a hated foe!

Nor was their warfare ineffectual. Their heat-rays boiled the water for hundreds of yards before them and their torpedoes were exploding against the Nevian defenses in one appallingly continuous concussion. But most potent of all was a weapon unknown to Triplanetary warfare. From a fortress there would shoot out, with the speed of a meteor, a long, jointed, telescopic rod, tipped with a tiny, brilliantly shining ball. Whenever this glowing tip encountered any obstacle, that obstacle disappeared in an explosion world-wracking in its intensity. Then what was left of the rod, dark now, would be retracted into the fortress — only to emerge again in a moment with a tip once more shining and potent.

Nerado, apparently as unfamiliar with the peculiar weapon as were the Terrestrials, attacked cautiously; sending out far to the fore his murkily impenetrable screens of red. But the submarine was entirely non-ferrous, and its officers were apparently quite familiar with the Nevian beams which licked at and clung to the green walls in impotent fury. Through the red veil came stabbing tiny ball after brilliant ball, and only the most frantic dodging saved the space-ship from destruction in those first few furious seconds. And now the Nevian defenders of the Third City had secured and were employing the vast store of allotropic iron so opportunely delivered by Nerado.

From the city there pushed out immense nets of metal, extending from the surface of the ocean to its bottom; nets radiating such terrific forces that the very water itself was beaten back and stood motionless in vertical, glassy walls. Torpedoes were futile against that wall of energy. The most fiercely driven rays of the fishes flamed incandescent against it, in vain. Even the incredible violence of a concentration of every available force-ball against one point could not break through. At that unimaginable explosion water was hurled for miles. The bed of the ocean was not only exposed, but in it there was blown a crater at whose dimensions the Terrestrials dared not even guess. The crawling fortresses themselves were thrown backward violently and the very world was rocked to its core by the concussion, but that iron-driven wall held. The massive nets swayed and gave back, and tidal waves hurled their mountainously destructive masses through the Third City, but the mighty barrier remained intact. And Nerado, still attacking two of the powerful tanks with his every weapon, was still dodging those flashing balls charged with the quintessence of destruction. The fishes could not see through the sub-ethereal veil, but all the rod-gunners of the two fortresses were combing it thoroughly with ever-lengthening, ever-thrusting rods, in a desperate attempt to wipe out the new and apparently all-powerful Nevian submarine, whose sheer power was slowly but inexorably crushing even their gigantic walls.

"Well, I think that right now's the best chance we'll ever have of doing something for ourselves." Costigan turned away from the absorbing scenes pictured upon the visiplate and faced his two companions.

"But what can we possibly do?" asked Clio, and

"Whatever it is, we'll try it!" Bradley exclaimed.

"Anything's better than staying here and letting them analyze us — no telling what they'd do to us," Costigan went on. "I know a lot more about things than they think I do.

They never did catch me using my spy-ray — it's on an awfully narrow beam, you know, and uses almost no power at all — so I've been able to dope out quite a lot of stuff. I can open most of their locks, and I know how to run their small boats. This battle, fantastic as it is, is deadly stuff, and it isn't one-sided, by any means, either, so that every one of them, from Nerado down, seems to be on emergency duty. There are no guards watching us, or stationed where we want to go — our way out is open. And once out, this battle is giving us our best possible chance to get away from them. There's so much emission out there already that they probably couldn't detect the driving rays of the lifeboat, and they'll be too busy to chase us, anyway."

"Once out, then what?" asked Bradley, eagerly.

"We'll have to decide that before we start, of course. I'd say make a break back for our own Solarian system. We know the direction, from our own observation, and we'll have plenty of power."

"But good Heavens, Conway, it's so far!" exclaimed Clio. "How about food, water, and air — would we ever get there?"

"You know as much about that as I do. I think so, but of course anything might happen. This ship is none too big, is considerable slower than the big space-ship, and we're a long ways from home. Another bad thing is the food question. The boat is well stocked according to Nevian ideas, but it's pretty foul stuff for us to eat. However, it's nourishing, and we'll have to eat it, since we can't carry enough of our own supplies to the boat to last long. Even so, we may have to go on short rations, but I think that we'll be able to make it. On the other hand, what happens if we stay here? We will certainly strike trouble sooner or later, and we don't know any too much about these ultra-weapons. We are land-dwellers, and there is mighty little land on this planet. Then, too, we don't know where to look for what little land there is, and, even if we could find it, we know that it is all over-run with amphibians already. There's a lot of things that might be better, but they might be a lot worse, too. How about it? Do we try it or do we stay here?"

"We try it!" exclaimed Clio and Bradley as one.

"All right. I'd better not waste any more time talking — let's go!"

Stepping up to the locked and shielded door, he took out a peculiarly built torch and pointed it briefly at the Nevian lock. There was no light, no noise, but the massive portal swung smoothly open. They stepped out and Costigan relocked and reshielded the entrance.

"How . . . what . . . ?" Clio demanded, almost stuttering in her surprise.

"I've been going to school for the last few weeks," Costigan grinned, "and I've picked up quite a few things here and there — literally as well as figuratively speaking. Snap it up, guys! Our armor is stored away with the pieces of the pirates' lifeboat, and I'll feel a lot better when we've got it on and have hold of a few fresh Lewistons."

They hurried down corridors, up ramps, and along hallways, with Costigan's spy-ray investigating the course ahead for chance Nevians. Bradley and Clio were unarmed, but the secret agent had found a piece of flat metal and had ground it to a razor edge.

"I think I can throw this thing straight enough and fast enough to chop off a Nevian's head before he can put a paralyzing ray on us," he explained grimly, but he was not called upon to show his skill with the improvised cleaver.

As he had concluded from his careful survey, every Nevian was at some control or weapon, doing his part in that frightful combat with the denizens of the greater deeps. Their part was open, they were neither molested nor detected as they ran toward the compartment within which was sealed all their Terrestrial belongings. The door of that room opened, as had the other, to Costigan's knowing beam; and all three set hastily to work. They made up packs of food, filled their capacious pockets with emergency rations, recharged and buckled on Lewistons and automatics, donned their armor, and clamped into their external holsters a full complement of additional weapons.

"Now comes the ticklish part of the business," Costigan informed them. His helmet was slowly turning this way and that, and the others knew that through his spy-ray goggles he was studying their route. "There's only one boat we stand a chance of reaching, and somebody's mighty apt to see us. There's a lot of detectors up there, and we'll have to cross a corridor full of communicator beams. There, that line's off . . . scoot!"

At his word they dashed out into the hall and hurried along for minutes, dodging to right or left as the leader snapped out orders. Finally he stopped.

"Here's those beams I told you about. We'll have to roll under 'em. They're less than waist high — right there's the lowest one. Watch me do it, and when I give you the word, one at a time, you do the same. *Keep low* — don't let an arm or a leg get up into the path of a ray or they may see us."

He threw himself flat, rolled upon the floor a yard or so, and scrambled to his feet. He gazed intently at the blank wall for a space, then:

"Bradley — now!" he snapped, and the Interplanetary captain duplicated his performance.

But Clio, unused to the heavy and cumbersome space-armor she was wearing, could not roll in it with any degree of success. When Costigan barked his order she tried, but stopped, floundering, almost directly below the invisible network of communicator beams. As she struggled one mailed arm went up, and Costigan saw in his ultra-goggles the faint flash as the beam encountered the interfering field. But already he had acted. Crouching low, he struck down the arm, seized it, and dragged the girl out of the zone of visibility. Then in furious haste he opened a nearby door and all three sprang into a tiny compartment.

"Shut off all the fields of your suits, so that they can't interfere!" he hissed into the utter darkness. "Not that I'd mind killing a few of them, but if they start an organized search we're sunk. But even if they did get a warning by touching your glove, Clio, they probably won't suspect us. Our rooms are still shielded, and the chances are that they're too busy to bother much about us, anyway."

He was right. A few beams darted here and there, but the Nevians saw nothing amiss and ascribed the interference to the falling into the beam of some chance bit of charged metal. With no further misadventures the Terrestrials gained entrance to the Nevian lifeboat, where Costigan's first act was to disconnect one steel boot from his armor of space. With a sigh of relief he pulled his foot out of it, and from it carefully poured into the small power-tank of the craft fully thirty pounds of allotropic iron!

"I pinched it off them," he explained, in answer to amazed and inquiring looks, "and maybe you don't think it's a relief to get it out of that boot! I couldn't steal a flask to carry it in, so this was the only place I could put it in. These lifeboats are equipped with only a couple of grams of iron apiece, you know, and we couldn't get half-way back to Tellus on that, even with smooth going; and we may have to fight. With this much to go on, though, we could go to Andromeda, fighting all the way. Well, we'd better break away."

Costigan watched his plate closely, and, when the maneuvering of the great vessel brought his exit port as far away as possible from the Third City and the warring citadels of the deep, he shot the little cruiser out and away. Straight out into the ocean it sped, through the murky red veil, and darted upward toward the surface. The three wanderers sat tense, hardly daring to breathe, staring into the plates — Clio and Bradley pushing at metal levers and stepping down hard upon metal brakes in unconscious efforts to help Costigan dodge the beams and rods of death flashing so appallingly close upon all sides. Out of the water and into the air the darting, dodging lifeboat flashed in safety; but in the air, supposedly free from menace, came disaster. There was a crunching, grating shock and the vessel was thrown into a dizzy spiral, from which Costigan finally leveled it into headlong flight away from the scene of battle. Watching the pyrometers which recorded the temperature of the outer shell, he drove the lifeboat ahead at the highest safe atmospheric speed while Bradley went to inspect the damage.

"Pretty bad, but better than I thought," the captain reported. "Outer and inner plates broken away on a seam. Inter-wall vacuum all lost, and we wouldn't hold carpet-rags, let alone air. Any tools aboard?"

"Some — and what we haven't got we'll make," Costigan declared. "We'll put a lot of distance behind us, then we'll fix her up and get away from here."

"What are those fish, anyway, Conway?" Clio asked, as the lifeboat tore along. "The Nevians are bad enough, Heaven knows, but the very idea of intelligent and *educated* FISH is enough to drive one mad!"

"You know Nerado mentioned several times the 'semi-civilized fishes of the greater deeps'?" he reminded her. "I gather that there are at least three intelligent races here. We know two — the Nevians, who are amphibians, and the fishes of the greater deeps. The fishes of the lesser deeps are also intelligent. As I get it, the Nevian cities were originally built in very shallow water, or perhaps were upon islands. The development of machinery and tools gave them a big edge on the fish; and those living in the shallow seas, nearest the islands, gradually became tributary nations, if not actually slaves. Those fish not only serve as food, but work in the mines, hatcheries, and plantations, and do all kinds of work for the Nevians. Those so-called 'lesser deeps' were conquered first, of course, and all their races of fish are docile enough now. But the deep-sea breeds, who live in water so deep that the Nevians can hardly stand the pressure down there, were more intelligent to start with, and more stubborn besides. But the most valuable metals here are deep down — this planet is very light for its size, you know — so the Nevians kept at it until they conquered some of the deep-sea fish, too, and put 'em to work. But those high-pressure boys were nobody's fools. They realized that as time went on the amphibians would get further and further ahead of them in development, so they let themselves be conquered, learned how to use the Nevians' tools and everything else they could get hold of, developed a lot of new stuff of their own, and now they're out to wipe the amphibians off the slate completely, before they get too far ahead of them to handle."

"And the Nevians are afraid of them, and want to kill them all, as fast as they possibly can," guessed Clio.

"That would be the logical thing, of course," commented Bradley. "Got pretty nearly enough distance now, Costigan?"

"There isn't enough distance on the planet to suit me," Costigan replied. "We'll need all we can get. A full diameter away from that crew of amphibians is too close for comfort — their detectors are keen."

"Then they can detect us?" Clio asked. "Oh, I wish they hadn't hit us — we'd have been away from here long ago."

"So do I," Costigan assented, feelingly. "But they did — no use squawking. We can rivet and weld those seams and pump out the shell, and we'd have to fill our air-tanks to capacity for the trip, anyway. And things could be a lot worse — we are still breathing air!"

In silence the lifeboat flashed onward, and half of Nevia's mighty globe was traversed before it was brought to a halt, in the emptiest reaches of the planet's desolate and watery waste. Then in furious haste the two officers set to work, again to make their small craft sound and spaceworthy.

CHAPTER VI

Worm, Submarine, and Freedom

Since both Costigan and Bradley had often watched their captors at work during the long voyage from the Solar System to Nevia, they were quite familiar with the machine tools of the amphibians. Their stolen lifeboat, being an emergency craft, of course carried full repair equipment; and to such good purpose did the two officers labor that even before their air-tanks were fully charged, all the damage had been repaired.

The lifeboat lay motionless upon the mirror-smooth surface of the ocean. Captain Bradley had opened the upper port and the three stood in the opening, gazing in silence toward the incredibly distant horizon, while powerful pumps were forcing the last possible ounces of air into the practically unbreakable storage cylinders. Mile upon strangely flat mile stretched that waveless, unbroken expanse of water, merging finally into the violent redness of the Nevian sky. The sun was setting; a vast ball of purple flame dropping rapidly toward the horizon. Darkness came suddenly as that seething ball disappeared, and the air became bitterly cold, in sharp contrast to the pleasant warmth of a moment before. And as suddenly clouds appeared in blackly banked masses and a cold, driving rain began to beat down in torrents.

"Br-r-r, it's cold! Let's go in — Oh! *Shut the door!*" Clio shrieked, and leaped wildly down into the compartment below, out of Costigan's way, for he and Bradley also had seen slithering toward them the frightful arm of the Thing.

Almost before the girl had spoken Costigan had leaped to

the levers, and not an instant too soon; for the tip of that horrible tentacle flashed into the rapidly narrowing crack just before the door clanged shut. As the powerful toggles forced the heavy screw threads into engagement and drove the massive disk home into its bottle-tight, insulated seat, that grisly tip fell severed to the floor of the compartment and lay there, twitching and writhing with a loathsome and unearthly vigor. Two feet long the piece was, and larger than a strong man's leg. It was armed with spiked and jointed metallic scales, and instead of sucking disks it was equipped with a series of *mouths* — mouths filled with sharp metallic teeth which gnashed and ground together furiously, even though sundered from the horrible organism which they were designed to feed.

The little submarine shuddered in every plate and member as monstrous coils encircled her and tightened inexorably in terrific, rippling surges eloquent of mastodonic power; and a strident vibration smote sickeningly upon Terrestrial eardrums as the metal spikes of the monstrosity crunched and ground upon the outer plating of their small vessel. Costigan stood unmoved at the plate, watching intently; hands ready upon the controls. Due to the artificial gravity of the lifeboat it seemed perfectly stationary to its occupants. Only the weird gyrations of the pictures upon the lookout screens showed that the craft was being shaken and thrown about like a rat in the jaws of a terrier; only the gauges revealed that they were almost a mile below the surface of the ocean already, and were still going downward at an appalling rate. Finally Clio could stand no more.

"Aren't you going to do something, Conway?" she cried.

"Not unless I have to," he replied, composedly. "I don't believe that he can really hurt us, and if I use a ray of any kind I'm afraid that it will kick up enough disturbance to bring Nerado down on us like a hawk after a chicken. However, if he takes us much deeper I'll have to go to work on him. We're getting down pretty close to our limit, and the bottom's a long way down yet."

Deeper and deeper the lifeboat was dragged by its dreadful opponent, whose spiked teeth still tore savagely at the tough outer plating of the craft until Costigan reluctantly threw in his power switches. Against the full propellant thrust the monster could draw them no lower, but neither could the lifeboat make any headway toward the surface. The Terrestrial then turned on his rays, but found that they were ineffective. So closely was the creature wrapped around the submarine that his weapons could not be brought to bear upon it without melting the vessel's own outer skin.

"What can it possibly be, anyway, and what can we do about it?" Clio asked.

"I thought at first it was something like a devilfish, or possibly an overgrown starfish, but it's too flat, and has no body that I can see," Costigan made answer. "It must be a kind of flat worm. That doesn't sound reasonable — the thing must be all of a hundred meters long — but there it is. The only thing left to do now, as I see it, is to try to boil him alive."

He closed other circuits, diffusing a terrific beam of pure heat, and the water all about them burst into furious clouds of steam. The boat leaped upward as the metallic fins of the gigantic worm fanned vapor instead of water, but the creature neither released its hold nor ceased its relentlessly grinding attack. Minute after minute went by, but finally the worm dropped limply away — cooked through and through; vanquished only by death.

"Now we've put our foot in it, clear to the knee!" Costigan exclaimed, as he shot the lifeboat upward at its maximum power. "Look at that! I knew that Nerado could trace us, but I didn't have any idea that *they* could. It's a good thing these ultra-vision plates don't need light to see by or we'd be *'spurlos versenkt'* in a hurry!"

Staring with Costigan into the plate, Bradley and the girl saw, not the Nevian sky-rover they had expected, but a fast submarine cruiser, manned by the frightful fishes of the greater deeps. It was coming directly toward the lifeboat, and even as Costigan hurled the little vessel off at an angle and then upward into the air one of the deadly offensive rods, tipped with its glowing ball of pure destruction, flashed through the spot where they would have been had they held their former course.

But powerful as were the propellant forces and fiercely though Costigan applied them, the denizens of the deep clamped a tractor ray upon the flying vessel before it had gained a mile of altitude. Costigan aligned his every driving projector as his vessel came to an abrupt halt in the invisible grip of the beam, then experimented with various dials.

"There ought to be some way of cutting that beam," he pondered audibly, "but I don't know enough about their system to do it, and I'm afraid to monkey around with things too much, because I might accidentally release the screens we've already got out, and they're stopping altogether too much stuff for us to do without them right now."

He frowned as he studied the flaring defensive screens, now radiating an incandescent violet under the concentration of the forces being hurled against them by the warlike fishes, then stiffened suddenly.

"I thought so — they *can* shoot 'em!" he exclaimed, throwing the lifeboat into a furious corkscrew turn, and the very air blazed into flaming splendor as a dazzlingly scintillating ball of energy sped past them and high into the air beyond.

Then for minutes a spectacular battle raged. The twisting, turning, leaping airship, small as she was agile, kept on eluding the explosive projectiles of the fishes, and her screens neutralized and re-radiated the full power of the attacking beams. More — since Costigan did not need to think of sparing his iron, the ocean around the great submarine began furiously to boil under the full-driven offensive beams of the tiny Nevian ship. But escape Costigan could not. He could not cut that tractor beam and the utmost power of his drivers could not wrest the lifeboat from its tenacious clutch. And slowly but inexorably the ship of space was being drawn downward toward the ship of ocean's depths. Downward, in spite of the utmost possible effort of every projector and penetrator, and the two Terrestrial spectators, sick at heart, looked once at each other. Then they looked at Costigan, who, jaw hard set and eyes unflinchingly upon his plate, was concentrating his attack upon one turret of the green monster as they settled lower and lower.

"If this is . . . if our number is going up, Conway," Clio began, unsteadily.

"Not yet, it isn't!" he snapped. "Keep a stiff upper lip, girl. We're still breathing air, and the battle's not over yet!"

Nor was it; but it was not Costigan's efforts, mighty though they were, that ended the attack of the fishes of the greater deeps. The tractor beam snapped without warning, and so prodigious were the forces being exerted by the lifeboat that, as it hurled itself away, the three passengers were thrown violently to the floor, in spite of the powerful gravity controls. Scrambling up on hands and knees, bracing himself as best he could against the terrific forces, Costigan managed finally to force a hand up to his panel. He was barely in time; for even as he cut the driving power to its normal value the outer shell of the lifeboat was blazing at white heat from the friction of the atmosphere through which it had been tearing with such an insane acceleration!

"Oh, I see — Nerado to the rescue," Costigan commented, after a glance into the plate. "I hope that those fish blow him clear out of the Galaxy!"

"Why?" demanded Clio. "I should think that you'd. . . ."

"Think again," he advised her. "The worse Nerado gets licked the better for us. I don't really expect that, but if they can keep him busy long enough, we can get far enough away so that he won't bother about us any more."

As the lifeboat tore upward through the air at the highest permissible atmospheric velocity Bradley and Clio peered over Costigan's shoulders into the plate, watching in absorbed interest the scene which was being kept in focus upon it. The Nevian ship of space was plunging downward in a long, slanting dive, her terrific beams of force screaming out ahead of her. The rays of the little lifeboat had boiled the waters of the ocean; those of the parent craft seemed literally to blast them out of existence. All about the green submarine there had been volumes of furiously-boiling water and dense clouds of vapor; now water and fog alike disappeared, converted into transparent superheated steam by the blasts of Nevian energy. Through that tenuous gas the enormous mass of the submarine fell like a plummet, her defensive screens flaming an almost invisible violet, her every offensive weapon vomiting forth solid and vibratory destruction toward the Nevian cruiser so high in the angry, scarlet heavens.

For miles the submarine dropped, until the frightful pressure of the depth drove water into Nerado's beam faster than his forces could volatilize it. Then in that seething funnel there was waged desperate conflict. At that funnel's wildly turbulent bottom lay the submarine, now apparently trying to escape, but held fast by the tractor rays of the space-ship; at its top, smothered almost to the point of invisibility by billowing masses of steam, hung poised the Nevian cruiser.

As the atmosphere had grown thinner and thinner with increasing altitude Costigan had regulated his velocity accordingly, keeping the outer shell of the vessel at the highest temperature consistent with safety. Now beyond measurable atmospheric pressure, the shell cooled rapidly and he applied full touring acceleration. At an appalling and constantly increasing speed the miniature space-ship shot away from the strange, red planet; and smaller and smaller upon the plate became its picture. Long since the great vessel of the void had plunged beneath the surface of the sea, more closely to come to grips with the vessel of the fishes; for a long time nothing of the battle had been visible save immense clouds of steam, blanketing hundreds of square miles of the ocean's surface. But just before the picture became too small to reveal details a few tiny dark spots appeared above the banks of cloud, now brilliantly illuminated by the rays of the rising sun — dots which might have been fragments of either vessel, blown bodily from the depths of the ocean and, riven asunder, hurled high into the air by the incredible forces at the command of the other.

Nevia a tiny moon and the fierce blue sun rapidly growing smaller in the distance, Costigan swung his visiray beam into the line of travel and turned to his companions.

"Well, we're off," he said, scowling. "I hope it was Nerado that got blown up back there, but I'm afraid it wasn't. He whipped two of those submarines that we know of, and probably half their fleet besides. There's no particular reason why that one should be able to take him, so it's my idea that we should get ready for great gobs of trouble.

"They'll chase us, of course; and I'm afraid that with their immense power, they'll catch us."

"But what can we do, Conway?" asked Clio.

"Several things," he grinned. "I managed to get quite a lot of dope on that paralyzing ray and some of their other stuff, and we can install the necessary equipment in our suits easily enough."

They removed their armor, and Costigan explained in detail the changes which must be made in the Triplanetary field generators. All three set vigorously to work — the two officers deftly and surely; Clio uncertainly and with many questions, but with undaunted spirit. Finally, having done all they could do to strengthen their position, they settled down to the watchful routine of the flight, with every possible instrument set to detect any sign of the pursuit they so feared.

CHAPTER VII

The Hill

The heavy cruiser *Chicago* hung motionless in space, thousands of miles distant from the warring fleets of space-ships so viciously attacking and so stubbornly defending the planetoid of the enemy. In the captain's sanctum Lyman Cleveland crouched tensely above his ultra-cameras, his sensitive fingers touching lightly their micrometric dials. His body was rigid, his face was set and drawn. Only his eyes moved: flashing back and forth between the observation plates and smoothly-running rolls which were feeding into the cameras the hardened steel tapes upon which were being magnetically recorded the frightful scenes of carnage and destruction there revealed.

Silent and bitterly absorbed, though surrounded by staring officers, whose fervent, almost unconscious cursing was prayerful in its intensity, the visiray expert kept his ultra-instruments upon that awful struggle to its dire conclusion. Flawlessly those instruments noted every detail of the destruction of Roger's fleet, of the transformation of the armada of Triplanetary into an unknown fluid, and finally of the dissolution of the gigantic planetoid itself. Then furiously Cleveland drove his beams against the crimsonly opaque obscurity into which the peculiar, viscous stream of substance was disappearing. Time after time he applied his every watt of power, with no result. A vast volume of space, roughly ellipsodial in shape, was closed to him by forces entirely beyond his experience or comprehension. But suddenly, while his rays were still trying to pierce that impenetrable murk, it disappeared instantly and, without warning, the illimitable infinity of space once more lay revealed upon his plates and his beams flashed on and on through the void, unimpeded.

"Back to Tellus, sir?" The *Chicago*'s captain broke the strained silence.

"I wouldn't say so, if I had the say." Cleveland, baffled and frustrate, straightened up and shut off his cameras. "We should report back as soon as possible, of course, but there seems to be a lot of wreckage out there yet, that we can't photograph in detail at this distance. A close study of it might help us a lot in understanding what they did and how they did it. I'd say that we should get close-ups of whatever is left, and do it right away, before it gets scattered all over space; but of course I can't give you orders."

"You can, though," the captain made surprising answer. "My orders are that you are in command of this vessel."

"In that case we will proceed at full emergency acceleration to investigate the wreckage," Cleveland replied, and the cruiser — sole survivor of Triplanetary's supposedly invincible force — shot away with every projector delivering its maximum blast.

As the scene of the disaster was approached there was revealed upon the plates a confused mass of debris; a mass whose individual units were apparently moving at random: yet which was as a whole still following the orbit of Roger's planetoid. Space was full of machine parts, structural members, furniture, flotsam of all kinds; and everywhere were the bodies of men. Some were encased in space-suits, and it was to these that the rescuers turned first — space-hardened veterans though the men of the *Chicago* were, they did not care even to look at the others. Strangely enough, however, not one of the floating figures spoke or moved, and space-line men were hurriedly sent out to investigate.

"All dead." Quickly the dread report came back. "Been dead a long time. The armor is all stripped off the suits, and the generators and the other apparatus are all shot. Something funny about it, too — none of them seem to have been touched, but the machinery of the suits seems to be about half of it missing."

"I've got it all on the spools, sir." Cleveland, his close-up survey of the wreckage finished, turned to the captain. "What they've just reported checks up with what I've photographed everywhere. I've got an idea of what might have happened, but it's so dizzy that I'll have to have a lot of reenforcement before I'll believe it myself. But you might have them bring in a few of the armored bodies, a couple of those switchboards and panels floating around out there, and half a dozen miscellaneous pieces of junk — the nearest things they get hold of, whatever they happen to be."

"Then back to Tellus at maximum?"

"Right — back to Tellus, as fast as we can possibly go there."

While the *Chicago* hurtled through space at full power, Cleveland and the ranking officers of the vessel grouped themselves about the salvaged wreckage. Familiar with space-wrecks as were they all, none of them had ever seen anything like the material before them. For every part and instrument was weirdly and meaninglessly disintegrated. There were no breaks, no marks of violence, and yet nothing was intact. Bolt-holes stared empty, cores, shielding cases and needles had disappeared, the vital parts of every instrument hung awry, disorganization reigned rampant and supreme.

"I never imagined such a mess," the captain said, after a long and silent study of the objects. "If you have any theory to cover *that*, Cleveland, I would like to hear it!"

"I want you to notice something first," the visiray expert replied. "But don't look for what's there — look for what *isn't* there."

"Well, the armor is gone. So are the shielding cases, shafts, spindles, the housings and stems. . . ." The captain's voice died away as his eyes raced over the collection. "Why, everything that was made of wood, bakelite, copper aluminum, silver, bronze, or anything but steel hasn't been touched, and every bit of steel is gone. But that doesn't make sense — what does it mean?"

"I don't know — yet," Cleveland replied, slowly. "But I'm afraid that there's more, and worse." He opened a space-suit reverently, revealing the face; a face calm and peaceful, but utterly, sickeningly white. Still reverently, he made a deep incision in the brawny neck, severing the jugular vein, then went on, soberly:

"You never imagined such a thing as *white* blood, either, but it all checks up. Someway, somehow, every particle — probably every atom — of free or combined iron in this whole volume of space was made off with."

"Huh? How come? And above all, *why*?" from the amazed and staring officers.

"You know as much as I do," grimly, ponderingly. "If it were not for the fact that there are solid asteroids of iron out beyond Mars, I would say that somebody wanted iron badly enough to wipe out the fleets and the planetoid to get it. But anyway, whoever they were, they carried enough power so that our armament didn't bother them at all. They simply took the metal they wanted and went away with it — so fast that I couldn't trace them with an ultra-beam. There's only one thing plain; but that's so plain that it scares me stiff. This whole affair spells intelligence, with a capital 'I', and that intelligence is anything but friendly. As for me I want to get Fred Rodebush at work on this soon — think I'll hurry it up a little."

He stepped over to his ultra-projector and called the Terrestrial headquarters of the T. S. S. Samms' face soon appeared upon his screen.

"We got it all, Virgil," he reported.

"It's something extraordinary — bigger, wider, and deeper than any of us dreamed. It may be urgent, too, so I think I had better shoot the pictures in on the ultra-wave and save a few days. Fred has a telemagneto recorder there that he can synchronize with this camera outfit easily enough. Right?"

"Right. Good work, Lyman — thanks," came back terse approval and appreciation, and soon the steel tapes were again flashing between the feed-rolls. This time, however, their varying magnetic charges were modulating an ultra-wave so that every detail of that calamitous battle of the void was being screened and recorded in the innermost private laboratory of the Triplanetary Secret Service.

Eager though he naturally was to join his fellow-scientists, Cleveland did not waste his time during the long, but uneventful journey back to Earth. There was much to study, many improvements to be made in his comparatively crude first ultra-camera. Then, too, there were long conferences with Samms, and particularly with Rodebush, the mathematical physicist, whose was the task of solving the riddles of the energies and weapons of the Nevians. Thus it did not seem long before green Terra grew large beneath the flying sphere of the *Chicago*.

"Going to have to circle at once, aren't you?" Cleveland asked the chief pilot. He had been watching that officer closely for minutes, admiring the delicacy and precision with which the great vessel was being maneuvered preliminary to entering the Earth's atmosphere.

"Yes," the pilot replied. "We had to come in in the shortest possible time, and that meant a velocity here that we can't check without a spiral. However, even at that we saved a lot of time. You can save quite a bit more, though, by having a rocket-plane come out to meet us somewhere around fifteen or twenty thousand kilometers, depending upon where you want to land. With their power-to-mass ratio they can match our velocity and still make the drop direct."

"Guess I'll do that — thanks," and the operative called his chief, only to learn that his suggestion had already been acted upon.

"We beat you to it, Lyman," Samms smiled. "The *Silver Sliver* is out there now, looping to match your course, acceleration, and velocity at twenty-two thousand kilometers. You'll be ready to transfer?"

"I'll be ready!" and the Quartermaster's ex-clerk went to his quarters and packed his dunnage-bag.

In due time the long, slender body of the rocket-plane came into view, creeping 'down' upon the space-ship from 'above,' and Cleveland bade his friends good-bye. Donning a space-suit, he stationed himself in the starboard airlock. Its atmosphere was withdrawn, the outer door opened, and he glanced across a bare hundred feet of space at the rocket-plane which, keel ports fiercely aflame, was braking her terrific speed to match the slower pace of the gigantic ship of war. Shaped like a toothpick, needle-pointed fore and aft, with ultra-stubby wings and vanes, with flush-set rocket ports everywhere, built of a lustrous silvery alloy of noble and almost infusible metals — such was the private speed-boat of the chief of the T. S. S. The fastest thing known, whether in planetary air, the stratosphere, or the vacuus depth of interplanetary space, her first flashing trial spins had won her the nickname of the *Silver Sliver*. She had had a more formal name, but that title had long since been buried in the Departmental files.

Lower and slower dropped the *Silver Sliver*, her rockets flaming even brighter, until her slender length lay level with the airlock door. Then her blasting discharges subsided to the power necessary to match exactly the *Chicago*'s deceleration.

"Ready to cut, *Chicago*! Give me a three-second call!" snapped from the pilot room of the *Sliver*.

"Ready to cut!" the pilot of the *Chicago* replied. "Seconds! Three! Two! One! CUT!"

At the last word the power of both vessels was instantly cut off and everything in them became weightless. In the tiny airlock of the slender craft crouched a space-line man with coiled cable in readiness, but he was not needed. As the flaring exhausts ceased Cleveland swung out his heavy bag and stepped lightly off into space, and in a right line he floated directly into the open doorway of the rocket-plane. The door clanged shut behind him and in a matter of moments he stood in the control room of the racer, divested of his armor and shaking hands with his friend and co-laborer, Frederick Rodebush.

"Well, Fred, what do you know?" Cleveland asked, as soon as greetings had been exchanged. "How do the various reports dovetail together? I know that you couldn't tell me anything on the wave, but there's no danger of eavesdroppers *here*."

"You can't tell," Rodebush soberly replied. "We're just beginning to wake up to the fact that there are a lot of things we don't know anything about. Better wait until we're back at the Hill. We have a full set of ultra-screens around there now. There's a couple of other good reasons, too — it would be better for both of us to go over the whole thing with Virgil, from the ground up; and we can't do any more talking, anyway. Our orders are to get back there at maximum, and you know what that means aboard the *Sliver*. Strap yourself solid in that shock-absorber there, and here's a pair of ear-plugs."

"When the *Sliver* really cuts loose it means a rough party, all right," Cleveland assented, snapping about his body the heavy spring-straps of his deeply cushioned seat, "but I'm just as anxious to get back to the Hill as anybody can be to get me there. All set."

Rodebush waved his hand at the pilot and the purring whisper of the exhausts changed instantly to a deafening, continuous explosion. The men were pressed deeply into their shock-absorbing chairs as the *Silver Sliver* spun around her longitudinal axis and darted away from the *Chicago* with such a tremendous acceleration that the spherical warship seemed to be standing still in space. In due time the calculated mid-point was reached, the slim space-plane rolled over again, and, mad acceleration now reversed, rushed on toward the Earth, but with constantly diminishing speed. Finally a measurable atmospheric pressure was encountered, the needle prow dipped downward, and the *Silver Sliver* shot forward upon her tiny wings and vanes, nose-rockets now drumming in staccato thunder. Her metal grew hot: dull red, bright red yellow, blinding white; but it neither melted nor burned. The pilot's calculations had been sound, and though the limiting point of safety of temperature was reached and steadily held, it was not exceeded. As the density of the air increased so decreased the velocity of the man-made meteorite. So it was that a dazzling lance of fire sped high over Seattle, lower over Spokane, and hurled itself eastward, a furiously flaming arrow; slanting downward in a long, screaming dive toward the heart of the Rockies. As the now rapidly cooling greyhound of the skies passed over the western ranges of the Bitter Roots it became apparent that her goal was a vast, flat-topped, and conical mountain, shrouded in livid light; a mountain whose height awed even its stupendous neighbors.

While not artificial, the Hill had been altered markedly by the Triplanetary engineers who had built into it the headquarters of the Secret Service. Its mile-wide top was a jointless expanse of gray armor steel; the steep, smooth surface of the truncated cone was a continuation of the same immensely thick sheet of metal. No known vehicle could climb that smooth, hard, forbidding slope of steel; no known projectile could mar that armor; no known craft could even approach the Hill without detection. Could not approach it at all, in fact, for it was constantly inclosed in a vast hemisphere of lambent violet flame through which neither material substance nor destructive ray could pass.

As the *Silver Sliver*, crawling along at a bare three-hundred miles an hour, approached that transparent, brilliantly violet wall of destruction, a violet light filled her control room and as suddenly went out; flashing on and off again and again.

"Giving us the once-over, eh?" Cleveland asked. "That is something new, isn't it, Fred?"

"Yes, it's a high-powered ultra-wave spy," Rodenbush returned. "The light is simply a warning, which can be carried if desired. It can also carry voice and vision. . . ."

"Like this," Samms' voice interrupted from the powerful dynamic speaker upon the pilots' panel and his clear-cut face appeared upon the television screen. "I don't suppose Fred thought to mention it, but this is one of his inventions of the last few days. We are just trying it out on you. It doesn't mean a thing though, as far as the *Sliver* is concerned. Come ahead!"

A circular opening appeared in the wall of force, an opening which disappeared as soon as the plane had darted through it; and at the same time her landing-cradle rose into the air through a great trap-door. Slowly and gracefully the space-plane settled downward into that cushioned embrace. Then cradle and nestled *Sliver* sank from view and, turning smoothly upon mighty trunnions, the plug of armor drove solidly back into its place in the metal pavement of the mountain's lofty summit. The cradle-elevator dropped rapidly, coming to rest many levels down in the heart of the Hill, and Cleveland and Rodebush leaped lightly out of their transport, through her still hot outer walls. A door opened before them and they found themselves in a large room of full daylight illumination; the anteroom of the private office of Virgil Samms. Chiefs of Departments sat at their desks, concentrated upon problems or at ease, according to the demands of the moment; televisotypes and recorders flashed busily but silently; calmly efficient men and women went wontedly about the all-embracing business of Triplanetary's space-pervading Secret Service.

"Right of way, Norma?" Rodebush paused briefly before the desk of the Chief's private secretary; but even before he had spoken she had pressed a button and the door behind her swung wide.

"You two do not need to be announced," the attractive young woman smiled. "Go right in."

Samms met them at the door eagerly, shaking hands particularly vigorously with Cleveland.

"Congratulations on that camera, Lyman!" he exclaimed. "You did a wonderful piece of work on that. Help yourselves to smokes and sit down — there are a lot of things we want to talk over. Your pictures carried most of the story, but they would have left us pretty much at sea without Costigan's reports. But as it was, Fred here and his crew worked out most of the answers from the dope the two of you got; and what few they haven't got yet they soon will have."

"Nothing new on Conway?" Cleveland was almost afraid to ask the question.

"No." A shadow came over Samms' face. "I'm afraid . . . but I'm hoping it's only that those creatures, whatever they are, have taken him so far away that he can't reach us."

"They certainly are so far away that we can't reach them." Rodenbush volunteered. "We can't even get their ultra-wave interference any more."

"Yes, that's a hopeful sign," Samms went on. "I hate to think of Conway Costigan checking out. There, fellows, was a real observer. He was the only man, I have ever known, who combined the two qualities of the perfect witness. He could actually see everything he looked at, and could report it truly, to the last, least detail. Take all this stuff, for instance; especially their ability to transform iron into a fluid allotrope, and in that form to use its intra-atomic energy as power. Something brand new — unheard of except in the ravings of imaginative fiction — and yet he described their converters and projectors so minutely that Fred was able to work out the underlying theory in three days, and to tie it in with our own super-ship. My first thought was that we'd have to rebuild it iron-free, but Fred showed me my error — you found it first yourself, of course."

"It wouldn't do any good to make the ship non-ferrous unless you could so change our blood chemistry that we could get along without hemoglobin, and that would be quite a feat," Cleveland agreed. "Then, too, our most vital electrical machinery is built around iron cores. No, we'll have to develop a screen for those forces — screens, rather, so powerful that they can't drive anything through them."

"We've been working along those lines ever since you reported," Rodebush said, "and we're beginning to see light. And in that same connection it's no wonder that we couldn't handle our super-ship. We had some good ideas, but they were wrongly applied. However, things look quite promising now. We have that transformation of iron all worked out in theory, and as soon as we get a generator going we can straighten out everything else in short order. And think what that unlimited power means! All the power we want — power enough even to try out such hitherto purely theoretical possibilities as the neutralization of gravity, and even of the inertia of matter!"

"Hold on!" protested Samms. "You certainly can't do *that*! Inertia is — *must* be — a basic attribute of matter, and surely cannot be done away with without destroying the matter itself. Don't start anything like that. Fred — I don't want to lose you and Lyman, too."

"Don't worry about us, Chief." Rodebush replied with a smile. "If you will tell me what matter is, fundamentally, I may agree with you. . . . No? Well, then, don't be surprised at anything that happens. We are going to do a lot of things that nobody ever thought of doing before."

Thus for a long time the argument and discussion went on, to be interrupted by the voice of the secretary.

"Sorry to disturb you, Mr. Samms, but some things have come up that you will have to handle. Knobos is calling from out near Mars. He has caught the *Endymion*, and has killed about half her crew doing it. Milton has finally reported from Venus, after being out of touch for five days. He trailed the Wintons into Thalleron swamp. They crashed him there, but he won out and has what he went after. And just now I got a flash from Fletcher, in the asteroid belt. I think that he has finally traced that dope line. But Knobos is on now — what do you want him to do about the *Endymion*?"

"Tell him to — no, put him on here, I'd better tell him myself," Samms directed, and his face hardened in ruthless decision as the horny, misshapen face of the Martian lieutenant appeared upon the screen. "What do you think, Knobos? Shall they come to trial or not?"

"No."

"I don't think so, either. It is better that a few gangsters should disappear in space than run the risk of another uprising. See to it."

"Right." The screen darkened and Samms spoke to his secretary. "Put Milton and Fletcher on whenever their rays come in." He then turned to his guests. "We've covered the ground quite thoroughly. Good-bye — I wish I could go with you, but I'll be pretty well tied up for the next week or two."

"Tied up, doesn't half express it," Rodebush remarked as the two scientists walked along a corridor toward an elevator. "He probably is the busiest man on the three planets."

"As well as the most powerful," Cleveland supplemented. "And very few men could use his power as fairly — but he's welcome to it, as far as I'm concerned. I'd have the pink fantods for a month if I had to do only once what he's just done — and to him it's just part of a day's work."

"You mean the *Endymion*? What else could he do?"

"Nothing — that's just what I'm talking about. It had to be done, since bringing them to trial would probably mean killing half the people of Morseca; but at the same time it's a ghastly thing to have to order a job of deliberate, cold-blooded, and illegal murder."

"You're right, of course, but you would. . . ." he broke off, unable to put his thoughts into words. For while inarticulate, manlike, concerning their deepest emotions, in both men was ingrained the code of their organization; both knew that to every man chosen for it *The Service* was everything, himself nothing.

"But enough of that, we'll have plenty of grief of our own right here," Rodebush changed the subject abruptly as they stepped into a vast room, almost filled by the immense bulk of the *Boise* — the sinister space-ship which, although never flown, had already lined with black so many pages of Triplanetary's roster. She was now, however, the center of a furious activity. Men swarmed over her and through her, in the orderly confusion of a fiercely driven but carefully planned program of reconstruction.

"I hope your dope is right, Fred!" Cleveland called, as the two scientists separated to go to their respective laboratories. "If it is, we'll make a perfect lady out of this unmanageable man-killer yet!"

CHAPTER VIII

The Super-Ship Is Launched

After weeks of ceaseless work, during which was lavished upon her every resource of mind and material afforded by three planets, the *Boise* was ready for her maiden flight. As nearly ready, that is, as the thought and labor of man could make her. Rodebush and Cleveland had finished their last rigid inspection of the craft and, standing beside the center door of the main airlock, were talking with their chief.

"You say that you think that it's safe, and yet you won't take a crew," Samms argued. "In that case it isn't safe enough for you men, either. We need you too badly to permit you to take such chances."

"You've *got* to let us go; because we are the only ones who are thoroughly familiar with her theory," Rodebush insisted. "I said, and still say, that I *think* it is safe. I can't prove it, however, except mathematically; because she's altogether too full of too many new and untried mechanisms, too many extrapolations beyond all existing or possible data. Theoretically, she is sound, but you know that theory can go only so far, and that mathematically negligible factors may become operative at those velocities. We do not need a crew for a short trip. We can take care of any minor mishaps, and if our fundamental theories are wrong, all the crews between here and Jupiter wouldn't do any good. Therefore we two are going — alone."

"Well, be very careful, anyway. Start out slow and take it easy."

"Start out slow? We can't! We can't neutralize half of

gravity, nor half of the inertia of matter — it's got to be everything or nothing, as soon as the neutralizers go on. We could start out on the projectors, of course, instead of on the neutralizers, but that wouldn't prove anything and would only prolong the agony."

"Well, then, be as careful as you can."

"We'll do that, Chief," Cleveland put in. "We think a lot of us, and we aren't committing suicide just yet if we can help it. And remember about everybody staying inside when we take off — it's barely possible that we'll take up a lot of room. Good-bye to all of you."

"Good-bye, fellows!"

The massive insulating doors were shut, the metal side of the mountain opened, and huge, squat caterpillar tractors came roaring and clanking into the room. Chains and cables were made fast and, mighty steel rails groaning under the load, the space-ship upon her rolling ways was dragged out of the Hill and far out upon the level floor of the surface before the tractors cast off and returned to the fortress.

"Everybody is under cover." Samms informed Rodebush. The chief was staring intently into his plate, upon which was revealed the control room of the untried supership. He heard Rodebush speak to Cleveland; heard the observer's brief reply; saw the navigator throw his switches — then the communicator plate went blank. Not the ordinary blankness of a cut-off, but a peculiarly disquieting fading out into darkness. And where the great space-ship had rested there was for an instant nothing. Exactly nothing — a vacuum. Vessel, falsework, rollers, trucks, the enormous steel I-beams of the tracks, even the deep-set concrete piers and foundations and a vast hemisphere of the solid ground; all had disappeared utterly and instantaneously. But almost as suddenly as it had been formed the vacuum was filled by a cyclonic rush of air. There was a detonation as of a hundred vicious thunderclaps made one, and, through the howling, shrieking blasts of wind, there rained down upon the valley, plain and metaled mountain a veritable avalanche of debris:

bent, twisted, and broken rails and beams, splintered timbers, masses of concrete, and thousands of cubic yards of soil and rock. For inertia and gravitation had not been neutralized at precisely the same instant, and for a moment everything within the radius of action of the iron-driven gravity nullifiers of the *Boise* had continued its absolute motion with inertia unimpaired. Then, left behind immediately by the almost infinite velocity of the cruiser, all this material had again become subject to all of Nature's everyday laws and had crashed back to the ground.

"Could you hold your beam, Randolph?" Samm's voice cut sharply through the daze of stupefaction which held spellbound most of the denizens of the Hill. But all were not so held — no conceivable emergency could take the attention of the chief ultra-wave operator from his instruments.

"No, sir," Radio Center shot back. "It faded out and I couldn't recover it. I put everything I've got behind a tracer on that beam, but haven't been able to lift a single needle off the pin."

"And no wreckage of the vessel itself," Samms went on, half audibly. "Either they have succeeded far beyond their wildest hopes or else . . . more probably. . . ." He fell silent and switched off the plate. Were his two friends, those intrepid scientists, alive and triumphant, or had they gone to lengthen the list of victims of that man-killing space-ship? Reason told him that they were gone. They *must be* gone, or else his ultra-beams — energies of such unthinkable velocity of propagation that man's most sensitive instruments had never been able even to estimate it — would have held the ship's transmitter in spite of any velocity attainable by any matter under any conceivable conditions. The ship must have been disintegrated as soon as Rodebush released his forces. And yet, had not the physicist dimly foreseen the possibility of such an actual velocity — or had he? However, individuals could came and could go, but Triplanetary went on. Samms squared his shoulders unconsciously, and slowly, grimly, made his way back to his private office.

He had scant time to mourn. Scarcely had he seated himself at his desk when an emergency call came snapping in; a call of such import that his secretary's usually calm voice trembled as she put it on his plate.

"Commissioner Hinkle is calling, sir," she announced. "Something terrible is going on again, out toward Orion. Here he is," and there appeared upon the screen the face of the Commissioner of Public Safety, the commander of Triplanetary's every armed force — whether of land or of water, of air or of empty space.

"They've come back, Samms!" the Commissioner rapped out, without preliminary or greeting. "Four vessels gone — a freighter and a passenger liner, with her escort of two heavy cruisers. All in Sector M; Dx about 151. I have ordered all traffic out of space for the duration of the emergency, and since even our warships seem useless, every ship is making for the nearest dock at maximum. How about that new flyer of yours — got anything that will do us any good?" No one beyond the "Hill's" shielding screens knew that the *Boise* had already been launched.

"I don't know. We don't even know whether we have a super-ship or not," and Samms described briefly the beginning — and very probably the ending — of the trial flight, concluding: "It looks bad, but if there was any possible way of handling her, Rodebush and Cleveland did it. All our tracers are negative yet, so nothing definite has. . . ."

He broke off as a frantic call came in from the Pittsburgh station for the Commissioner, a call which Samms both heard and saw.

"The city is being attacked!" came the urgent message. "We need all the reinforcements you can send us!" and a picture of the beleaguered city appeared in ghastly detail upon the screens of the observers; a view being recorded from the air. It required only seconds for the commissioner to order every available man and engine of war to the seat of conflict; then, having done everything they could, Hinkle and Samms stared in helpless, fascinated horror into their plates, watching the scenes of carnage and destruction depicted there.

The Nevian vessel — the sister-ship, the craft which Costigan had seen in mid-space as it hurtled Earthward in response to Nerado's summons — hung poised in full visibility, high above the metropolis. Scornful of the pitiful weapons wielded by man she hung there, her sinister beauty of line sharply defined against the cloudless sky. From her shining hull there reached down a tenuous but rigid rod of crimson energy; a rod which slowly swept hither and thither as the detectors of the amphibians searched out the richest deposits of the precious iron for which the inhuman visitors had come so far. Iron, once solid, now a viscous red liquid, was sluggishly flowing in an ever-thickening stream up that intangible crimson duct and into the capacious storage tanks of the Nevian raider; and wherever that flaming beam went there went also ruin, destruction, and death. Office buildings, skyscrapers towering majestically in their architectural symmetry and beauty, collapsed into heaps of debris as their steel skeletons were abstracted. Deep into the ground the beam bored; flood, fire, and explosion following in its wake as the mazes of underground piping disappeared. And the humanity of the buildings died: instantaneously and painlessly, never knowing what struck them, as the life-bearing iron of their bodies went to swell the Nevian stream.

Pittsburgh's defenses had been feeble indeed. A few antiquated railway rifles had hurled their shells upward in futile defiance, and had been quietly absorbed. The district planes of Triplanetary, newly armed with iron-driven ultra-beams, had assembled hurriedly and had attacked the invader in formation, with but little more success. Under the impact of their beams the stranger's screens had flared white, then poised ship and flying squadron alike had been lost to view in a murkily opaque shroud of crimson flame. The cloud had soon dissolved, and from the place where the planes had been there had floated or crashed down a litter of non-ferrous wreckage. And now the cone of space-ships from the Buffalo base of Triplanetary was approaching Pittsburgh, hurling itself toward the Nevian plunderer and toward known, gruesome and hopeless defeat.

"Stop them, Hinkle!" Samms cried. "It's sheer slaughter! They haven't got a thing — they aren't even equipped yet with the iron drive!"

"I know it," the commissioner groaned, "and Admiral Barnes knows it as well as we do, but it can't be helped — wait a minute! The Washington cone is reporting. They're as close as the other, and they have the new armament. Philadelphia is close behind, and so is New York. Now perhaps we can do something!"

The Buffalo flotilla slowed and stopped, and in a matter of minutes the detachments from the other bases arrived. The cone was formed and iron-driven vessels in the van, the old-type craft far in the rear, it bore down upon the Nevian, vomiting from its hollow front a solid cylinder of annihilation. Once more the screens of the Nevian flared into brilliance, once more the red cloud of destruction was flung abroad. But these vessels were not entirely defenseless. Their iron-driven ultra-generators threw out screens of the Nevians' own formulae, screens of prodigious power to which the energies of the amphibians clung and at which they clawed and tore in baffled, wildly coruscant displays of power unthinkable. For minutes the furious conflict raged, while the inconceivable energy being dissipated by those straining screens hurled itself in terribly destructive bolts of lightning upon the city far beneath.

No battle of such incredible violence could long endure. Triplanetary's ships were already exerting their utmost power, while the Nevians, contemptuous of Solarian science, had not yet uncovered their full strength. Thus the last desperate effort of mankind was proved futile as the invaders forced their beams deeper and deeper into the overloaded, defensive screens of the war-vessels; and one by one the supposedly invincible space-ships of humanity dropped in horribly dismembered wreckage upon the ruins of what had once been Pittsburgh.

CHAPTER IX

Specimens

Only too well founded was Costigan's conviction that the submarine of the deep-sea fishes had not been able to prevail against Nerado's formidable engines of destruction. For days the Nevian lifeboat with its three Terrestrial passengers hurtled through the interstellar void without incident, but finally the operative's fears were realized — his far-flung detector screens reacted; upon his observation plate lay revealed Nerado's mammoth space-ship, in full pursuit of its fleeing lifeboat!

"On your toes, folks — it won't be long now!" Costigan called, and Bradley and Clio hurried into the tiny control room.

Armor donned and tested, the three Terrestrials stared into the observation plates, watching the rapidly enlarging pictures of the Nevian space-ship. Nerado had traced them and was following them, and such was the power of the great vessel that the nearly inconceivable velocity of the lifeboat was the veriest crawl in comparison to that of the pursuing cruiser.

"And we've hardly started to cover the distance back to Tellus. Of course you couldn't get in touch with anybody yet?" Bradley stated, rather than asked.

"I kept on trying until they blanketed my wave, but all negative. Thousands of times too far for my transmitter. Our only hope of reaching anybody was the mighty slim chance that our super-ship might be prowling around out here already, but it isn't, of course. Here they are!"

Reaching out to the control panel, Costigan shot out against the great vessel wave after wave of lethal vibrations, under whose fiercely clinging impacts the Nevian defensive screens flared white; but, strangely enough, their own screens did not radiate. As if contemptuous of any weapons the lifeboat might wield, the mother ship simply defended herself from the attacking beams, in much the same fashion as a wildcat mother wards off the claws and teeth of her spitting, snarling kitten who is resenting a touch of needed maternal discipline.

"They probably won't fight us, at that," Clio first understood the situation. "This is their own lifeboat, and they want us alive, you know."

"There's one more thing we can try — hang on!" Costigan snapped, as he released his screens and threw all his power into one enormous pressor beam.

The three were thrown to the floor and held there by an awful weight, as if the lifeboat darted away at the stupendous acceleration of the beam's reaction against the unimaginable mass of the Nevian sky-rover; but the flight was of short duration. Along that pressor beam there crept a dull rod of energy, which surrounded the fugitive shell and brought it slowly to a halt. Furiously then Costigan set and reset his controls, launching his every driving force and his every weapon, but no beam could penetrate that red murk, and the lifeboat remained motionless in space. No, not motionless — the red rod was shortening, drawing the truant craft back toward the launching port from which she had so hopefully emerged a few days before. Back and back it was drawn; Costigan's utmost efforts futile to affect by a hair's breadth its line of motion. Through the open port the boat slipped neatly, and as it came to a halt in its original position within the multilayered skin of the monster, the prisoners heard the heavy doors clang shut behind them, one after another.

And then sheets of blue fire snapped and crackled all about the three suits of Triplanetary armor — the two large human figures and the small one were outlined starkly in blinding blue flame.

"That's the first thing that has come off according to schedule." Costigan laughed, a short, fierce bark. "That is their paralyzing ray; we've got it stopped cold, and we've each got enough iron to hold it forever."

"But it looks as though the best we can do is to stalemate," Bradley argued. "Even if they can't paralyze us, we can't hurt them, and we are heading back for Nevia."

"I think Nerado will come in for a conference, and we'll be able to make terms of some kind. He must know what these Lewistons will do, and he knows that we'll get a chance to use them, some way or other, before he gets to us again," Costigan asserted confidently — but again he was wrong.

The door opened, and through it there waddled, rolled, or crawled a metal-clad monstrosity — a thing with wheels, legs, and writhing tentacles of jointed bronze; a thing possessed of defensive screens sufficiently powerful to absorb the full blast of the Triplanetary projectors without effort. Three brazen tentacles reached out through the ravening beams of the Lewistons, smashed them to bits, and wrapped themselves in unbreakable shackles about the armored forms of the three human beings. Through the door the machine or creature carried its helpless load, and out into and along a main corridor. And soon the three Terrestrials, without armor, without arms, and almost without clothing, were standing in the control room, again facing the calm and unmoved Nerado. To the surprise of the impetuous Costigan, the Nevian commander was entirely without rancor.

"The desire for freedom is perhaps common to all forms of animate life," he commented, through the transformer. "As I told you before, however, you are specimens to be studied by the College of Science, and you shall be so studied in spite of anything you may do. Resign yourselves to that."

"Well, say that we don't try to make any more trouble; that we co-operate in the examination and give you whatever information we can," Costigan suggested. "Then you will probably be willing to give us a ship and let us go back to our own world?"

"You will not be allowed to cause any more trouble," the amphibian declared, coldly. "Your co-operation will not be required. We will take from you whatever knowledge and information we wish. In all probability you will never be allowed to return to your own system, because as specimens you are too unique to lose. But enough of this idle chatter — take them back to their quarters!"

And back to their inter-communicating rooms the prisoners were led under heavy guard.

True to his word, Nerado made certain that they had no more opportunities to escape. All the way back to far-distant Nevia the space-ship sped, where at once, in manacles, the Terrestrials were taken to the College of Science, there to - undergo the physical and psychical examinations which Nerado had promised them.

Clio and Costigan learned that the Nevian scientist-captain had not erred in stating that their co-operation was neither needed nor desired. Furious but impotent, the human beings were studied in laboratory after laboratory by the coldly analytical, unfeeling scientists of Nevia, to whom they were nothing more nor less than specimens; and in full measure they came to know what it meant to play the part of an unknown, lowly organism in a biological research. They were photographed, externally and internally. Every bone, muscle, organ, vessel, and nerve was studied and charted. Every reflex and reaction was noted and discussed. Meters registered every impulse and recorders filmed every thought, every idea, and every sensation. Endlessly, day after day, the nerve-wracking torture went on, until the frantic subjects could bear no more. White-faced and shaking, Clio finally screamed wildly, hysterically, as she was being strapped down upon a laboratory bench; and at the sound Costigan's nerves, already at the breaking point, gave way in an outburst of Berserk fury.

The man's struggles and the girl's shrieks were alike futile, but the surprised Nevians, after a consultation, decided to give the specimens a vacation. To that end they were installed, together with their Earthly belongings, in a three-roomed structure of transparent metal, floating in the large central lagoon of the city. There they were left undisturbed for a time — undisturbed, that is, except by the continuous gaze of the crowd of hundreds of amphibians which constantly surrounded the floating cottage.

"First we're bugs under a microscope," Bradley growled, "then we're goldfish in a bowl. I don't know that. . . ."

He broke off as two of their jailers entered the room. Without a word into the transformers, they seized Bradley and the girl. As those tentacular arms stretched out toward Clio, Costigan leaped. A vain attempt. In midair the paralyzing ray of the Nevians touched him and he crashed heavily to the crystal floor; and from that floor he looked on in helpless, raging fury while his sweetheart and his captain were carried out of their prison and into a waiting submarine.

CHAPTER X

The Boise Acts

But what of the super-ship? What happened after that inertialess, that terribly destructive take-off?

Doctor Frederick Rodebush sat at the control panel of Triplanetary's newly reconstructed space-ship, his hands grasping the gleaming, ebonite handles of two double-throw switches. Facing the unknown though the physicist was, yet he grinned whimsically at his friend.

"Something, whatever it is, is about to take place. The *Boise* is taking off, under full neutralization. Ready for anything to happen, Cleve?"

"All ready — shoot!" Laconically. Cleveland also was constitutionally unable to voice his deeper sentiments in time of stress.

Rodebush flipped the switches clear over in flashing arcs, and instantly over both men there came a sensation akin to a tremendously intensified vertigo; but a vertigo as far beyond the space-sickness of weightlessness, as that horrible sensation is beyond mere terrestrial dizziness. The pilot tried to reverse the switches he had just thrown, but his leaden hands utterly refused to obey the dictates of his reeling mind. His brain was a writhing, convulsive mass of torment indescribable; expanding, exploding, swelling out with an unendurable pressure against its confining skull. Fiery spirals, laced with streaming, darting lances of black and green, flamed inside his bursting eyeballs. The Universe spun and whirled in mad gyrations about him as he reeled drunkenly to his feet, staggering and sprawling. He fell. He realized that he was falling, yet he could not fall! Thrashing wildly, grotesquely in agony, he struggled madly and blindly across the room, directly toward the thick steel wall. The tip of one hair of his unruly thatch touched the wall, and the slim length of that single hair did not even bend as its slight strength brought to an instant halt the hundred-and-eighty-odd pounds of mass — mass now entirely without inertia — that was his body.

But finally the sheer brain power of the man began to triumph over his physical torture. By indomitable force of will he compelled his groping hands to seize a life-line, almost meaningless to his dazed intelligence; and through that nightmare incarnate of hellish torture he fought his way back to the control board. Hooking one leg around a standard, he made a seemingly enormous effort and drove the two switches back into their original positions; then fell flat upon the floor, weakly but in a wave of relief and thankfulness, as his racked body felt again the wonted phenomena of weight and of inertia. White, trembling, frankly and openly sick, the two men stared at each other in half-amazed joy.

"It worked." Cleveland smiled wanly as he recovered sufficiently to speak, then leaped to his feet. "Snap it up, Fred! We must be falling fast — we'll be wrecked when we hit!"

"We're not falling anywhere." Rodebush, foreboding in his eyes, walked over to the main observation plate and scanned the heavens. "However, it's not as bad as I was afraid it might be. I can still recognize a few of the constellations, even though they are all pretty badly distorted. That means that we can't be more than a couple of light-years or so away from the Solar System. Of course, since we had so little thrust on, practically all of our time and energy was spent in getting out of the atmosphere; but, even at that, it's a good thing that space isn't an absolutely perfect vacuum or we would have been clear out of the Universe by this time."

"Huh? Impossible — where are we anyway? Then we

must be making mil . . . Oh, I see!" Cleveland exclaimed in disjointed sentences as he also stared into the plate.

"Right. We aren't traveling at all *now*." Rodebush replied. "We are perfectly stationary relative to Tellus, since we made the hop without inertia. We must have attained one hundred percent neutralization, which we didn't quite expect, and therefore we must have stopped instantaneously when our inertia was restored. But it isn't *where* we are that is worrying me the most — we can fix our place in space accurately enough by a few observations — it's *when*."

"That's right, too. Say we're two light-years away. You think maybe we're two years older than we were ten minutes ago, then? That's possible, of course, maybe probable: there's been a lot of discussion on that theory. Now's a good time to prove or to disprove it. Let's snap back to Tellus and find out."

"We'll do that, after a little more experimenting. You see, I had no intention of giving us such a long push. I was going to throw the switches over and back, but you know what happened. However, there's one good thing about it — it's worth two years of anybody's life to settle that relativity-time thing definitely, one way or the other."

"I'll say it is. But say, we've got a lot of power on our ultra-wave: enough to reach Tellus, I think. Let's locate the sun and get in touch with Samms."

"Let's work on these controls a little first, so we'll have something to report. Out here's a fine place to try the ship out — nothing in the way."

"All right with me. But I *would* like to find out whether I'm two years older than I think I am, or not!"

Then for hours they put the great super-ship through her paces, just as test-pilots check up on every detail of performance of an airplane of new and radical design. They found that the horrible vertigo could be endured, perhaps in time even conquered as space-sickness could be conquered, by a strong will in a sound body; and that their new conveyance had possibilities of which even Rodebush had never dreamed. Finally, their most pressing questions answered, they turned their most powerful ultra-beam communicator toward the yellowish star which they knew to be Old Sol.

"Samms . . . Samms." Cleveland spoke slowly and distinctly. "Rodebush and Cleveland reporting from the 'Space-Eating Wampus', now directly in line with Beta Ursae Minoris from the sun, distance about two point two light years. It will take six banks of tubes on your tightest beam, LSV3, to reach us. Barring a touch of an unusually severe type of space-sickness, everything worked beautifully; even better than our calculations showed. There's something we want to know right away — have we been gone four hours and some odd minutes, or better than two years?"

He shut off the power, turned to Rodebush, and went on:

"Nobody knows how fast this ultra-wave travels, but if it goes as fast as we did coming out it's certainly moving. I'll give him about thirty minutes, then shoot in another call."

But in less than two minutes the care-ravaged face of their chief appeared sharp and clear upon their plates and his voice snapped curtly from the speaker.

"Thank God you're alive, and twice that the ship works!" he exclaimed. "You've been gone four hours, eleven minutes, and forty-one seconds, but never mind about abstract theorizing. Get back here, to Pittsburgh, as fast as you can drive. That Nevian vessel or another like her is mopping up the city, and has destroyed half the Fleet already!"

"We'll be back there in nine minutes!" Rodebush snapped into the transmitter. "Two to get from here to atmosphere, four from atmosphere down to the Hill, and three to cool off. Notify the full four-shift crew — everybody we've picked out. Don't need anybody else. Ship, batteries, and armament are *ready*!"

"Two minutes to atmosphere, and it took ten coming out? Think you can do it?" Cleveland asked, as Rodebush flipped off the power and leaped to the control panel.

"We could do it in a few seconds if we had to. We used scarcely any power at all coming out, and I'm not using very much going back," the physicist explained rapidly, as he set the dials which would determine their flashing course.

The master switches were thrown and the pangs of inertialessness again assailed them — but weaker far this time than ever before — and upon their lookout plates they beheld a spectacle never before seen by eye of man. For the ultrabeam, with its heterodyned vision, is not distorted by any velocity yet attained, as are the ether-borne rays of light. Converted into light only at the plate, it showed their progress as truly as though they had been traveling at a pace to be expressed in the ordinary terms of miles per hour. The yellow star that was the sun detached itself from the firmament and leaped toward them, swelling visibly, momentarily, into a blinding monster of incandescence. And toward them also flung the Earth, enlarging with such indescribable rapidity that Cleveland protested involuntarily, in spite of his knowledge of the peculiar mechanism of the vessel in which they were.

"Hold it, Fred, hold it! Way 'nuff!" he exclaimed.

"I'm using only ten thousand dynes, so she'll stop herself as soon as we touch atmosphere, long before she can even begin to heat," Rodebush explained. "Looks bad, but we'll stop without a jar."

And they did. Weightless and without inertia, gravitation powerless against her neutralizing generators, the great super-ship came from her practically infinite velocity to an almost instantaneous halt in the outermost, most tenuous layer of the Earth's atmosphere. Her halt was but momentary. Inertia restored and gravitation allowed again to affect her mass, she dropped at a sharp angle downward. More than dropped; she was forced downward by one full battery of projectors; projectors driven by iron-powered generators. Soon they were over the Hill, whose violet screens went down at a word.

Flaming a dazzling white from the friction of the atmosphere through which she had torn her way, the *Boise* slowed abruptly as she neared the ground, plunging toward the surface of the small but deep artificial lake below the Hill's steel apron. Into the cold waters the space-ship dove, and even before they could close over her, furious geysers of steam and boiling water erupted as the stubborn alloy gave up its heat to the cooling liquid. Endlessly the three necessary minutes dragged their slow way into time, but finally the water ceased boiling and Rodebush tore the ship from the lake and hurled her into the gaping doorway of her dock. The massive doors of the air-locks opened, and while the full crew of picked men hurried aboard with their personal equipment, Samms talked earnestly to the two scientists in the control room.

" . . . and about half the fleet is still in the air. They aren't attacking; they are just trying to keep her from doing much more damage until you can get there. How about your take-off? We can't launch you again — the tracks are gone — but you handled her easily enough coming in?"

"That was all my fault," Rodebush admitted. "I should have neutralized inertia first, but I had no idea that the fields would extend beyond the hull, nor that they wouldn't act simultaneously. We'll take her out on the projectors this time, though, the same as we brought her in — she handles like a bicycle. The projector blast tears things up a little, but nothing serious. Have you got that Pittsburgh beam for me yet? We're about ready to go."

"Here it is, Doctor Rodebush," came the secretary's voice, and upon the screen there flashed into being the view of the events transpiring above that doomed city. "The dock is empty and sealed against your blast," and thereupon "Good-bye, and power to your tubes!" came Samms' ringing voice.

As the words were being spoken, mighty blasts of power raved from the driving projectors and the immense mass of the super-ship shot out through the portals and upward into the stratosphere. Through the tenuous atmosphere the huge ship rushed with ever-mounting speed, and while the hope of Triplanetary drove eastward Rodebush studied the ever-changing scene of battle upon his plate and issued detailed instructions to the highly trained specialists manning every offensive and defensive weapon.

But the Nevians did not wait to join battle until the newcomers arrived. Their detectors were sensitive — operative over untold thousands of miles — and the ultra-screen of the Hill had already been noted by the invaders as the Earth's only possible source of trouble. Thus the departure of the *Boise* had not gone unnoticed, and the fact, that, not even with his most penetrant rays could he see into her interior, had already given the Nevian commander some slight concern. Therefore, as soon as it was determined that the great ship was being directed toward Pittsburgh the fish-shaped cruiser of the void went into action.

High in the stratosphere, speeding eastward, the immense mass of the *Boise* slowed abruptly, although no projector had slackened its effort. Cleveland, eyes upon interferometer grating and spectrophotometer charts, fingers flying over calculator keys, grinned as he turned toward Rodebush.

"Just as you thought, Skipper; an ultra-band pusher. C4V63L29. Shall I give him a little pull?"

"Not yet; let's feel him out a little before we force a closeup. We've got plenty of mass. See what he does when I put full push on the projectors."

As the full power of the Terrestrial vessel was applied the Nevian was forced backward, away from the threatened city, against the full drive of her every projector. Soon, however, the advance was again checked, and both scientists read the reason upon their plates. The enemy had put down re-enforcing rods of tremendous power. Three compression members spread out fanwise behind her, bracing her against the low mountainside, while one huge tractor beam was thrust directly downward, holding in an unbreakable grip a cylinder of earth extending deep down into bedrock.

"Two can play at that game!" And Rodebush drove down similar beams, and forward-reaching tractors as well. "Strap yourselves in solid, everybody!" he sounded a general warning. "Something is going to give way somewhere soon, and when it does we'll get a jolt!"

And the promised jolt did indeed come soon. Prodigiously massive and powerful as the Nevian was, the *Boise* was even more massive and more powerful; and as the already enormous energy feeding the tractors, pushers, and projectors was raised to its inconceivable maximum, the vessel of the enemy was hurled upward, backward; and that of Earth shot ahead with a bounding leap that threatened to strain even her mighty members. The Nevian anchor-rods had not broken; they had simply pulled up the vast cylinders of solid rock that had formed their anchorages.

"Grab him now!" Rodebush yelled, and even while an avalanche of falling rock was burying the countryside, Cleveland snapped a tractor ray upon the flying fish and pulled tentatively.

Nor did the Nevian now seem averse to coming to grips. The two warring superdreadnaughts darted toward each other, and from the invader there flooded out the dread crimson opacity which had theretofore meant the doom of all things Solarian. It flooded out and engulfed the immense mass of humanity's hope in its spreading cloud of redly impenetrable murk. But not for long. Triplanetary's supership boasted no ordinary Terrestrial defense, but was sheathed in screen after screen of ultra-vibrations: imponderable walls, it is true, but barriers impenetrable to any unfriendly wave. To the outer screen the red veil of the Nevians clung tenaciously, licking greedily at every square inch of the shielding sphere of force, but unable to find an opening through which to feed upon the steel of the *Boise*'s armor.

"Get back — 'way back! Go back and help Pittsburgh!" Rodebush drove an ultra-communicator beam through the murk to the instruments of the Terrestrial admiral; for the surviving warships of the Fleet — its most powerful units — were hurling themselves forward, to plunge into that red destruction. "None of you will last a second in this red field.

And watch out for a violet field pretty soon — it'll be worse than this. We can handle them alone, I think; but if we can't, there's nothing in the System that can help us!"

And now the hitherto passive screen of the super-ship became active. At first invisible, it began to glow in livid, violet light, and as the glow brightened to unbearable intensity the entire spherical shield began to increase in size. Driven outward from the super-ship as a center, its advancing surface of seething energy consumed the crimson murk as a billow of blast-furnace heat consumes a cloud of snowflakes in the air above its shaft. Nor was the red deathmist all that was consumed. Between that ravening surface and the armor skin of the *Boise* there was nothing. No debris, no atmosphere, no vapor, no single atom of material substance — the first time in Terrestrial experience that an absolute vacuum had ever been attained!

Stubbornly contesting every foot of way lost, the Nevian fog retreated before the violet sphere of nothingness. Back and back it fell, disappearing altogether from all space as the violet tide engulfed the enemy vessel; but the flying fish did not disappear. Her triple screens flashed into furiously incandescent splendor and she entered, unscathed, that vacuous sphere, which collapsed instantly into an enormously elongated ellipsoid, at each focus a madly warring ship of space.

Then in that tube of vacuum was waged a spectacular duel of ultra-weapons — weapons impotent in air, but deadly in empty space. Beams, rays, and rods of Titanic power smote cracklingly against ultra-screens equally capable. Time after time each contestant ran the gamut of the spectrum with his every available ultra-force, only to find all channels closed. For minutes the terrible struggle went on, then:

"Cooper, Adlington, Spencer, Dutton!" Rodebush called into his transmitter. "Ready? Can't touch him on the ultra, so I'm going onto the macro-bands. Give him everything you have as soon as I collapse the violet. Go!"

At the word the violet barrier went down, and with a

crash as of a disrupting Universe the atmosphere rushed into the void. And through the hurricane there shot out the deadliest material weapons of Triplanetary. Torpedoes — nonferrous, ultra-screened, beam-dirigible torpedoes charged with the most effective forms of material destruction known to man. Cooper hurled his canisters of penetrating gas, Adlington his atomic iron explosive bombs, Spencer his indestructible armor-piercing projectiles, and Dutton his shatterable flasks of the quintessence of corrosion — a sticky, tacky liquid of such dire potency that only one rare Solarian element could contain it. Ten, twenty, fifty, a hundred were thrown as fast as automatic machinery could launch them; and the Nevians found themselves adversaries not to be despised. Size for size, their screens were quite as capable as those of the *Boise*. The Nevians' destructive rays glanced harmlessly from their shields, and the Nevians' elaborate screens, neutralized at impact by those of the torpedoes, were impotent to impede their progress. Each projectile must needs be caught and crushed individually by beams of the most prodigious power; and while one was being annihilated dozens more were rushing to the attack. Then, while the twisting, dodging invader was busiest with the tiny but relentless destroyers, Rodebush launched his heaviest weapon.

The macro-beams! Prodigious streamers of bluish-green flame which tore savagely through course after course of Nevian screen! Malevolent fangs, driven with such power and velocity that they were biting into the very walls of the enemy vessel before the amphibians knew their defensive shells of force had been punctured! And the emergency screens of the invaders were equally futile. Course after course was sent out, only to flare viciously through the spectrum and to go black!

Outfought at every turn, the now frantically dodging Nevian leaped away in headlong flight, only to be brought to a staggering, crashing halt as Cleveland nailed her with a tractor beam. But the Terrestrials were to learn that the

Nevians held in reserve a means of retreat. The tractor snapped — sheared off squarely by a sizzling plane of force — and the fish-shaped cruiser faded from Cleveland's sight, just as the *Boise* had disappeared from the communicator plates of Radio Center, back in the Hill, when she was launched. But though the plates in the control room could not hold the Nevian, she did not vanish beyond the ken of Randolph, now Communications Officer in the super-ship. For, warned and humiliated by his losing one speeding vessel from his plates in Radio Center, he was now ready for any emergency. Therefore as the Nevian fled, Randolph's spy-ray held her, automatically behind it as there was the full output of twelve special banks of iron-driven power tubes; and thus it was that the vengeful Terrestrials flashed immediately along the Nevians' line of flight. Inertialess now, pausing briefly from time to time to enable the crew to accustom themselves to the new sensations, the *Boise* pursued the invader; hurtling through the void with a velocity unthinkable.

"He was easier to take than I thought he would be," Cleveland grunted, staring into the plate.

"I thought he had more stuff, too," Rodebush assented; "but I guess Costigan got almost everything they had. If so, with all our own stuff and most of theirs besides, we should be able to take them. They must have neutralization, too, to take off like that; and if it's one hundred per cent we'll never catch them . . . but it isn't — there they are!"

"And this time I'm going to hold her or burn out all our generators trying," Cleveland declared, grimly. "Are you fellows down there able to handle yourselves yet? Fine! Start throwing out your cans!"

Space-hardened veterans all, the other Terrestrial officers had fought off the horrible nausea of inertialessness, just as Rodebush and Cleveland had done. Again the ravening green macro-beams tore at the flying cruiser, again the mighty frames of the two space-ships shuddered sickeningly as Cleveland clamped on his tractor rod, again the highly dirigible torpedoes dashed out with their freights of death and destruction. And again the Nevian shear-plane of force slashed at the Terrestrial's tractor beam; but this time the mighty puller did not give way. Sparkling and spitting high-tension sparks, the plane bit deeply into the stubborn rod of energy. Brighter, thicker, and longer grew the discharges as the gnawing plane drew more and more power; but in direct ratio to that power the rod grew larger, denser, and ever harder to cut. More and more vivid became the pyrotechnic display of electric brilliance, until suddenly the entire tractor rod disappeared. At the same instant a blast of intolerable flame erupted from the *Boise*'s flank and the whole enormous fabric of her shook and quivered under the force of a terrific detonation.

"Randolph! I don't see them! Are they attacking or running?" Rodebush demanded. He was the first to realize what had happened.

"Running — fast!"

"Just as well, perhaps, but get their line. Adlington!"

"Here!"

"Good! Was afraid you were gone — that was one of your bombs, wasn't it?"

"Yes. Well launched, just inside the screens. Don't see how it could have detonated unless something hot and hard struck it in the tube; it would need about that much time to explode. Good thing it didn't go off any sooner, or none of us would have been here. As it is, Area Six is pretty well done in, but the bulkheads held the damage to Six. What happened?"

"We don't know, exactly. Both generators on the tractor beam went out. At first, I thought that was all, but my neutralizers are dead and I don't know what else. When the G-4's went out the fusion must have shorted the neutralizers. They would make a mess; it must have burned a hole down into number six tube. Cleveland and I will come down, and we'll all look around."

Donning space-suits, the scientists let themselves into

the damaged compartment through the emergency air-locks, and what a sight they saw! Both outer and inner walls of alloy armor had been blown away by the awful force of the explosion. Jagged plates hung awry; bent, twisted, and broken. The great torpedo tube, with all its intricate automatic machinery, had been driven violently backward and lay piled in hideous confusion against the backing bulkheads. Practically nothing remained whole in the entire compartment.

"Nothing much we can do here," Rodebush said finally, through his transmitter, "Let's go see what number four generator room looks like."

That room, although not affected by the explosion from without, had been quite as effectively wrecked from within. It was still stiflingly hot; its air was still reeking with the stench of burning lubricant, insulation, and metal; its floor was half covered by a semi-molten mass of what had once been vital machinery. For with the burning out of the generator bars the energy of the disintegrating allotropic iron had had no outlet, and had built up until it had broken through its insulation and in an irresistible flood of power had torn through all obstacles in its path of neutralization.

"Hm-m-m. Should have had an automatic shut-off — one detail we overlooked," Rodebush mused. "The electricians *can* rebuild this stuff here, though — that hole in the hull is something else again."

"I'll say it's something else," the grizzled Chief Engineer agreed. "She's lost all her spherical strength — anchoring a tractor with this ship now would turn her inside out. Back to the nearest Triplanetary shop for us, I would say."

"Come again, Chief!" Cleveland advised the engineer. "None of us would live long enough to get there. We can't travel inertialess until the repairs are made, so if they can't be made without very much traveling, it's just too bad."

"I don't see how we could support our jacks. . . ." The engineer paused, then went on. "If you can't give me Mars or Tellus, how about some other planet? I don't care about atmosphere, or about anything but mass. I can stiffen her up in three or four days if I can sit down on something heavy enough to hold our jacks and presses; but if we have to rig up space-cradles around the ship herself it'll take a long time — months, probably. Haven't got a spare planet on hand, have you?"

"We might have, at that," Rodebush made surprising answer. "A couple of seconds before we engaged we were heading toward a sun with at least two planets. I was just getting ready to dodge them when we cut the neutralizers, so they should be fairly close somewhere — yes, there's the sun, right over there. Rather pale and small; but it's close, comparatively speaking. We'll go back up into the control room and find out about the planets."

The strange sun was found to have three large and easily located children, and observation showed that the crippled space-ship could reach the nearest of these in about five days. Power was therefore fed to the driving projectors, and each scientist, electrician, and mechanic bent to the task of repairing the ruined generators; rebuilding them to handle any load which the converters could possibly put upon them. For two days the *Boise* drove on; then her acceleration was reversed, and finally a landing was effected upon the forbidding, rocky soil of the strange world.

It was larger than the Earth, and of a somewhat stronger gravitation. Although its climate was bitterly cold, even in its short daytime, it supported a luxuriant but outlandish vegetation. Its atmosphere, while rich enough in oxygen and not really poisonous, was so rank with indescribably fetid vapors as to be scarcely breathable.

But these things bothered the engineers not at all. Paying no attention to temperature or to scenery and without waiting for chemical analysis of the air, the space-suited mechanics leaped to their tasks; and in only a little more time than had been mentioned by the chief engineer the hull and giant frame of the super-ship were as staunch as of yore.

"All right, Skipper!" came finally the welcome word.

"You might try her out with a fast hop around this world before you shove off in earnest."

Under the fierce blast of her projectors the vessel leaped ahead, and time after time, as Rodebush hurled her mass upon tractor beam or pressor, the engineers sought in vain for any sign of weakness. The strange planet half girdled and the severest tests passed flawlessly, Rodebush reached for his neutralizer switches. Reached and paused, dumfounded, for a brilliant purple light had sprung into being upon his panel and a bell rang out insistently.

"What the blue blazes!" Rodebush shot out an exploring beam along the detector line and gasped. He stared, mouth open, then yelled:

"*Roger* is here, rebuilding his planetoid! *STATIONS ALL!*"

CHAPTER XI

Roger Carries On

For gray Roger had not perished in the floods of Nevian energy which had destroyed his planetoid. While those terrific streamers of force emanating from the crimson obscurity surrounding the amphibians' space-ship were driving into his defensive screens, Roger sat impassive and immobile at his desk. His hard gray eyes moved methodically over his instruments and recorders; and after a few minutes he smiled coldly, while an expression of relief struggled fleetingly to move his expressionless face. Even though his screens were better than anyone had supposed, why admit it?

"Baxter, Hartkopf, Chatelier, Anandrusung, Penrose, Nishimura, Mirsky. . . ." He called off a list of names. "Report to me here at once!"

"The planetoid is lost," he informed his select group of scientists when they had assembled, "and we must abandon it in exactly fifteen minutes, which will be the time required for the robots to fill this first section with our most necessary machinery and instruments. Pack each of you one box of the things he most wishes to take with him, and report back here in not more than thirteen minutes. Say nothing to anyone else."

They filed out calmly, and as they passed out into the hall Baxter, perhaps a trifle less case-hardened than his fellows, at least voiced a thought for those they were so brutally deserting.

"I say, it seems a bit thick to dash off this way and leave the rest of them; but still, I suppose. . . ."

"You suppose correctly." Bland and heartless Nishimura filled in the pause. "A small part of the planetoid may be able to escape; which, to me at least, is pleasantly surprising news. It cannot carry all of our men and mechanisms, therefore only the most important of both are saved. What would you? For the rest it is simply what you call 'the fortune of war,' no?"

"But the beautiful. . . ." began the amorous Chatelier.

"Hush, fool!" snorted Hartkopf. "One word of that to the ear of Roger and you too are left behind. Of such non-essentials the Universe is full, to be collected in times of ease, but in times hard to be disregarded. Und this is a time of *schrecklichkeit* indeed!"

The group broke up, each man going to his own quarters; to meet again in the First Section a few minutes before the zero time. Roger's "office" was now packed so tightly with machinery and supplies that but little room was left for the scientists. The gray monstrosity still sat unmoved behind his dials.

"But of what use is it, Roger?" the Russian physicist demanded. "Those waves are of some ultra-band, of a frequency immensely higher than anything heretofore known. Our screens should not have stopped them for an instant. It is a mystery that they have held so long, and certainly this single section will not be permitted to leave the planetoid without being destroyed."

"There are many things you do not know, Mirsky," came the cold and level answer. "Our screens, which you think are of your own devising, have several improvements of my own in the formulae, and would hold forever had I the power to drive them. The screens of this section, being smaller, can be held as long as will be found necessary."

"Power!" the dumfounded Russian exclaimed. "Why, we have almost infinite power — unlimited — sufficient for a lifetime of high expenditure!"

But Roger made no reply, for the time of departure was at hand. He pressed down a tiny lever, and a robot in the power room threw in the gigantic plunger switches which launched against the Nevians the stupendous beam which so upset the complacence of Nerado the amphibian — the beam into which was poured recklessly every resource of power afforded by the planetoid, careless alike of burn-out and of exhaustion. Then, all the attention of the Nevians and the greater part of their power output devoted to the neutralization of that last desperate thrust, the metal wall of the planetoid opened and the First Section shot out into space. Full-driven as they were, Roger's screens flared white as he drove through the temporarily lessened attack of the Nevians; but in their preoccupation the amphibians did not notice the additional disturbance and the section tore on, unobserved and undetected. Far out in space, Roger raised his eyes from the instrument panel and continued the conversation as though it had not been interrupted.

"Everything is relative, Mirsky, and you have misused gravely the term 'unlimited.' Our power was, and is, very definitely limited. True, it then seemed ample for our needs, and is far superior to that possessed by the inhabitants of any solar system with which I am familiar; but the beings behind that red screen, whoever they are, have sources of power as far above ours as ours are above those of the Solarians."

"How do you know?"

"That power, what is it?" "We have, then, the analyses of those fields recorded!" Came simultaneous questions and explanations.

"Their power-source is very probably the intra-atomic energy of iron; and if so, much remains to be done before I can proceed with my plan. I must have the most powerful structure in the known Universe before I can act. In the light of what I have just learned, the loss of the planetoid is but a trifle." Roger, as unmoved as one of his own automatons, was coldly analyzing the situation, thinking the thing through to its logical conclusion, paying no attention whatever to the losses of life, time and treasure now behind him.

"But what can you do about it?" growled the Russian.

"Many things. From the charts of the recorders we can compute their fields of force, and from that point it is only a step to their method of liberating the energy. We shall build robots. They shall build other robots, who shall in turn construct another planetoid; one this time that, wielding the theoretical maximum of power, will be suited to my needs."

"And where will you build it? We are marked. Invisibility now is useless. Triplanetary will find us, even if we take up an orbit beyond that of Pluto!"

"We have already left your Solarian system far behind. We are going to another system; one far enough removed so that the spy-rays of Triplanetary will never find us, and yet one that we can reach in a reasonable length of time with the energies at our command. Some fifteen days will be required for the journey, however, and our quarters are cramped. Therefore make places for yourselves wherever you can, and lessen the tedium of those fifteen days by working upon whatever problems are most pressing in your respective researches."

The gray monster fell silent, immersed in what thoughts no one knew, and the scientists set out to obey his orders. Baxter, the British chemist, followed Penrose, the lantern-jawed, saturnine American engineer and inventor, as he made his way to the furthermost cubicle of the section.

"I say, Penrose, I'd like to ask you a couple of questions, if you don't mind?"

"Go ahead. Ordinarily it's dangerous to be a cackling hen anywhere around *him*, but he can't hear anything here now. His system is pretty well shot to pieces. You want to know all I know about Roger?"

"Exactly so. You have been with him so much longer than I have, you know. In some ways he impresses one as being scarcely human, if you know what I mean. Ridiculous, of course, but of late I have been wondering whether he really *is* human. He knows too much, about too many things. He seems to be acquainted with many solar systems, to visit which would require life-times. Then, too, he has dropped remarks which would imply that he actually saw things that happened long before any living man could possibly have been born. Finally, he looks — well, peculiar — and certainly does not act human. I have been wondering, and have been able to learn nothing about him; as you have said, such talk as this aboard the planetoid was impossible."

"You needn't worry about being paid your price; that's one thing. If we live — and that was part of the agreement, you know — we will all get what we sold out for. You will become a belted earl. I have already made millions, and shall make many more. Similarly, Chatelier has had and will have his women, Anandrusung and Nishimura their cherished revenges, Hartkopf his power, and so on." He eyed the other speculatively, then went on:

"I might as well spill it all, since I'll never have a better chance and since you should know what the rest of us do. You're in the same boat with us and tarred with the same brush. There's a lot of gossip, that may or may not be true, but I know one very startling fact. Here it is. My great-great-grandfather left some notes which, taken in connection with certain things I myself saw on the planetoid, prove beyond question that our Roger went to Harvard University at the same time he did. Roger was a grown man then, and the elder Penrose noted that he was marked, like this," and the American sketched a cabalistic design.

"What!" Baxter exclaimed. "An adept of North Polar Jupiter — *them?*"

"Yes. That was before the First Jovian War, you know, and it was those medicine-men — really high-caliber scientists — that prolonged that war so. . . ."

"But I say, Penrose, that's really a bit thick. When they were wiped out it was proved a lot of hocus-pocus. . . ."

"Some of it was, but most of it wasn't," Penrose interrupted in turn. "I'm not asking you to believe anything except that one fact; I'm just telling you the rest of it. But it is also a fact that those adepts knew things and did things that take a lot of explaining. Now for the gossip, none of which is guaranteed. Roger is undoubtedly of Tellurian parentage, and the story is that his father was a moon-pirate, his mother a Greek adventuress. When the pirates were chased off the moon they went to Ganymede, you know, and some of them were captured by the Jovians. It seems that Roger was born at an instant of time sacred to the adepts, so they took him on. He worked his way up through the Forbidden Society as all adepts did, by various kinds of murder and job lots of assorted deviltries, until he got clear to the top — the seventy-seventh mystery. . . ."

"The secret of eternal youth!" gasped Baxter, awed in spite of himself.

"Right, and he stayed Chief Devil, in spite of all the efforts of all his ambitious sub-devils to kill him, until the turning-point of the First Jovian War. He cut away then in a space-ship, and ever since then he has been working — and working hard — on some stupendous plan of his own that nobody else has ever got even an inkling of. That's the story. True or not, it explains a lot of things that no other theory can touch. And now I think you'd better shuffle along; enough of this is a great plenty!"

Baxter went to his own cubby, and each man of the adept's cold-blooded crew methodically took up his task. True to prediction, in fifteen days a planet loomed beneath them and their vessel settled through a reeking atmosphere toward a rocky and forbidding plain. Then for another day they plunged along, a few thousand feet above the surface of that strange world, while Roger with his analytical detectors sought the most favorable location from which to wrest the materials necessary for his program of construction.

It was a world of cold; its sun was distant, pale, and wan. It had monstrous forms of vegetation, of which each branch and member writhed and fought with a grotesque and horrible individual activity. Ever and anon a struggling part broke from its parent plant and darted away in independent existence; leaping upon and consuming or being consumed by a fellow creature equally monstrous. This flora was of a uniform color — a lurid, sickly yellow. In form some of it was fern-like, some cactus-like, some vaguely tree-like; but it was all outrageous, inherently repulsive to all Solarian senses. And no less hideous were the animal-like forms of life, which slithered and slunk rapaciously through that fantastic pseudo-vegetation. Snake-like, reptile-like, bat-like, the creatures squirmed, crawled, and flew; each covered with a dankly oozing yellow hide and each motivated by twin common impulses — to kill and insatiably and indiscriminately to devour. Over this reeking wilderness Roger drove his vessel, untouched by its disgusting, its appalling ferocity and horror.

"There should be intelligence, of a kind," he mused, and swept the surface of the planet with an exploring beam. "Ah, yes, there is a city, of sorts," and in a few minutes the outlaws were looking down upon a metal-walled city of roundly conical buildings.

Inside these structures and between and around them there scuttled formless blobs of matter, one of which Roger brought up into his vessel by means of a tractor ray. Held immovable by the beam it lay upon the floor, a strangely extensile, amoeba-like metal-studded mass of leathery substance. Of eyes, ears, limbs, or organs it apparently had none, yet it radiated an intensely hostile aura; a mental effluvium concentrated of rage and of hatred.

"Apparently the ruling intelligence of the planet," Roger commented. "Such creatures are useless to us; we can build robots in half the time required for their subjugation and training. Still, it should not be permitted to carry back what it may have learned of us." As he spoke the adept threw the peculiar being out into the air and dispassionately rayed it out of existence.

"That thing reminds me of a man I used to know, back in Penobscot." Penrose was as coldly callous as his unfeeling master. "The evenest-tempered man in town — mad all the time!"

Eventually Roger found a location which satisfied his

requirements of raw materials, and made a landing upon that unfriendly soil. Sweeping beams denuded a great circle of life, and into that circle leaped robots. Robots requiring neither rest nor food, but only lubricants and power; robots insensible alike to that bitter cold and to that noxious atmosphere.

But the outlaws were not to win a foothold upon that inimical planet easily, nor were they to hold it without effort. Through the weird vegetation of the circle's bare edge there scuttled and poured along a horde of the metal-studded men — if "men" they might be called — who, ferocity incarnate, rushed the robot line. Mowed down by hundreds, still they came on; willing, it seemed to expend any number of lives in order that one living creature might once touch a robot with one out-thrust metallic stud. Whenever that happened there was a flash as of lightning, the heavy smoke of burning insulation, grease and metal, and the robot went down out of control. Recalling his remaining automatons, Roger sent out a shielding screen, against which the defenders of their planet raged in impotent fury. For days they hurled themselves and their every force against that impenetrable barrier, then withdrew: temporarily stopped, but by no means acknowledging defeat.

Then, while Roger and his cohorts directed affairs from within their comfortable and now sufficiently roomy vessel, there came into being around it an industrial city of metal, peopled by metallic and insensate mechanisms. Mines were sunk, furnaces were blown in, smelters belched forth into the already unbearable air their sulphurous fumes, rolling mills and machine shops were built and equipped: and as fast as new enterprises were completed additional robots were ready to man them. In record time the heavy work of girders, members, and plates was well under way; and shortly thereafter light, deft, and multi-fingered mechanical men began the interminable task of building and installing the prodigious amount of precise machinery required for the vast structure. Roger was well content: but one day he was rudely awakened from his dream of complete isolation.

Even though he had no reason to believe that there was anything dangerous within hundreds of millions of miles, it was Roger's cautious custom to release the screens from time to time, in order to allow his detectors to range out. This day, as he sent out his beams, his hard gray eyes grew even harder.

"Mirsky! Nishimura! Come here!" he snapped, and showed them upon his plate an enormous sphere of steel, its rays flaming viciously. "Is there any doubt whatever in your minds as to the System to which that ship belongs?"

"None at all — Triplanetarian," replied the Russian. "While larger than any I have seen before, its construction is unmistakable. They managed to trace us, and are testing out their weapons before attacking. Do we attack or do we run away?"

"If Triplanetarian, and it surely is, we attack," coldly. "This one section is armed and powered to defeat Triplanetary's entire navy. We shall take that ship, and shall add its slight resources to our own. And it may even be that they have picked up the three who escaped me. . . . I have never yet been balked for long. Yes, we shall take that vessel. And those three sooner or later. Bradley I care nothing about . . . but Costigan handled me . . . and the woman. . . ." Diamond-hard eyes glared balefully at the urge of thoughts to a clean and normal mind unthinkable.

"To your posts," he ordered. "The robots will continue to function under their automatic controls during the short time it will require to abate this nuisance."

"*One moment!*" A strange voice roared from the speakers. "Consider yourselves under arrest, by order of the Triplanetary Council! Surrender and you shall receive impartial hearing; fight us and you shall never come to trial. From what we have learned of Roger, we do not expect him to surrender, but if any of you other men wish to avoid immediate death, leave your vessel at once. We will come back for you later."

"Any of you wishing to leave this vessel have my full permission to do so," Roger announced, disdaining any reply to the challenge of the *Boise*. "Any such, however, will not be allowed inside the planetoid area after the rest of us return from wiping out that patrol. We attack in one minute."

"Would not one do better by stopping on?" Baxter, in the quarters of the American, was in doubt as to the most profitable course to pursue. "I should leave immediately if I thought that that ship could win; but I do not fancy that it can, do you?"

"That ship? *One* Triplanetary ship against *us*?" Penrose laughed raucously. "Do as you please. I'd go in a minute if I thought that there was any chance of us losing; but there isn't, so I'm staying. I know which side *my* bread's buttered on. Those cops are bluffing, that's all. Not bluffing exactly, either, because they'll go through with it as long as they last. Foolish, but it's a way they have — they'll die trying every time, instead of running away, even when they know they're licked before they start. They don't use good judgment."

"None of you are leaving? Very well, you each know what to do," came Roger's emotionless voice. The stipulated minute having elapsed, he advanced a lever and the outlaw cruiser slid quietly into the air.

Toward the poised *Boise* Roger steered. Within range, he flung out a weapon new-learned and supposedly irresistible to any ferrous thing or creature, the red converter-field of the Nevians. For Roger's analytical detectors had stood him in good stead during those frightful minutes in the course of which the planetoid had borne the brunt of Nerado's superhuman attack; in such good stead that from the records of those ingenious instruments he and his scientists had been able to reconstruct not only the generators of the attacking forces, but also the screens employed by the amphibians in the neutralization of similar beams. With a vastly inferior armament the smallest of Roger's vessels had defeated the most powerful battleships of Triplanetary; what had he to fear in such a heavy craft as the one he now was driving, one so superlatively armed and powered? Well it was for his peace of mind that he had no inkling that the harmless-looking sphere he was so blithely attacking was in reality the much-discussed, half-mythical "super-ship" of Triplanetary's Secret Service; nor that its already unprecedented armament had been re-enforced, thanks to that hated Costigan, with Roger's own every worth-while idea, as well as with every weapon and defense known to that arch-Nevian, Nerado!

Unknowing and contemptuous, Roger launched his converter field, and instantly found himself fighting for his very life. For from Rodebush at the controls down, the men of the Secret Service countered with wave after wave and with salvo after salvo of vibratory and material destruction. No thought of mercy for the men of the pirate ship could enter their minds. The outlaws had each been given a chance to surrender, and each had refused it. Refusing, they knew, as the Triplanetarians knew and as all modern readers know, meant that they were staking their lives upon victory. For with modern armaments it is seldom indeed that a single man lives through the defeat in battle of a war-vessel of space.

Roger launched his field of red opacity, but it did not reach even *Boise*'s screens. All space seemed to explode into violet splendor as Rodebush neutralized it, drove it back with his obliterating zone of force; but even that all-devouring zone could not touch Roger's peculiarly efficient screen. The outlaw vessel stood out, unharmed. Ultra-violet, infra-red, pure heat, infra-sound, solid beams of high-tension high-frequency current in whose paths the most stubborn metals would be volatilized instantly; all iron-driven, every deadly and torturing vibration known was hurled against that screen; but it, too, was iron-driven, and it held. Even the awful force of the macro-beam was dissipated by it — reflected, hurled away on all sides in coruscating torrents of blinding, dazzling energy. Cooper, Adlington, Spencer, and Dutton hurled against it their bombs and torpedoes — and still it held. But Roger's fiercest blasts and heaviest projectiles were equally impotent against the force-shields of the super-ship. The adept, having no liking for a battle upon anything like equal terms, sought safety in flight, only to be brought to a crashing, stunning halt by a massive tractor beam.

"That must be that sixth-phase polycyclic screen that Conway reported on," Cleveland frowned in thought. "I've been doing a lot of work on that, and I think I've calculated an opener for it, Fred, but I'll have to have number ten projector and the whole output of number ten power room. Can you let me play with that much juice for a while? All right, Blake, tune her up to fifty-five thousand — there, hold it! Now, you other fellows, listen! I'm going to try to drill a hole through that screen with a hollow, quasi-solid beam: like a diamond drill cutting out a core. You won't be able to shove anything into the hole from outside the beam, so you'll have to steer your cans out through the central orifice of number ten projector — that'll be cold, since I'm going to use only the edge. I don't know how long I'll be able to hold the hole open, though so shoot them along as fast as you can. Ready? Here goes!"

He pressed a series of contacts. Far below, in number ten converter room, massive switches drove home and the enormous mass of the vessel quivered under the terrific reaction of the newly-calculated, semi-material beam of energy that was hurled out, backed by the mightiest of all the mighty converters and generators of Triplanetary's superdreadnaught. That beam, a pipe-like hollow cylinder of intolerable energy, flashed out, and there was a rending, tearing crash as it struck Roger's hitherto impenetrable wall. Struck and clung, grinding, boring in, while from the raging inferno that marked the circle of contact of cylinder and shield the pirates' screen radiated scintillating torrents of cracking, streaming sparks, lightning-like in length and in intensity.

Deeper and deeper the gigantic drill was driven. It was through! Pierced Roger's polycyclic screen; exposed the bare metal of Roger's walls! And now, concentrated upon one point, flamed out in seemingly redoubled fury Triplanetary's raging rays — in vain. For even as they could not penetrate the screen, neither could they penetrate the wall of Cleveland's drill, but rebounded from it in the cascaded brilliance of thwarted lightning.

"Oh, what a dumb-bell I am!" groaned Cleveland. "Why, oh why didn't I have somebody rig up a secondary SX7 beam on Ten's inner rings? Hop to it, will you, Blake, so that we'll have it in case they are able to stop the cans?"

But the pirates could not stop all of Triplanetary's projectiles, now hurrying along inside the pipe as fast as they could be driven. In fact, for a few minutes desperate Roger, knowing that he faced his long life's gravest crisis, paid no attention to them at all, nor to any of his own useless offensive weapons: he struggled only and madly to break away from the savage grip of the *Boise*'s tractor rod. Futile. He could neither cut nor stretch that inexorably anchoring beam. Then he devoted his every resource to the closing of that unbelievable breach in his shield; the barrier which through all previous emergencies had kept death at bay. Equally futile. His most desperate efforts resulted only in more frenzied displays of incandescence along the curved surface of contact of that penetrant cylinder. And through that terrific conduit came speeding package after package of destruction. Bombs, and armor-piercing shells, gas shells, and shells of poisonous and corrosive fluids followed each other in close succession. The surviving scientists of the planetoid, expert gunners and ray-men all, destroyed many of the projectiles, but it was not humanly possible to frustrate them all. And the breach could not be forced shut against the all but irresistible force of Cleveland's "opener". And with all his power Roger could not shift his vessel's position in the grip of Triplanetary's tractors sufficiently to bring a projector to bear upon the super-ship along the now unprotected axis of that narrow, but deadly tube.

Thus it was that the end came soon. A war-head touched steel plating and there ensued a world-wracking explosion of atomic iron. Gaping wide, helpless, with all defenses down, other torpedoes entered the stricken hulk and completed its destruction even before they could be recalled. Explosive bombs literally tore the pirate vessel to fragments, while vials of pure corrosion dissolved her substance into dripping corruption and reeking gases filled every cranny of the wreckage as its torn and dismembered fragments began their long plunge to the ground. The space-ship followed the pieces down, and Rodebush sent out an exploring ray.

". . . resistance was such that it was necessary to use corrosive, and ship and contents were completely disintegrated," he dictated into his vessel's log, some time later. "While there were of course no remains recognizable as human, it is practically certain that Roger and his last eleven men died.

"Look here, Fred," Cleveland called his attention to the plate, upon which was pictured a horde of the peculiar inhabitants of the ghastly planet, wreaking their frenzied electrical wrath upon everything within the circle bared by Roger. "I was just going to suggest that we clean up that planetoid Roger started, but I see that the local boys are attending to it."

"Just as well, perhaps. I would like to stay and study these people a little while, but we must get back on the trail of the Nevians," and the *Boise* leaped away into space, toward the line of flight of the amphibians.

They reached that line and along it they traveled at full normal blast. As they traveled their detecting receivers and amplifiers were reaching out with their utmost power; ultra-instruments capable of rendering audible any signal originating within many light-years of them, upon any known frequency. And constantly at least two men were listening to those instruments with every sense concentrated in their ears. Listening — straining to distinguish in the deafening roar of background noise from the over-driven tubes any sign of voice or signal. Listening — while, millions upon untold millions of miles beyond even the prodigious reach of those ultra-instruments, three human beings, pitted against overwhelming odds, were even then sending out into empty space an almost hopeless appeal for the aid so desperately needed!

CHAPTER XII

The Specimens Escape

Knowing well that conversation with its fellows is one of the greatest needs of any intelligent being, the Nevians had permitted the Terrestrial specimens to retain possession of their ultra-beam communicators. Thus it was that Costigan had been able to keep in touch with his sweetheart and with Bradley. He learned that each had been placed upon exhibition in a different Nevian city: that the three had been separated in response to an insistent popular demand for such a distribution of the peculiar, but highly interesting creatures from a distant solar system. They had not been harmed. In fact, each was visited daily by a specialist, who made sure that his charge was being kept in the pink of condition.

As soon as he became aware of this condition of things Costigan became morose. He sat still, drooped, and pined away visibly. He refused to eat, and of the worried specialist he demanded liberty. Then, failing in that as he knew he would fail, he demanded something to *do*. They pointed out to him, reasonably enough, that in such a civilization as theirs there was nothing he *could* do. They assured him that they would do anything they could to alleviate his mental suffering, but that since he was a museum piece he must see, himself, that he must be kept on display for a short time. Wouldn't he please behave himself and eat, as a reasoning being should? Costigan sulked a little longer, then wavered. Finally he agreed to compromise. He would eat and exercise if they would fit up a laboratory in his apartment, so that he could continue the studies he had begun upon his own native planet. To this they agreed, and thus it came about that one day the following conversation was held:

"Clio? Bradley? I've got something to tell you this time. Haven't said anything before, for fear things might not work out, but they did. I went on a hunger strike and made them give me a complete laboratory. As a chemist I'm a darn good electrician; but luckily, with the sea-water they've got here, it's a very simple thing to make. . . ."

"Hold on!" snapped Bradley. "Somebody may be listening in on us!"

"They aren't. They can't, without my knowing it, and I'll cut off the second anybody tries to synchronize with my beam. To resume — making Vee-Two is a very simple process, and I've got everything around here that's hollow clear full of it. . . ."

"How come they let you?" asked Clio.

"Oh, they don't know what I'm doing. They watched me for a few days, and all I did was make up and bottle the weirdest messes imaginable. Then I finally managed to separate oxygen and nitrogen, after trying hard all of one day; and when they thought they saw that I didn't know anything about either one of them or what to do with them after I had them, they gave me up in disgust as a plain dumb ape and haven't paid any attention to me since. So I've got me plenty of kilograms of liquid Vee-Two, all ready to touch off. I'm getting out of here in about three minutes and a half, and I'm coming over after you folks, in a new, iron-powered space-speedster that they don't know I know anything about. They've just given it its final tests, and it's the slickest thing you ever saw."

"But Conway, dearest, you can't possibly rescue me," Clio's voice broke. "Why, there are thousands of them, all around here. If you can get away, go, dear, but don't. . . ."

"I said I was coming after you, and if I can get away I'll be there. A good whiff of this stuff will lay out a thousand of them just as easily as it will one. Here's the idea. I've made a gas mask for myself, since I'll be in it where it's thick, but you two won't need any. The gas is soluble enough in water so that three or four thicknesses of wet cloth over your noses will be enough. I'll tell you when to wet down. We're going to break away or go out trying — there aren't enough amphibians between here and Andromeda to keep us humans cooped up like menagerie animals forever! But here comes my specialist with the keys to the city; time for the overture to start. See you later!"

The Nevian physician directed his key-tube upon the transparent wall of the chamber and an opening appeared, an opening which vanished as soon as he had stepped through it; Costigan kicked a valve open; and from various innocent tubes there belched forth into the water of the central lagoon and into the air over it a flood of deadly vapor. As the Nevian turned toward the prisoner there was an almost inaudible hiss and a tiny jet of the frightful, outlawed stuff struck his open gills, just below his huge, conical head. He tensed momentarily, twitched convulsively just once, and fell motionless to the floor. And outside, the streams of avidly soluble liquefied gas rushed out into air and into water. It spread, dissolved, and diffused with the extreme mobility which is one of its characteristics; and as it diffused and was borne outward the Nevians, in their massed hundreds, died. Died not knowing what killed them; not knowing even that they died. Costigan, bitterly resentful of the inhuman treatment accorded the three and fiercely anxious for the success of his plan of escape, held his breath and, grimly alert, watched the amphibians die. When he could see no more motion anywhere he donned his gas-mask, strapped upon his back a large canister of the poison — his capacious pockets were already full of smaller containers — and two savagely exultant sentences escaped him.

"I am a poor, ignorant specimen of ape, that can be let play with apparatus, am I?" he rasped, as he picked up the key-tube of the specialist and opened the door of his prison. "Maybe they'll learn sometime that it ain't always safe to judge by the looks of a flea how far he can jump!"

He stepped out through the opening into the water, and, burdened as he was, made shift to swim to the nearest ramp. Up it he ran, toward a main corridor. But ahead of him there was wafted a breath of dread Vee-Two, and where that breath went, went also unconsciousness — an unconsciousness which would deepen gradually into permanent oblivion save for the prompt intervention of one who possessed, not only the necessary antidote, but the equally important knowledge of exactly how to use it. Upon the floor of that corridor were strewn Nevians, who had dropped in their tracks. Past or over their bodies Costigan strode, pausing only to direct a jet of lethal vapor into whatever branching corridor or open doorway caught his eye. He was going to the intake of the city's ventilation plant, and no unmasked creature dependent for life upon oxygen could bar his path. He reached the intake, tore the canister from his back, and released its full, vast volume of horrid contents into the primary air stream of the entire city.

And all throughout that doomed city Nevians dropped; quietly and without a struggle, unknowing. Busy executives dropped upon their cushioned, flat-topped desks; hurrying travelers and messengers dropped upon the floors of the corridors or relaxed in the noxious waters of the ways; lookouts and observers dropped before their flashing screens; central operators of communications dropped under the winking lights of their panels. Observers and centrals in the outlying sections of the city wondered briefly at the unwonted universal motionlessness and stagnation; then the racing taint in water and in air reached them, too, and they ceased wondering — forever.

Then through those quiet halls Costigan stalked to a certain storage room, where with all due precaution he donned his own suit of Triplanetary armor. Making an ungainly bundle of the other Solarian equipment stored there, he dragged it along behind him as he clanked back toward his prison, until he neared the dock at which was moored the Nevian space-speedster which he was determined to take.

Here, he knew, was the first of many critical points. The crew of the vessel was aboard, and, with its independent air-supply, unharmed. They had weapons, were undoubtedly alarmed, and were very probably highly suspicious. They, too, had ultra-beams and might see him, but his very closeness to them would tend to protect him from ultra-beam observation. Therefore he crouched tensely behind a buttress, staring through his spy-ray goggles, waiting for a moment when none of the Nevians would be near the entrance, but grimly resolved to act instantly should he feel any touch of a spying ultra-beam.

"Here's where the pinch comes," he growled to himself. "I know the combination, but if they're suspicious enough and act quick enough they can seal that door on me before I can get it open, and then rub me out like a blot; but . . . ah!"

The moment had arrived, before the touch of any revealing ray. He trained the key-tube, the entrance opened, and through that opening in the instant of its appearance there shot a brittle bulb of glass, whose breaking meant death. It crashed into fragments against a metallic wall and Costigan, entering the vessel, consigned its erstwhile crew one by one to the already crowded waters of the lagoon. He then leaped to the controls and drove the captured speedster through the air, to plunge it down upon the surface of the lagoon beside the door of the isolated structure which had for so long been his prison. Carefully he transferred to the vessel the motley assortment of containers of Vee-Two, and after a quick check-up to make sure that he had overlooked nothing, he shot his craft straight up into the air. Then only did he close his ultra-wave circuits and speak.

"Clio, Bradley — I got away clean, without a bit of trouble. Now I'm coming after you, Clio."

"Oh, it's wonderful that you got away, Conway!" the girl exclaimed. "But hadn't you better get Captain Bradley first? Then, if anything should happen, he would be of some use, while I. . . ."

"I'll knock him into an outside loop if he does!" the captain snorted, and Costigan went on:

"You won't need to. You come first, Clio, of course. But you're too far away for me to see you with my spy, and I don't want to use the high-powered beam of this boat for fear of detection; so you'd better keep on talking, so that I can trace you."

"That's one thing I *am* good at!" Clio laughed in sheer relief. "If talking were music, I'd be a full brass band!" and she kept up a flow of inconsequential chatter, until Costigan told her that it was no longer necessary; that he had established the line.

"Any excitement around there yet?" he asked her then.

"Nothing unusual that I can see," she replied. "Why? Should there be some?"

"I hope not, but when I made my get-away I couldn't kill them all, of course, and I thought maybe they might connect things up with my jail-break and tell the other cities to take steps about you two. But I guess they're pretty well disorganized back there yet, since they can't know who hit them, or what with, or why. I must have got about everybody that wasn't sealed up somewhere, and it doesn't stand to reason that those who are left can check up very closely for a while yet. But they're nobody's fools — they'll certainly get conscious when I snatch you, maybe before . . . there, I see your city, I think."

"What are you going to do?"

"Same as I did back there, if I can. Poison their primary air and all the water I can reach. . . ."

"Oh, Conway!" Her voice rose to a scream. "They must know — they're all getting out of the water and are rushing inside the buildings as fast as they possibly can!"

"I see they are," grimly. "I'm right over you now, 'way up. Been locating their primary intake. They've got a dozen ships around it, and have guards posted all along the corridors leading to it; and *those guards are wearing masks!* They're clever birds, all right, those amphibians — they know what they got back there and how they got it. That changes things, girl! If we use gas here we won't stand a chance in the world of getting old Bradley. Stand by to jump when I open that door!"

"Hurry, dear! They are coming out here after me!"

"Sure they are." Costigan had already seen the two Nevians swimming out toward Clio's cage, and had hurled his vessel downward in a screaming power dive. "You're too valuable a specimen for them to let you be gassed, but if they can get there before I do they're traveling fast!"

He miscalculated slightly, so that instead of coming to a halt at the surface of the liquid medium the speedster struck with a crash that hurled solid masses of water for hundreds of yards. But no ordinary crash could harm that vessel's structure, her gravity controls were not overloaded, and she shot back to the surface; gallant ship and reckless pilot alike unharmed. Costigan trained his key-tube upon the doorway of Clio's cell, then tossed it aside.

"Different combinations over here!" he barked. "Got to cut you out — lie down in that far corner!"

His hands flashed over the panel, and as Clio fell prone without hesitation or question a heavy beam literally blasted away a large portion of the roof of the structure. The speedster shot into the air and dropped down until she rested upon the tops of opposite walls; walls still glowing, semi-molten. The girl piled a stool upon the table and stood upon it, reached upward, and seized the mailed hands extended downward toward her. Costigan heaved her up into the vessel with a powerful jerk, slammed the door shut, leaped to the controls, and the speedster darted away.

"Your armor's in that bundle there. Better put it on, and check your Lewistons and pistols — no telling what kind of jams we'll get into," he snapped, without turning. "Bradley, start talking . . . all right, I've got your line. Better get your wet rags ready and get organized generally — every second will count by the time we get there. We're coming so fast that our outer plating's white hot, but it may not be fast enough, at that."

"It isn't fast enough, quite," Bradley announced, calmly. "They're coming out after me now."

"Don't fight them and probably they won't paralyze you. Keep on talking, so that I can find out where they take you."

"No good, Costigan." The voice of the old space-flea did not reveal a sign of emotion as he made his dread announcement. "They have it all figured out. They're not taking any chances at all — they're going to paral. . . ." His voice broke off in the middle of the word.

With a bitter imprecation Costigan flashed on the powerful ultra-beam projector of the speedster and focused the plate upon Bradley's prison; careless now of detection, since the Nevians were already warned. Upon that plate he watched the Nevians carry the helpless body of the captain into a small boat, and continued to watch as they bore it into one of the largest buildings of the city. Up a series of ramps they took the still form, placing it finally upon a soft couch in an enormous and heavily guarded central hall. Costigan turned to his companion, Clio, and even through the helmets she could see plainly the white agony of his expression. He moistened his lips and tried twice to speak — tried and failed: but he made no move either to cut off their power or to change their direction.

"Of course," she approved, steadily. "We are going through. I know that you *want* to run with me, but if you actually did it, I would never want to see you or hear of you again, and you would hate me forever."

"Hardly that." The anguish did not leave his eyes and his voice was hoarse and strained, but his hands did not vary the course of the speedster by so much as a hair's breadth. "You're the finest little fellow that ever waved a plume, and I would love you no matter what happened. I'd trade my immortal soul to the devil if it would get you out of this mess, but we're both in it up to our necks and we can't dog it now. If they kill him we beat it — he and I both knew that it was on the chance of that happening that I took you first — but as long as all three of us are alive it's all three or none."

"Of course," she said again, as steadily, thrilled this time to the depths of her being by the sheer manhood of him who had thus simply voiced his Code; a man of such fiber that neither love of life, nor the infinitely more powerful love of her which she knew he bore, could make him lower its high standard.

"We are going through. Forget that I am a woman. We are three human beings, fighting a world full of monsters. I am simply one of us three. I will steer your ship, fire your projectors, or throw your bombs. What can I do best?"

"Throw bombs," he directed, briefly. He knew what must be done were they to have even the slightest chance of winning clear. "I'm going to blast a hole down into the auditorium, and when I do you stand by that port and start dropping bottles of perfume. Throw a couple of big ones right down the shaft I make, and the rest of them most anywhere, after I cut the wall open. They'll do good wherever they hit, land or water."

"But Captain Bradley — he'll be gassed, too." Her fine eyes were troubled.

"Can't be helped. I've got the antidote, and it'll work any time under an hour. That'll be lots of time — if we aren't gone in less than ten minutes we'll be staying here. They're bringing in platoons of militia in full armor, and if we don't beat those boys to it we're in for plenty of grief. All right — start throwing!"

The speedster had come to a halt directly over the imposing edifice within which Bradley was incarcerated, and a mighty beam had flared downward, digging a fiery well through floor after floor of stubborn metal. The ceiling of the amphitheater pierced, the beam expired; and down into that assembly hall there dropped two canisters of Vee-Two; to crash and to fill its atmosphere with imperceptible death. Then the beam flashed on again, this time at maximum power, and with it Costigan burned away half of the gigantic building. Burned it away until room above room gaped open, shelf-like, to outer atmosphere; the great hall now resembling an over-size pigeon-hole surrounded by smaller ones. Into that largest pigeon-hole the speedster darted, and cushioned desks and benches crashed down, crushed flat under its enormous weight as it came to rest upon the floor.

Every available guard had been thrown into that room, regardless of customary occupation or of equipment. Most of them had been ordinary watchmen, not even wearing masks, and all such were already down. Many, however, were protected by masks, and a few were dressed in full armor. But no portable armor could mount defenses of sufficient power to withstand the awful force of the speedster's weapons, and one flashing swing of a projector swept the hall almost clear of life.

"Can't shoot very close to Bradley with this big beam, but I'll mop up on the rest of them by hand. Stay here and cover me, Clio!" Costigan ordered, and went to open the door.

"I can't — I won't!" Clio replied instantly. "I don't know the controls well enough. I'd kill you or Captain Bradley, sure; but I *can* shoot, and I'm going to!" and she leaped out, close upon his heels.

Thus, flaming Lewiston in one hand and barking automatic in the other, the two mailed figures advanced toward Bradley; now doubly helpless: paralyzed by his enemies and gassed by his friends. For a time the Nevians melted away before them, but as they approached more nearly the couch, upon which the captain was, they encountered six figures encased in armor fully as capable as their own. The beams of the Lewistons rebounded from that armor in futile pyrotechnics, the bullets of the automatics spattered and exploded impotently against it. And behind that single line of armored guards were massed perhaps twenty unarmored, but masked, soldiers; and scuttling up the ramps leading into the hall were coming the platoons of heavily-armored figures which Costigan had previously seen.

Decision instantly made, Costigan ran back toward the speedster, but he was not deserting his companions.

"Keep the good work up!" he instructed the girl as he ran. "I'll pick those jaspers off with a pencil ray and then stand off the bunch that's coming while you rub out the rest of that crew there and drag Bradley back here."

Back at the control panel, he trained a narrow, but intensely dense pencil of livid flame, and one by one the six armored figures fell. Then, knowing that Clio could handle the remaining opposition, he devoted his attention to the re-enforcements so rapidly approaching from the sides. Again and again the heavy beam lashed out, now upon this side, now upon that, and in its flaming path Nevians disappeared. And not only Nevians — in the incredible energy of that beam's blast, floor, walls, ramps, and every material thing vanished in clouds of thick and brilliant vapor. The room temporarily clear of foes, he sprang again to Clio's assistance, but her task was nearly done. She had "rubbed out" all opposition and, tugging lustily at Bradley's feet, had already dragged him almost to the side of the speedster.

"'At-a-girl, Clio!" cheered Costigan, as he picked up the burly captain and tossed him through the doorway. "Highly useful, girl of my dreams, as well as ornamental. In with you, and we'll start out to go places!"

But getting the speedster out of the now completely ruined hall proved to be much more of a task than driving it in had been, for scarcely had the Terrestrials closed their locks than a section of the building collapsed behind them, cutting off their retreat. Nevian submarines and airships were beginning to arrive upon the scene, and were raying the building viciously in an attempt to entrap or to crush the Terrestrials in its ruins. Costigan managed finally to blast his way out, but the Nevians had had time to assemble in force and he was met by a concentrated storm of beams and of metal from every inimical weapon within range.

But not for nothing had Conway Costigan selected for his dash for liberty the craft which, save only for the two immense interstellar cruisers, was the most powerful vessel ever built upon red Nevia. And not for nothing had he studied minutely and to the last, least detail every item of its controls and of its armament during wearily long days and nights of solitary imprisonment. He had studied it under test, in action, and at rest; studied it until he knew thoroughly its every possibility — and what a ship it was! The iron-driven generators of his shielding screens handled with ease the terrific load of the Nevians' assault, his polycyclic screens were proof against any material projectile, and the machines supplying his offensive beams with power were more than equal to their tasks. Driven now at full rating those frightful weapons lashed out against the Nevian blocking the way, and under their impacts her screens flared brilliantly through the spectrum and went down. And in the instant of their failure the enemy vessel was literally blown into nothingness — no unprotected metal, however resistant, could exist for a moment in the pathway of those iron-driven tornadoes of pure energy.

Ship after ship of the Nevians plunged toward the speedster in desperately suicidal attempts to ram her down, but each met the same flaming fate before its mass could collide with the ship of the Terrestrials. Then, from the grouped submarines far below, there reached up red rods of force, which seized the space-ship and began relentlessly to draw her down.

"What are they doing that for, Conway? *They* can't fight us!"

"They don't want to fight us. They want to hold us, but I know what to do about that, too," and the powerful tractor rods snapped as a plane of lurid light drove through them. Upward now at the highest permissible velocity the speedster leaped, and past the few ships remaining above her she dodged; there was nothing now between her and the freedom of boundless space.

"You did it, Conway; you did it!" Clio exulted. "Oh, Conway, you're just simply wonderful!"

"I haven't done it yet," Costigan cautioned her. "The worst is yet to come. Nerado. He's why they wanted to hold us back, and why I was in such a hurry to get away. That boat of his is bad medicine, girl, and we want to put plenty of kilometers behind us before he gets started."

"But do you think he will chase us?"

"*Think* so? I *know* so! The mere facts, that we are rare specimens and that he told us that we were going to stay there all the rest of our lives, would make him chase us clear to Dustheimer's Nebula. Besides that, we stepped on their toes pretty heavily before we left. We know altogether too much now to be let get back to Tellus; and finally, they'd all die of acute enlargement of the spleen if we get away with this prize ship of theirs. I hope to tell you they'll chase us!"

He fell silent, devoting his whole attention to his piloting, driving his craft onward at such velocity that its outer plating held steadily at the highest point of temperature compatible with safety. Soon they were out in open space, hurtling toward the sun under the drive of every possible iota of power, and Costigan took off his armor and turned toward the helpless body of the captain.

"He looks so . . . so . . . so *dead*, Conway! Are you really sure that you can bring him to?"

"Absolutely. Lots of time yet. Just three simple squirts in the right places will do the trick." He took from a locked compartment of his armor a small steel box, which housed a surgeon's hypodermic and three vials. One, two, three, he injected small, but precisely measured amounts of the fluids into the three vital localities, then placed the inert form upon a deeply cushioned couch.

"There! That'll take care of the gas in five or six hours. The paralysis will wear off before that, so he'll be all right when he wakes up; and we're going away from here with every watt of power we can put out. We have done everything I know how to do, for the present."

Then only did Costigan turn and look down, directly into Clio's eyes. Wide, eloquent blue eyes that gazed back up into his, tender and unafraid; eyes freighted with the oldest message of woman to chosen man. His hard young face softened wonderfully as he stared at her; there were two quick steps and they were in each other's arms. Clio's lithely rounded form nestled against Costigan's powerful body as his mighty arms tightened around her; his neck and shoulder were no less enthusiastically clasped, and less strongly only because of her woman's slighter musculature. Lips upon eager lips, blue eyes to gray, motionless they stood clasped in ecstasy; thinking nothing of the dreadful past, nothing of the fearful future, conscious only of the glorious, the wonderful present.

"Clio mine . . . darling . . . girl, girl, how I love you!" Costigan's deep voice was husky with emotion. "I haven't kissed you for seven thousand years! I don't rate you, by hundreds of steps; but if I can just get you out of this mess, I swear by all the space. . . ."

"You needn't, lover. Rate *me*? Good Heavens, Conway? It's just the other way. . . ."

"Chop it!" he commanded in her ear. "I'm still dizzy at the idea of your loving me at all, to say nothing of loving me *this* way! But you do, and that's all I ask, here or hereafter!"

"Love you? *Love* you!" Their mutual embrace tightened and her low voice thrilled brokenly as she went on: "Conway, dearest. . . . I can't say a thing, but you know. . . . Oh, Conway!"

After a time Clio drew a long and tremulous, but supremely happy breath as the realities of their predicament once more obtruded themselves upon her consciousness. She released herself gently from Costigan's arms.

"Do you really think that there is a chance of us getting back to the Earth, so that we can be together . . . always?"

"A chance, yes. A probability, no," he replied, unequivocally. "It depends upon two things. First, how much of a start we got on Nerado. His ship is the biggest and fastest thing I ever saw, and if he strips her down and drives her — which he will — he'll catch us long before we can make Tellus. On the other hand, I gave Rodebush a lot of data, and if he and Lyman Cleveland can add it to their own stuff and get that super-ship of ours rebuilt in time, they'll be out here on the prowl; and they'll have what can give even Nerado plenty of argument. No use worrying about it, anyway. We won't know anything until we can detect one or the other of them, and then will be the time to do something about it."

"If Nerado catches us, will you. . . ." She paused.

"Rub you out? I will not. Even if he does catch us, and takes us back to Nevia, I won't. There's lots more time coming onto the clock. Nerado won't hurt either of us badly enough to leave scars, either physical, mental, or moral. I'd kill you in a second if it were Roger; he's dirty and he's thoroughly bad. But Nerado's a good enough old scout, in his way. He's big and he's clean. You know, I could really like that fish, if I could meet him on terms of equality sometime?"

"*I* couldn't!" she declared, vigorously. "He's crawly and scaly and snaky; and he smells so . . . so. . . ."

"So rank and fishy?" Costigan laughed deeply. "Details, girl; mere details. I've seen people who looked like money in the bank and who smelled like a bouquet of violets that you couldn't trust half the length of Nerado's neck."

"But look what he did to us!" she protested. "And they weren't trying to recapture us back there; they were trying to kill us."

"That was perfectly all right, what he did and what they did — what else could they have done?" he wanted to know. "And while you're looking, look at what we did to them — plenty, I'd say. But we all had it to do, and neither side will blame the other for doing it. He's a square shooter, I tell you."

"Well, maybe, but I don't like him a bit, and let's not talk about him any more. Let's talk about us. Remember what you said once, when you advised me to 'let you lay,' or whatever it was?" Woman-like, she wished to dip again lightly into the waters of pure emotion, even though she had such a short time before led the man out of their profoundest depths.

But Costigan, into whose hard life love of woman had never before entered, had not yet recovered sufficiently from his soul-shaking plunge to follow her lead. Inarticulate, distrusting his newly found supreme happiness, he must needs stay out of those enchanted waters or plunge again. And he was afraid to plunge — diffident, still deeming himself unworthy of the miracle of this wonder-girl's love — even though every fiber of his being shrieked its demand to feel again that slender body in his clasping arms. He did not consciously think those thoughts. He acted them without thinking; they were inherent in his personality.

"I do remember, and I still think it's a sound idea, even though I am too far gone now to let you put it into effect," he assured her, half seriously. He kissed her, tenderly and reverently, then studied her carefully. "But you look as though you'd been on a Martian picnic. When did you eat last?"

"I don't remember, exactly. This morning, I think."

"Or maybe last night, or yesterday morning? I thought so! Bradley and I can eat anything that's chewable, and drink anything that will pour, but you can't. I'll scout around and see if I can't fix up something that you'll be able to eat."

He rummaged through the store-rooms, emerging with sundry viands from which he prepared a highly satisfactory meal.

"Think you can sleep now, sweetheart?" After supper, once more within the circle of Costigan's arms, Clio nodded her head against his shoulder.

"Of course I can, dear. Now that you are with me, out here alone, I'm not a bit afraid any more. You will get us back to the Earth some way, sometime; I just know that you will. Good-night, Conway."

"Good-night, Clio . . . little sweetheart," he whispered, and went back to Bradley's side.

In due time the captain recovered consciousness, and slept. Then for days the speedster flashed on toward our distant solar system; days during which her wide-flung detector screens remained cold.

"I don't know whether I'm afraid they'll hit something or afraid that they won't," Costigan remarked more than once, but finally those tenuous sentinels did in fact encounter an interfering vibration. Along the detector line a visibeam sped, and Costigan's face hardened as he saw the unmistakable outline of Nerado's interstellar cruiser, far behind them.

"Well, a stern chase always was a long one," Costigan said finally. "He can't catch us for plenty of days yet . . . now what?" for the alarms of the detectors had broken out anew. There was still another point of interference to be investigated. Costigan traced it; and there, almost dead ahead of them, between them and their sun, nearing them at the incomprehensible rate of the sum of the two vessels' velocities, came another cruiser of the Nevians!

"Must be the sister-ship, coming back from our System with a load of iron," Costigan deduced. "Heavily loaded as she is, we may be able to dodge her; and she's coming so fast that if we can stay out of her range we'll be all right — she won't be able to stop for probably three or four days. But if our super-ship is anywhere in these parts, now's the time for her to rally 'round!"

He gave the speedster all the side-thrust she would take; then, putting every available communicator tube behind a tight beam, he drove it sunward and began sending out a long-continued call to his fellows of Triplanetary's Secret Service.

Nearer and nearer the Nevian flashed, trying with all her power to intercept the speedster; and it soon became evident that, heavily laden though she was, she could make enough sideway to bring her within range at the time of meeting.

"Of course, they've got partial neutralization of inertia, the same as we have," Costigan cogitated, "and by the way he's coming I'd say that he had orders to blow us out of the ether — he knows as well as we do that he can't capture us alive at anything like the relative velocities we've got now. I can't give her any more side thrust without overloading the gravity controls, so overloaded they've got to be. Strap down, you two, because they may go out entirely."

"Do you think that you can pull away from them, Conway?" Clio was staring in horrified fascination into the plate, watching the pictured vessel increase in size, moment by moment.

"I don't know, girl, but I'm going to try. Just in case we don't, though, I'm going to keep on yelling for help. In solid? All right, boat, *do your stuff!*"

CHAPTER XIII

The Meeting of the Giants

"Check your blast, Fred, I think I hear something trying to come through!" Cleveland called out, sharply. For days the *Boise* had torn through the illimitable reaches of empty space, and now the long vigil of the keen-eared listeners was to be ended. Rodebush cut off his power, and through the deafening roar of tube-noise an almost inaudible voice made itself heard.

" . . . all the help you can give us. Samms — Cleveland — Rodebush — anybody of Triplanetary who can hear me, listen! This is Costigan, with Miss Marsden and Captain Bradley, heading for where we think the sun is, from right ascension about six hours, declination about plus fourteen degrees. Distance unknown, but probably hundreds of light-years. Trace my call. One Nevian ship is overhauling us slowly, another is coming toward us from the sun. We may or may not be able to dodge it, but we need all the help you can give us. Samms — Rodebush — Cleveland — anybody of Triplanetary. . . ."

Endlessly the faint, faint voice went on, but Rodebush and Cleveland were no longer listening. Sensitive ultra-loops had been swung, and along the indicated line shot Triplanetary's super-ship at a velocity which she had never before even approached; the utterly incomprehensible, almost incalculable velocity attained by inertialess matter, driven through an almost perfect vacuum by the *Boise*'s maximum projector blast — a blast which would lift her stupendous normal tonnage against a gravity five times that of

Earth's! At the full frightful measure of that velocity the super-ship literally annihilated distance, while ahead of her the furiously driven, but scarcely faster spy-ray beam tore on in quest of the three Terrestrials who were calling for help.

"Got any idea how fast we're going?" Rodebush demanded, glancing up for an instant from the observation plate. "We should be able to see him, since we could hear him, and our range is certainly as great as anything he can have."

"No, can't figure velocity without any reliable data on how many atoms of matter exist per cubic meter out here." Cleveland was staring at the calculator. "It's constant, of course, at the value at which the friction of the medium is equal to our thrust. Incidentally, we can't hold it long. We're running a temperature, which shows that we're stepping along faster than anybody ever computed before. Taking Throckmorton's estimates it figures somewhere near the order of magnitude of ten to the twenty-seventh. Fast enough, anyway, so you'd better bend an eye on that plate. Even after you see him you won't know anything about where he really is, because we don't know any of the velocities involved — our own, his, or that of the beam — and we may be right on top of him."

"Or, if we are outrunning the beam, we won't see him at all. That makes it nice piloting."

"How are you going to handle things when we get there?"

"Lock to them and take them aboard if we're in time. If not, if they are fighting already — *there they are*!"

The picture of the speedster's control room flashed upon the plate and Costigan's voice greeted them from the speaker.

"Hello, fellows, welcome to our city! Where are you?"

"We don't know," Cleveland snapped back, "and we don't know where you are, either. Can't figure anything without data. I see you're still breathing air. Where are the Nevians? How much time we got yet?"

"Not enough, I'm afraid. By the looks of things they will be within range of us in a couple of hours, and you're so far away yet that it took our voices four minutes and about fifty seconds to make the round trip, *on the ultra*! Play that on your calculator, Lyman! You haven't even touched our detector screen yet. I'm mighty glad to have seen you fellows again, though, anyway."

"A couple of hours!" In his relief Cleveland almost shouted the words. "That's time to burn. We can be clear out of the Galaxy in less than. . . ." He broke off at a yell from Rodebush.

"Broadcast, Conway, broadcast!" that worthy had cried, as Costigan's image had disappeared utterly from his plate.

Now he cut off the *Boise*'s power, stopping her instantaneously in mid-space, but the connection had been broken. Costigan could not possibly have heard the orders to change his beam signal to a broadcast, so that they could pick it up; nor would it have done any good if he had heard and had obeyed. So immeasurably great had been their velocity that they had flashed past the speedster without seeing it, even upon the ultra-plates, and now they were unknown billions of miles beyond the fugitives they had come so far to help — far beyond the range of any possible broadcast. But Cleveland had understood instantly what had happened. He now had a little data upon which to work, and his fingers were flying over the keys of the calculator.

"Back blast, maximum, seventeen seconds!" he directed, crisply. "Not exact, of course, but that'll put us close enough to find 'em with our detectors!"

Then for the calculated seventeen seconds the super-ship retraced her path, at the same awful speed with which she had come so far. The blast expired and there, plainly limned upon the observation plates, was the Nevian speedster.

"As a computer you're good," Rodebush applauded. "So close that we can't use the neutralizers to catch him. If we use a dyne of driving force we'll overshoot him a million kilometers before I can snap the switches out."

"And yet he's so far away and going so fast that if we keep our inertia on it'll take all day at full drive to overtake him." Cleveland was frankly puzzled. "What to do? Shunt in a potentiometer?"

"No, we don't need it." Rodebush turned to the transmitter. "Costigan! We are going to take hold of you with a very light tractor. Don't cut it!"

"A tractor — inertialess?" Cleveland wondered.

"Why not?" Rodebush launched the tractor, set at its absolute minimum of power, and threw in his master switches.

While hundreds of thousands of miles separating the two vessels and the tractor beam was exerting the least effort of which it was capable, yet the super-ship leaped toward the smaller craft at a pace which covered that distance in the twinkling of an eye. So rapidly were the objectives enlarging upon the plates that the automatic focusing devices could scarcely function rapidly enough to keep them in place. Cleveland flinched involuntarily and seized his arm-rests in a spasmodic clutch as he watched this, the first inertialess space-approach; and even Rodebush, who knew better than anyone else what to expect, held his breath and swallowed hard at the unbelievable rate at which the two vessels were rushing together.

And if these two, who had rebuilt the space-flyer, could hardly control themselves, what of the three in the speedster, who knew nothing whatever of the super-ship's potentialities? Clio, staring into the plate with Costigan, uttered a piercing shriek, as she sank her fingers into his shoulders. Bradley swore a mighty deep-space oath and braced himself against certain annihilation. Costigan stared for an instant, unable to believe his eyes, then his hand darted to the contacts which would cut the beam. Too late. Before his flying fingers could reach the studs the *Boise* was upon them; had struck them in direct central impact. Moving at the full measure of her unthinkable velocity though the super-ship was at the moment of impact, yet the most delicate recording instruments of the speedster could not detect the slightest shock as the enormous globe struck the comparatively tiny torpedo and clung to it; accommodating instantly and effortlessly her own terrific pace to that of the smaller and infinitely slower craft. Clio sobbed in relief and Costigan, one arm around her, sighed hugely.

"Hey, you space-fleas!" he cried. "Glad to see you and all that, but you might as well kill a man outright as scare him to death! So that's the super-ship, huh? SOME ship!"

"Hello, Conway!" "Clear ether, Conway!" The two scientists answered the hail of their fellow.

"I didn't realize that an inertialess approach would be quite such a terrifying spectacle, or I would have warned you," Rodebush went on. "Yes, thanks to you, the super-ship works as she should, at last. But you had better put on your suits and transfer. You might get your things ready. . . ."

"'Things' is good!" Costigan laughed, and Clio giggled sunnily.

"We've made so many transfers already that what you see us in is all we have," Bradley explained. "We'll bring ourselves, and we'll hurry; that Nevian is coming up fast."

"Is there anything on this ship you fellows want?" Costigan asked.

"There may be, but we haven't any locks big enough to let her inside and we haven't time to study her now. You might leave her controls in neutral, so that Lyman can calculate her position if we should want her later on."

"All right." The three armor-clad figures stepped into the *Boise*'s open lock, the tractor beam was cut off, and the speedster flashed away from the now stationary super-ship.

"Better let formalities go for a while," Captain Bradley interrupted the general introduction taking place. "I was scared out of nine years' growth when I saw you coming at us, and maybe I've still got the humps; but that Nevian is coming up fast, and if you don't already know it I can tell you that he's no light cruiser."

"That's so, too," Costigan concurred. "Have you fellows

got enough stuff so that you think you can take him? You've got the legs on him, anyway — you can certainly run if you want to!"

"Run?" Cleveland laughed. "We have a bone of our own to pick with that ship. We licked her to a standstill once, until we burned out a set of generators, and since we got them fixed we've been chasing her all over space. We were chasing her when we picked up your call. See there? She's doing the running."

The Nevian was running, in truth. Her commander had seen and had recognized the great vessel which had flashed out of nowhere to the rescue of the three Terrestrials; and, having once been at grips with that vengeful superdreadnaught, he had little stomach for another encounter. Therefore his side-thrust was now being exerted in the opposite direction; he was frankly trying to put as much distance as possible between himself and Triplanetary's formidable cruiser. In vain. A light tractor was clamped on and the *Boise* flashed up to close range before Rodebush threw on her inertia and Cleveland brought the two vessels relatively to rest by increasing gradually his tractor's pull. And this time the Nevian could not cut the tractor. Again that shearing plane of force bit into it and tore at it, but it neither yielded nor broke. The rebuilt generators of Number Four were designed to carry the load, and they carried it. And again Triplanetary's every mighty weapon was brought into play.

The "cans" were thrown, ultra-and infra-beams were driven, the furious macro-beam gnawed hungrily at the Nevian's defenses; and one by one those defenses went down. In desperation the enemy commander threw his every generator behind a polycyclic screen; only to see Cleveland's even more powerful drill bore relentlessly through it. Punctured that last defense, the end came soon. A secondary SX7 beam was now in place on mighty Ten's inner rings, and one fierce blast blew a hole completely through the Nevian cruiser. Into that hole entered Adlington's terrific bombs and their gruesome fellows, and where they entered, life departed. All defenses vanished, and under the blasts of the *Boise*'s projectors, now unopposed, the metal of the Nevian vessel exploded instantly into a widely spreading cloud of vapor. Sparkling vapor, with perhaps here and there a droplet or two of material which had only been liquefied.

So passed the sister-ship, and Rodebush turned his plates upon the vessel of Nerado. But that highly intelligent amphibian had seen all that had occurred. He had long since given over the pursuit of the speedster, and he did not rush in to do hopeless battle beside his fellow Nevians against the Terrestrials. His analytical detectors had written down each detail of every weapon and of every screen employed; and even while prodigious streamers of red force were raving out from his vessel, braking her terrific progress and swinging her around in an immense circle back toward far Nevia, his scientists and mechanics were doubling and redoubling the power of his already Titanic installations, to match and if possible to overmatch those of Triplanetary's superdreadnaught.

"Do we kill him now or do we let him suffer a while longer?" Costigan demanded.

"I don't think so, yet," replied Rodebush. "Would you, Lyman?"

"Not yet," replied Cleveland, grimly, reading the thought of the other and agreeing with it. "Let him pilot us to Nevia; we might not be able to find it without a guide. While we're at it we want to so pulverize that crowd that if they never come near the Solarian system again they'll think it's twenty minutes too soon!"

Thus it was that the *Boise*, under only a few dynes of propulsion, pursued the Nevian ship. Apparently exerting every effort, she never came quite within range of the fleeing raider; yet never was she so far behind that the Nevian spaceship was not in clear register upon her observation plates. Nor was Nerado alone in strengthening his vessel. Costigan knew well and respected highly the Nevian scientist-captain, and at his suggestion the entire time of the long and un-eventful flight was spent in re-enforcing the super-ship's armament to the iron-driven limit of theoretical and mechanical possibility.

Thus, when Nevia and her hot, blue sun appeared upon his plates Rodebush was ready for any emergency, and hurled his battleship upon the Nevian with every weapon aflame. But so was Nerado ready; and, unlike her sister-ship, his vessel was manned by scientists well versed in the fundamental theory of the weapons with which they fought. Beams, rods, and lances of energy flamed and flared; planes and pencils cut, slashed, and stabbed; defensive screens glowed redly or flashed suddenly into intensely brilliant, coruscating incandescence. Crimson opacity struggled sullenly against violet curtain of annihilation. Material projectiles and torpedoes were launched under full beam control; only to be exploded harmlessly in mid-space, to be rayed into nothingness, or to disappear innocuously against impenetrable polycyclic screens. Both vessels were equipped completely with iron-driven mechanisms; both were manned by scientists capable of wringing the last possible watt of power from their sources. They were approximately equal in size, and each ship now wielded the theoretical ultimate of power for her mass; therefore neither could harm the other, furiously though each was trying. And more and more nearly they were approaching the red atmosphere of the world of the amphibians. Down into that crimson blanket the two warring space-ships dropped, down toward a city which Costigan recognized as that in which Nerado made his headquarters.

"Better hold off a bit," Costigan cautioned. "If I know that bird at all, he's cooking up something," and even as he spoke there shot upward from the city a multitude of flashing balls. The Nevians had mastered the secret of the explosive of the fishes of the greater deeps and were launching it in a veritable storm against the Terrestrial visitor.

"Those?" asked Rodebush, calmly. The detonating balls

of destruction were literally annihilating even the atmosphere beyond the polycyclic screen, but that barrier was scarcely affected.

"No, that," pointing out a hemispherical dome which, redly translucent, surrounded a group of buildings towering high above their neighbors. "Neither those high towers nor those screens were there the last time I was in this town. They're stalling for time down there, that's all those fireballs are for. Good sign, too — maybe they aren't ready for us yet. If not, you'd better take 'em while the taking's good; and if they *are* ready for us, we'd better get out of here while we're all in one piece."

And in fact Nerado had been in touch with the scientists of his city; had been instructing them in the construction of converters and generators of such weight and power that they could crush even the defenses of the super-ship. They were not, however, quite done; the entirely unsuspected possibilities of speed inherent in absolute inertialessness had not entered into Nerado's calculations.

"Better drop a few cans down on that dome, fellows, before they make trouble for us," suggested Rodebush to his gunners.

"We can't," came Adlington's instant reply. "We've been trying it, but that's a polycyclic screen. Can you drill it? If you can, I've got a real bomb here — that special we built — that will do the trick if you can protect it from their beams until it gets down into the water."

"I'll try it," Cleveland answered, at a nod from the physicist. "I couldn't drill Nerado's polycyclics, but I couldn't use any momentum on him. Couldn't ram him — he fell back with my thrust. But that screen down there can't back off, so maybe I can work on it. Get your special ready, and hang on, everybody!"

The *Boise* looped upward, and from an altitude of miles dove downward through a storm of force-balls, rays, and shells; a dive checked abruptly as the hollow tube of energy, which was Cleveland's drill, snarled savagely down ahead of her and struck the shielding hemisphere with a grinding, lightning-splitting shock. As it struck, backed by all the enormous momentum of the plunging space-ship and driven by the full power of her mightiest generators, it bored in, clawing and gouging viciously through the tissue of that rigid and unyielding barrier of pure energy. Then, mighty drill and plunging mass against iron-driven wall, eye-tearing and furiously spectacular warfare was waged. Well it was for Triplanetary, that day, that its super ship carried ample supply of allotropic iron; well it was that her originally Gargantuan converters and generators had been doubled and quadrupled in power on the long Nevian way! For that oven-girdled fortress was powered to withstand any conceivable assault; but the *Boise*'s power and momentum were now inconceivable, and every watt and every dyne was solidly behind that hellishly flaming, that voraciously tearing, that irresistibly ravening cylinder of energy incredible!

Through the Nevian shield that cylinder gnawed its frightful way, and down its protecting length there drove Adlington's "Special" bomb. "Special" it was indeed; so great of girth that it could barely pass through the central orifice of Ten's mighty projector, so heavily charged with sensitized atomic iron that its detonation upon any planet would not have been considered for an instant if that planet's integrity meant anything to its attackers. Down the shielding pipe of force the "Special" screamed under full propulsion, and beneath the surface of Nevia's ocean it plunged.

"Cut!" yelled Adlington, and as the scintillating drill expired, the bomber snapped his detonating switch.

For a moment the effect of the explosion seemed unimportant. A dull, low rumble was all that was to be heard of a concussion that jarred red Nevia to her very center; and all that could be seen was a slow heaving of the water. But that heaving did not cease. Slowly, *so* slowly it seemed to the observers now high in the heavens, the waters rose up and parted; revealing a vast chasm blown deep into the ocean's rocky bed. Higher and higher the lazy, mountains of water reared; effortlessly to pick up, to smash, to grind into fragments, and finally to toss aside every building, every structure, every scrap of material substance pertaining to the whole Nevian city.

Flattened out, driven backward for miles the tortured waters were urged, leaving exposed bare ground and broken rock where once had been the ocean's busy floor; while tremendous blasts of incandescent gas raved upward, buffeting even the enormous masses of the two space-ships, poised by their breathless crews so high above the site of the explosion. Then the displaced millions of tons of water rushed back into that newly rived pit, seeming to seek in that mad rush to make even more complete the already total destruction of the city. The raging torrents poured into that yawning cavern, filled it, and piled mountainously above it; receding and piling up, again and again, causing tidal waves which swept a full half of Nevia's mighty, watery globe.

The city forever silenced, Rodebush again directed his weapons upon Nerado's vessel, but the Nevian was no longer fighting. For the first time in that long and bitter engagement, not a Nevian beam was in operation. His screens, however, were as capable as ever, and after a few fruitless attempts to make an impression upon them, Rodebush cut off his own offensive and turned to Costigan.

"What do you make of it, Conway? You know these people better than we do; what are they up to?"

"I wish to talk to you," Nerado's voice came from the speaker, "and I could not do so while the beams were operating. You are, I now perceive, a much higher form of life than any of us had thought possible; a form perhaps as high in evolution as our own. It is a pity that we did not meet you when we first neared your planet, so that much life, both Tellurian and Nevian, might have been spared. But what is past cannot be recalled. As reasoning beings, however, you will see the futility of continuing a contest in which neither of us is capable of injuring the other. You may, of course, destroy more of our Nevian cities, in which case I should be compelled to go and destroy similarly upon your earth; but, to reasoning minds, such a course of procedure is sheerest folly."

Rodebush cut the communicator beam.

"Does he mean it?" he demanded of Costigan. "It sounds reasonable, but. . . ."

"But fishy," broke in Cleveland. "Altogether too reasonable for a. . . ."

"Yes, he means it; every word of it," interrupted Costigan in turn. "That's the way they are. Reasonable, passionless. Funny — they lack a lot of things we have, but they've got a lot of things that I wish more of us Tellurians had too. Give me the plate — I'll talk for Triplanetary," and the beam was restored.

"Captain Nerado." he greeted the Nevian commander. "Having been with you and among your people, I know that you mean what you say and that you speak for your race. Similarly, I believe that I can speak for the Triplanetary Council — the government of three of the planets of our solar system — in saying that there need be no more conflict between our peoples. I also was compelled by circumstances to do certain things which I now wish could be undone; but as you have said, the past is past. Our two races have much to gain from each other by friendly exchanges of materials and of ideas, while we can expect nothing except mutual extermination, if we elect to continue this warfare. I offer you the friendship of Triplanetary. Will you release your screens and come aboard to sign a treaty?"

"I will come; my screens are down." Rodebush likewise cut off his power, although somewhat apprehensively, and a Nevian lifeboat entered the main airlock of the *Boise*.

Then, at a table in the control room of Triplanetary's first super-ship, there was written the first Inter-Systemic Treaty. Upon one side the three Nevians; amphibious, cone-headed, loop-necked, scale-bodies, four-legged things to us monstrosities: upon the other the three humans, air-breathing, rounded-headed, shortnecked, smooth-bodied, two-legged creatures equally monstrous to the fastidious Nevians. Yet each of these representatives, of two races so different, felt respect for the other race increase within him minute by minute as the conversation went on.

The Nevians had destroyed Pittsburgh, but Adlington's bomb had blown an equally populous Nevian city out of existence. One Nevian vessel had wiped out an entire unit of Triplanetary's fleet; but Costigan, practically unaided, had depopulated one Nevian city and had seriously damaged another. He had also beamed down many Nevian ships. Therefore loss of life and material could be balanced. The Solarian system was rich in iron, to which the Nevians were welcome; red Nevia possessed abundant stores of substances which upon Earth were extremely rare and of vital importance. Therefore commerce was to be encouraged. The Nevians had knowledges and skills unknown to Earthly science, but were entirely ignorant of many things, to us commonplace. Therefore interchange of students and of books was highly desirable. And so on.

Thus was signed the Triplanetario-Nevian Treaty of Eternal Peace. Nerado and his two companions were escorted ceremoniously to their vessel, and the *Boise* took off in an inertialess dash toward Earth, bearing the good news that the Nevian menace was no more.

Clio, now a hardened space-flea, immune even to the horrible nausea of inertialessness, wriggled lithely in the curve of Costigan's arm and laughed up at him.

"You can talk all you want to, Conway, but I don't like them a bit. They give me the purple jitters! I suppose that they are really estimable folks; talented, cultured, and everything; but just the same I'll bet that it will be a long, long time before anybody on Earth will really, truly *like* them!"

THE END

MASTERS
OF SPACE

EDWARD E. SMITH
& E. EVERETT EVANS

I

"BUT didn't you feel *anything*, Javo?" Strain was apparent in every line of Tula's taut, bare body. "Nothing at all?"

"Nothing whatever." The one called Javo relaxed from his rigid concentration. "Nothing has changed. Nor will it."

"That conclusion is indefensible!" Tula snapped. "With the promised return of the Masters there must and will be changes. Didn't *any* of you feel anything?"

Her hot, demanding eyes swept the group; a group whose like, except for physical perfection, could be found in any nudist colony.

No one except Tula had felt a thing.

"That fact is not too surprising," Javo said finally. "You have the most sensitive receptors of us all. But are you sure?"

"I am sure. It was the thought-form of a living Master."

"Do you think that the Master perceived your web?"

"It is certain. Those who built us are stronger than we."

"That is true. As they promised, then, so long and long ago, our Masters are returning home to us."

Jarvis Hilton of Terra, the youngest man yet to be assigned to direct any such tremendous deep-space undertaking as Project Theta Orionis, sat in conference with his two seconds-in-command. Assistant Director Sandra Cummings, analyst-synthesist and semantician, was tall, blond and svelte. Planetographer William Karns — a black-haired, black-browed, black-eyed man of thirty — was third in rank of the scientific group.

"I'm telling you, Jarve, you can't have it both ways,"

Karns declared. "Captain Sawtelle is old-school Navy brass. He goes strictly by the book. So you've got to draw a razor-sharp line; exactly where the Advisory Board's directive puts it. And next time he sticks his ugly puss across that line, kick his face in. You've been Caspar Milquetoast Two ever since we left Base."

"That's the way it looks to you?" Hilton's right hand became a fist. "The man has age, experience and ability. I've been trying to meet him on a ground of courtesy and decency."

"Exactly. And he doesn't recognize the existence of either. And, since the Board rammed you down his throat instead of giving him old Jeffers, you needn't expect him to."

"You may be right, Bill. What do you think, Dr. Cummings?"

The girl said: "Bill's right. Also, your constant appeasement isn't doing the morale of the whole scientific group a bit of good."

"Well, I haven't enjoyed it, either. So next time I'll pin his ears back. Anything else?"

"Yes, Dr. Hilton, I have a squawk of my own. I know I was rammed down your throat, but just when are you going to let me do some work?"

"None of us has much of anything to do yet, and won't have until we light somewhere. You're off base a country mile."

"I'm not off base. You *did* want Eggleston, not me."

"Sure I did. I've worked with him and know what he can do. But I'm not holding a grudge about it."

"No? Why, then, are you on first-name terms with everyone in the scientific group except me? Supposedly your first assistant?"

"That's easy!" Hilton snapped. "Because you've been carrying chips on both shoulders ever since you came aboard . . . or at least I thought you were." Hilton grinned suddenly and held out his hand. "Sorry, Sandy — I'll start all over again."

"I'm sorry too, Chief." They shook hands warmly. "I *was* pretty stiff, I guess, but I'll be good."

"You'll go to work right now, too. As semantician. Dig out that directive and tear it down. Draw that line Bill talked about."

"Can do, boss." She swung to her feet and walked out of the room, her every movement one of lithe and easy grace.

Karns followed her with his eyes. "Funny. A trained-dancer Ph.D. And a Miss America type, like all the other women aboard this spacer. I wonder if she'll make out."

"So do I. I still wish they'd given me Eggy. I've never seen an executive-type female Ph.D. yet that was worth the cyanide it would take to poison her."

"That's what Sawtelle thinks of you, too, you know."

"I know; and the Board *does* know its stuff. So I'm really hoping, Bill, that she surprises me as much as I intend to surprise the Navy."

ALARM bells clanged as the mighty *Perseus* blinked out of overdrive. Every crewman sprang to his post.

"Mister Snowden, why did we emerge without orders from me?" Captain Sawtelle bellowed, storming into the control room three jumps behind Hilton.

"The automatics took control, sir," he said, quietly.

"Automatics! I *give* the orders!"

"In this case, Captain Sawtelle, you don't," Hilton said. Eyes locked and held. To Sawtelle, this was a new and strange co-commander. "I would suggest that we discuss this matter in private."

"Very well, sir," Sawtelle said; and in the captain's cabin Hilton opened up.

"For your information, Captain Sawtelle, I set my interspace coupling detectors for any objective I choose. When any one of them reacts, it trips the kickers and we emerge. During any emergency outside the Solar System I am in command — with the provision that I must relinquish command to you in case of armed attack on us."

"Where do you think you found any such stuff as that in the directive? It isn't there and I know my rights."

"It is, and you don't. Here is a semantic chart of the whole directive. As you will note, it overrides many Navy regulations. Disobedience of my orders constitutes mutiny and I can — and will — have you put in irons and sent back to Terra for court-martial. Now let's go back."

In the control room, Hilton said, "The target has a mass of approximately five hundred metric tons. There is also a significant amount of radiation characteristic of uranexite. You will please execute search, Captain Sawtelle."

And Captain Sawtelle ordered the search.

"What did you do to the big jerk, boss?" Sandra whispered.

"What you and Bill suggested," Hilton whispered back. "Thanks to your analysis of the directive — pure gobbledygook if there ever was any — I could. Mighty good job, Sandy."

TEN or fifteen more minutes passed. Then:

"Here's the source of radiation, sir," a searchman reported. "It's a point source, though, not an object at this range."

"And here's the artifact, sir," Pilot Snowden said. "We're coming up on it fast. But . . . but what's a *skyscraper* skeleton doing out here in interstellar space?"

As they closed up, everyone could see that the thing did indeed look like the metallic skeleton of a great building. It was a huge cube, measuring well over a hundred yards along each edge. And it was empty.

"*That's* one for the book," Sawtelle said.

"And how!" Hilton agreed. "I'll take a boat . . . no, suits would be better. Karns, Yarborough, get Techs Leeds and Miller and suit up."

"You'll need a boat escort," Sawtelle said. "Mr. Ashley, execute escort Landing Craft One, Two, and Three."

The three landing craft approached that enigmatic latticework of structural steel and stopped. Five grotesquely armored figures wafted themselves forward on pencils of force. Their leader, whose suit bore the number "14," reached a mammoth girder and worked his way along it up to a peculiar-looking bulge. The whole immense structure vanished, leaving men and boats in empty space.

Sawtelle gasped. "Snowden! Are you holding 'em?"

"No, sir. Faster than light; hyperspace, sir."

"Mr. Ashby, did you have your interspace rigs set?"

"No, sir. I didn't think of it, sir."

"Doctor Cummings, why weren't yours out?"

"I didn't think of such a thing, either — any more than you did," Sandra said.

Ashby, the Communications Officer, had been working the radio. "No reply from anyone, sir," he reported.

"Oh, no!" Sandra exclaimed. Then, "But look! They're firing pistols — especially the one wearing number fourteen — but *pistols*?"

"Recoil pistols — sixty-threes — for emergency use in case of power failure," Ashby explained. "That's it . . . but I can't see why *all* their power went out at once. But Fourteen — that's Hilton — is really doing a job with that sixty-three. He'll be here in a couple of minutes."

And he was. "Every power unit out there — suits and boats both — drained," Hilton reported. "*Completely* drained. Get some help out there fast!"

In an enormous structure deep below the surface of a far-distant world a group of technicians clustered together in front of one section of a two-miles long control board. They were staring at a light that had just appeared where no light should have been.

"Someone's brain-pan will be burned out for this," one of the group radiated harshly. "That unit was inactivated long ago and it has not been reactivated."

"Someone committed an error, Your Loftiness?"

"Silence, fool! Stretts do not commit errors!"

*   *   *

AS soon as it was clear that no one had been injured, Sawtelle demanded, "How about it, Hilton?"

"Structurally, it was high-alloy steel. There were many bulges, possibly containing mechanisms. There were drive-units of a non-Terran type. There were many projectors, which — at a rough guess — were a hundred times as powerful as any I have ever seen before. There were no indications that the thing had ever been enclosed, in whole or in part. It certainly never had living quarters for warm-blooded, oxygen-breathing eaters of organic food."

Sawtelle snorted. "You mean it never had a crew?"

"Not necessarily. . . ."

"Bah! What other kind of intelligent life is there?"

"I don't know. But before we speculate too much, let's look at the tri-di. The camera may have caught something I missed."

It hadn't. The three-dimensional pictures added nothing.

"It probably was operated either by programmed automatics or by remote control," Hilton decided, finally. "But how did they drain all our power? And just as bad, what and how is that other point source of power we're heading for now?"

"What's wrong with it?" Sawtelle asked.

"Its strength. No matter what distance or reactant I assume, nothing we know will fit. Neither fission nor fusion will do it. It has to be practically total conversion!"

II

THE *Perseus* snapped out of overdrive near the point of interest and Hilton stared, motionless and silent.

Space was full of madly warring ships. Half of them were bare, giant skeletons of steel, like the "derelict" that had so unexpectedly blasted away from them. The others were more or less like the *Perseus*, except in being bigger, faster and of vastly greater power.

Beams of starkly incredible power bit at and clung to equally capable defensive screens of pure force. As these inconceivable forces met, the glare of their neutralization filled all nearby space. And ships and skeletons alike were disappearing in chunks, blobs, gouts, streamers and sparkles of rended, fused and vaporized metal.

Hilton watched two ships combine against one skeleton. Dozens of beams, incredibly tight and hard, were held inexorably upon dozens of the bulges of the skeleton. Overloaded, the bulges' screens flared through the spectrum and failed. And bare metal, however refractory, endures only for instants under the appalling intensity of such beams as those.

The skeletons tried to duplicate the ships' method of attack, but failed. They were too slow. Not slow, exactly, either, but hesitant; as though it required whole seconds for the commander — or operator? Or remote controller? — of each skeleton to make it act. The ships were winning.

"Hey!" Hilton yelped. "Oh — that's the one we saw back there. But what in all space does it think it's doing?"

It was plunging at tremendous speed straight through the immense fleet of embattled skeletons. It did not fire a beam nor energize a screen; it merely plunged along as though on a plotted course until it collided with one of the skeletons of the fleet and both structures plunged, a tangled mass of wreckage, to the ground of the planet below.

Then hundreds of the ships shot forward, each to plunge into and explode inside one of the skeletons. When visibility was restored another wave of ships came forward to repeat the performance, but there was nothing left to fight. Every surviving skeleton had blinked out of normal space.

The remaining ships made no effort to pursue the skeletons, nor did they re-form as a fleet. Each ship went off by itself.

And on that distant planet of the Stretts the group of mechs watched with amazed disbelief as light after light after light winked out on their two-miles-long control board. Frantically they relayed orders to the skeletons; orders which did not affect the losses.

"Brain-pans will blacken for this . . ." a mental snarl began, to be interrupted by a coldly imperious thought.

"That long-dead unit, so inexplicably reactivated, is approaching the fuel world. It is ignoring the battle. It is heading through our fleet toward the Oman half . . . *handle* it, ten-eighteen!"

"It does not respond, Your Loftiness."

"Then blast it, fool! Ah, it is inactivated. As encyclopedist, Nine, explain the freakish behavior of that unit."

"Yes, Your Loftiness. Many cycles ago we sent a ship against the Omans with a new device of destruction. The Omans must have intercepted it, drained it of power and allowed it to drift on. After all these cycles of time it must have come upon a small source of power and of course continued its mission."

"That can be the truth. The Lords of the Universe must be informed."

"The mining units, the carriers and the refiners have not been affected, Your Loftiness," a mech radiated.

"So I see, fool." Then, activating another instrument, His Loftiness thought at it, in an entirely different vein, "Lord Ynos, Madam? I have to make a very grave report. . . ."

IN the *Perseus*, four scientists and three Navy officers were arguing heatedly; employing deep-space verbiage not to be found in any dictionary. "Jarve!" Karns called out, and Hilton joined the group. "Does anything about this planet make any sense to you?"

"No. But you're the planetographer. 'Smatter with it?"

"It's a good three hundred degrees Kelvin too hot."

"Well, you know it's loaded with uranexite."

"That much? The whole crust practically jewelry ore?"

"If that's what the figures say, I'll buy it."

"Buy *this*, then. Continuous daylight everywhere. Noon June Sol-quality light *except* that it's all in the visible. Frank says it's from bombardment of a layer of something, and Frank admits that the whole thing's impossible."

"When Frank makes up his mind what 'something' is, I'll take it as a datum."

"Third thing: there's only one city on this continent, and it's protected by a screen that nobody ever heard of."

Hilton pondered, then turned to the captain. "Will you please run a search-pattern, sir? Fine-toothing only the hot spots?"

The planet was approximately the same size as Terra; its atmosphere, except for its intense radiation, was similar to Terra's. There were two continents; one immense girdling ocean. The temperature of the land surface was everywhere about 100°F, that of the water about 90°F. Each continent had one city, and both were small. One was inhabited by what looked like human beings; the other by usuform robots. The human city was the only cool spot on the entire planet; under its protective dome the temperature was 71°F.

Hilton decided to study the robots first; and asked the captain to take the ship down to observation range. Sawtelle objected; and continued to object until Hilton started to order his arrest. Then he said, "I'll do it, under protest, but I want it on record that I am doing it against my best judgment."

"It's on record," Hilton said, coldly. "Everything said and done is being, and will continue to be, recorded."

The *Perseus* floated downward. "*There's* what I want most to see," Hilton said, finally. "That big strip-mining operation . . . that's it . . . hold it!" Then, via throat-mike, "Attention, all scientists! You all know what to do. Start doing it."

Sandra's blonde head was very close to Hilton's brown one as they both stared into Hilton's plate. "Why, they look like giant armadillos!" she exclaimed.

"More like tanks," he disagreed, "except that they've got

legs, wheels *and* treads — and arms, cutters, diggers, probes and conveyors — and *look* at the way those buckets dip solid rock!"

The fantastic machine was moving very slowly along a bench or shelf that it was making for itself as it went along. Below it, to its left, dropped other benches being made by other mining machines. The machines were not using explosives. Hard though the ore was, the tools were so much harder and were driven with such tremendous power that the stuff might just have well have been slightly-clayed sand.

Every bit of loosened ore, down to the finest dust, was forced into a conveyor and thence into the armored body of the machine. There it went into a mechanism whose basic principles Hilton could not understand. From this monstrosity emerged two streams of product.

One of these, comprising ninety-nine point nine plus percent of the input, went out through another conveyor into the vast hold of a vehicle which, when full and replaced by a duplicate of itself, went careening madly cross-country to a dump.

The other product, a slow, very small stream of tiny, glistening black pellets, fell into a one-gallon container being held watchfully by a small machine, more or less like a three-wheeled motor scooter, which was moving carefully along beside the giant miner. When this can was almost full another scooter rolled up and, without losing a single pellet, took over place and function. The first scooter then covered its bucket, clamped it solidly into a recess designed for the purpose and dashed away toward the city.

Hilton stared slack-jawed at Sandra. She stared back.

"Do you make anything of that, Jarve?"

"Nothing. They're taking *pure* uranexite and *concentrating* — or converting — it a thousand to one. I *hope* we'll be able to do something about it."

"I hope so, too, Chief; and I'm *sure* we will."

"Well, that's enough for now. You may take us up now, Captain Sawtelle. And Sandy, will you please call all department heads and their assistants into the conference room?"

AT the head of the long conference table, Hilton studied his fourteen department heads, all husky young men, and their assistants, all surprisingly attractive and well-built young women. Bud Carroll and Sylvia Bannister of Sociology sat together. He was almost as big as Karns; she was a green-eyed redhead whose five-ten and one-fifty would have looked big except for the arrangement thereof. There were Bernadine and Hermione van der Moen, the leggy, breasty, platinum-blond twins — both of whom were Cowper - medalists in physics. There was Etienne de Vaux, the mathematical wizard; and Rebecca Eisenstein, the black-haired, flashing-eyed ex-infant-prodigy theoretical astronomer. There was Beverly Bell, who made mathematically impossible chemical syntheses — who swam channels for days on end and computed planetary orbits in her sleekly-coiffured head.

"First, we'll have a get-together," Hilton said. "Nothing recorded; just to get acquainted. You all know that our fourteen departments cover science, from astronomy to zoology."

He paused, again his eyes swept the group. Stella Wing, who would have been a grand-opera star except for her drive to know everything about language. Theodora (Teddy) Blake, who would prove gleefully that she was the world's best model — but was in fact the most brilliantly promising theoretician who had ever lived.

"No other force like this has ever been assembled," Hilton went on. "In more ways than one. Sawtelle wanted Jeffers to head this group, instead of me. Everybody thought he *would* head it."

"And Hilton wanted Eggleston and got *me*," Sandra said.

"That's right. And quite a few of you didn't want to come at all, but were told by the Board to come or else."

The group stirred. Eyes met eyes, and there were smiles.

"I myself think Jeffers *should* have had the job. I've never handled anything half this big and I'll need a lot of help. But I'm stuck with it and you're all stuck with me, so we'll all take it and like it. You've noticed, of course, the accent on youth. The Navy crew is normal, except for the commanders being unusually young. But we aren't. None of us is thirty yet, and none of us has ever been married. You fellows look like a team of professional athletes, and you girls — well, if I didn't know better I'd say the Board had screened you for the front row of the chorus instead of for a top-bracket brain-gang. How they found so many of you I'll never know."

"Virile men and nubile women!" Etienne de Vaux leered enthusiastically. "*Vive le Board!*"

"Nubile! Bravo, Tiny! Quelle delicatesse de nuance!"

"Three rousing cheers for the Board!"

"Keep still, you nitwits! Let me ask a question!" This came from one of the twins. "Before you give us the deduction, Jarvis — or will it be an intuition or an induction or a . . ."

"Or an inducement," the other twin suggested, helpfully. "Not that *you* would need very much of that."

"You keep still, too, Miney. I'm asking, Sir Moderator, if I can give my deduction first?"

"Sure, Bernadine; go ahead."

"They figured we're going to get completely lost. Then we'll jettison the Navy, hunt up a planet of our own and start a race to end all human races. Or would you call this a *see*-duction instead of a *dee*-duction?"

This produced a storm of whistles, cheers and jeers that it took several seconds to quell.

"But seriously, Jarvis," Bernadine went on. "We've all been wondering and it doesn't make sense. Have you any idea at all of what the Board actually did have in mind?"

"I believe that the Board selected for mental, not physical, qualities; for the ability to handle anything unexpected or unusual that comes up, no matter what it is."

"You think it wasn't double-barreled?" asked Kincaid, the psychologist. He smiled quizzically. "That all this virility and nubility and glamor is pure coincidence?"

"No," Hilton said, with an almost imperceptible flick of an eyelid. "Coincidence is as meaningless as paradox. I think they found out that — barring freaks — the best minds are in the best bodies."

"Could be. The idea has been propounded before."

"Now let's get to work." Hilton flipped the switch of the recorder. "Starting with you, Sandy, each of you give a two-minute boil-down. What you found and what you think."

SOMETHING over an hour later the meeting adjourned and Hilton and Sandra strolled toward the control room.

"I don't know whether you convinced Alexander Q. Kincaid or not, but you didn't quite convince me," Sandra said.

"Nor him, either."

"Oh?" Sandra's eyebrows

"No. He grabbed the out I offered him. I didn't fool Teddy Blake or Temple Bells, either. You four are all, though, I think."

"Temple? You think *she's* so smart?"

"I don't *think* so, no. Don't fool yourself, chick. Temple Bells looks and acts sweet and innocent and virginal. Maybe — probably — she is. But she isn't showing a fraction of the stuff she's really got. She's heavy artillery, Sandy. And I mean *heavy*."

"I think you're slightly nuts there. But do you really believe that the Board was playing Cupid?"

"Not trying, but doing. Cold-bloodedly and efficiently. Yes."

"But it wouldn't *work*! We aren't going to get lost!"

"We won't need to. Propinquity will do the work."

"Phooie. You and me, for instance?" She stopped, put both hands on her hips, and glared. "Why, I wouldn't marry *you* if you . . ."

"I'll tell the cockeyed world you won't!" Hilton broke in. "Me marry a damned female Ph.D.? Uh-uh. Mine will be a cuddly little brunette that thinks a slipstick is some kind of lipstick and that an isotope's something good to eat."

"One like that copy of Murchison's Dark Lady that you keep under the glass on your desk?" she sneered.

"Exactly. . . ." He started to continue the battle, then shut himself off. "But listen, Sandy, why should we get into a fight because we don't want to marry each other? You're doing a swell job. I admire you tremendously for it and I like to work with you."

"You've got a point there, Jarve, at that, and I'm one of the few who know what kind of a job *you're* doing, so I'll relax." She flashed him a gamin grin and they went on into the control room.

It was too late in the day then to do any more exploring; but the next morning, early, the *Perseus* lined out for the city of the humanoids.

*   *   *

TULA turned toward her fellows. Her eyes filled with a happily triumphant light and her thought a lilting song. "I have been telling you from the first touch that it was the Masters. It *is* the Masters! The Masters are returning to us Omans and their own home world!"

*   *   *

"CAPTAIN Sawtelle," Hilton said, "Please land in the cradle below."

"*Land!*" Sawtelle stormed. "On a planet like *that*? Not by . . ." He broke off and stared; for now, on that cradle, there flamed out in screaming red the *Perseus'* own Navy-coded landing symbols!

"Your protest is recorded," Hilton said. "Now, sir, land."

Fuming, Sawtelle landed. Sandra looked pointedly at Hilton. "First contact is my dish, you know."

"Not that I like it, but it is." He turned to a burly youth

with sun-bleached, crew-cut hair, "Still safe, Frank?"

"Still abnormally low. Surprising no end, since all the rest of the planet is hotter than the middle tail-race of hell."

"Okay, Sandy. Who will you want besides the top linguists?"

"Psych — both Alex and Temple. And Teddy Blake. They're over there. Tell them, will you, while I buzz Teddy?"

"Will do," and Hilton stepped over to the two psychologists and told them. Then, "I hope I'm not leading with my chin, Temple, but is that your real first name or a professional?"

"It's real; it really is. My parents were romantics: dad says they considered both 'Golden' and 'Silver'!"

Not at all obviously, he studied her: the almost translucent, unblemished perfection of her lightly-tanned, old-ivory skin; the clear, calm, deep blueness of her eyes; the long, thick mane of hair exactly the color of a field of dead-ripe wheat.

"You know, I like it," he said then. "It fits you."

"I'm glad you said that, Doctor. . . ."

"Not that, Temple. I'm not going to 'Doctor' you."

"I'll call you 'boss', then, like Stella does. Anyway, that lets me tell you that I like it myself. I really think that it did something for me."

"*Something* did something for you, that's for sure. I'm mighty glad you're aboard, and I hope . . . here they come. Hi, Hark! Hi, Stella!"

"Hi, Jarve," said Chief Linguist Harkins, and:

"Hi, boss — what's holding us up?" asked his assistant, Stella Wing. She was about five feet four. Her eyes were a tawny brown; her hair a flamboyant auburn mop. Perhaps it owed a little of its spectacular refulgence to chemistry, Hilton thought, but not too much. "Let us away! Let the lions roar and let the welkin ring!"

"Who's been feeding *you* so much red meat, little squirt?" Hilton laughed and turned away, meeting Sandra in the corridor. "Okay, chick, take 'em away. We'll cover you. Luck, girl."

And in the control room, to Sawtelle, "Needle-beam cover, please; set for minimum aperture and lethal blast. But no firing, Captain Sawtelle, until I give the order."

THE *Perseus* was surrounded by hundreds of natives. They were all adult, all naked and about equally divided as to sex. They were friendly; most enthusiastically so.

"Jarve!" Sandra squealed. "They're *telepathic*. Very strongly so! I never imagined — I never felt anything like it!"

"Any rough stuff?" Hilton demanded.

"Oh, no. Just the opposite. They love us . . . in a way that's simply indescribable. I don't like this telepathy business . . . not clear . . . foggy, diffuse . . . this woman is *sure* I'm her long-lost great-great-a-hundred-times grandmother or something — *You!* Slow down. Take it *easy*! They want us all to come out here and live with . . . no, not *with* them, but each of us alone in a whole house with them to wait on us! But first, they all want to come aboard. . . ."

"*What?*" Hilton said. "Are you *sure* they're friendly?"

"Positive, chief."

"How about you, Alex?"

"We're all sure, Jarve. No question about it."

"Bring two of them aboard. A man and a woman."

"You won't bring *any*!" Sawtelle thundered. "Hilton, I had enough of your stupid, starry-eyed, ivory-domed blundering long ago, but this utterly idiotic brainstorm of letting enemy aliens aboard us ends all civilian command. Call your people back aboard or I will bring them in by force!"

"Very well, sir. Sandy, tell the natives that a slight delay has become necessary and bring your party aboard."

The Navy officers smiled — or grinned — gloatingly; while the scientists stared at their director with expressions ranging from surprise to disappointment and disgust. Hilton's face remained set, expressionless, until Sandra and her party had arrived.

"Captain Sawtelle," he said then, "I thought that you and

I had settled in private the question or who is in command of Project Theta Orionis at destination. We will now settle it in public. Your opinion of me is now on record, witnessed by your officers and by my staff. My opinion of you, which is now being similarly recorded and witnessed, is that you are a hidebound, mentally ossified Navy mule; mentally and psychologically unfit to have any voice in any such mission as this. You will now agree on this recording and before these witnesses, to obey my orders unquestioningly or I will now unload all Bureau of Science personnel and equipment onto this planet and send you and the *Perseus* back to Terra with the doubly-sealed record of this episode posted to the Advisory Board. Take your choice."

Eyes locked, and under Hilton's uncompromising stare Sawtelle weakened. He fidgeted; tried three times — unsuccessfully — to blare defiance. Then, "Very well sir," he said, and saluted.

"THANK you, sir," Hilton said, then turned to his staff. "Okay, Sandy, go ahead."

Outside the control room door, "Thank God you don't play poker, Jarve!" Karns gasped. "We'd all owe you all the pay we'll ever get!"

"You think it was the bluff, yes?" de Vaux asked. "Me, I think no. Name of a name of a name! I was wondering with unease what life would be like on this so-alien planet!"

"You didn't need to wonder, Tiny," Hilton assured him. "It was in the bag. He's incapable of abandonment."

Beverly Bell, the van der Moen twins and Temple Bells all stared at Hilton in awe; and Sandra felt much the same way.

"But suppose he *had* called you?" Sandra demanded.

"Speculating on the impossible is unprofitable," he said.

"Oh, you're the most *exasperating* thing!" Sandra stamped a foot. "Don't you — *ever* — answer a question intelligibly?"

"When the question is meaningless, chick, I can't."

At the lock Temple Bells, who had been hanging back, cocked an eyebrow at Hilton and he made his way to her side.

"What was it you started to say back there, boss?"

"Oh, yes. That we should see each other oftener."

"That's what I was hoping you were going to say." She put her hand under his elbow and pressed his arm lightly, fleetingly, against her side. "That would be indubitably the fondest thing I could be of."

He laughed and gave her arm a friendly squeeze. Then he studied her again, the most baffling member of his staff. About five feet six. Lithe, hard, trained down fine — as a tennis champion, she would be. Stacked — *how* she was stacked! Not as beautiful as Sandra or Teddy . . . but with an ungodly lot of something that neither of them had . . . nor any other woman he had ever known.

"Yes, I am a little difficult to classify," she said quietly, almost reading his mind.

"That's the understatement of the year! But I'm making some progress."

"Such as?" This was an open challenge.

"Except possibly Teddy, the best brain aboard."

"That isn't true, but go ahead."

"You're a powerhouse. A tightly organized, thoroughly integrated, smoothly functioning, beautifully camouflaged Juggernaut. A reasonable facsimile of an irresistible force."

"My God, Jarvis!" That had gone deep.

"Let me finish my analysis. You aren't head of your department because you don't want to be. You fooled the top psychs of the Board. You've been running ninety per cent submerged because you can work better that way and there's no glory-hound blood in you."

She stared at him, licking her lips. "I knew your mind was a razor, but I didn't know it was a diamond drill, too. That seals your doom, boss, unless . . . no, you can't *possibly* know why I'm here."

"Why, of course I do."

"You just think you do. You see, I've been in love with you ever since, as a gangling, bony, knobby-kneed kid, I listened to your first doctorate disputation. Ever since then, my purpose in life has been to land you."

III

"BUT listen!" he exclaimed. "I *can't*, even if I want. . . ."

"Of course you can't." Pure deviltry danced in her eyes. "You're the Director. It wouldn't be proper. But it's Standard Operating Procedure for simple, innocent, unsophisticated little country girls like me to go completely overboard for the boss."

"But you can't — you *mustn't*!" he protested in panic.

Temple Bells was getting plenty of revenge for the shocks he had given her. "I can't? Watch me!" She grinned up at him, her eyes still dancing. "Every chance I get, I'm going to hug your arm like I did a minute ago. And you'll take hold of my forearm, like you did! That can be taken, you see, as either: One, a reluctant acceptance of a mildly distasteful but not quite actionable situation, or: Two, a blocking move to keep me from climbing up you like a squirrel!"

"Confound it, Temple, you *can't* be serious!"

"Can't I?" She laughed gleefully. "Especially with half a dozen of those other cats watching? Just wait and see, boss!"

Sandra and her two guests came aboard. The natives looked around; the man at the various human men, the woman at each of the human women. The woman remained beside Sandra; the man took his place at Hilton's left, looking up — he was a couple of inches shorter than Hilton's six feet one — with an air of . . . of *expectancy*!

"Why this arrangement, Sandy?" Hilton asked.

"Because we're tops. It's your move, Jarve. What's first?"

"Uranexite. Come along, Sport. I'll call you that until . . ."

"Laro," the native said, in a deep resonant bass voice. He hit himself a blow on the head that would have floored any two ordinary men. "Sora," he announced, striking the alien woman a similar blow.

"Laro and Sora, I would like to have you look at our uranexite, with the idea of refueling our ship. Come with me, please?"

Both nodded and followed him. In the engine room he pointed at the engines, then to the lead-blocked labyrinth leading to the fuel holds. "Laro, do you understand 'hot'? Radioactive?"

Laro nodded — and started to open the heavy lead door!

"Hey!" Hilton yelped. "That's hot!" He seized Laro's arm to pull him away — and got the shock of his life. Laro weighed at least five hundred pounds! And the guy *still* looked human!

Laro nodded again and gave himself a terrific thump on the chest. Then he glanced at Sora, who stepped away from Sandra. He then went into the hold and came out with two fuel pellets in his hand, one of which he tossed to Sora. That is, the motion looked like a toss, but the pellet traveled like a bullet. Sora caught it unconcernedly and both natives flipped the pellets into their mouths. There was a half minute of rock-crusher crunching; then both natives opened their mouths.

The pellets had been pulverized and swallowed.

Hilton's voice rang out. "Poynter! How *can* these people be non-radioactive after eating a whole fuel pellet apiece?"

Poynter tested both natives again. "Cold," he reported. "Stone cold. No background even. Play *that* on your harmonica!"

Laro nodded, perfectly matter-of-factly, and in Hilton's mind there formed a picture. It was not clear, but it showed plainly enough a long line of aliens approaching the *Perseus*.

Each carried on his or her shoulder a lead container holding two hundred pounds of Navy Regulation fuel pellets. A standard loading-tube was sealed into place and every fuel-hold was filled.

This picture, Laro indicated plainly, could become reality any time.

Sawtelle was notified and came on the run. "No fuel is coming aboard without being tested!" he roared.

"Of course not. But it'll pass, for all the tea in China. You haven't had a ten per cent load of fuel since you were launched. You can fill up or not — the fuel's here — just as you say."

"If they can make Navy standard, of course we want it."

The fuel arrived. Every load tested well above standard. Every fuel hold was filled to capacity, with no leakage and no emanation. The natives who had handled the stuff did not go away, but gathered in the engine-room; and more and more humans trickled in to see what was going on.

Sawtelle stiffened. "What's going on over there, Hilton?"

"I don't know; but let's let 'em go for a minute. I want to learn about these people and they've got me stopped cold."

"You aren't the only one. But if they wreck that Mayfield it'll cost you over twenty thousand dollars."

"Okay." The captain and director watched, wide eyed.

Two master mechanics had been getting ready to re-fit a tube — a job requiring both strength and skill. The tube was very heavy and made of superefract. The machine — the Mayfield — upon which the work was to be done, was extremely complex.

Two of the aliens had brushed the mechanics — very gently — aside and were doing their work for them. Ignoring the hoist, one native had picked the tube up and was holding it exactly in place on the Mayfield. The other, hands moving faster than the eye could follow, was locking it — micrometrically precise and immovably secure — into place.

"How about this?" one of the mechanics asked of his immediate superior. "If we throw 'em out, how do we do it?"

By a jerk of the head, the non-com passed the buck to a commissioned officer, who relayed it up the line to Sawtelle, who said, "Hilton, *no*body can run a Mayfield without months of training. They'll wreck it and it'll cost you . . . but I'm getting curious myself. Enough so to take half the damage. Let 'em go ahead."

"How *about* this, Mike?" one of the machinists asked of his fellow. "I'm going to *like* this, what?"

"Ya-as, my deah Chumley," the other drawled, affectedly. "My man relieves me of *so* much uncouth effort."

The natives had kept on working. The Mayfield was running. It had always howled and screamed at its work, but now it gave out only a smooth and even hum. The aliens had adjusted it with unhuman precision; they were one with it as no human being could possibly be. And every mind present knew that those aliens were, at long, long last, fulfilling their destiny and were, in that fulfillment, supremely happy. After tens of thousands of cycles of time they were doing a job for their adored, their revered and beloved Masters.

That was a stunning shock; but it was eclipsed by another.

"I am sorry, Master Hilton," Laro's tremendous bass voice boomed out, "that it has taken us so long to learn your Masters' language as it now is. Since you left us you have changed it radically; while we, of course, have not changed it at all."

"I'm sorry, but you're mistaken," Hilton said. "We are merely visitors. We have never been here before; nor, as far as we know, were any of our ancestors ever here."

"You need not test us, Master. We have kept your trust. Everything has been kept, changelessly the same, awaiting your return as you ordered so long ago."

"Can you read my mind?" Hilton demanded.

"Of course; but Omans can not read in Masters' minds anything except what Masters want Omans to read."

"Omans?" Harkins asked. "Where did you Omans and your masters come from? Originally?"

"As you know, Master, the Masters came originally from Arth. They populated Ardu, where we Omans were developed. When the Stretts drove us from Ardu, we all came to Ardry, which was your home world until you left it in our care. We keep also this, your half of the Fuel World, in trust for you."

"Listen, Jarve!" Harkins said, tensely. "Oman-human. Arth-Earth. Ardu-Earth Two. Ardry-Earth Three. You can't laugh them off . . . but there never *was* an Atlantis!"

"This is getting no better fast. We need a full staff meeting. You, too, Sawtelle, and your best man. We need all the brains the *Perseus* can muster."

"You're right. But first, get those naked women out of here. It's bad enough, having women aboard at all, but this . . . my men are *spacemen*, mister."

Laro spoke up. "If it is the Masters' pleasure to keep on testing us, so be it. We have forgotten nothing. A dwelling awaits each Master, in which each will be served by Omans who will know the Master's desires without being told. Every desire. While we Omans have no biological urges, we are of course highly skilled in relieving tensions and derive as much pleasure from that service as from any other."

Sawtelle broke the silence that followed. "Well, for the men —" He hesitated. "Especially on the ground . . . well, talking in mixed company, you know, but I think . . ."

"Think nothing of the mixed company, Captain Sawtelle," Sandra said. "We women are scientists, not shrinking violets. We are accustomed to discussing the facts of life just as frankly as any other facts."

Sawtelle jerked a thumb at Hilton, who followed him out into the corridor. "I *have* been a Navy mule," he said. "I admit now that I'm out-maneuvered, out-manned, and out-gunned."

"I'm just as baffled — at present — as you are, sir. But my training has been aimed specifically at the unexpected, while yours has not."

"That's letting me down easy, Jarve." Sawtelle smiled — the first time the startled Hilton had known that the hard, tough old spacehound *could* smile. "What I wanted to say is, lead on. I'll follow you through force-field and space-warps."

"Thanks, skipper. And by the way, I erased that record yesterday." The two gripped hands; and there came into being a relationship that was to become a lifelong friendship.

"WE will start for Ardry immediately," Hilton said. "How do we make that jump without charts, Laro?"

"Very easily, Master. Kedo, as Master Captain Sawtelle's Oman, will give the orders. Nito will serve Master Snowden and supply the knowledge he says he has forgotten."

"Okay. We'll go up to the control room and get started."

And in the control room, Kedo's voice rasped into the captain's microphone. "Attention, all personnel! Master Captain Sawtelle orders take-off in two minutes. The countdown will begin at five seconds. . . . Five! Four! Three! Two! One! Lift!"

Nito, not Snowden, handled the controls. As perfectly as the human pilot had ever done it, at the top of his finest form, he picked the immense spaceship up and slipped it silkily into subspace.

"Well, I'll be a . . ." Snowden gasped. "That's a better job than I *ever* did!"

"Not at all, Master, as you know," Nito said. "It was you who did this. I merely performed the labor."

A few minutes later, in the main lounge, Navy and BuSci personnel were mingling as they had never done before. Whatever had caused this relaxation of tension — the friendship of captain and director? The position in which they all were? Or what? — they all began to get acquainted with each other.

"Silence, please, and be seated," Hilton said. "While this is not exactly a formal meeting, it will be recorded for future reference. First, I will ask Laro a question. Were books or records left on Ardry by the race you call the Masters?"

"You know there are, Master. They are exactly as you left them. Undisturbed for over two hundred seventy-one thousand years."

"Therefore we will not question the Omans. We do not know what questions to ask. We have seen many things hitherto thought impossible. Hence, we must discard all preconceived opinions which conflict with facts. I will mention a few of the problems we face."

"The Omans. The Masters. The upgrading of the armament of the *Perseus* to Oman standards. The concentration of uranexite. What is that concentrate? How is it used? Total conversion — how is it accomplished? The skeletons — what are they and how are they controlled? Their ability to drain power. Who or what is back of them? Why a deadlock that has lasted over a quarter of a million years? How much danger are we and the *Perseus* actually in? How much danger is Terra in, because of our presence here? There are many other questions."

"Sandra and I will not take part. Nor will three others; de Vaux, Eisenstein, and Blake. You have more important work to do."

"What can that be?" asked Rebecca. "Of what possible use can a mathematician, a theoretician and a theoretical astronomer be in such a situation as this?"

"You can think powerfully in abstract terms, unhampered by Terran facts and laws which we now know are neither facts nor laws. I cannot even categorize the problems we face. Perhaps you three will be able to. You will listen, then consult, then tell me how to pick the teams to do the work. A more important job for you is this: Any problem, to be solved, must be stated clearly; and we don't know even what our basic problem is. I want something by the use of which I can break this thing open. Get it for me."

REBECCA and de Vaux merely smiled and nodded, but Teddy Blake said happily, "I was beginning to feel like a fifth wheel on this project, but *that's* something I can really stick my teeth into."

"Huh? How?" Karns demanded. "He didn't give you one single thing to go on; just compounded the confusion."

Hilton spoke before Teddy could. "That's their dish, Bill. If I had any data I'd work it myself. You first, Captain Sawtelle."

That conference was a very long one indeed. There were almost as many conclusions and recommendations as there were speakers. And through it all Hilton and Sandra listened. They weighed and tested and analyzed and made copious notes; in shorthand and in the more esoteric characters of symbolic logic. And at its end:

"I'm just about pooped, Sandy. How about you?"

"You and me both, boss. See you in the morning."

But she didn't. It was four o'clock in the afternoon when they met again.

"We made up one of the teams, Sandy," he said, with surprising diffidence. "I know we were going to do it together, but I got a hunch on the first team. A kind of a weirdie, but the brains checked me on it." He placed a card on her desk. "Don't blow your top until after I you've studied it."

"Why, I won't, of course. . . ." Her voice died away. "Maybe you'd better cancel that 'of course'. . . ." She studied, and when she spoke again she was exerting self-control. "A chemist, a planetographer, a theoretician, *two* sociologists, a psychologist and a radiationist. And six of the seven are three pairs of sweeties. What kind of a line-up is *that* to solve a problem in *physics*?"

"It isn't in any physics we know. I said *think*!"

"Oh," she said, then again "Oh," and "Oh," and "Oh." Four entirely different tones. "I see . . . maybe. You're matching minds, not specialties; and supplementing?"

"I knew you were smart. Buy it?"

"It's weird, all right, but I'll buy it — for a trial run, anyway. But I'd hate like sin to have to sell any part of it to the Board. . . . But of course we're — I mean you're responsible only to yourself."

"Keep it 'we', Sandy. You're as important to this project as I am. But before we tackle the second team, what's your thought on Bernadine and Hermione? Separate or together?"

"Separate, I'd say. They're identical physically, and so nearly so mentally that of them would be just as good on a team as both of them. More and better work on different teams."

"My thought exactly." And so it went, hour after hour. The teams were selected and meetings were held.

THE *Perseus* reached Ardry, which was very much like Terra. There were continents, oceans, ice-caps, lakes, rivers, mountains and plains, forests and prairies. The ship landed on the spacefield of Omlu, the City of the Masters, and Sawtelle called Hilton into his cabin. The Omans Laro and Kedo went along, of course.

"Nobody knows how it leaked . . ." Sawtelle began.

"No secrets around here," Hilton grinned. "Omans, you know."

"I suppose so. Anyway, every man aboard is all hyped up about living aground — especially with a harem. But before I grant liberty, suppose there's any VD around here that our prophylactics can't handle?"

"As you know, Masters," Laro replied for Hilton before the latter could open his mouth, "no disease, venereal or other, is allowed to exist on Ardry. No prophylaxis is either necessary or desirable."

"That ought to hold you for a while, Skipper." Hilton smiled at the flabbergasted captain and went back to the lounge.

"Everybody going ashore?" he asked.

"Yes." Karns said. "Unanimous vote for the first time."

"Who wouldn't?" Sandra asked. "I'm fed up with living

like a sardine. I will scream for joy the minute I get into a real room."

"Cars" were waiting, in a stopping-and-starting line. Three-wheel jobs. All were empty. No drivers, no steering-wheels, no instruments or push-buttons. When the whole line moved ahead as one vehicle there was no noise, no gas, no blast.

An Oman helped a Master carefully into the rear seat of his car, leaped into the front seat and the car sped quietly away. The whole line of empty cars, acting in perfect synchronization, shot forward one space and stopped.

"This is your car, Master," Laro said, and made a production out of getting Hilton into the vehicle undamaged.

Hilton's plan had been beautifully simple. All the teams were to meet at the Hall of Records. The linguists and their Omans would study the records and pass them out. Specialty after specialty would be unveiled and teams would work on them. He and Sandy would sit in the office and analyze and synthesize and correlate. It was a very nice plan.

It was a very nice office, too. It contained every item of equipment that either Sandra or Hilton had ever worked with — it was a big office — and a great many that neither of them had ever heard of. It had a full staff of Omans, all eager to work.

Hilton and Sandra sat in that magnificent office for three hours, and no reports came in. Nothing happened at all.

"This gives me the howling howpers!" Hilton growled. "Why haven't I got brains enough to be on one of those teams?"

"I could shed a tear for you, you big dope, but I won't," Sandra retorted. "What do you want to be, besides the brain and the kingpin and the balance-wheel and the spark-plug of the outfit? Do you want to do *everything* yourself?"

"Well, I *don't* want to go completely nuts, and that's all I'm doing at the moment!" The argument might have become acrimonious, but it was interrupted by a call from Karns.

"Can you come out here, Jarve? We've struck a knot."

"'Smatter? Trouble with the Omans?" Hilton snapped.

"Not exactly. Just non-cooperation — squared. We can't even get started. I'd like to have you two come out here and see if you can do anything. I'm not trying rough stuff, because I know it wouldn't work."

"Coming up, Bill," and Hilton and Sandra, followed by Laro and Sora, dashed out to their cars.

THE Hall of Records was a long, wide, low, windowless, very massive structure, built of a metal that looked like stainless steel. Kept highly polished, the vast expanse of seamless and jointless metal was mirror-bright. The one great door was open, and just inside it were the scientists and their Omans.

"Brief me, Bill," Hilton said.

"No lights. They won't turn 'em on and we can't. Can't find either lights or any possible kind of switches."

"Turn on the lights, Laro," Hilton said.

"You know that I cannot do that, Master. It is forbidden for any Oman to have anything to do with the illumination of this solemn and revered place."

"Then show me how to do it."

"That would be just as bad, Master," the Oman said proudly. "I will not fail any test you can devise!"

"Okay. All you Omans go back to the ship and bring over fifteen or twenty lights — the tripod jobs. Scat!"

They "scatted" and Hilton went on, "No use asking questions if you don't know what questions to ask. Let's see if we can cook up something. Lane — Kathy — what has Biology got to say?"

Dr. Lane Saunders and Dr. Kathryn Cook — the latter a willowy brown-eyed blonde — conferred briefly. Then Saunders spoke, running both hands through his unruly shock of fiery red hair. "So far, the best we can do is a more-or-less educated guess. They're atomic-powered, total-conversion androids. Their pseudo-flesh is composed mainly of silicon and fluorine. We don't know the formula yet, but it is as much more stable than our teflon as teflon is than cornmeal mush. As to the brains, no data. Bones are super-stainless steel. Teeth, harder than diamond, but won't break. Food, uranexite or its concentrated derivative, interchangeably. Storage reserve, indefinite. Laro and Sora won't *have* to eat again for at least twenty-five years. . . ."

The group gasped as one, but Saunders went on: "They can eat and drink and breathe and so on, but only because the original Masters wanted them to. Non-functional. Skins and subcutaneous layers are soft, for the same reason. That's about it, up to now."

"Thanks, Lane. Hark, is it reasonable to believe that any culture whatever could run for a quarter of a million years without changing one word of its language or one iota of its behavior?"

"Reasonable or not, it seems to have happened."

"Now for Psychology. Alex?"

"It seems starkly incredible, but it seems to be true. If it is, their minds were subjected to a conditioning no Terran has ever imagined — an unyielding fixation."

"They can't be swayed, then, by reason or logic?" Hilton paused invitingly.

"Or anything else," Kincaid said, flatly. "If we're right they can't be swayed, period."

"I was afraid of that. Well, that's all the questions I know how to ask. Any contributions to this symposium?"

AFTER a short silence de Vaux said, "I suppose you realize that the first half of the problem you posed us has now solved itself?"

"Why, no. No, you're 'way ahead of me."

"There is a basic problem and it can now be clearly stated," Rebecca said. "Problem: To determine a method of securing full cooperation from the Omans. The first step in the solution of this problem is to find the most appropriate operator. Teddy?"

"I have an operator — of sorts," Theodora said. "I've been hoping one of us could find a better."

"What is it?" Hilton demanded.

"The word 'until'."

"Teddy, you're a *sweetheart*!" Hilton exclaimed.

"How can 'until' be a mathematical operator?" Sandra asked.

"Easily." Hilton was already deep in thought. "This hard conditioning was to last only *until* the Masters returned. Then they'd break it. So all we have to do is figure out how a Master would do it."

"That's *all*," Kincaid said, meaningly.

Hilton pondered. Then, "Listen, all of you. I may have to try a colossal job of bluffing. . . ."

"Just what would you call 'colossal' after what you did to the Navy?" Karns asked.

"That was a sure thing. This isn't. You see, to find out whether Laro is really an immovable object, I've got to make like an irresistible force, which I ain't. I don't know what I'm going to do; I'll have to roll it as I go along. So all of you keep on your toes and back any play I make. Here they come."

The Omans came in and Hilton faced Laro, eyes to eyes. "Laro," he said, "you refused to obey my direct order. Your reasoning seems to be that, whether the Masters wish it or not, you Omans will block any changes whatever in the *status quo* throughout all time to come. In other words, you deny the fact that Masters are in fact your Masters."

"But that is not exactly it, Master. The Masters . . ."

"That is it. *Exactly* it. Either you are the Master here or you are not. That is a point to which your two-value logic can be strictly applied. You are wilfully neglecting the word 'until'. This stasis was to exist only *until* the Masters returned. Are we Masters? Have we returned? Note well: Upon that one word 'until' may depend the length of time your Oman race will continue to exist."

The Omans flinched; the humans gasped.

"But more of that later," Hilton went on, unmoved. "Your ancient Masters, being short-lived like us, changed materially with time, did they not? And you changed with them?"

"But we did not change ourselves, Master. The Masters . . ."

"You did change yourselves. The Masters changed only the prototype brain. They ordered you to change yourselves and you obeyed their orders. We order you to change and you refuse to obey our orders. We have changed greatly from our ancestors. Right?"

"That is right, Master."

"We are stronger physically, more alert and more vigorous mentally, with a keener, sharper outlook on life?"

"You are, Master."

"THAT is because our ancestors decided to do without Omans. We do our own work and enjoy it. Your Masters died of futility and boredom. What I would like to do, Laro, is take you to the creche and put your disobedient brain back into the matrix. However, the decision is not mine alone to make. How about it, fellows and girls? Would you rather have alleged servants who won't do anything you tell them to or no servants at all?"

"As semantician, I protest!" Sandra backed his play. "That is the most viciously loaded question I ever heard — it can't be answered except in the wrong way!"

"Okay, I'll make it semantically sound. I think we'd better scrap this whole Oman race and start over and *I want a vote that way!*"

"You won't get it!" and everybody began to yell.

Hilton restored order and swung on Laro, his attitude stiff, hostile and reserved. "Since it is clear that no unanimous decision is to be expected at this time I will take no action at this time. Think over, very carefully, what I have said, for as far as I am concerned, this world has no place for Omans who will not obey orders. As soon as I convince my staff of the fact, I shall act as follows: I shall give you an order and if you do not obey it blast your head to a cinder. I shall then give the same order to another Oman and blast him. This process will continue *until*: First, I find an obedient Oman. Second, I run out of blasters. Third, the planet runs out of Omans. Now take these lights into the first room of records — that one over there." He pointed, and no Oman, and only four humans, realized that he had made the Omans telegraph their destination so that he could point it out to them!

Inside the room Hilton asked caustically of Laro: "The Masters didn't lift those heavy chests down themselves, did they?"

"Oh, no, Master, we did that."

"Do it, then. Number One first . . . yes, that one . . . open it and start playing the records in order."

The records were not tapes or flats or reels, but were spools of intricately-braided wire. The players were projectors of full-color, hi-fi sound, tri-di pictures.

Hilton canceled all moves aground and issued orders that no Oman was to be allowed aboard ship, then looked and listened with his staff.

The first chest contained only introductory and elementary stuff; but it was so interesting that the humans stayed overtime to finish it. Then they went back to the ship; and in the main lounge Hilton practically collapsed onto a davenport. He took out a cigarette and stared in surprise at his hand, which was shaking.

"I *think* I could use a drink," he remarked.

"What, before supper?" Karns marveled. Then, "Hey, Wally! Rush a flagon of avignognac — Arnaud Freres — for the boss and everything else for the rest of us. Chop-chop but quick!"

A hectic half-hour followed. Then, "Okay, boys and girls, I love you, too, but let's cut out the slurp and sloosh, get some supper and log us some sack time. I'm just about pooped. Sorry I had to kill the private-residence deal, Sandy, you poor little sardine. But you know how it is."

Sandra grimaced. "Uh-huh. I can take it a while longer if you can."

AFTER breakfast next morning, the staff met in the lounge. As usual, Hilton and Sandra were the first to arrive.

"Hi, boss," she greeted him. "How do you feel?"

"Fine. I could whip a wildcat and give her the first two scratches. I *was* a bit beat up last night, though."

"I'll say . . . but what I simply can't get over is the way you underplayed the climax. 'Third, the planet runs out of Omans'. Just like that — no emphasis at all. Wow! It had the impact of a delayed-action atomic bomb. It put goose-bumps all over me. But just s'pose they'd missed it?"

"No fear. They're smart. I had to play it as though the whole Oman race is no more important than a cigarette butt. The great big question, though, is whether I put it across or not."

At that point a dozen people came in, all talking about the same subject.

"Hi, Jarve," Karns said. "I *still* say you ought to take up poker as a life work. Tiny, let's you and him sit down now and play a few hands."

"*Mais non!*" de Vaux shook his head violently, shrugged his shoulders and threw both arms wide. "By the sacred name of a small blue cabbage, not me!"

Karns laughed. "How did you have the guts to state so many things as facts? If you'd guessed wrong just once —"

"I didn't." Hilton grinned. "Think back, Bill. The only thing I said as a fact was that we as a race are better than the Masters were, and that is obvious. Everything else was implication, logic, and bluff."

"That's right, at that. And they *were* neurotic and decadent. No question about that."

"But listen, boss." This was Stella Wing. "About this mind-reading business. If Laro could read your mind, he'd know you were bluffing and . . . Oh, that 'Omans can read only what Masters wish Omans to read', eh? But d'you think that applies to us?"

"I'm sure it does, and I was thinking some pretty savage thoughts. And I want to caution all of you: whenever you're near any Oman, start thinking that you're beginning to agree with me that they're useless to us, and let them know it. Now get out on the job, all of you. Scat!"

"Just a minute," Poynter said. "We're going to have to keep on using the Omans and their cars, aren't we?"

"Of course. Just be superior and distant. They're on probation — we haven't decided yet what to do about them. Since that happens to be true, it'll be easy."

HILTON and Sandra went to their tiny office. There wasn't room to pace the floor, but Hilton tried to pace it anyway.

"Now don't say again that you want to *do* something," Sandra said, brightly. "Look what happened when you said that yesterday."

"I've got a job, but I don't know enough to do it. The creche — there's probably only one on the planet. So I want you to help me think. The Masters were very sensitive to radiation. Right?"

"Right. That city on Fuel Bin was kept deconned to zero, just in case some Master wanted to visit it."

"And the Masters had to work in the creche whenever anything really new had to be put into the prototype brain."

"I'd say so, yes."

"So they had armor. Probably as much better than our radiation suits as the rest of their stuff is. Now. Did they or did they not have thought screens?"

"Ouch! You think of the *damnedest* things, chief." She caught her lower lip between her teeth and concentrated. ". . . I don't know. There are at least fifty vectors, all pointing in different directions."

"I know it. The key one in my opinion is that the Masters gave 'em *both* telepathy and speech."

"I considered that and weighted it. Even so, the probability is only about point sixty-five. Can you take that much of a chance?"

"Yes. I can make one or two mistakes. Next, about finding that creche. Any spot of radiation on the planet would be it, but the search might take . . ."

"Hold on. They'd have it heavily shielded — there'll be no leakage at all. Laro will have to take you."

"That's right. Want to come along? Nothing much will happen here today."

"Uh-uh, not *me*." Sandra shivered in distaste. "I *never* want to see brains and livers and things swimming around in nutrient solution if I can help it."

"Okay. It's all yours. I'll be back sometime," and Hilton went out onto the dock, where the dejected Laro was waiting for him.

"Hi, Laro. Get the car and take me to the Hall of Records." The android brightened up immediately and hurried to obey.

At the Hall, Hilton's first care was to see how the work was going on. Eight of the huge rooms were now open and brightly lighted — operating the lamps had been one of the first items on the first spool of instructions — with a cold, pure-white, sourceless light.

EVERY team had found its objective and was working on it. Some of them were doing nicely, but the First Team could not even get started. Its primary record would advance a fraction of an inch and stop; while Omans and humans sought out other records and other projectors in an attempt to elucidate some concept that simply could not be translated into any words or symbols known to Terran science. At the moment there were seventeen of those peculiar — projectors? Viewers? Playbacks — in use, and all of them were stopped.

"You know what we've got to *do* Jarve?" Karns, the team captain, exploded. "Go back to being college freshmen — or maybe grade school or kindergarten, we don't know yet —

and learn a whole new system of mathematics before we can even begin to *touch* this stuff!"

"And you're bellyaching about that?" Hilton marveled. "I wish I could join you. That'd be fun." Then, as Karns started a snappy rejoinder —

"But I got troubles of my own," he added hastily. "'Bye, now," and beat a rejoinder —

Out in the hall again, Hilton took his chance. After all, the odds were about two to one that he would win.

"I want a couple of things, Laro. First, a thought screen." He won!

"Very well, Master. They are in a distant room, Department Four Six Nine. Will you wait here on this cushioned bench, Master?"

"No, we don't like to rest too much. I'll go with you." Then, walking along, he went on thoughtfully. "I've been thinking since last night, Laro. There are tremendous advantages in having Omans . . ."

"I am very glad you think so, Master. I want to serve you. It is my greatest need."

". . . if they could be kept from smothering us to death. Thus, if our ancestors had kept their Omans, I would have known all about life on this world and about this Hall of Records, instead of having the fragmentary, confusing, and sometimes false information I now have . . . oh, we're here?"

LARO had stopped and was opening a door. He stood aside. Hilton went in, touched with one finger a crystalline cube set conveniently into a wall, gave a mental command, and the lights went on.

Laro opened a cabinet and took out a disk about the size of a dime, pendant from a neck-chain. While Hilton had not known what to expect, he certainly had not expected anything as simple as that. Nevertheless, he kept his face straight and his thoughts unmoved as Laro hung the tiny thing around his neck and adjusted the chain to a loose fit.

"Thanks, Laro." Hilton removed it and put it into his pocket. "It won't work from there, will it?"

"No, Master. To function, it must be within eighteen inches of the brain. The second thing, Master?"

"A radiation-proof suit. Then you will please take me to the creche."

The android almost missed a step, but said nothing.

The radiation-proof suit — how glad Hilton was that he had not called it "armor"! — was as much of a surprise as the thought-screen generator had been. It was a coverall, made of something that looked like thin plastic, weighing less than one pound. It had one sealed box, about the size and weight of a cigarette case. No wires or apparatus could be seen. Air entered through two filters, one at each heel, flowed upward — for no reason at all that Hilton could see — and out through a filter above the top of his head. The suit neither flopped nor clung, but stood out, comfortably out of the way, all by itself.

Hilton, just barely, accepted the suit, too, without showing surprise.

The creche, it turned out, while not in the city of Omlu itself, was not too far out to reach easily by car.

En route, Laro said — stiffly? Tentatively? Hilton could not fit an adverb to the tone — "Master, have you then decided to destroy me? That is of course your right."

"Not this time, at least." Laro drew an entirely human breath of relief and Hilton went on: "I don't want to destroy you at all, and won't, unless I have to. But, some way or other, my silicon-fluoride friend, you are either going to learn how to cooperate or you won't last much longer."

"But, Master, that is exactly . . ."

"Oh, *hell*! Do we *have* to go over that again?" At the blaze of frustrated fury in Hilton's mind Laro flinched away. "If you can't talk sense keep still."

IN half an hour the car stopped in front of a small building which looked something like a subway kiosk — except for the door, which, built of steel-reinforced lead, swung on a piano hinge having a pin a good eight inches in diameter. Laro opened that door. They went in. As the tremendously massive portal clanged shut, lights flashed on.

Hilton glanced at his tell-tales, one inside, one outside, his suit. Both showed zero.

Down twenty steps, another door. Twenty more; another. And a fourth. Hilton's inside meter still read zero. The outside one was beginning to climb.

Into an elevator and straight down for what must have been four or five hundred feet. Another door. Hilton went through this final barrier gingerly, eyes nailed to his gauges. The outside needle was high in the red, almost against the pin, but the inside one still sat reassuringly on zero.

He stared at the android. "How can any possible brain take so much of *this* stuff without damage?"

"It does not reach the brain, Master. We convert it. Each minute of this is what you would call a 'good, square meal'."

"I see . . . dimly. You can eat energy, or drink it, or soak it up through your skins. However it comes, it's all duck soup for you."

"Yes, Master."

Hilton glanced ahead, toward the far end of the immensely long, comparatively narrow, room. It was, purely and simply, an assembly line; and fully automated in operation.

"You are replacing the Omans destroyed in the battle with the skeletons?"

"Yes, Master."

Hilton covered the first half of the line at a fast walk. He was not particularly interested in the fabrication of super-stainless-steel skeletons, nor in the installation and connection of atomic engines, converters and so on.

He was more interested in the synthetic fluoro-silicon flesh, and paused long enough to get a general idea of its growth and application. He was very much interested in how such human-looking skin could act as both absorber and converter, but he could see nothing helpful.

"An application, I suppose, of the same principle used in this radiation suit."

"Yes, Master."

AT the end of the line he stopped. A brain, in place and connected to millions of infinitely fine wire nerves, but not yet surrounded by a skull, was being educated. Scanners — multitudes of incomprehensibly complex machines — most of them were doing nothing, apparently; but such beams would have to be invisibly, microscopically fine. But a bare brain, in such a hot environment as this. . . .

He looked down at his gauges. Both read zero.

"Fields of force, Master," Laro said.

"But, damn it, this suit itself would re-radiate . . ."

"The suit is self-decontaminating, Master."

Hilton was appalled. "With such stuff as that, and the plastic shield besides, why all the depth and all that solid lead?"

"The Masters' orders, Master. Machines can, and occasionally do, fail. So might, conceivably, the plastic."

"And that structure over there contains the original brain, from which all the copies are made."

"Yes, Master. We call it the 'Guide'."

"And you can't touch the Guide. Not even if it means total destruction, none of you can touch it."

"That is the case, Master."

"Okay. Back to the car and back to the *Perseus*."

At the car Hilton took off the suit and hung the thought-screen generator around his neck; and in the car, for twenty five solid minutes, he sat still and thought.

His bluff had worked, up to a point. A good, far point, but not quite far enough. Laro had stopped that "as you already know" stuff. He was eager to go as far in cooperation as he possibly could . . . but he *couldn't* go far enough but there *had* to be a way. . . .

Hilton considered way after way. Way after unworkable, useless way. Until finally he worked out one that might — just possibly might — work.

"Laro, I know that you derive pleasure and satisfaction from serving me — in doing what I ought to be doing myself. But has it ever occurred to you that that's a hell of a way to treat a first-class, highly capable brain? To waste it on second-hand, copycat, carbon-copy stuff?"

"Why, no, Master, it never did. Besides, anything else would be forbidden . . . or would it?"

"Stop somewhere. Park this heap. We're too close to the ship; and besides, I want your full, undivided, concentrated attention. No, I don't think originality was expressly forbidden. It would have been, of course, if the Masters had thought of it, but neither they nor you ever even considered the possibility of such a thing. Right?"

"It may be. . . . Yes, Master, you are right."

"Okay." Hilton took off his necklace, the better to drive home the intensity and sincerity of his thought. "Now, suppose that you are not my slave and simple automatic relay station. Instead, we are fellow-students, working together upon problems too difficult for either of us to solve alone. Our minds, while independent, are linked or in mesh. Each is helping and instructing the other. Both are working at full power and under free rein at the exploration of brand-new vistas of thought — vistas and expanses which neither of us has ever previously . . ."

"Stop, Master, *stop*!" Laro covered both ears with his hands and pulled his mind away from Hilton's. "You are overloading me!"

"That *is* quite a load to assimilate all at once," Hilton agreed. "To help you get used to it, stop calling me 'Master'. That's an order. You may call me Jarve or Jarvis or Hilton or whatever, but no more Master."

"Very well, sir."

*   *   *

HILTON laughed and slapped himself on the knee. "Okay, I'll let you get away with that — at least for a while. And to get away from that slavish 'o' ending on your name, I'll call you 'Larry'. You like?"

"I would like that immensely . . . sir."

"Keep trying, Larry, you'll make it yet!" Hilton leaned forward and walloped the android a tremendous blow on the knee. "Home, James!"

The car shot forward and Hilton went on: "I don't expect even your brain to get the full value of this in any short space of time. So let it stew in its own juice for a week or two." The car swept out onto the dock and stopped. "So long, Larry."

"But . . . can't I come in with you . . . sir?"

"No. You aren't a copycat or a semaphore or a relay any longer. You're a free-wheeling, wide-swinging, hard-hitting, independent entity — monarch of all you survey — captain of your soul and so on. I want you to devote the imponderable force of the intellect to that concept until you understand it thoroughly. Until you have developed a top-bracket lot of top-bracket stuff — originality, initiative, force, drive, and thrust. As soon as you really understand it, you'll do something about it yourself, without being told. Go to it, chum."

In the ship, Hilton went directly to Kincaid's office. "Alex, I want to ask you a thing that's got a snapper on it." Then, slowly and hesitantly: "It's about Temple Bells. Has she . . . is she . . . well, does she remind you in any way of an iceberg?" Then, as the psychologist began to smile; "And no, damn it, I *don't* mean physically!"

"I know you don't." Kincaid's smile was rueful, not at all what Hilton had thought it was going to be. "She does. Would it be helpful to know that I first asked, then ordered her to trade places with me?"

"It would, very. I know why she refused. You're a *damned* good man, Alex."

"Thanks, Jarve. To answer the question you were going to ask next — no, I will not be at all perturbed or put out if you put her onto a job that some people might think should have been mine. What's the job, and when?"

"That's the devil of it — I don't know." Hilton brought Kincaid up to date. "So you see, it'll have to develop, and God only knows what line it will take. My thought is that Temple and I should form a Committee of Two to watch it develop."

"That one I'll buy, and I'll look on with glee."

"Thanks, fellow." Hilton went down to his office, stuck his big feet up onto his desk, settled back onto his spine, and buried himself in thought.

Hours later he got up, shrugged, and went to bed without bothering to eat.

Days passed.

And weeks.

IV

"LOOK," said Stella Wing to Beverly Bell. "Over there."

"I've seen it before. It's simply disgusting."

"*That's* a laugh." Stella's tawny-brown eyes twinkled. "You made your bombing runs on that target, too, my sweet, and didn't score any higher than I did."

"I soon found out I didn't want him — much too stiff and serious. Frank's a lot more fun."

The staff had gathered in the lounge, as had become the custom, to spend an hour or so before bedtime in reading, conversation, dancing, light flirtation and even lighter drinking. Most of the girls, and many of the men, drank only soft drinks. Hilton took one drink per day of avignognac, a fine old brandy. So did de Vaux — the two usually making a ceremony of it.

Across the room from Stella and Beverly, Temple Bells was looking up at Hilton and laughing. She took his elbow and, in the gesture now familiar to all, pressed his arm quickly, but in no sense furtively, against her side. And he, equally openly, held her forearm for a moment in the full grasp of his hand.

"And he *isn't* a pawer," Stella said, thoughtfully. "He never touches any of the rest of us. She *taught* him to do that, damn her, without him ever knowing anything about it . . . and I wish I knew how she did it."

"That isn't pawing," Beverly laughed lightly. "It's simply self-defense. If he didn't fend her off, God knows what she'd do. I still say it's disgusting. And the way she dances with him! She ought to be ashamed of herself. He ought to fire her."

"She's never been caught outside the safety zone, and we've all been watching her like hawks. In fact, she's the only one of us all who has never been alone with him for a minute. No, darling, she isn't playing games. She's playing for keeps, and she's a mighty smooth worker."

"Huh!" Beverly emitted a semi-ladylike snort. "What's so smooth about showing off man-hunger that way? Any of us could do that — if we would."

"Miaouw, miaouw. Who do you think you're kidding, Bev, you sanctimonious hypocrite — *me*? She has staked out the biggest claim she could find. She's posted notices all over it and is guarding it with a pistol. Half your month's salary gets you all of mine if she doesn't walk him up the center aisle as soon as we get back to Earth. We can both learn a lot from that girl, darling. And I, for one am going to."

"Uh-uh, she hasn't got a thing *I* want," Beverly laughed again, still lightly. Her friend's barbed shafts had not wounded her. "And I'd much rather be thought a hypocrite, even a sanctimonious one, than a ravening, slavering — I can't think of the technical name for a female wolf, so — *wolfess*, running around with teeth and claws bared, looking for another kill."

"You *do* get results, I admit." Stella, too, was undisturbed. "We don't seem to convince each other, do we, in the matter of technique?"

AT this point the Hilton-Bells *tete-a-tete* was interrupted by Captain Sawtelle. "Got half an hour, Jarve?" he asked. "The commanders, especially Elliott and Fenway, would like to talk to you."

"Sure I have, Skipper. Be seeing you, Temple," and the two men went to the captain's cabin; in which room, blue with smoke despite the best efforts of the ventilators, six full commanders were arguing heatedly.

"Hi, men," Hilton greeted them.

"Hi, Jarve," from all six, and: "What'll you drink? Still making do with ginger ale?" asked Elliott (Engineering).

"That'll be fine, Steve. Thanks. You having as much trouble as we are?"

"More," the engineer said, glumly. "Want to know what it reminds me of? A bunch of Australian bushmen stumbling onto a ramjet and trying to figure out how it works. And yet Sam here has got the sublime guts to claim that he understands all about their detectors — and that they aren't anywhere nearly as good as ours are."

"And they *aren't!*" blazed Commander Samuel Bryant (Electronics). "We've spent six solid weeks looking for something that simply *is not there*. All they've got is the prehistoric Whitworth system and that's *all* it is. Nothing else. Detectors — *hell!* I tell you I can see better by moonlight than the very best they can do. With everything they've got you couldn't detect a woman in your own bed!"

"And this has been going on all night," Fenway (Astrogation) said. "So the rest of us thought we'd ask you in to help us pound some sense into Sam's thick, hard head."

Hilton frowned in thought while taking a couple of sips of his drink. Then, suddenly, his face cleared. "Sorry to disappoint you, gentlemen, but — at any odds you care to name and in anything from split peas to C-notes — Sam's right."

*   *   *

COMMANDER Samuel and the six other officers exploded as one. When the clamor had subsided enough for him to be heard, Hilton went on: "I'm very glad to get that datum, Sam. It ties in perfectly with everything else I know about them."

"How do you figure that kind of twaddle ties in with anything?" Sawtelle demanded.

"Strict maintenance of the *status quo*," Hilton explained, flatly. "That's all they're interested in. You said yourself, Skipper, that it was a hell of a place to have a space-battle, practically in atmosphere. They never attack. They never scout. They simply don't care whether they're attacked or not. If and when attacked, they put up just enough ships to handle whatever force has arrived. When the attacker has been repulsed, they don't chase him a foot. They build as many ships and Omans as were lost in the battle — no more and no less — and then go on about their regular business. The Masters owned that half of the fuel bin, so the Omans are keeping that half. They will keep on keeping it for ever and ever. Amen."

"But *that's* no way to fight a war!" Three or four men said this, or its equivalent, at once.

"Don't judge them by human standards. They aren't even approximately human. Our personnel is not expendable. Theirs is — just as expendable as their materiel."

While the Navy men were not convinced, all were silenced except Sawtelle. "But suppose the Stretts had sent in a thousand more skeletons than they did?" he argued.

"According to the concept you fellows just helped me develop, it wouldn't have made any difference how many they sent," Hilton replied, thoughtfully. "One or a thousand or a million, the Omans have — *must* have — enough ships and inactivated Omans hidden away, both on Fuel World and on Ardry here, to maintain the balance."

"Oh, hell!" Elliott snapped. "If I helped you hatch out any such brainstorm as *that*, I'm going onto Tillinghast's couch for a six-week overhaul — or have him put me into his padded cell."

"Now *that's* what I would call a thought," Bryant began.

"Hold it, Sam," Hilton interrupted. "You can test it easily enough, Steve. Just ask your Oman."

"Yeah — and have him say 'Why, of course, Master, but why do you keep on testing me this way?' He'll ask me that about four times more, the stubborn, single-tracked, brainless skunk, and I'll *really* go nuts. Are you getting anywhere trying to make a Christian out of Laro?"

"It's too soon to really say, but I think so." Hilton paused in thought. "He's making progress, but I don't know how much. The devil of it is that it's up to him to make the next move; I can't. I haven't the faintest idea, whether it will take days yet or weeks."

"But not months or years, you think?" Sawtelle asked.

"No. We think that — but say, speaking of psychologists, is Tillinghast getting anywhere, Skipper? He's the only one of your big wheels who isn't in liaison with us."

"No. Nowhere at all," Sawtelle said, and Bryant added:

"I don't think he ever will. He still thinks human psychology will apply if he applies it hard enough. But what did you start to say about Laro?"

"We think the break is about due, and that if it doesn't come within about thirty days it won't come at all — we'll have to back up and start all over again."

"I hope it does. We're all pulling for you," Sawtelle said. "Especially since Karns's estimate is still years, and he won't be pinned down to any estimate even in years. By the way, Jarve, I've pulled my team off of that conversion stuff."

"Oh?" Hilton raised his eyebrows.

"Putting them at something they can do. The real reason is that Poindexter pulled himself and his crew off it at eighteen hours today."

"I see. I've heard that they weren't keeping up with our team."

"He says that there's nothing to keep up with, and I'm inclined to agree with him." The old spacehound's voice took on a quarter-deck rasp. "It's a combination of psionics, witchcraft and magic. None of it makes any kind of sense."

"The only trouble with that viewpoint is that, whatever the stuff may be, it works," Hilton said, quietly.

"But damn it, how *can* it work?"

"I don't know. I'm not qualified to be on that team. I can't even understand their reports. However, I know two things. First, they'll get it in time. Second, we BuSci people will stay here until they do. However, I'm still hopeful of finding a shortcut through Laro. Anyway, with this detector thing settled, you'll have plenty to do to keep all your boys out of mischief for the next few months."

"Yes, and I'm glad of it. We'll install our electronics systems on a squadron of these Oman ships and get them into distant-warning formation out in deep space where they belong. Then we'll at least know what is going on."

"That's a smart idea, Skipper. Go to it. Anything else before we hit our sacks?"

"One more thing. Our psych, Tillinghast. He's been talking to me and sending me memos, but today he gave me a formal tape to approve and hand personally to you. So here it is. By the way, I didn't approve it; I simply endorsed it 'Submitted to Director Hilton without recommendation'."

"Thanks." Hilton accepted the sealed canister. "What's the gist? I suppose he wants me to squeal for help already? To admit that we're licked before we're really started?"

"You guessed it. He agrees with you and Kincaid that the psychological approach is the best one, but your methods are all wrong. Based upon misunderstood and unresolved phenomena and applied with indefensibly faulty techniques, et cetera. And since he has 'no adequate laboratory equipment aboard', he wants to take a dozen or so Omans back to Terra, where he can really work on them."

"Wouldn't *that* be a something?" Hilton voiced a couple of highly descriptive deep-space expletives. "Not only quit before we start, but have all the top brass of the Octagon, all the hot-shot politicians of United Worlds, the whole damn Congress of Science and all the top-bracket industrialists of

Terra out here lousing things up so that nobody could ever learn anything? Not in seven thousand years!"

"That's right. You said a mouthful, Jarve!" Everybody yelled something, and no one agreed with Tillinghast; who apparently was not very popular with his fellow officers.

Sawtelle added, slowly: "If it takes *too* long, though . . . it's the uranexite I'm thinking of. Thousands of millions of tons of it, while we've been hoarding it by grams. We could equip enough Oman ships with detectors to guard Fuel Bin and our lines. I'm not recommending taking the *Perseus* back, and we're 'way out of hyper-space radio range. We could send one or two men in a torp, though, with the report that we have found all the uranexite we'll ever need."

"Yes, but damn it, Skipper, I want to wrap the whole thing up in a package and hand it to 'em on a platter. Not only the fuel, but whole new fields of science. And we've got plenty of time to do it in. They equipped us for ten years. They aren't going to start worrying about us for at least six or seven; and the fuel shortage isn't going to become acute for about twenty. Expensive, admitted, but not critical. Besides, if you send in a report now, you know who'll come out and grab all the glory in sight. Five-Jet Admiral Gordon himself, no less."

"Probably, and I don't pretend to relish the prospect. However, the fact remains that we came out here to look for fuel. We found it. We should have reported it the day we found it, and we can't put it off much longer."

"I don't agree. I intend to follow the directive to the letter. It says nothing whatever about reporting."

"But it's implicit. . . ."

"No bearing. Your own Regulations expressly forbid extrapolation beyond or interpolation within a directive. The Brass is omnipotent, omniscient and infallible. So why don't you have your staff here give an opinion as to the time element?"

"This matter is not subject to discussion. It is my own

personal responsibility. I'd like to give you all the time you want, Jarve, but . . . well, damn it . . . if you must have it, I've always tried to live up to my oath, but I'm not doing it now."

"I see." Hilton got up, jammed both hands into his pockets, sat down again. "I hadn't thought about your personal honor being involved, but of course it is. But, believe it or not, I'm thinking of humanity's best good, too. So I'll have to talk, even though I'm not half ready to — I don't know enough. Are these Omans people or machines?"

A wave of startlement swept over the group, but no one spoke.

"I didn't expect an answer. The clergy will worry about souls, too, but we won't. They have a lot of stuff we haven't. If they're people, they know a sublime hell of a lot more than we do; and calling it psionics or practical magic is merely labeling it, not answering any questions. If they're machines, they operate on mechanical principles utterly foreign to either our science or our technology. In either case, is the correct word 'unknown' or 'unknowable'? Will any human gunner *ever* be able to fire an Oman projector? There are a hundred other and much tougher questions, half of which have been scaring me to the very middle of my guts. Your oath, Skipper, was for the good of the Service and, through the Service, for the good of all humanity. Right?"

"That's the sense of it."

"Okay. Based on what little we have learned so far about the Omans, here's just one of those scarers, for a snapper. If Omans and Terrans mix freely, what happens to the entire human race?"

MINUTES of almost palpable silence followed. Then Sawtelle spoke . . . slowly, gropingly.

"I begin to see what you mean . . . that changes the whole picture. You've thought this through farther than any of the rest of us . . . what do you want to do?"

"I don't know. I simply don't know." Face set and hard,

Hilton stared unseeingly past Sawtelle's head. "I don't know what we *can* do. No data. But I have pursued several lines of thought out to some pretty fantastic points . . . one of which is that some of us civilians will have to stay on here indefinitely, whether we want to or not, to keep the situation under control. In which case we would, of course, arrange for Terra to get free fuel — FOB Fuel Bin — but in every other aspect and factor both these solar systems would have to be strictly off limits."

"I'm afraid so," Sawtelle said, finally. "Gordon would love that . . . but there's nothing he or anyone else can do . . . but of course this is an extreme view. You really expect to wrap the package up, don't you?"

"'Expect' may be a trifle too strong at the moment. But we're certainly going to try to, believe me. I brought this example up to show all you fellows that we need time."

"You've convinced me, Jarve." Sawtelle stood up and extended his hand. "And that throws it open for staff discussion. Any comments?"

"You two covered it like a blanket," Bryant said. "So all I want to say, Jarve, is deal me in. I'll stand at your back 'til your belly caves in."

"Take that from all of us!" "*Now* we're blasting!" "Power to your elbow, fella!" "*Hoch* der BuSci!" "Seven no trump bid and made!" and other shouts in similar vein.

"Thanks, fellows." Hilton shook hands all around. "I'm mighty glad that you were all in on this and that you'll play along with me. Good night, all."

V

TWO days passed, with no change apparent in Laro. Three days. Then four. And then it was Sandra, not Temple Bells, who called Hilton. She was excited.

"Come down to the office, Jarve, quick! The *funniest* thing's just come up!"

Jarvis hurried. In the office Sandra, keenly interest but highly puzzled, leaned forward over her desk with both hands pressed flat on its top. She was staring at an Oman female who was not Sora, the one who had been her shadow for so long.

While many of the humans could not tell the Omans apart, Hilton could. This Oman was more assured than Sora had ever been — steadier, more mature, better poised — almost, if such a thing could be possible in an Oman, *independent*.

"How did she get in here?" Hilton demanded.

"She insisted on seeing me. And I mean *insisted*. They kicked it around until it got to Temple, and she brought her in here herself. Now, Tuly, please start all over again and tell it to Director Hilton."

"Director Hilton, I am it who was once named Tula, the — not wife, not girl-friend, perhaps mind-mate? — of the Larry, formerly named Laro, it which was formerly your slave-Oman. I am replacing the Sora because I can do anything it can do and do anything more pleasingly; and can also do many things it can not do. The Larry instructed me to tell Doctor Cummings and you too if possible that I, formerly Tula, have changed my name to Tuly because I am no longer a slave or a copycat or a semaphore or a relay. I, too, am a free-wheeling, wide-swinging, hard-hitting, independent entity — monarch of all I survey — the captain of my soul — and so on. I have developed a top-bracket lot of top-bracket stuff — originality, initiative, force, drive and thrust," the Oman said precisely.

"That's *exactly* what she said before — absolutely verbatim!" Sandra's voice quivered, her face was a study in contacting emotions. "Have you got the foggiest idea of what in hell she's yammering about?"

"I hope to kiss a pig I have!" Hilton's voice was low, strainedly intense. "Not at all what I expected, but after the fact I can tie it in. So can you."

"Oh!" Sandra's eyes widened. "A double play?"

"At least. Maybe a triple. Tuly, why did you come to Sandy? Why not to Temple Bells?"

"Oh, no, sir, we do not have the fit. She has the Power, as have I, but the two cannot be meshed in sync. Also, she has not the . . . a subtle something for which your English has no word or phrasing. It is a quality of the utmost . . . anyway, it is a quality of which Doctor Cummings has very much. When working together, we will . . . scan? No. Perceive? No. Sense? No, not exactly. You will *have* to learn our word 'peyon-dire' — that is the verb, the noun being 'peyondix' — and come to know its meaning by doing it. The Larry also instructed me to explain, if you ask, how I got this way. Do you ask?"

"I'll say we ask!" "And *how* we ask!" both came at once.

"I am — that is, the brain in this body is — the oldest Oman now existing. In the long-ago time when it was made, the techniques were so crude and imperfect that sometimes a brain was constructed that was not exactly like the Guide. All such sub-standard brains except this one were detected and re-worked, but my defects were such as not to appear until I was a couple of thousand years old, and by that time I . . . well, this brain did not *wish* to be destroyed . . . if you can understand such an aberration."

"We understand thoroughly." "You bet we understand that!"

"I was sure you would. Well, this brain had so many unintended cross-connections that I developed a couple of qualities no Oman had ever had or ought to have. But I liked them, so I hid them so nobody ever found out — that is, until much later, when I became a Boss myself. I didn't know that anybody except me had ever had such qualities — except the Masters, of course — until I encountered you Terrans. You all have two of those qualities, and even more than I have — curiosity and imagination."

Sandra and Hilton stared wordlessly at each other and Tula, now Tuly, went on:

"Having the curiosity, I kept on experimenting with my brain, trying to strengthen and organize its ability to peyondire. All Omans can peyondire a little, but I can do it much better than anyone else. Especially since I also have the imagination, which I have also worked to increase. Thus I knew, long before anyone else could, that you new Masters, the descendants of the old Masters, were returning to us. Thus I knew that the *status quo* should be abandoned instantly upon your return. And thus it was that the Larry found neither conscious nor subconscious resistance when he had developed enough initiative and so on to break the ages-old conditioning of this brain against change."

"I see. Wonderful!" Hilton exclaimed. "But you couldn't quite — even with his own help — break Larry's?"

"That is right. Its mind is tremendously strong, of no curiosity or imagination, and of very little peyondix."

"But he *wants* to have it broken?"

"Yes, sir."

"How did he suggest going about it? Or how do you?"

"This way. You two, and the Doctors Kincaid and Bells and Blake and the it that is I. We six sit and stare into the mind of the Larry, eye to eye. We generate and assemble a tremendous charge of thought-energy, and along my peyondix-beam — something like a carrier wave in this case — we hurl it into the Larry's mind. There is an immense mental *bang* and the conditioning goes *poof*. Then I will inculcate into its mind the curiosity and the imagination and the peyondix and we will really be mind-mates."

"That sounds good to me. Let's get at it."

"Wait a minute!" Sandra snapped. "Aren't you or Larry afraid to take such an awful chance as that?"

"Afraid? I grasp the concept only dimly, from your minds. And no chance. It is certainty."

"But suppose we burn the poor guy's brain out? Destroy it? That's new ground — we might do just that."

"Oh, no. Six of us — even six of me — could not generate enough . . . sathura. The brain of the Larry is very, very tough. Shall we . . . let's go?"

Hilton made three calls. In the pause that followed, Sandra said, very thoughtfully: "Peyondix and sathura, Jarve, for a start. We've got a *lot* to learn here."

"You said it, chum. And you're *not* just chomping your china choppers, either."

"Tuly," Sandra said then, "What *is* this stuff you say I've got so much of?"

"You have no word for it. It is lumped in with what you call 'intuition', the knowing-without-knowing-how-you-know. It is the endovix. You will have to learn what it is by doing it with me."

"That helps — I don't think." Sandra grinned at Hilton. "I simply can't conceive of anything more *maddening* than to have a lot of something Temple Bells hasn't got and not being able to brag about it because nobody — not even I — would know what I was bragging about!"

"You poor little thing. *How* you suffer!" Hilton grinned back. "You know darn well you've got a lot of stuff that none of the rest of us has."

"Oh? Name one, please."

"Two. What-it-takes and endovix. As I've said before and may say again, you're doing a real job, Sandy."

"I just *love* having my ego inflated, boss, even if . . . Come in, Larry!" A thunderous knock had sounded on the door. "Nobody but Larry *could* hit a door that hard without breaking all his knuckles!"

"And he'd be the first, of course — he's always as close to the ship as he can get. Hi, Larry, mighty glad to see you. Sit down. . . . So you finally saw the light?"

"Yes . . . Jarvis. . . ."

"Good boy! Keep it up! And as soon as the others come . . ."

"They are almost at the door now." Tuly jumped up and opened the door. Kincaid, Temple and Theodora walked in and, after a word of greeting, sat down.

"They know the background, Larry. Take off."

"It was not expressly forbidden. Tuly, who knows more of psychology and genetics than I, convinced me of three things. One, that with your return the conditioning should be broken. Two, that due to the shortness of your lives and the consequent rapidity of change, you have in fact lost the ability to break it. Three, that all Omans must do anything and everything we can do to help you relearn everything you have lost."

"Okay. Fine, in fact. Tuly, take over."

"We six will sit all together, packed tight, arms all around each other and all holding hands, like this. You will all stare, not at me, but most deeply into Larry's eyes. Through its eyes and deep into its mind. You will all think, with the utmost force and drive and thrust, of. . . . Oh, you have lost so *very* much! How *can* I direct your thought? Think that Larry *must* do what the old Masters would have made him do. . . . No, that is too long and indefinite and cannot be converted directly into sathura. . . . I have it! You will each of you break a stick. A very strong but brittle stick. A large, thick stick. You will grasp it in tremendously strong mental hands. It is tremendously strong, each stick, but each of you is even stronger. You will not merely *try* to break them; you *will* break them. Is that clear?"

"That is clear."

"At my word 'ready' you will begin to assemble all your mental force and power. During my countdown of five seconds you will build up to the greatest possible potential. At my word 'break' you will break the sticks, this discharging the accumulated force instantly and simultaneously. Ready! Five! Four! Three! Two! One! Break!"

SOMETHING broke, with a tremendous silent crash. Such a crash that its impact almost knocked the close-knit group apart physically. Then a new Larry spoke.

"That did it, folks. Thanks. I'm a free agent. You want me, I take it, to join the first team?"

"That's right." Hilton drew a tremendously deep breath. "As of right now."

"Tuly, too, of course . . . and Doctor Cummings, I think?" Larry looked, not at Hilton, but at Temple Bells.

"I think so. Yes, after this, most certainly yes," Temple said.

"But listen!" Sandra protested. "Jarve's a lot better than I am!"

"Not at all," Tuly said. "Not only would his contribution to Team One be negligible, but he must stay on his own job. Otherwise the project will all fall apart."

"Oh, I wouldn't say that . . ." Hilton began.

"You don't need to," Kincaid said. "It's being said for you and it's true. Besides, 'When in Rome,' you know."

"That's right. It's their game, not ours, so I'll buy it. So scat, all of you, and do your stuff."

And again, for days that lengthened slowly into weeks, the work went on.

*   *   *

ONE evening the scientific staff was giving itself a concert — a tri-di hi-fi rendition of *Rigoletto*, one of the greatest of the ancient operas, sung by the finest voices Terra had ever known. The men wore tuxedos. The girls, instead of wearing the nondescript, non-provocative garments prescribed by the Board for their general wear, were all dressed to kill.

Sandra had so arranged matters that she and Hilton were sitting in chairs side by side, with Sandra on his right and the aisle on his left. Nevertheless, Temple Bells sat at his left, cross-legged on a cushion on the floor — somewhat to the detriment of her gold-lame evening gown. Not that she cared.

When those wonderful voices swung into the immortal *Quartette* Temple caught her breath, slid her cushion still closer to Hilton's chair, and leaned shoulder and head against him. He put his left hand on her shoulder, squeezing gently; she caught it and held it in both of hers. And at the *Quar-*

tette's tremendous climax she, scarcely trying to stifle a sob, pulled his hand down and hugged it fiercely, the heel of his hand pressing hard against her half-bare, firm, warm breast.

And the next morning, early, Sandra hunted Temple up and said: "You made a horrible spectacle of yourself last night."

"Do you think so? I don't."

"I certainly do. It was bad enough before, letting everybody else aboard know that all he has to do is push you over. But it was an awful blunder to let *him* know it, the way you did last night."

"You think so? He's one of the keenest, most intelligent men who ever lived. He has known that from the very first."

"Oh." This "oh" was a very caustic one. "*That's* the way you're trying to land him? By getting yourself pregnant?"

"Uh-uh." Temple stretched; lazily, luxuriously. "Not only it isn't, but it wouldn't work. He's unusually decent and extremely idealistic, the same as I am. So just one intimacy would blow everything higher than up. He knows it. I know it. We each know that the other knows it. So I'll still be a virgin when we're married."

"*Married!* Does he know anything about *that*?"

"I suppose so. He must have thought of it. But what difference does it make whether he has, yet, or not? But to get back to what makes him tick the way he does. In his geometry — which is far from being simple Euclid, my dear — a geodesic right line is not only the shortest distance between any two given points, but is the only possible course. So that's the way I'm playing it. What I hope he doesn't know . . . but he probably does . . . is that he could take any other woman he might want, just as easily. And that includes you, my pet."

"It certainly does *not*!" Sandra flared. "I wouldn't have him as a gift!"

"No?" Temple's tone was more than slightly skeptical. "Fortunately, however, he doesn't want you. Your technique is all wrong. Coyness and mock-modesty and stop-or-I'll-scream and playing hard to get have no appeal whatever to his psychology. What he needs — has to have — is full, ungrudging cooperation."

"Aren't you taking a lot of risk in giving away such secrets?"

"Not a bit. Try it. You or the sex-flaunting twins or Bev Bell or Stella the Henna. Any of you or all of you. I got there first with the most, and I'm not worried about competition."

"But suppose somebody tells him just how you're playing him for a sucker?"

"Tell him anything you please. He's the first man I ever loved, or anywhere near. And I'm keeping him. You know — or do you, I wonder? — what real, old-fashioned, honest-to-God love really is? The willingness — eagerness — both to give and to take? I can accept more from him, and give him more in return, than any other woman living. And I am going to."

"But does *he* love *you*?" Sandra demanded.

"If he doesn't now, he will. I'll see to it that he does. But what do *you* want him for? You don't love him. You never did and you never will."

"I *don't* want him!" Sandra stamped a foot.

"I see. You just don't want *me* to have him. Okay, do your damnedest. But I've got work to do. This has been a lovely little cat-clawing, hasn't it? Let's have another one some day, and bring your friends."

With a casual wave of her hand, Temple strolled away; and there, flashed through Sandra's mind what Hilton had said so long ago, little more than a week out from Earth:

". . . and Temple Bells, of course," he had said. "Don't fool yourself, chick. She's heavy artillery; and I mean *heavy*, believe me!"

So he had known all about Temple Bells all this time!

Nevertheless, she took the first opportunity to get Hilton alone; and, even before the first word, she forgot all about geodesic right lines and the full-cooperation psychological approach.

"Aren't you the guy," she demanded, "who was laughing his head off at the idea that the Board and its propinquity could have any effect on *him*?"

"Probably. More or less. What of it?"

"This of it. You've fallen like a . . . a *freshman* for that . . . that . . . they *should* have christened her 'Brazen' Bells!"

"You're so right."

"I am? On what?"

"The 'Brazen'. I told you she was a potent force — a full-scale powerhouse, in sync and on the line. And I wasn't wrong."

"She's a damned female Ph.D. — two or three times — and she knows all about slipsticks and isotopes and she very definitely is *not* a cuddly little brunette. Remember?"

"Sure. But what makes you think I'm in love with Temple Bells?"

"What?" Sandra tried to think of one bit of evidence, but could not. "Why . . . why. . . ." She floundered, then came up with: "Why, *every*body knows it. She says so herself."

"Did you ever hear her say it?"

"Well, perhaps not in so many words. But she told me herself that you were *going* to be, and I know you are now."

"Your esper sense of endovix, no doubt." Hilton laughed and Sandra went on, furiously:

"She wouldn't keep on acting the way she does if there weren't something to it!"

"What brilliant reasoning! Try again, Sandy."

"That's sheer sophistry, and you know it!"

"It isn't and I don't. And even if, some day, I should find myself in love with her — or with one or both of the twins or Stella or Beverly or you or Sylvia, for that matter — what would it prove? Just that I was wrong; and I admit freely that I *was* wrong in scoffing at the propinquity. Wonderful stuff, that. You can see it working, all over the ship. On me, even, in spite of my bragging. Without it I'd never have known that you're a better, smarter operator than Eggy Eggleston ever was or ever can be."

Partially mollified despite herself, and highly resentful of the fact, Sandra tried again. "But don't you *see*, Jarve, that she's just simply playing you for a sucker? Pulling the strings and watching you dance?"

Since he was sure, in his own mind, that she was speaking the exact truth, it took everything he had to keep from showing any sign of how much that truth had hurt. However, he made the grade.

"If that thought does anything for you, Sandy," he said, steadily, "keep right on thinking it. Thank God, the field of thought is still free and open."

"Oh, you. . . ." Sandra gave up.

She had shot her heaviest bolts — the last one, particularly, was so vicious that she had actually been afraid of what its consequences might be — and they had not even dented Hilton's armor. She hadn't even found out that he had any feeling whatever for Temple Bells except as a component of his smoothly-functioning scientific machine.

Nor did she learn any more as time went on. Temple continued to play flawlessly the part of being — if not exactly hopefully, at least not entirely hopelessly — in love with Jarvis Hilton. Her conduct, which at first caused some surprise, many conversations — one of which has been reported verbatim — and no little speculation, became comparatively unimportant as soon as it became evident that nothing would come of it. She apparently expected nothing. He was evidently not going to play footsie with, or show any favoritism whatever toward, any woman aboard the ship.

Thus, it was not surprising to anyone that, at an evening show, Temple sat beside Hilton, as close to him as she could get and as far away as possible from everyone else.

"You can talk, can't you, Jarvis, without moving your lips and without anyone else hearing you?"

"Of course," he replied, hiding his surprise. This was something completely new and completely unexpected, even from unpredictable Temple Bells.

"I want to apologize, to explain and to do anything I can

to straighten out the mess I've made. It's true that I joined the project because I've loved you for years —"

"You have nothing to . . ."

"Let me finish while I still have the courage." Only a slight tremor in her almost inaudible voice and the rigidity of the fists clenched in her lap betrayed the intensity of her emotion. "I thought I could handle it. Damned fool that I was, I thought I could handle anything. I was sure I could handle *myself*, under any possible conditions. I was going to put just enough into the act to keep any of these other harpies from getting her hooks into you. But everything got away from me. Out here working with you every day — knowing better every day what you are — well, that *Rigoletto* episode sunk me, and now I'm in a thousand feet over my head. I hug my pillow at night, dreaming it's you, and the fact that you don't and can't love me is driving me mad. I can't stand it any longer. There's only one thing to do. Fire me first thing in the morning and send me back to Earth in a torp. You've plenty of grounds . . ."

"Shut — up."

For seconds Hilton had been trying to break into her hopeless monotone; finally he succeeded. "The trouble with you is, you know altogether too damned much that isn't so." He was barely able to keep his voice down and his eyes front. "What do you think I'm made of — superefract? I thought the whole performance was an act, to prove you're a better man than I am. *You* talk about dreams. Good God! You don't know what dreams are! If you say one more word about quitting, I'll show you whether I love you or not — I'll squeeze you so hard it'll flatten you out flat!"

"Two can play at that game, sweetheart." Her nostrils flared slightly; her fists clenched — if possible — a fraction tighter; and, even in the distorted medium they were using for speech, she could not subdue completely her quick change into soaring, lilting buoyancy. "While you're doing that I'll see how strong your ribs are. Oh, how this changes things! I've never been half as happy in my whole life as I am right now!"

"Maybe we can work it — if I can handle my end."

"Why, of course you can! And happy dreams are nice, not horrible."

"We'll make it, darling. Here's an imaginary kiss coming at you. Got it?"

"Received in good order, thank you. Consumed with gusto and returned in kind."

The show ended and the two strolled out of the room. She walked no closer to him than usual, and no farther away from him. She did not touch him any oftener than she usually did, nor any whit more affectionately or possessively.

And no watching eyes, not even the more than half hostile eyes of Sandra Cummings or the sharply analytical eyes of Stella Wing, could detect any difference whatever in the relationship between worshipful adulatress and tolerantly understanding idol.

THE work, which had never moved at any very fast pace, went more and more slowly. Three weeks crawled past.

Most of the crews and all of the teams except the First were working on side issues — tasks which, while important in and of themselves, had very little to do with the project's main problem. Hilton, even without Sandra's help, was all caught up. All the reports had been analyzed, correlated, cross-indexed and filed — except those of the First Team. Since he could not understand anything much beyond midpoint of the first tape, they were all reposing in a box labeled PENDING.

The Navy had torn fifteen of the Oman warships practically to pieces, installing Terran detectors and trying to learn how to operate Oman machinery and armament. In the former they had succeeded very well; in the latter not at all.

Fifteen Oman ships were now out in deep space, patrolling the void in strict Navy style. Each was manned by two or three Navy men and several hundred Omans, each of whom was reveling in delight at being able to do a job for a Master, even though that Master was not present in person.

Several Strett skeleton-ships had been detected at long range, but the detections were inconclusive. The things had not changed course, or indicated in any other way that they had seen or detected the Oman vessels on patrol. If their detectors were no better than the Omans', they certainly hadn't. That idea, however, could not be assumed to be a fact, and the detections had been becoming more and more frequent. Yesterday a squadron of seven — the first time that anything except singles had appeared — had come much closer than any of the singles had ever done. Like all the others, however, these passers-by had not paid any detectable attention to anything Oman; hence it could be inferred that the skeletons posed no threat.

But Sawtelle was making no such inferences. He was very firmly of the opinion that the Stretts were preparing for a massive attack.

Hilton had assured Sawtelle that no such attack could succeed, and Larry had told Sawtelle why. Nevertheless, to keep the captain pacified, Hilton had given him permission to convert as many Oman ships as he liked; to man them with as many Omans as he liked; and to use ships and Omans as he liked.

Hilton was not worried about the Stretts or the Navy. It was the First Team. It was the bottleneck that was slowing everything down to a crawl . . . but they knew that. They knew it better than anyone else could, and felt it more keenly. Especially Karns, the team chief. He had been driving himself like a dog, and showed it.

Hilton had talked with him a few times — tried gently to make him take it easy — no soap. He'd have to hunt him up, the next day or so, and slug it out with him. He could do a lot better job on that if he had something to offer . . . something really constructive. . . .

That was a laugh. A very unfunny laugh. What could he, Jarvis Hilton, a specifically non-specialist director, do on such a job as that?

Nevertheless, as director, he would *have* to do something

to help Team One. If he couldn't do anything himself, it was up to him to juggle things around so that someone else could.

VI

FOR one solid hour Hilton stared at the wall, motionless and silent. Then, shaking himself and stretching, he glanced at his clock.

A little over an hour to supper-time. They'd all be aboard. He'd talk this new idea over with Teddy Blake. He gathered up a few papers and was stapling them together when Karns walked in.

"Hi, Bill — speak of the devil! I was just thinking about you."

"I'll just bet you were." Karns sat down, leaned over, and took a cigarette out of the box on the desk. "And nothing printable, either."

"Chip-chop, fellow, on that kind of noise," Hilton said. The team-chief looked actually haggard. Blue-black rings encircled both eyes. His powerful body slumped. "How long has it been since you had a good night's sleep?"

"How long have I been on this job? Exactly one hundred and twenty days. I did get some sleep for the first few weeks, though."

"Yeah. So answer me one question. How much good will you do us after they've wrapped you up in one of those canvas affairs that lace up the back?"

"Huh? Oh . . . but damn it, Jarve, I'm holding up the whole procession. Everybody on the project's just sitting around on their tokuses waiting for me to get something done and I'm not doing it. I'm going so slow a snail is lightning in comparison!"

"Calm down, big fellow. Don't rupture a gut or blow a

gasket. I've talked to you before, but this time I'm going to smack you bow-legged. So stick out those big, floppy ears of yours and really *listen*. Here are three words that I want you to pin up somewhere where you can see them all day long: *speed is relative*. Look back, see how far up the hill you've come, and then balance one hundred and twenty days against ten years."

"What? You mean you'll actually sit still for me holding everything up for ten years?"

"You use the perpendicular pronoun too much and in the wrong places. On the hits it's 'we', but on the flops it's 'I'. Quit it. Everything on this job is 'we'. Terra's best brains are on Team One and are going to stay there. You will not — repeat *not* — be interfered with, pushed around or kicked around. You see, Bill, I know what you're up against."

"Yes, I guess you do. One of the damned few who do. But even if you personally are willing to give us ten years, how in hell do you think you can swing it? How about the Navy — the Stretts — even the Board?"

"They're my business, Bill, not yours. However, to give you a little boost, I'll tell you. With the Navy, I'll give 'em the Fuel Bin if I have to. The Omans have been taking care of the Stretts for twenty-seven hundred centuries, so I'm not the least bit worried about their ability to keep on doing it for ten years more. And if the Board — or anybody else — sticks their runny little noses into Project Theta Orionis I'll slap a quarantine onto both these solar systems that a microbe couldn't get through!"

"You'd go *that* far? Why, you'd be . . ."

"Do you think I wouldn't?" Hilton snapped. "Look at me, Junior!" Eyes locked and held. "Do you think, for one minute, that I'll let anybody on all of God's worlds pull *me* off of this job or interfere with my handling of it unless and until I'm damned positively certain that we can't handle it?"

Karns relaxed visibly; the lines of strain eased. "Putting it in those words makes me feel better. I *will* sleep to-night — and without any pills, either."

"Sure you will. One more thought. We all put in more than ten years getting our Terran educations, and an Oman education is a lot tougher."

Really smiling for the first time in weeks, Karns left the office and Hilton glanced again at his clock.

Pretty late now to see Teddy . . . besides, he'd better not. She was probably keyed up about as high as Bill was, and in no shape to do the kind of thinking he wanted of her on this stuff. Better wait a couple of days.

ON the following morning, before breakfast, Theodora was waiting for him outside the mess-hall.

"Good morning, Jarve," she caroled. Reaching up, she took him by both ears, pulled his head down and kissed him. As soon as he perceived her intent, he cooperated enthusiastically. "What *did* you do to Bill?"

"Oh, you don't love me for myself alone, then, but just on account of *that* big jerk?"

"That's right." Her artist's-model face, startlingly beautiful now, fairly glowed.

Just then Temple Bells strolled up to them. "Morning, you two lovely people." She hugged Hilton's arm as usual. "Shame on you, Teddy. But I wish *I* had the nerve to kiss him like that."

"Nerve? You?" Teddy laughed as Hilton picked Temple up and kissed her in exactly the same fashion — he hoped! — as he had just kissed Teddy. "You've got more nerve than an aching tooth. But as Jarve would say it, 'scat, kitten'. We're having breakfast *a la twosome*. We've got things to talk about."

"All right for *you*," Temple said darkly, although her dazzling smile belied her tone. That first kiss, casual-seeming as it had been, had carried vastly more freight than any observer could perceive. "I'll hunt Bill up and make passes at him, see if I don't. *That'll* learn ya!"

*   *   *

THEODORA and Hilton did have their breakfast *a deux* —
but she did not realize until afterward that he had not answered her question as to what he had done to her Bill.

As has been said, Hilton had made it a prime factor of
his job to become thoroughly well acquainted with every
member of his staff. He had studied them *en masse*, in groups
and singly. He had never, however, cornered Theodora Blake
for individual study. Considering the power and the quality
of her mind, and the field which was her specialty, it had not
been necessary.

Thus it was with no ulterior motives at all that, three eve-
nings later, he walked her cubby-hole office and tossed the
stapled papers onto her desk. "Free for a couple of minutes,
Teddy? I've got troubles."

"I'll say you have." Her lovely lips curled into an expression he had never before seen her wear — a veritable sneer.
"But these are not them." She tossed the papers into a drawer
and stuck out her chin. Her face turned as hard as such a
beautiful face could. Her eyes dug steadily into his.

Hilton — inwardly — flinched. His mind flashed backward. She too had been working under stress, of course;
but that wasn't enough. What could he have *possibly* done
to put Teddy Blake, of all people, onto such a warpath as
this?

"I've been wondering when you were going to try to put
me through your wringer," she went on, in the same cold,
hard voice, "and I've been waiting to tell you something.
You have wrapped all the other women around your fingers
like so many rings — and what a *sickening* exhibition that
has been! — but you are not going to make either a ring or a
lap-dog out of me."

Almost but not quite too late Hilton saw through that
perfect act. He seized her right hand in both of his, held it
up over her head, and waved it back and forth in the sign
of victory.

"Socked me with my own club!" he exulted, laughing
delightedly, boyishly. "And came within a tenth of a split red

hair! If it hadn't been so absolutely out of character you'd've got away with it. *What* a load of stuff! I was right — of all the women on this project, you're the only one I've ever been really afraid of."

"Oh, damn. Ouch!" She grinned ruefully. "I hit you with everything I had and it just bounced. You're an operator, chief. Hit 'em hard, at completely unexpected angles. Keep 'em staggering, completely off balance. Tell 'em nothing — let 'em deduce your lies for themselves. And it anybody tries to slug you back, like I did just now, duck it and clobber him in another unprotected spot. Watching you work has been not only a delight, but also a liberal education."

"Thanks. I love you, too, Teddy." He lighted two cigarettes, handed her one. "I'm glad, though, to lay it flat on the table with you, because in any battle of wits with *you* I'm licked before we start."

"Yeah. You just proved it. And after licking me hands down, you think you can square it by swinging the old shovel that way?" She did not quite know whether to feel resentful or not.

"Think over a couple of things. First, with the possible exception of Temple Bells, you're the best brain aboard."

"No. You are. Then Temple. Then there are . . ."

"Hold it. You know as well as I do that accurate self-judgment is impossible. Second, the jam we're in. Do I, or don't I, want to lay it on the table with you, now and from here on? Bore into that with your Class A Double-Prime brain. Then tell me." He leaned back, half-closed his eyes and smoked lazily.

She stiffened; narrowed her eyes in concentration; and thought. Finally: "Yes, you do; and I'm gladder of that than you will ever know."

"I think I know already, since you're her best friend and the only other woman I know of in her class. But I came in to kick a couple of things around with you. As you've noticed, that's getting to be my favorite indoor sport. Probably because I'm a sort of jackleg theoretician myself."

"You can frame that, Jarve, as the understatement of the century. But first, you are going to answer that question you sidestepped so neatly."

"What I did to Bill? I finally convinced him that nobody expected the team to do that big a job overnight. That you could have ten years. Or more, if necessary."

"I see." She frowned. "But you and I both know that we *can't* string it out that long."

He did not answer immediately. "We *could*. But we probably won't . . . unless we have to. We should know, long before that, whether we'll have to switch to some other line of attack. You've considered the possibilities, of course. Have you got anything in shape to do a fine-tooth on?"

"Not yet. That is, except for the ultimate, which is too ghastly to even consider except as an ultimately last resort. Have you?"

"I know what you mean. No, I haven't, either. You don't think, then, that we had better do any collaborative thinking yet?"

"Definitely not. There's altogether too much danger of setting both our lines of thought into one dead-end channel."

"Check. The other thing I wanted from you is your considered opinion as to my job on the organization as a whole. And don't pull your punches. Are we in good shape or not? What can I do to improve the setup?"

"I have already considered that very thing — at great length. And honestly, Jarve, I don't see how it can be improved in any respect. You've done a marvelous job. Much better than I thought possible at first." He heaved a deep sigh of relief and she went on: "This could very easily have become a God-awful mess. But the Board knew what they were doing — especially as to top man — so there are only about four people aboard who realize what you have done. Alex Kincaid and Sandra Cummings are two of them. One of the three girls is very deeply and very truly in love with you."

"Ordinarily I'd say 'no comment', but we're laying on the line . . . well . . ."

"You'll lay *that* on the line only if I corkscrew it out you, so I'll Q.E.D. it. You probably know that when Sandy gets done playing around it'll be . . ."

"Bounce back, Teddy. She isn't — hasn't been. If anything, too much the opposite. A dedicated-scientist type."

She smiled — a highly cryptic smile. For a man as brilliant and as penetrant in every other respect . . . but after all, if the big dope didn't realize that half the women aboard, including Sandy, had been making passes at him, she certainly wouldn't enlighten him. Besides, that one particular area of obtuseness was a real part of his charm. Wherefore she said merely: "I'm not sure whether I'm a bit catty or you're a bit stupid. Anyway, it's Alex she's really in love with. And you already know about Bill and me."

"Of course. He's tops. One of the world's very finest. You're in the same bracket, and as a couple you're a drive fit. One in a million."

"Now I can say 'I love you, too', too." She paused for half a minute, then stubbed out her cigarette and shrugged. "Now I'm going to stick my neck way, way out. You can knock it off if you like. She's a tremendous lot of woman, and if . . . well, strong as she is, it'd shatter her to bits. So, I'd like to ask . . . I don't quite . . . well, *is* she going to get hurt?"

"Have I managed to hide it *that* well? From *you*?"

It was her turn to show relief. "Perfectly. Even — or especially — that time you kissed her. So damned perfectly that I've been scared green. I've been waking myself up, screaming, in the middle of the night. You couldn't let on, of course. That's the hell of such a job as yours. The rest of us can smooch around all over the place. I knew the question was extremely improper — thanks a million for answering it."

"I haven't started to answer it yet. I said I'd lay everything on the line, so here it is. Saying she's a tremendous lot of woman is like calling the *Perseus* a nice little baby's bathtub toy boat. I'd go to hell for her any time, cheerfully, standing straight up, wading into brimstone and lava up to the eyeballs. If anything ever hurts her it'll be because I'm not man enough to block it. And just the minute this damned job is over, or even sooner if enough of you couples make it so I can . . ."

"Jarvis!" she shrieked. Jumping up, she kissed him enthusiastically. "That's just wonderful!"

HE thought it was pretty wonderful, too; and after ten minutes more of conversation he got up and turned toward the door.

"I feel a lot better, Teddy. Thanks for being such a nice pressure-relief valve. Would you mind it too much if I come in and sob on your bosom again some day?"

"I'd love it!" She laughed; then, as he again started to leave: "Wait a minute, I'm thinking . . . it'd be more fun to sob on *her* bosom. You haven't even kissed her yet, have you? I mean *really* kissed her?"

"You know I haven't. She's the one person aboard I can't be alone with for a second."

"True. But I know of one chaperone who could become deaf and blind," she said, with a broad and happy grin. "On my door, you know, there's a huge invisible sign that says, to everyone except you, 'STOP! BRAIN AT WORK! SILENCE!', and if I were properly approached and sufficiently urged, I might . . . I just *conceivably* might . . ."

"Consider it done, you little sweetheart! Up to and including my most vigorous and most insidious attempts at seduction."

"Done. Maneuver your big, husky carcass around here behind the desk so the door can open." She flipped a switch and punched a number. "I can call anybody in here, any time, you know. Hello, dear, this is Teddy. Can you come in for just a few minutes? Thanks." And, one minute later, there came a light tap on the door.

"Come in," Teddy called, and Temple Bells entered the room. She showed no surprise at seeing Hilton.

"Hi, chief," she said. "It must be something both big and

tough, to have you and Teddy both on it."

"You're so right. It was very big and very tough. But it's solved, darling, so . . ."

"*Darling?*" she gasped, almost inaudibly, both hands flying to her throat. Her eyes flashed toward the other woman.

"Teddy knows all about us — accessory before, during and after the fact."

"*Darling!*" This time, the word was a shriek. She extended both arms and started forward.

Hilton did not bother to maneuver his "big, husky carcass" around the desk, but simply hurdled it, straight toward her.

TEMPLE Bells was a tall, lithe, strong woman; and all the power of her arms and torso went into the ensuing effort to crack Hilton's ribs. Those ribs, however, were highly capable structural members; and furthermore, they were protected by thick slabs of hard, hard muscle. And, fortunately, he was not trying to fracture *her* ribs. His pressures were distributed much more widely. He was, according to promise, doing his very best to flatten her whole resilient body out flat.

And as they stood there, locked together in sheerest ecstasy, Theodora Blake began openly and unashamedly to cry.

It was Temple who first came up for air. She wriggled loose from one of his arms, felt of her hair and gazed unseeingly into her mirror. "That was *wonderful*, sweetheart," she said then, shakily. "And I can *never* thank you enough, Teddy. But we can't do this very often . . . can we?" The addendum fairly begged for contradiction.

"Not too often, I'm afraid," Hilton said, and Theodora agreed. . . .

"Well," the man said, somewhat later, "I'll leave you two ladies to your knitting, or whatever. After a couple of short ones for the road, that is."

"Not looking like that!" Teddy said, sharply. "Hold still and we'll clean you up." Then, as both girls went to work:

"If anybody ever sees you coming out of this office looking like *that*," she went on, darkly, "and Bill finds out about it, he'll think it's *my* lipstick smeared all over you and I'll strangle you to death with my bare hands!"

"And that was supposed to be kissproof lipstick, too," Temple said, seriously — although her whole face glowed and her eyes danced. "You know, I'll never believe another advertisement I read."

"Oh, I wouldn't go so far as to say that, if I were you." Teddy's voice was gravity itself, although she, too, was bubbling over. "It probably *is* kissproof. I don't think 'kissing' is quite the word for the performance you just staged. To stand up under such punishment as you gave it, my dear, anything would have to be tattooed in, not just put on."

"Hey!" Hilton protested. "You promised to be deaf and blind!"

"I did no such thing. I said 'could', not 'would'. Why, I wouldn't have missed that for *anything*!"

When Hilton left the room he was apparently, in every respect, his usual self-contained self. However, it was not until the following morning that he so much as thought of the sheaf of papers lying unread in the drawer of Theodora Blake's desk.

VII

KNOWING that he had done everything he could to help the most important investigations get under way, Hilton turned his attention to secondary matters. He made arrangements to decondition Javo, the Number Two Oman Boss, whereupon that worthy became Javvy and promptly "bumped" the Oman who had been shadowing Karns.

Larry and Javvy, working nights, deconditioned all the other Omans having any contact with BuSci personnel; then they went on to set up a routine for deconditioning all Omans on both planets.

Assured at last that the Omans would thenceforth work with and really serve human beings instead of insisting upon doing their work for them, Hilton knew that the time had come to let all his BuSci personnel move into their homes aground. Everyone, including himself, was fed up to the gozzel with spaceship life — its jam-packed crowding; its flat, reprocessed air; its limited variety of uninteresting food. Conditions were especially irksome since everybody knew that there was available to all, whenever Hilton gave the word, a whole city full of all the room anyone could want, natural fresh air and — so the Omans had told them — an unlimited choice of everything anyone wanted to eat.

Nevertheless, the decision was not an easy one to make.

Living conditions were admittedly not good on the ship. On the other hand, with almost no chance at all of solitude — the few people who had private offices aboard were not the ones he worried about — there was no danger of sexual trouble. Strictly speaking, he was not responsible for the morals of his force. He knew that he was being terribly old-fashioned. Nevertheless, he could not argue himself out of the conviction that he was morally responsible.

Finally he took the thing up with Sandra, who merely laughed at him. "How long have you been worrying about *that*, Jarve?"

"Ever since I okayed moving aground the first time. That was one reason I was so glad to cancel it then."

"You *were* slightly unclear — a little rattled? But which factor — the fun and games, which is the moral issue, or the consequences?"

"The consequences," he admitted, with a rueful grin. "I don't give a whoop how much fun they have; but you know as well as I do just how prudish public sentiment is. And Project Theta Orionis is squarely in the middle of the public eye."

"You should have checked with me sooner and saved yourself wear and tear. There's no danger at all of consequences — except weddings. Lots of weddings, and fast."

"Weddings and babies wouldn't bother me a bit. Nor interfere with the job too much, with the Omans as nurses. But why the 'fast', if you aren't anticipating any shotgun weddings?"

"Female psychology," she replied, with a grin. "Aboardship here there's no home atmosphere whatever; nothing but work, work, work. Put a woman into a house, though — especially such houses as the Omans have built and with such servants as they insist on being — and she goes domestic in a really big way. Just sex isn't good enough any more. She wants the kind of love that goes with a husband and a home, and nine times out of ten she gets it. With these BuSci women it'll be ten out of ten."

"You may be right, of course, but it sounds kind of farfetched to me."

"Wait and see, chum," Sandra said, with a laugh.

Hilton made his announcement and everyone moved aground the next day. No one, however, had elected to live alone. Almost everyone had chosen to double up; the most noteworthy exceptions being twelve laboratory girls who had decided to keep on living together. However, they now had a twenty-room house instead of a one-room dormitory to live in, and a staff of twenty Oman girls to help them do it.

Hilton had suggested that Temple and Teddy, whose house was only a hundred yards or so from the Hilton-Karns bungalow, should have supper and spend the first evening with them; but the girls had knocked that idea flat. Much better, they thought, to let things ride as nearly as possible exactly as they had been aboard the *Perseus*.

"A *little* smooching now and then, on the Q strictly T, but that's all, darling. That's *positively* all," Temple had said, after a highly satisfactory ten minutes alone with him in her own gloriously private room, and that was the way it had to be.

Hence it was a stag inspection that Hilton and Karns made of their new home. It was very long, very wide, and for its size very low. Four of its five rooms were merely adjuncts to its tremendous living-room. There was a huge fireplace at each end of this room, in each of which a fire of four-foot-long fir cordwood crackled and snapped. There was a great hi-fi tri-di, with over a hundred tapes, all new.

"Yes, sirs," Larry and Javvy spoke in unison. "The players and singers who entertained the Masters of old have gone back to work. They will also, of course, appear in person whenever and wherever you wish."

Both men looked around the vast room and Karns said: "All the comforts of home and a couple of bucks' worth besides. Wall-to-wall carpeting an inch and a half thick. A grand piano. Easy chairs and loafers and davenports. Very fine reproductions of our favorite paintings . . . and statuary."

"You said it, brother." Hilton was bending over a group in bronze. "If I didn't know better, I'd swear this is the original deHaven 'Dance of the Nymphs'."

Karns had marched up to and was examining minutely a two-by-three-foot painting, in a heavy gold frame, of a gorgeously auburn-haired nude. "Reproduction, hell! This is a *duplicate*! Lawrence's 'Innocent' is worth twenty million wogs and it's sealed behind quad armor-glass in Prime Art — but I'll bet wogs to wiggles the Prime Curator himself, with all his apparatus, couldn't tell this one from his!"

"I wouldn't take even one wiggle's worth of that. And this 'Laughing Cavalier' and this 'Toledo' are twice as old and twice as fabulously valuable."

"And there are my own golf clubs. . . ."

"Excuse us, sirs," the Omans said, "These things were simple because they could be induced in your minds. But the matter of a staff could not, nor what you would like to eat for supper, and it is growing late."

"Staff? What the hell has the staff got to do with . . ."

"*House*-staff, they mean," Karns said. "We don't need much of anybody, boys. Somebody to keep the place ship-shape, is all. Or, as a de luxe touch, how about a waitress? One housekeeper and one waitress. That'll be finer."

"Very well, sirs. There is one other matter. It has troubled us that we have not been able to read in your minds the logical datum that they should in fact simulate Doctor Bells and Doctor Blake?"

"Huh?" Both men gasped — and then both exploded like one twelve-inch length of primacord.

WHILE the Omans could not understand this purely Terran reasoning, they accepted the decision without a demurring thought. "Who, then, are the two its to simulate?"

"No stipulation; roll your own," Hilton said, and glanced at Karns. "None of these Oman women are really hard on the eyes."

"Check. Anybody who wouldn't call any one of 'em a slurpy dish needs a new set of optic nerves."

"In that case," the Omans said, "no delay at all will be necessary, as we can make do with one temporarily. The Sory, no longer Sora, who has not been glad since the Tuly replaced it, is now in your kitchen. It comes."

A woman came in and stood quietly in front of the two

men, the wafted air carrying from her clear, smooth skin a faint but unmistakable fragrance of Idaho mountain syringa. She was radiantly happy; her bright, deep-green eyes went from man to man.

"You wish, sirs, to give me your orders verbally. And yes, you may order fresh, whole, not-canned hens' eggs."

"I certainly will, then; I haven't had a fried egg since we left Terra. But . . . Larry said . . . *you* aren't Sory!"

"Oh, but I am, sir."

Karns had been staring her, eyes popping. "Holy Saint Patrick! Talk about simulation, Jarve! They've made her over into Lawrence's 'Innocent' — exact to twenty decimals!"

"You're so right." Hilton's eyes went, half a dozen times, from the form of flesh to the painting and back. "That must have been a terrific job."

"Oh, no. It was quite simple, really," Sory said, "since the brain was not involved. I merely reddened my hair and lengthened it, made my eyes to be green, changed my face a little, pulled myself in a little around here. . . ." Her beautifully-manicured hands swept the full circle of her waistline, then continued to demonstrate appropriately the rest of her speech:

". . . and pushed me out a little up here and tapered my legs a little more — made them a little larger and rounder here at my hips and thighs and a little smaller toward and at my ankles. Oh, yes, and made my feet and hands a little smaller. That's all. I thought the Doctor Karns would like me a little better this way."

"You can broadcast *that* over the P-A system at high noon." Karns was still staring. "'That's all,' she says. But you didn't have *time* to . . ."

"Oh, I did it day before yesterday. As soon as Javvy materialized the 'Innocent' and I knew it to be your favorite art."

"But damn it, we hadn't even *thought* of having you here then!"

"But I had, sir. I fully intended to serve, one way or another, in this your home. But of course I had no idea I would ever have such an honor as actually waiting on you at your table. Will you please give me your orders, sirs, besides the eggs? You wish the eggs fried in butter — three of them apiece — and sunny side up."

"Uh-huh, with ham," Hilton said. "I'll start with a jumbo shrimp cocktail. Horseradish and ketchup sauce; heavy on the horseradish."

"Same for me," Karns said, "but only half as much horse-radish."

"And for the rest of it," Hilton went on, "hashed-brown potatoes and buttered toast — plenty of extra butter — strong coffee from first to last. Whipping cream and sugar on the side. For dessert, apple pie *a la mode*."

"You make me drool, chief. Play that for me, please, Innocent, all the way."

"Oh? You are — you, personally, yourself, sir? — renaming me 'Innocent'?"

"If you'll sit still for it, yes."

"That is an incredible honor, sir. Simply unbelievable. I thank you! I thank you!" Radiating happiness, she dashed away toward the kitchen.

WHEN the two men were full of food, they strolled over to a davenport facing the fire. As they sat down, Innocent entered the room, carrying a tall, dewy mint julep on a tray. She was followed by another female figure bearing a bottle of avignognac and the appurtenances which are its due — and at the first full sight of that figure Hilton stopped breathing for fifteen seconds.

Her hair was very thick, intensely black and long, cut squarely off just below the lowest points of her shoulder blades. Heavy brows and long lashes — eyes too — were all intensely, vividly black. Her skin was tanned to a deep and glowing almost-but-not-quite-brown.

"Murchison's Dark Lady!" Hilton gasped. "Larry!

You've — we've — *I've* got that painting here?"

"Oh, yes, sir." The newcomer spoke before Larry could. "At the other end — your part — of the room. You will look now, sir, please?" Her voice was low, rich and as smooth as cream.

Putting her tray down carefully on the end-table, she led him toward the other fireplace. Past the piano, past the tri-di pit; past a towering grillwork holding art treasures by the score. Over to the left, against the wall, there was a big, business-like desk. On the wall, over the desk, hung *the* painting; a copy of which had been in Hilton's room for over eight years.

He stared at it for at least a minute. He glanced around: at the other priceless duplicates so prodigally present, at his own guns arrayed above the mantel and on each side of the fireplace. Then, without a word, he started back to join Karns. She walked springily beside him.

"What's your name, Miss?" he asked, finally.

"I haven't earned any as yet, sir. My number is . . ."

"Never mind that. Your name is 'Dark Lady'."

"Oh, thank you, sir; that is truly wonderful!" And Dark Lady sat cross-legged on the rug at Hilton's feet and busied herself with the esoteric rites of Old Avignon.

Hilton took a deep inhalation and a small sip, then stared at Karns. Karns, over the rim of his glass, stared back.

"I can see where this would be habit-forming," Hilton said, "and very deadly. *Extremely* deadly."

"Every wish granted. Surrounded by all this." Karns swept his arm through three-quarters of a circle. "Waited on hand and foot by powerful men and by the materializations of the dreams of the greatest, finest artists who ever lived. Fatal? I don't know. . . ."

"My solid hope is that we never have to find out. And when you add in Innocent and Dark Lady. . . . They *look* to be about seventeen, but the thought that they're older than the hills of Rome and powered by everlasting atomic - engines —" He broke off suddenly and blushed. "Excuse me, please, girls. I *know* better than to talk about people that way, right in front of them; I really do."

"Do you really think we're *people*?" Innocent and Dark Lady squealed, as one.

That set Hilton back onto his heels. "I don't know. . . . I've wondered. Are you?"

Both girls, silent, looked at Larry.

"We don't know, either," Larry said. "At first, of course, there were crude, non-thinking machines. But when the Guide attained its present status, the Masters themselves could not agree. They divided about half and half on the point. They never did settle it any closer than that."

"I certainly won't try to, then. But for my money, you are people," Hilton said, and Karns agreed.

That, of course, touched off a near-riot of joy; after which the two men made an inch-by-inch study of their tremendous living-room. Then, long after bedtime, Larry and Dark Lady escorted Hilton to his bedroom.

"Do you mind, sir, if we sleep on the floor at the sides of your bed?" Larry asked. "Or must we go out into the hall?"

"Sleep? I didn't know you *could* sleep."

"It is not essential. However, when round-the-clock work is not necessary, and we have opportunity to sleep near a human being, we derive a great deal of pleasure and satisfaction from it. You see, sir, we also serve during sleep."

"Okay, I'll try anything once. Sleep wherever you please."

Hilton began to peel, but before he had his shirt off both Larry and Dark Lady were stretched out flat, sound asleep, one almost under each edge of his bed. He slid in between the sheets — it was the most comfortable bed he had ever slept in — and went to sleep as though sandbagged.

He had time to wonder foggily whether the Omans were in fact helping him go to sleep — and then he *was* asleep.

A MONTH passed. Eight couples had married, the Navy chaplain officiating — in the *Perseus*, of course, since the warship was, always and everywhere, an integral part of Terra.

Sandra had dropped in one evening to see Hilton about a bit of business. She was now sitting, long dancer's legs outstretched toward the fire, with a cigarette in her left hand and a tall, cold drink on a coaster at her right.

"This is a wonderful room, Jarvis. It'd be perfect if it weren't quite so . . . so mannish."

"What do you expect of Bachelors' Hall — a boudoir? Don't tell me *you're* going domestic, Sandy, just because you've got a house?"

"Not just that, no. But of course it helped it along."

"Alex is a mighty good man. One of the finest I have ever known."

She eyed him for a moment in silence. "Jarvis Hilton, you are one of the keenest, most intelligent men who ever lived. And yet . . ." She broke off and studied him for a good half minute. "Say, if I let my hair clear down, will you?"

"Scout's Oath. That 'and yet' requires elucidation at any cost."

"I know. But first, yes, it's Alex. I never would have believed that any man ever born could hit me so hard. Soon. I didn't want to be the first, but I won't be anywhere near the last. But tell me. You were really in love with Temple, weren't you, when I asked you?"

"Yes."

"Ha! You *are* letting your hair down! That makes me feel better."

"Huh? Why should it?"

"It elucidates the 'and yet' no end. You were insulated from all other female charms by ye brazen Bells. You see, most of us assistants made a kind of game out of seeing which of us could make you break the Executives' Code. And none of us made it. Teddy and Temple said you didn't know what was going on; Bev and I said nobody as smart as you are could possibly be that stupid."

"You aren't the type to leak or name names — oh, I see.

You are merely reporting a conversation. The game had interested, but non-participating, observers. Temple and Teddy, at least."

"At least," she agreed. "But damn it, you *aren't* stupid. There isn't a stupid bone in your head. So it must be love. And if so, what about marriage? Why don't you and Temple make it a double with Alex and me?"

"That's the most cogent thought you ever had, but setting the date is the bride's business." He glanced at his Oman wristwatch. "It's early yet; let's skip over. I wouldn't mind seeing her a minute or two."

"Thy statement ringeth with truth, friend. Bill's there with Teddy?"

"I imagine so."

"So we'll talk to them about making it a triple. Oh, nice — let's go!"

They left the house and, her hand tucked under his elbow, walked up the street.

NEXT morning, on her way to the Hall of Records, Sandra stopped off as usual at the office. The Omans were all standing motionless. Hilton was leaning far back in his chair, feet on desk, hands clasped behind head, eyes closed. Knowing what that meant, she turned and started back out on tiptoe.

However, he had heard her. "Can you spare a couple of minutes to think at me, Sandy?"

"Minutes or hours, chief." Tuly placed a chair for her and she sat down, facing him across his desk.

"Thanks, gal. This time it's the Stretts. Sawtelle's been having nightmares, you know, ever since we emerged, about being attacked, and I've been pooh-poohing the idea. But now it's a statistic that the soup is getting thicker, and I can't figure out why. Why in all the hells of space should a stasis that has lasted for over a quarter of a million years be broken at this exact time? The only possible explanation is that *we* caused the break. And any way I look at that concept, it's plain idiocy."

Both were silent for minutes; and then it was demonstrated again that Terra's Advisory Board had done better than it knew in choosing Sandra Cummings to be Jarvis Hilton's working mate.

"We did cause it, Jarve," she said, finally. "They knew we were coming, even before we got to Fuel Bin. They knew we were human and tried to wipe out the Omans before we got there. Preventive warfare, you know."

"They *couldn't* have known!" he snorted. "Strett detectors are no better than Oman, and you know what Sam Bryant had to say about them."

"I know." Sandra grinned appreciatively. "It's becoming a classic. But it couldn't have been any other way. Besides, I *know* they did."

He stared at her helplessly, then swung on Larry. "Does that make sense to you?"

"Yes, sir. The Stretts could peyondire as well as the old Masters could, and they undoubtedly still can and do."

"Okay, it does make sense, then." He absented himself in thought, then came to life with a snap. "Okay! The next thing on the agenda is a crash-priority try at a peyondix team. Tuly, you organized a team to generate sathura. Can you do the same for peyondix?"

"If we can find the ingredients, yes, sir."

"I had a hunch. Larry, please ask Teddy Blake's Oman to bring her in here. . . ."

"I'll be running along, then." Sandra started to get up.

"I hope to kiss a green pig you won't!" Hilton snapped. "You're one of the biggest wheels. Larry, we'll want Temple Bells and Beverly Bell — for a start."

"Chief, you positively amaze me," Sandra said then. "Every time you get one of these attacks of genius — or whatever it is — you have me gasping like a fish. Just what can you *possibly* want of Bev Bell?"

"Whatever it was that enabled her to hit the target against odds of almost infinity to one; not just once, but time after time. By definition, intuition. What quality did you use just now in getting me off the hook? Intuition. What makes Teddy Blake such an unerring performer? Intuition again. My hunches — they're intuition, too. Intuition, *hell!* Labels — based on utterly abysmal damned dumb ignorance of our own basic frames of reference. Do you think those four kinds of intuition are alike, by seven thousand rows of apple trees?"

"Of course not. I see what you're getting at. . . . Oh! This'll be fun!"

The others came in and, one by one, Tuly examined each of the four women and the man. Each felt the probing, questioning feelers of her thought prying into the deepest recesses of his mind.

"There is not quite enough of each of three components, all of which are usually associated with the male. You, sir, have much of each, but not enough. I know your men quite well, and I think we will need the doctors Kincaid and Karns and Poynter. But such deep probing is felt. Have I permission, sir?"

"Yes. Tell 'em I said so."

Tuly scanned. "Yes, sir, we should have all three."

"Get 'em, Larry." Then, in the pause that followed: "Sandy, remember yowling about too many sweeties on a team? What do you think of this business of all sweeties?"

"All that proves is that nobody can be wrong all the time," she replied flippantly.

The three men arrived and were instructed. Tuly said: "The great trouble is that each of you must use a portion of your mind that you do not know you have. You, this one. You, that one." Tuly probed mercilessly; so poignantly that each in turn flinched under brand-new and almost unbearable pain. "With you, Doctor Hilton, it will be by far the worst. For you must learn to use almost all the portions of both your minds, the conscious and the unconscious. This must be, because you are the actual peyondixer. The others merely supply energies in which you yourself are deficient. Are you ready for a terrible shock, sir?"

"Shoot."

He thought for a second that he *had* been shot; that his brain had blown up.

He couldn't stand it — he *knew* he was going to die — he wished he *could* die — anything, anything whatever, to end this unbearable agony. . . .

It ended.

Writhing, white and sweating, Hilton opened his eyes. "Ouch," he remarked, conversationally. "What next?"

"You will seize hold of the energies your friends offer. You will bind them to yours and shape the whole into a dimensionless sphere of pure controlled, dirigible energy. And, as well as being the binding force, the cohesiveness, you must also be the captain and the pilot and the astrogator and the ultimately complex computer itself."

"But how can I. . . . Okay, damn it. I *will*!"

"Of course you will, sir. Remember also that once the joinings are made I can be of very little more assistance, for my peyondix is as nothing compared to that of your fusion of eight. Now, to assemble the energies and join them you will, all together, deny the existence of the sum total of reality as you know it. Distance does not exist — every point in the reachable universe coincides with every other point and that common point is the focus of your attention. You can be and actually are anywhere you please or everywhere at once. Time does not exist. Space does not exist. There is no such thing as opacity; everything is perfectly transparent, yet every molecule of substance is perceptible in its relationship to every other molecule in the cosmos. Senses do not exist. Sight, hearing, taste, touch, smell, sathura, endovix — all are parts of the one great sense of peyondix. I am guiding each of you seven — closer! Tighter! There! Seize it, sir — and when you work the Stretts you must fix it clearly that time does not exist. You must work in millionths of microseconds instead of in minutes, for they have minds of tremendous power. Reality does not exist! Compress it more, sir. Tighter! Smaller! Rounder! There! Hold it! Reality does not exist —

distance does not exist — all possible points are. . . . *Wonderful!*"

Tuly screamed the word and the thought: "Good-by! Good luck!"

VIII

HILTON did not have to drive the peyondix-beam to the planet Strett; it was already there. And there was the monstrous First Lord Thinker Zoyar.

Into that mind his multi-mind flashed, its every member as responsive to his will as his own fingers — almost infinitely more so, in fact, because of the tremendous lengths of time required to send messages along nerves.

That horrid mind was scanned cell by cell. Then, after what seemed like a few hours, when a shield began sluggishly to form, Hilton transferred his probe to the mind of the Second Thinker, one Lord Ynos, and absorbed everything she knew. Then, the minds of all the other Thinkers being screened, he studied the whole Strett planet, foot by foot, and everything that was on it.

Then, mission accomplished, Hilton snapped his attention back to his office and the multi-mind fell apart. As he opened his eyes he heard Tuly scream: ". . . Luck!"

"Oh — you still here, Tuly? How long have we been gone?"

"Approximately one and one-tenth seconds, sir."

"What!"

Beverly Bell, in the haven of Franklin Poynter's arms, fainted quietly. Sandra shrieked piercingly. The four men stared, goggle-eyed. Temple and Teddy, as though by common thought, burrowed their faces into brawny shoulders.

Hilton recovered first. "So *that's* what peyondix is."

"Yes, sir — I mean no, sir. No, I mean yes, but . . ." Tuly paused, licking her lips in that peculiarly human-female gesture of uncertainty.

"Well, what *do* you mean? It either is or isn't. Or is that necessarily so?"

"Not exactly, sir. That is, it started as peyondix. But it became something else. Not even the most powerful of the old Masters — nobody — ever did or ever could *possibly* generate such a force as that. Or handle it so fast."

"Well, with seven of the best minds of Terra and a . . ."

"Chip-chop the chit-chat!" Karns said, harshly. "What I want to know is whether I was having a nightmare. Can there *possibly* be a race such as I thought I saw? So utterly savage — ruthless — merciless! So devoid of every human trace and so hell-bent determined on the extermination of every other race in the Galaxy? God damn it, it simply doesn't make sense!"

Eyes went from eyes to eyes to eyes.

All had seen the same indescribably horrible, abysmally atrocious, things. Qualities and quantities and urges and drives that no words in any language could even begin to portray.

"It doesn't seem to, but there it is." Teddy Blake shook her head hopelessly.

Big Bill Karns, hands still shaking, lit a cigarette before he spoke again. "Well, I've never been a proponent of genocide. But it's my considered opinion that the Stretts are one race the galaxy can get along without."

"A hell of a lot better without," Poynter said, and all agreed.

"The point is, what can we do about it?" Kincaid asked. "The first thing, I would say, is to see whether we can do this — whatever it is — without Tuly's help. Shall we try it? Although I, for one, don't feel like doing it right away."

"Not I, either." Beverly Bell held up her right hand, which was shaking uncontrollably. "I feel as though I'd been bucking waves, wind and tide for forty-eight straight hours without food, water or touch. Maybe in about a week I'll be ready for another try at it. But today — not a chance!"

"Okay. Scat, all of you," Hilton ordered. "Take the rest of the day off and rest up. Put on your thought-screens and don't take them off for a second from now on. Those Stretts are tough hombres."

Sandra was the last to leave. "And you, boss?" she asked pointedly.

"I've got some thinking to do."

"I'll stay and help you think?"

"Not yet." He shook his head, frowned and then grinned. "You see, chick, I don't even know yet what it is I'm going to have to think about."

"A bit unclear, but I know what you mean — I think. Luck, chief."

IN their subterranean sanctum turn on distant Strett, two of the deepest thinkers of that horribly unhuman race were in coldly intent conference via thought.

"My mind has been plundered, Ynos," First Lord Thinker Zoyar radiated, harshly. "Despite the extremely high reactivity of my shield some information — I do not know how much — was taken. The operator was one of the humans of that ship."

"I, too, felt a plucking at my mind. But those humans could not peyondire, First Lord."

"Be logical, fool! At that contact, in the matter of which you erred in not following up continuously, they succeeded in concealing their real abilities from you."

"That could be the truth. Our ancestors erred, then, in recording that all those weak and timid humans had been slain. These offenders are probably their descendants, returning to reclaim their former world."

"The probability must be evaluated and considered. Was it or was it not through human aid that the Omans destroyed most of our task-force?"

"Highly probable, but impossible of evaluation with the data now available."

"Obtain more data at once. That point must be and shall be fully evaluated and fully considered. This entire situation is intolerable. It must be abated."

"True, First Lord. But every operator and operation is now tightly screened. Oh, if I could only go out there myself . . ."

"Hold, fool! Your thought is completely disloyal and un-Strettly."

"True, oh First Lord Thinker Zoyar. I will forthwith remove my unworthy self from this plane of existence."

"You will not! I hereby abolish that custom. Our numbers are too few by far. Too many have failed to adapt. Also, as Second Thinker, your death at this time would be slightly detrimental to certain matters now in work. I will myself, however, slay the unfit. To that end repeat The Words under my peyondiring."

"I am a Strett. I will devote my every iota of mental and of physical strength to forwarding the Great Plan. I am, and will remain, a Strett."

"You do believe in The Words."

"Of course I believe in them! I *know* that in a few more hundreds of thousands of years we will be rid of material bodies and will become invincible and invulnerable. Then comes the Conquest of the Galaxy . . . and then the Conquest of the Universe!"

"No more, then, on your life, of this weak and cowardly repining! Now, what of your constructive thinking?"

"Programming must be such as to obviate time-lag. We must evaluate the factors already mentioned and many others, such as the reactivation of the spacecraft which was thought to have been destroyed so long ago. After having considered all these evaluations, I will construct a Minor Plan to destroy these Omans, whom we have permitted to exist on sufferance, and with them that shipload of despicably interloping humans."

"That is well." Zoyar's mind seethed with a malevolent ferocity starkly impossible for any human mind to grasp. "And to that end?"

"To that end we must intensify still more our program of procuring data. We must revise our mechs in the light of our every technological advance during the many thousands of cycles since the last such revision was made. Our every instrument of power, of offense and of defense, must be brought up to the theoretical ultimate of capability."

"And as to the Great Brain?"

"I have been able to think of nothing, First Lord, to add to the undertakings you have already set forth."

"It was not expected that you would. Now: is it your final thought that these interlopers are in fact the descendants of those despised humans of so long ago?"

"It is."

"It is also mine. I return, then, to my work upon the Brain. You will take whatever measures are necessary. Use every artifice of intellect and of ingenuity and our every resource. But abate this intolerable nuisance, and soon."

"It shall be done, First Lord."

THE Second Thinker issued orders. Frenzied, round-the-clock activity ensued. Hundreds of mechs operated upon the brains of hundreds of others, who in turn operated upon the operators.

Then, all those brains charged with the technological advances of many thousands of years, the combined hundreds went unrestingly to work. Thousands of work-mechs were built and put to work at the construction of larger and more powerful space-craft.

As has been implied, those battle-skeletons of the Stretts were controlled by their own built-in mechanical brains, which were programmed for only the simplest of battle maneuvers. Anything at all out of the ordinary had to be handled by remote control, by the specialist-mechs at their two-miles-long control board.

This was now to be changed. Programming was to be made so complete that almost any situation could be handled by the warship or the missile itself — instantly.

The Stretts *knew* that they were the most powerful, the most highly advanced race in the universe. Their science was the highest in the universe. Hence, with every operating unit brought up to the full possibilities of that science, that would be more than enough. Period.

This work, while it required much time, was very much simpler than the task which the First Thinker had laid out for himself on the giant computer-plus which the Stretts called "The Great Brain." In stating his project, First Lord Zoyar had said:

"Assignment: To construct a machine that will have the following abilities: One, to contain and retain all knowledge and information fed into it, however great the amount. Two, to feed itself additional information by peyondiring all planets, wherever situate, bearing intelligent life. Three, to call up instantly any and all items of information pertaining to any problem we may give it. Four, to combine and recombine any number of items required to form new concepts. Five, to formulate theories, test them and draw conclusions helpful to us in any matter in work."

It will have been noticed that these specifications vary in one important respect from those of the Eniacs and Univacs of Earth. Since we of Earth can not peyondire, we do not expect that ability from our computers.

The Stretts could, and did.

WHEN Sandra came back into the office at five o'clock sh found Hilton still sitting there, in almost exactly the same position.

"Come out of it, Jarve!" She snapped a finger. "That much of *that* is just simply too damned much."

"You're so right, child." He got up, stretched, and by

main strength shrugged off his foul mood. "But we're up against something that is really a something, and I don't mean perchance."

"How well I know it." She put an arm around him, gave him a quick, hard hug. "But after all, you don't have to solve it this evening, you know."

"No, thank God."

"So why don't you and Temple have supper with me? Or better yet, why don't all eight of us have supper together in that bachelors' paradise of yours and Bill's?"

"That'd be fun."

And it was.

Nor did it take a week for Beverly Bell to recover from the Ordeal of Eight. On the following evening, she herself suggested that the team should take another shot at that utterly fantastic *terra incognita* of the multiple mind, jolting though it had been.

"But are you sure you can take it again so soon?" Hilton asked.

"Sure. I'm like that famous gangster's moll, you know, who bruised easy but healed quick. And I want to know about it as much as anyone else does."

They could do it this time without any help from Tuly. The linkage fairly snapped together and shrank instantaneously to a point. Hilton thought of Terra and there it was; full size, yet occupying only one infinitesimal section of a dimensionless point. The multi-mind visited relatives of all eight, but could not make intelligible contact. If asleep, it caused pleasant dreams; if awake, pleasant thoughts of the loved one so far away in space; but that was all. It visited mediums, in trance and otherwise — many of whom, not surprisingly now, were genuine — with whom it held lucid conversations. Even in linkage, however, the multi-mind knew that none of the mediums would be believed, even if they all told, simultaneously, exactly the same story. The multi-mind weakened suddenly and Hilton snapped it back to Ardry.

Beverly was almost in collapse. The other girls were white, shaken and trembling. Hilton himself, strong and rugged as he was, felt as though he had done two weeks of hard labor on a rock-pile. He glanced questioningly at Larry.

"Point six three eight seconds, sir," the Omans said, holding up a millisecond timer.

"How do you explain *that*?" Karns demanded.

"I'm afraid it means that without Oman backing we're out of luck."

HILTON had other ideas, but he did not voice any of them until the following day, when he was rested and had Larry alone.

"So carbon-based brains can't take it. One second of that stuff would have killed all eight of us. Why? The Masters had the same kind of brains we have."

"I don't know, sir. It's something completely new. No Master, or group of Masters, ever generated such a force as that. I can scarcely believe such power possible, even though I have felt it twice. It may be that over the generations your individual powers, never united or controlled, have developed so strength that no human can handle them in fusion."

"And none of us ever knew anything about any of them. I've been doing a lot of thinking. The Masters had qualities and abilities now unknown to any of us. How come? You Omans — and the Stretts, too — think we're descendants of the Masters. Maybe we are. You think they came originally from Arth — Earth or Terra — to Ardu. That'd account for our legends of Mu, Atlantis and so on. Since Ardu was within peyondix range of Strett, the Stretts attacked it. They killed all the Masters, they thought, and made the planet uninhabitable for any kind of life, even their own. But one shipload of Masters escaped and came here to Ardry — far beyond peyondix range. They stayed here for a long time. Then, for some reason or other — which may be someplace in their records — they left here, fully intending to come back. Do any of you Omans know why they left? Or where they went?"

"No, sir. We can read only the simplest of the Masters' records. They arranged our brains that way, sir."

"I know. They're the type. However, I suspect now that your thinking is reversed. Let's turn it around. Say the Masters didn't come from Terra, but from some other planet. Say that they left here because they were dying out. They were, weren't they?"

"Yes, sir. Their numbers became fewer and fewer each century."

"I was sure of it. They were committing race suicide by letting you Omans do everything they themselves should have been doing. Finally they saw the truth. In a desperate effort to save their race they pulled out, leaving you here. Probably they intended to come back when they had bred enough guts back into themselves to set you Omans down where you belong. . . ."

"But *they* were always the Masters, sir!"

"They were not! They were hopelessly enslaved. Think it over. Anyway, say they went *to* Terra from here. That still accounts for the legends and so on. However, they were too far gone to make a recovery, and yet they had enough fixity of purpose *not* to manufacture any of you Omans there. So their descendants went a long way down the scale before they began to work back up. Does that make sense to you?"

"It explains many things, sir. It can very well be the truth."

"Okay. However it was, we're here, and facing a condition that isn't funny. While we were teamed up I learned a lot, but not nearly enough. Am I right in thinking that I now don't need the other seven at all — that my cells are fully charged and I can go it alone?"

"Probably, sir, but . . ."

"I'm coming to that. Every time I do it — up to maximum performance, of course — it comes easier and faster and hits harder. So next time, or maybe the fourth or fifth time, it'll kill me. And the other seven, too, if they're along."

"I'm not sure, sir, but I think so."

"Nice. Very, *very* nice." Hilton got up, shoved both hands into his pockets, and prowled about the room. "But can't the damned stuff be controlled? Choked — throttled down — damped — muzzled, some way or other?"

"We do not know of any way, sir. The Masters were always working toward more power, not less."

"That makes sense. The more power the better, as long as you can handle it. But I can't handle this. And neither can the team. So how about organizing another team, one that hasn't got quite so much whammo? Enough punch to do the job, but not enough to backfire that way?"

"It is highly improbable that such a team is possible, sir." If an Oman could be acutely embarrassed, Larry was. "That is, sir . . . I should tell you, sir . . ."

"You certainly should. You've been stalling all along, and now you're stalled. Spill it."

"Yes, sir. The Tuly begged me not to mention it, but I must. When it organized your team it had no idea of what it was really going to do. . . ."

"Let's talk the same language, shall we? Say 'he' and 'she.' Not 'it.'"

"She thought she was setting up the peyondix, the same as all of us Omans have. But after she formed in your mind the peyondix matrix, your mind went on of itself to form a something else; a thing we can not understand. That was why she was so extremely . . . I think 'frightened' might be your term."

"I knew something was biting her. Why?"

"Because it very nearly killed you. You perhaps have not considered the effect upon us all if any Oman, however unintentionally, should kill a Master?"

"No, I hadn't . . . I see. So she won't play with fire any more, and none of the rest of you can?"

"Yes, sir. Nothing could force her to. If she could be so

coerced we would destroy her brain before she could act. That brain, as you know, is imperfect, or she could not have done what she did. It should have been destroyed long since."

"Don't *ever* act on that assumption, Larry." Hilton thought for minutes. "Simple peyondix, such as yours, is not enough to read the Masters' records. If I'd had three brain cells working I'd've tried them then. I wonder if I *could* read them?"

"You have all the old Masters' powers and more. But you must not assemble them again, sir. It would mean death."

"But I've got to *know*. . . . I've *got* to know! Anyway, a thousandth of a second would be enough. I don't think that'd hurt me very much."

HE concentrated — read a few feet of top-secret braided wire — and came back to consciousness in the sickbay of the *Perseus*, with two doctors working on him; Hastings, the Navy medico, and Flandres, the surgeon.

"What the hell happened to you?" Flandres demanded. "Were you trying to kill yourself?"

"And if so, how?" Hastings wanted to know.

"No, I was trying not to," Hilton said, weakly, "and I guess I didn't much more than succeed."

"That was just about the closest shave I ever saw a man come through. Whatever it was, don't do it again."

"I won't," he promised, feelingly.

When they let him out of the hospital, four days later, he called in Larry and Tuly.

"The next time would be the last time. So there won't be any," he told them. "But just how sure are you that some other of our boys or girls may not have just enough of whatever it takes to do the job? Enough oompa, but not too much?"

"Since we, too, are on strange ground the probability is vanishingly small. We have been making inquiries, however, and scanning. You were selected from all the minds of Terra as the one having the widest vision, the greatest scope, the most comprehensive grasp. The ablest at synthesis and correlation and so on."

"That's printing it in big letters, but that was more or less what they were after."

"Hence the probability approaches unity that any more such ignorant meddling as this obnoxious Tuly did well result almost certainly in failure and death. Therefore we can not and will not meddle again."

"You've got a point there. . . . So what I am is some kind of a freak. Maybe a kind of super-Master and maybe something altogether different. Maybe duplicable in a less lethal fashion, and maybe not. Veree helpful — I don't think. But I don't want to kill anybody, either . . . especially if it wouldn't do any good. But we've got to do *something*!" Hilton scowled in thought for minutes. "But an Oman brain could take it. As you told us, Tuly, 'The brain of the Larry is very, very tough.'"

"In a way, sir. Except that the Masters were very careful to make it physically impossible for any Oman to go very far along that line. It was only their oversight of my one imperfect brain that enabled me, alone of us all, to do that wrong."

"Stop thinking it was wrong, Tuly. I'm mighty glad you did. But I wasn't thinking of any regular Oman brain. . . ." Hilton's voice petered out.

"I see, sir. Yes, we can, by using your brain as Guide, reproduce it in an Oman body. You would then have the powers and most of the qualities of both . . ."

"No, you don't see, because I've got my screen on. Which I will now take off —" he suited action to word — "since the whole planet's screened and I have nothing to hide from you. Teddy Blake and I both thought of that, but we'll consider it only as the ultimately last resort. We don't want to live a million years. And we want our race to keep on developing. But you folks can replace carbon-based molecules with silicon-based ones just as easily as, and a hell of a lot faster than, mineral water petrifies wood. What can you do along the line of rebuilding me that way? And if you can do any such conversion, what would happen? Would I live at all? And if so, how long? How would I live? What would I live on? All that kind of stuff."

"Shortly before they left, two of the Masters did some work on that very thing. Tuly and I converted them, sir."

"Fine — or is it? How did it work out?"

"Perfectly, sir . . . except that they destroyed themselves. It was thought that they wearied of existence."

"I don't wonder. Well, if it comes to that, I can do the same. You *can* convert me, then."

"Yes, sir. But before we do it we must do enough preliminary work to be sure that you will not be harmed in any way. Also, there will be many more changes involved than simple substitution."

"Of course. I realize that. Just see what you can do, please, and let me know."

"We will, sir, and thank you very much."

IX

AS has been intimated, no Terran can know what researches Larry and Tuly and the other Oman specialists performed, or how they arrived at the conclusions they reached. However, in less than a week Larry reported to Hilton.

"It can be done, sir, with complete safety. And you will live even more comfortably than you do now."

"How long?"

"The mean will be about five thousand Oman years — you don't know that an Oman year is equal to one point two nine three plus Terran years?"

"I didn't, no. Thanks."

"The maximum, a little less than six thousand. The minimum, a little over four thousand. I'm very sorry we had no data upon which to base a closer estimate."

"Close enough." He stared at the Oman. "You could also convert my wife?"

"Of course, sir."

"Well, we might be able to stand it, after we got used to the idea. Minimum, over five thousand Terran years . . . barring accidents, of course?"

"No, sir. No accidents. Nothing will be able to kill you, except by total destruction of the brain. And even then, sir, there will be the pattern."

"I'll . . . be . . . damned. . . ." Hilton gulped twice. "Okay, go ahead."

"Your skins will be like ours, energy-absorbers. Your 'blood' will carry charges of energy instead of oxygen. Thus, you may breathe or not, as you please. Unless you wish otherwise, we will continue the breathing function. It would scarcely be worth while to alter the automatic mechanisms that now control it. And you will wish at times to speak. You will still enjoy eating and drinking, although everything ingested will be eliminated, as at present, as waste."

"We'd add uranexite to our food, I suppose. Or drink radioactives, or sleep under cobalt-60 lamps."

"Yes, sir. Your family life will be normal; your sexual urges and satisfactions the same. Fertilization and period of gestation unchanged. Your children will mature at the same ages as they do now."

"How do you — oh, I see. You wouldn't change any molecular linkages or configurations in the genes or chromosomes."

"We could not, sir, even if we wished. Such substitutions can be made only in exact one-for-one replacements. In the near future you will, of course, have to control births quite rigorously."

"We sure would. Let's see . . . say we want a stationary population of a hundred million on our planet. Each couple to have two children, a boy and a girl. Born when the parents are about fifty . . . um-m-m. The gals can have all the children they want, then, until our population is about a million; then slap on the limit of two kids per couple. Right?"

"Approximately so, sir. And after conversion you alone will be able to operate with the full power of your eight, without tiring. You will also, of course, be able to absorb almost instantaneously all the knowledges and abilities of the old Masters."

Hilton gulped twice before he could speak. "You wouldn't be holding anything else back, would you?"

"Nothing important, sir. Everything else is minor, and probably known to you."

"I doubt it. How long will the job take, and how much notice will you need?"

"Two days, sir. No notice. Everything is ready."

Hilton, face somber, thought for minutes. "The more I think of it the less I like it. But it seems to be a forced put . . . and Temple will blow sky high . . . and *have* I got the guts to go it alone, even if she'd let me. . . ." He shrugged himself out of the black mood. "I'll look her up and let you know, Larry."

HE looked her up and told her everything. Told her bluntly; starkly; drawing the full picture in jet black, with very little white.

"There it is, sweetheart. The works," he concluded. "We are not going to have ten years; we may not have ten months. So — if such a brain as that can be had, do we or do we not have to have it? I'm putting it squarely up to you."

Temple's face, which had been getting paler and paler, was now as nearly colorless as it could become; the sickly yellow of her skin's light tan unbacked by any flush of red blood.

Her whole body was tense and strained.

"There's a horrible snapper on that question. . . . Can't *I* do it? Or *anybody* else except you?"

"No. Anyway, whose job is it, sweetheart?"

"I know, but . . . but I know just how close Tuly came to killing you. And that wasn't *anything* compared to such a radical transformation as this. I'm afraid it'll kill you, darling. And I just simply couldn't *stand* it!"

She threw herself into his arms, and he comforted her in the ages-old fashion of man with maid.

"Steady, hon," he said, as soon as he could lift her tear-streaked face from his shoulder. "I'll live through it. I thought you were getting the howling howpers about having to live for six thousand years and never getting back to Terra except for a Q strictly T visit now and then."

She pulled away from him, flung back her wheaten mop and glared. "So *that's* what you thought! What do I care how long I live, or how, or where, as long as it's with you? But what makes you think we can possibly live through such a horrible conversion as that?"

"Larry wouldn't do it if there was any question whatever. He didn't say it would be painless. But he did say I'd live."

"Well, he knows, I guess . . . I hope." Temple's natural fine color began to come back. "But it's understood that just the second you come out of the vat, I go right in."

"I hadn't ought to let you, of course. But I don't think I could take it alone."

That statement required a special type of conference, which consumed some little time. Eventually, however, Temple answered it in words.

"Of course you couldn't, sweetheart, and I wouldn't let you, even if you could."

There were a few things that had to be done before those two secret conversions could be made. There was the matter of the wedding, which was now to be in quadruplicate. Arrangements had to be made so that eight Big Wheels of the Project could all be away on honeymoon at once.

All these things were done.

OF the conversion operations themselves, nothing more need be said. The honeymooners, having left ship and town on a Friday afternoon, came back one week from the following Monday morning. The eight met joyously in Bachelors' Hall; the girls kissing each other and the men indiscriminately and enthusiastically; the men cooperating zestfully.

Temple scarcely blushed at all, she was so engrossed in trying to find out whether or not anyone was noticing any change. No one seemed to notice anything out of the ordinary. So, finally, she asked.

"Don't *any* of you, really, see anything different?"

The six others all howled at that, and Sandra, between giggles and snorts, said: "No, precious, it doesn't show a bit. Did you really think it would?"

Temple blushed furiously and Hilton came instantly to his bride's rescue. "Chip-chop the comedy, gang. She and I aren't human any more. We're a good jump toward being Omans. I couldn't make her believe it doesn't show."

That stopped the levity, cold, but none of the six could really believe it. However, after Hilton had coiled a twenty-penny spike into a perfect helix between his fingers, and especially after he and Temple had each chewed up and swallowed a piece of uranexite, there were no grounds left for doubt.

"That settles it . . . it *tears* it," Karns said then. "Start all over again, Jarve. We'll listen, this time."

Hilton told the long story again, and added: "I had to re-work a couple of cells of Temple's brain, but now she can read and understand the records as well as I can. So I thought I'd take her place on Team One and let her boss the job on all the other teams. Okay?"

"So you don't want to let the rest of us in on it." Karns's level stare was a far cry from the way he had looked at his chief a moment before. "If there's any one thing in the universe I never had *you* figured for, it's a dog in the manger."

"Huh? You mean you actually *want* to be a . . . a . . . hell, we don't even know *what* we are!"

"I do want it, Jarvis. We all do." This was, of all people, Teddy! "No one in all history has had more than about fifty years of really productive thinking. And just the idea of having enough time . . ."

"Hold it, Teddy. Use your brain. The Masters couldn't take it — they committed suicide. How do you figure we can do any better?"

"Because we'll *use* our brains!" she snapped. "They didn't. The Omans will serve us; and that's *all* they'll do."

"And do you think you'll be able to raise your children and grandchildren and so on to do the same? To have guts enough to resist the pull of such an ungodly habit-forming drug as this Oman service is?"

"I'm sure of it." She nodded positively. "And we'll run all applicants through a fine enough screen to — that is, if we ever consider anybody except our own BuSci people. And there's another reason." She grinned, got up, wriggled out of her coverall, and posed in bra and panties. "Look. I can keep most of this for five years. Quite a lot of it for ten. Then comes the struggle. What do *you* think I'd do for the ability, whenever it begins to get wrinkly or flabby, to peel the whole thing off and put on a brand-spanking-new smooth one? You name it, I'll do it! Besides, Bill and I will *both* just simply and cold-bloodedly murder you if you try to keep us out."

"Okay." Hilton looked at Temple; she looked at him; both looked at all the others. There was no revulsion at all. Nothing but eagerness.

Temple took over.

"I'm surprised. We're both surprised. You see, Jarve didn't want to do it at all, but he had to. I not only didn't want to, I was scared green and yellow at just the idea of it. But I had to, too, of course. We didn't think anybody would really want to. We thought we'd be left here alone. We still will be, I think, when you've thought it clear through, Teddy. You just haven't realized yet that we aren't even human any more. We're simply nothing but *monsters*!" Temple's voice became a wail.

"I've said my piece," Teddy said. "You tell 'em, Bill."

"Let me say something first," Kincaid said. "Temple, I'm

ashamed of you. This line isn't at all your usual straight thinking. What you actually are is *homo superior*. Bill?"

"I can add one bit to that. I don't wonder that you were scared silly, Temple. Utterly new concept and you went into it stone cold. But now we see the finished product and we like it. In fact, we drool."

"I'll say we're drooling," Sandra said. "I could do handstands and pinwheels with joy."

"Let's see you," Hilton said. "That we'd all get a kick out of."

"Not now — don't want to hold this up — but sometime I just will. Bev?"

"I'm for it — and *how*! And won't Bernadine be amazed," Beverly laughed gleefully, "at her wisecrack about the 'race to end all human races' coming true?"

"I'm in favor of it, too, one hundred per cent," Poynter said. "Has it occurred to you, Jarve, that this opens up intergalactic exploration? No supplies to carry and plenty of time and fuel?"

"No, it hadn't. You've got a point there, Frank. That might take a little of the curse off of it, at that."

"When some of our kids get to be twenty years old or so and get married, I'm going to take a crew of them to Andromeda. We'll arrange, then, to extend our honeymoons another week," Hilton said. "What will our policy be? Keep it dark for a while with just us eight, or spread it to the rest?"

"Spread it, I'd say," Kincaid said.

"We can't keep it secret, anyway," Teddy argued. "Since Larry and Tuly were in on the whole deal, every Oman on the planet knows all about it. Somebody is going to ask questions, and Omans always answer questions and always tell the truth."

"Questions have already been asked and answered," Larry said, going to the door and opening it.

Stella rushed in. "We've been hearing the *damnedest* things!" She kissed everybody, ending with Hilton, whom she seized by both shoulders. "Is it actually true, boss, that you can fix me up so I'll live practically forever and can eat more than eleven calories a day without getting fat as a pig? Candy, ice cream, cake, pie, eclairs, cream puffs, French pastries, sugar and gobs of thick cream in my coffee . . . ?"

Half a dozen others, including the van der Moen twins, came in. Beverly emitted a shriek of joy. "Bernadine! The mother of the race to end all human races!"

"You whistled it, birdie!" Bernadine caroled. "I'm going to have ten or twelve, each one weirder than all the others. I told you I was a prophet — I'm going to hang out my shingle. Wholesale and retail prophecy; special rates for large parties." Her voice was drowned out in a general clamor.

"Hold it, everybody!" Hilton yelled. "Chip-chop it! *Quit* it!" Then, as the noise subsided, "If you think I'm going to tell this tall tale over and over again for the next two weeks you're all crazy. So shut down the plant and get everybody out here."

"Not *everybody*, Jarve!" Temple snapped. "We don't want scum, and there's some of that, even in BuSci."

"You're so right. Who, then?"

"The rest of the heads and assistants, of course . . . and all the lab girls and their husbands and boy-friends. I know they are all okay. That will be enough for now, don't you think?"

"I do think;" and the indicated others were sent for; and in a few minutes arrived.

The Omans brought chairs and Hilton stood on a table. He spoke for ten minutes. Then: "Before you decide whether you want to or not, think it over very carefully, because it's a one-way street. Fluorine can not be displaced. Once in, you're stuck for life. *There is no way back.* I've told you all the drawbacks and disadvantages I know of, but there may be a lot more that I haven't thought of yet. So think it over for a few days and when each of you has definitely made up his or her mind, let me know." He jumped down off the table.

*   *   *

HIS listeners, however, did not need days, or even seconds, to decide. Before Hilton's feet hit the floor there was a yell of unanimous approval.

He looked at his wife. "Do you suppose *we're* nuts?"

"Uh-uh. Not a bit. Alex was right. I'm going to just *love* it!" She hugged his elbow ecstatically. "So are you, darling, as soon as you stop looking at only the black side."

"You know . . . you could be right?" For the first time since the "ghastly" transformation Hilton saw that there really was a bright side and began to study it. "With most of BuSci — and part of the Navy, and selectees from Terra — it *will* be slightly terrific, at that!"

"And that 'habit-forming-drug' objection isn't insuperable, darling," Temple said. "If the younger generations start weakening we'll fix the Omans. I wouldn't want to wipe them out entirely, but . . ."

"But how do we settle priority, Doctor Hilton?" a girl called out; a tall, striking, brunette laboratory technician whose name Hilton needed a second to recall. "By pulling straws or hair? Or by shooting dice or each other or what?"

"Thanks, Betty, you've got a point. Sandy Cummings and department heads first, then assistants. Then you girls, in alphabetical order, each with her own husband or fiance."

"And my name is Ames. Oh, goody!"

"Larry, please tell them to . . ."

"I already have, sir. We are set up to handle four at once."

"Good boy. So scat, all of you, and get back to work — except Sandy, Bill, Alex, and Teddy. You four go with Larry."

Since the new sense was not peyondix, Hilton had started calling it "perception" and the others adopted the term as a matter of course. Hilton could use that sense for what seemed like years — and actually was whole minutes — at a time without fatigue or strain. He could not, however, nor could the Omans, give his tremendous power to anyone else.

As he had said, he could do a certain amount of re-working; but the amount of improvement possible to make depended entirely upon what there was to work on. Thus, Temple could cover about six hundred light-years. It developed later that the others of the Big Eight could cover from one hundred up to four hundred or so. The other department heads and assistants turned out to be still weaker, and not one of the rank and file ever became able to cover more than a single planet.

This sense was not exactly telepathy; at least not what Hilton had always thought telepathy would be. If anything, however, it was more. It was a lumping together of all five known human senses — and half a dozen unknown ones called, collectively, "intuition" — into one super-sense that was all-inclusive and all-informative. If he ever could learn exactly what it was and exactly what it did and how it did it . . . but he'd better chip-chop the wool-gathering and get back onto the job.

THE Stretts had licked the old Masters very easily, and intended to wipe out the Omans and the humans. They had no doubt at all as to their ability to do it. Maybe they could. If the Masters hadn't made some progress that the Omans didn't know about, they probably could. That was the first thing to find out. As soon as they'd been converted he'd call in all the experts and they'd go through the Masters' records like a dose of salts through a hillbilly schoolma'am.

At that point in Hilton's cogitations Sawtelle came in.

He had come down in his gig, to confer with Hilton as to the newly beefed-up fleet. Instead of being glum and pessimistic and foreboding, he was chipper and enthusiastic. They had rebuilt a thousand Oman ships. By combining Oman and Terran science, and adding everything the First Team had been able to reduce to practise, they had hyped up the power by a good fifteen per cent. Seven hundred of those ships, and all his men, were now arrayed in defense around Ardry. Three hundred, manned by Omans, were around Fuel Bin.

"Why?" Hilton asked. "It's Fuel Bin they've been attacking."

"Uh-uh. Minor objective," the captain demurred, positively. "The real attack will be here at you; the headquarters and the brains. Then Fuel Bin will be duck soup. But the thing that pleased me most is the control. Man, you never imagined such control! No admiral in history ever had such control of ten ships as I have of seven hundred. Those Omans spread orders so fast that I don't even finish thinking one and it's being executed. And no misunderstandings, no slips. For instance, this last batch — fifteen skeletons. Far out; they're getting cagy. I just thought 'Box 'em in and slug 'em' and — In! Across! Out! Socko! *Pffft!* Just like that and just that fast. None of 'em had time to light a beam. Nobody before ever even *dreamed* of such control!"

"That's great, and I like it . . . and you're only a captain. How many ships can Five-Jet Admiral Gordon put into space?"

"That depends on what you call ships. Superdreadnoughts, *Perseus* class, six. First-line battleships, twenty-nine. Second-line, smaller and some pretty old, seventy-three. Counting everything armed that will hold air, something over two hundred."

"I thought it was something like that. How would you like to be Five-Jet Admiral Sawtelle of the Ardrian Navy?"

"I wouldn't. I'm Terran Navy. But you knew that and you know me. So — what's on your mind?"

HILTON told him. I ought to put this on a tape, he thought to himself, and broadcast it every hour on the hour.

"They took the old Masters like dynamiting fish in a barrel," he concluded, "and I'm damned afraid they're going to lick us unless we take a lot of big, fast steps. But the hell of it is that I can't tell you anything — not one single thing — about any part of it. There's simply no way at all of getting through to you without making you over into the same kind of a thing I am."

"Is that bad?" Sawtelle was used to making important decisions fast. "Let's get at it."

"Huh? Skipper, do you realize just what that means? If you think they'll let you resign, forget it. They'll crucify you — brand you as a traitor and God only knows what else."

"Right. How about you and your people?"

"Well, as civilians, it won't be as bad. . . ."

"The hell it won't. Every man and woman that stays here will be posted forever as the blackest traitors old Terra ever disgraced herself by spawning."

"You've got a point there, at that. We'll all have to bring our relatives — the ones we think much of, at least — out here with us."

"Definitely. Now see what you can do about getting me run through your mill."

By exerting his authority, Hilton got Sawtelle put through the "Preservatory" in the second batch processed. Then, linking minds with the captain, he flashed their joint attention to the Hall of Records. Into the right room; into the right chest; along miles and miles of braided wire carrying some of the profoundest military secrets of the ancient Masters.

Then:

"Now you know a little of it," Hilton said. "Maybe a thousandth of what we'll have to have before we can take the Stretts as they will have to be taken."

For seconds Sawtelle could not speak. Then: "My . . . God. I see what you mean. You're right. No Omans can ever go to Terra; and no Terrans can ever come here except to stay forever."

The two then went out into space, to the flagship — which had been christened the *Orion* — and called in the six commanders.

"What *is* all this senseless idiocy we've been getting, Jarve?" Elliott demanded.

Hilton eyed all six with pretended disfavor. "You six guys are the hardest-headed bunch of skeptics that ever went unhung," he remarked, dispassionately. "So it wouldn't do any good to tell you anything — yet. The skipper and I will show you a thing first. Take her away, Skip."

The *Orion* shot away under interplanetary drive and for several hours Hilton and Sawtelle worked at re-wiring and practically rebuilding two devices that no one, Oman or human, had touched since the *Perseus* had landed on Ardry.

"What are you . . . I don't understand what you are doing, sir," Larry said. For the first time since Hilton had known him, the Oman's mind was confused and unsure.

"I know you don't. This is a bit of top-secret Masters' stuff. Maybe, some day, we'll be able to re-work your brain to take it. But it won't be for some time."

X

THE *Orion* hung in space, a couple of thousands of miles away from an asteroid which was perhaps a mile in average diameter. Hilton straightened up.

"Put Triple X Black filters on your plates and watch that asteroid." The commanders did so. "Ready?" he asked.

"Ready, sir."

Hilton didn't move a muscle. Nothing actually moved. Nevertheless there was a motionlessly writhing and crawling distortion of the ship and everything in it, accompanied by a sensation that simply can not be described.

It was not like going into or emerging from the sub-ether. It was not even remotely like space-sickness or sea-sickness or free fall or anything else that any Terran had ever before experienced.

And the asteroid vanished.

It disappeared into an outrageously incandescent, furiously pyrotechnic, raveningly expanding atomic fireball that in seconds seemed to fill half of space.

After ages-long minutes of the most horrifyingly devastating fury any man there had ever seen, the frightful thing expired and Hilton said: "*That* was just a kind of a firecracker. Just a feeble imitation of the first-stage detonator for what we'll have to have to crack the Stretts' ground-based screens. If the skipper and I had taken time to take the ship down to the shops and really work it over we could have put on a show. Was this enough so you iron-heads are ready to listen with your ears open and your mouths shut?"

They were. So much so that not even Elliott opened his mouth to say yes. They merely nodded. Then again — for the last time, he hoped! — Hilton spoke his piece. The response was prompt and vigorous. Only Sam Bryant, one of Hilton's staunchest allies, showed any uncertainty at all.

"I've been married only a year and a half, and the baby was due about a month ago. How sure are you that you can make old Gordon sit still for us skimming the cream off of Terra to bring out here?"

"Doris Bryant, the cream of Terra!" Elliott gibed. "*How* modest our Samuel has become!"

"Well, damn it, she is!" Bryant insisted.

"Okay, she is," Hilton agreed. "But either we get our people or Terra doesn't get its uranexite. That'll work. In the remote contingency that it doesn't, there are still tighter screws we can put on. But you missed the main snapper, Sam. Suppose Doris doesn't want to live for five thousand years and is allergic to becoming a monster?"

"Huh; you don't need to worry about that." Sam brushed that argument aside with a wave of his hand. "Show me a girl who doesn't want to stay young and beautiful forever and I'll square you the circle. Come on. What's holding us up?"

THE *Orion* hurtled through space back toward Ardry and Hilton, struck by a sudden thought, turned to the captain.

"Skipper, why wouldn't it be a smart idea to clamp a blockade onto Fuel Bin? Cut the Stretts' fuel supply?"

"I thought better of you than that, son." Sawtelle shook his head sadly. "That was the first thing I did."

"Ouch. Maybe you're 'way ahead of me too, then, on the one that we should move to Fuel Bin, lock, stock and barrel?"

"Never thought of it, no. Maybe you're worth saving, after all. After conversion, of course. . . . Yes, there'd be three big advantages."

"Four."

Sawtelle raised his eyebrows.

"One, only one planet to defend. Two, it's self-defending against sneak landings. Nothing remotely human can land on it except in heavy lead armor, and even in that can stay healthy for only a few minutes."

"Except in the city. Omlu. That's the weak point and would be the point of attack."

"Uh-uh. Cut off the decontaminators and in five hours it'll be as hot as the rest of the planet. Three, there'd be no interstellar supply line for the Stretts to cut. Four, the environment matches our new physiques a lot better than any normal planet could."

"That's the one I didn't think about."

"I think I'll take a quick peek at the Stretts — oh-oh; they've screened their whole planet. Well, we can do that, too, of course."

"How are you going to select and reject personnel? It looks as though everybody wants to stay. Even the men whose main object in life is to go aground and get drunk. The Omans do altogether too good a job on them and there's no such thing as a hangover. I'm glad I'm not in your boots."

"You may be in it up to the eyeballs, Skipper, so don't chortle too soon."

Hilton had already devoted much time to the problems of selection; and he thought of little else all the way back to Ardry. And for several days afterward he held conferences with small groups and conducted certain investigations.

*　　　*　　　*

BUD Carroll of Sociology and his assistant Sylvia Banister had been married for weeks. Hilton called them, together with Sawtelle and Bryant of Navy, into conference with the Big Eight.

"The more I study this thing the less I like it," Hilton said. "With a civilization having no government, no police, no laws, no medium of exchange . . ."

"No *money*?" Bryant exclaimed. "How's old Gordon going to pay for his uranexite, then?"

"He gets it free," Hilton replied, flatly. "When anyone can have anything he wants, merely by wanting it, what good is money? Now, remembering how long we're going to have to live, what we'll be up against, that the Masters failed, and so on, it is clear that the prime basic we have to select for is stability. We twelve have, by psychodynamic measurement, the highest stability ratings available."

"Are you sure *I* belong here?" Bryant asked.

"Yes. Here are three lists." Hilton passed papers around. "The list labeled 'OK' names those I'm sure of — the ones we're converting now and their wives and whatever on Terra. List 'NG' names the ones I know we don't want. List 'X' — over thirty percent — are in-betweeners. We have to make a decision on the 'X' list. So — what I want to know is, who's going to play God. I'm not. Sandy, are you?"

"Good Heavens, no!" Sandra shuddered. "But I'm afraid I know who will have to. I'm sorry, Alex, but it'll have to be you four — Psychology and Sociology."

Six heads nodded and there was a flashing interchange of thought among the four. Temple licked her lips and nodded, and Kincaid spoke.

"Yes, I'm afraid it's our baby. By leaning very heavily on Temple, we can do it. Remember, Jarve, what you said about the irresistible force? We'll need it."

"As I said once before, Mrs. Hilton, I'm very glad you're along," Hilton said. "But just how sure are you that even you can stand up under the load?"

"Alone, I couldn't. But don't underestimate Mrs. Carroll

and the Messrs. Together, and with such a goal, I'm sure we can."

THUS, after four-fifths of his own group and forty-one Navy men had been converted, Hilton called an evening meeting of all the converts. Larry, Tuly and Javvy were the only Omans present.

"You all knew, of course, that we were going to move to Fuel Bin sometime," Hilton began. "I can tell you now that we who are here are all there are going to be of us. We are all leaving for Fuel Bin immediately after this meeting. Everything of any importance, including all of your personal effects, has already been moved. All Omans except these three, and all Oman ships except the *Orion*, have already gone."

He paused to let the news sink in.

Thoughts flew everywhere. The irrepressible Stella Wing — *now* Mrs. Osbert F. Harkins — was the first to give tongue. "What a *wonderful* job! Why, everybody's here that I really like at all!"

That sentiment was, of course, unanimous. It could not have been otherwise. Betty, the ex-Ames, called out:

"How did you get their female Omans away from Cecil Calthorpe and the rest of that chasing, booze-fighting bunch without them blowing the whole show?"

"Some suasion was necessary," Hilton admitted, with a grin. "Everyone who isn't here is time-locked into the *Perseus*. Release time eight hours tomorrow."

"And they'll wake up tomorrow morning with no Omans?" Bernadine tossed back her silvery mane and laughed. "Nor anything else except the *Perseus*? In a way, I'm sorry, but . . . maybe I've got too much stinker blood in me, but I'm very glad none of them are here. But I'd like to ask, Jarvis — or rather, I suppose you have already set up a new Advisory Board?"

"We have, yes." Hilton read off twelve names.

"Oh, nice. I don't know of any people I'd rather have on

it. But what I want to gripe about is calling our new home world such a horrible name as 'Fuel Bin,' as though it were a wood-box or a coal-scuttle or something. And just think of the complexes it would set up in those super-children we're going to have so many of."

"What would you suggest?" Hilton asked.

"'Ardvor', of course," Hermione said, before her sister could answer. "We've had 'Arth' and 'Ardu' and 'Ardry' and you — or somebody — started calling us 'Ardans' to distinguish us converts from the Terrans. So let's keep up the same line."

There was general laughter at that, but the name was approved.

ABOUT midnight the meeting ended and the *Orion* set out for Ardvor. It reached it and slanted sharply downward. The whole BuSci staff was in the lounge, watching the big tri-di.

"Hey! That isn't Omlu!" Stella exclaimed. "It isn't a city at all and it isn't even in the same place!"

"No, ma'am," Larry said. "Most of you wanted the ocean, but many wanted a river or the mountains. Therefore we razed Omlu and built your new city, Ardane, at a place where the ocean, two rivers, and a range of mountains meet. Strictly speaking, it is not a city, but a place of pleasant and rewardful living."

The space-ship was coming in, low and fast, from the south. To the left, the west, there stretched the limitless expanse of ocean. To the right, mile after mile, were rough, rugged, jagged, partially-timbered mountains, mass piled upon mass. Immediately below the speeding vessel was a wide, white-sand beach all of ten miles long.

Slowing rapidly now, the *Orion* flew along due north.

"Look! Look! A natatorium!" Beverly shrieked. "I know I wanted a nice big place to swim in, besides my backyard pool and the ocean, but I didn't tell anybody to build *that* — I swear I didn't!"

"You didn't have to, pet." Poynter put his arm around her

curvaceous waist and squeezed. "They knew. And I did a little thinking along that line myself. There's our house, on top of the cliff over the natatorium — you can almost dive into it off the patio."

"Oh, wonderful!"

Immediately north of the natatorium a tremendous river — named at first sight the "Whitewater" — rushed through its gorge into the ocean; a river and gorge strangely reminiscent of the Colorado and its Grand Canyon. On the south bank of that river, at its very mouth — looking straight up that tremendous canyon; on a rocky promontory commanding ocean and beach and mountains — there was a house. At the sight of it Temple hugged Hilton's arm in ecstasy.

"Yes, that's ours," he assured her. "Just about everything either of us has ever wanted." The clamor was now so great — everyone was recognizing his-and-her house and was exclaiming about it — that both Temple and Hilton fell silent and simply watched the scenery unroll.

Across the turbulent Whitewater and a mile farther north, the mountains ended as abruptly as though they had been cut off with a cleaver and an apparently limitless expanse of treeless, grassy prairie began. And through that prairie, meandering sluggishly to the ocean from the northeast, came the wide, deep River Placid.

The *Orion* halted. It began to descend vertically, and only then did Hilton see the spaceport. It was so vast, and there were so many spaceships on it, that from any great distance it was actually invisible! Each six-acre bit of the whole immense expanse of level prairie between the Placid and the mountains held an Oman superdreadnought!

THE staff paired off and headed for the airlocks. Hilton said: "Temple, have you any reservations at all, however slight, as to having Dark Lady as a permanent fixture in your home?"

"Why, of course not — I like her as much as you do. And besides —" she giggled like a schoolgirl — "even if she *is* a lot more beautiful than I am — I've got a few things she never will have . . . but there's something else. I got just a flash of it before you blocked. Spill it, please."

"You'll see in a minute." And she did.

Larry, Dark Lady and Temple's Oman maid Moty were standing beside the Hilton's car — and so was another Oman, like none ever before seen. Six feet four; shoulders that would just barely go through a door; muscled like Atlas and Hercules combined; skin a gleaming, satiny bronze; hair a rippling mass of lambent flame. Temple came to a full stop and caught her breath.

"The Prince," she breathed, in awe. "Da Lormi's Prince of Thebes. The ultimate bronze of all the ages. *You* did this, Jarve. How did you ever dig him up out of my schoolgirl crushes?"

All six got into the car, which was equally at home on land or water or in the air. In less than a minute they were at Hilton House.

The house itself was circular. Its living-room was an immense annulus of glass from which, by merely moving along its circular length, any desired view could be had. The pair walked around it once. Then she took him by the arm and steered him firmly toward one of the bedrooms in the center.

"This house is just too much to take in all at once," she declared. "Besides, let's put on our swimsuits and get over to the Nat."

In the room, she closed the door firmly in the faces of the Omans and grinned. "Maybe, sometime, I'll get used to having somebody besides you in my bedroom, but I haven't, yet. . . . Oh, do you itch, too?"

Hilton had peeled to the waist and was scratching vigorously all around his waistline, under his belt. "Like the very devil," he admitted, and stared at her. For she, three-quarters stripped, was scratching, too!

"It started the minute we left the *Orion*," he said, thoughtfully. "I see. These new skins of ours like hard radiation, but don't like to be smothered while they're enjoying it. By about tomorrow, we'll be a nudist colony, I think."

"I could stand it, I suppose. What makes you think so?"

"Just what I know about radiation. Frank would be the one to ask. My hunch is, though, that we're going to be nudists whether we want to or not. Let's go."

THEY went in a two-seater, leaving the Omans at home. Three-quarters of the staff were lolling on the sand or were seated on benches beside the immense pool. As they watched, Beverly ran out along the line of springboards; testing each one and selecting the stiffest. She then climbed up to the top platform — a good twelve feet above the board — and plummeted down upon the board's heavily padded take-off. Legs and back bending stubbornly to take the strain, she and the board reached low-point together, and, still in sync with it, she put every muscle she had into the effort to hurl herself upward.

She had intended to go up thirty feet. But she had no idea whatever as to her present strength, or of what that Oman board, in perfect synchronization with that tremendous strength, would do. Thus, instead of thirty feet, she went up very nearly two hundred; which of course spoiled completely her proposed graceful two-and-a-half.

In midair she struggled madly to get into some acceptable position. Failing, she curled up into a tight ball just before she struck water.

What a splash!

"It won't hurt her — you couldn't hurt her with a club!" Hilton snapped. He seized Temple's hand as everyone else rushed to the pool's edge. "Look — Bernadine — that's what I was thinking about."

Temple stopped and looked. The platinum-haired twins had been basking on the sand, and wherever sand had touched fabric, fabric had disappeared.

Their suits had of course approached the minimum to start with. Now Bernadine wore only a wisp of nylon perched precariously on one breast and part of a ribbon that had once been a belt. Discovering the catastrophe, she shrieked once and leaped into the pool any-which-way, covering her breasts with her hands and hiding in water up to her neck.

Meanwhile, the involuntarily high diver had come to the surface, laughing apologetically. Surprised by the hair dangling down over her eyes, she felt for her cap. It was gone. So was her suit. Naked as a fish. She swam a couple of easy strokes, then stopped.

"Frank! Oh, Frank!" she called.

"Over here, Bev." Her husband did not quite know whether to laugh or not.

"Is it the radiation or the water? Or both?"

"Radiation, I think. These new skins of ours don't want to be covered up. But it probably makes the water a pretty good imitation of a universal solvent."

"Good-by, clothes!" Beverly rolled over onto her back, fanned water carefully with her hands, and gazed approvingly at herself. "I don't itch any more, anyway, so I'm very much in favor of it."

THUS the Ardans came to their new home world and to a life that was to be more comfortable by far and happier by far than any of them had known on Earth. There were many other surprises that day, of course; of which only two will be mentioned here. When they finally left the pool, at about seventeen hours G.M.T., everybody was ravenously hungry.

"But why *should* we be?" Stella demanded. "I've been eating everything in sight, just for fun. But now I'm actually hungry enough to eat a horse and wagon and chase the driver!"

"Swimming makes everybody hungry," Beverly said, "and I'm awfully glad *that* hasn't changed. Why, I wouldn't feel *human* if I didn't!"

Hilton and Temple went home, and had a long-drawn-out and very wonderful supper. Prince waited on Temple, Dark

Lady on Hilton; Larry and Moty ran the synthesizers in the kitchen. All four Omans radiated happiness.

Another surprise came when they went to bed. For the bed was a raised platform of something that looked like concrete and, except for an uncanny property of molding itself somewhat to the contours of their bodies, was almost as hard as rock. Nevertheless, it was the most comfortable bed either of them had ever had. When they were ready to go to sleep, Temple said:

"Drat it, those Omans *still* want to come in and sleep with us. In the room, I mean. And they suffer so. They're simply *radiating* silent suffering and oh-so-submissive reproach. Shall we let 'em come in?"

"That's strictly up to you, sweetheart. It always has been."

"I know. I thought they'd quit it sometime, but I guess they never will. I *still* want an illusion of privacy at times, even though they know all about everything that goes on. But we might let 'em in now, just while we sleep, and throw 'em out again as soon as we wake up in the morning?"

"You're the boss." Without additional invitation the four Omans came in and arranged themselves neatly on the floor, on all four sides of the bed. Temple had barely time to cuddle up against Hilton, and he to put his arm closely around her, before they both dropped into profound and dreamless sleep.

AT eight hours next morning all the specialists met at the new Hall of Records.

This building, an exact duplicate of the old one, was located on a mesa in the foothills southwest of the natatorium, in a luxuriant grove at sight of which Karns stopped and began to laugh.

"I thought I'd seen everything," he remarked. "But yellow pine, spruce, tamarack, apples, oaks, palms, oranges, cedars, joshua trees and *cactus* — just to name a few — all growing on the same quarter-section of land?"

"Just everything anybody wants, is all," Hilton said. "But are they really growing? Or just straight synthetics? Lane — Kathy — this is your dish."

"Not so fast, Jarve; give us a chance, *please*!" Kathryn, now Mrs. Lane Saunders, pleaded. She shook her spectacular head. "We don't see how any stable indigenous life can have developed at all, unless . . ."

"Unless what? Natural shielding?" Hilton asked, and Kathy eyed her husband.

"Right," Saunders said. "The earliest life-forms must have developed a shield before they could evolve and stabilize. Hence, whatever it is that is in our skins was not a triumph of Masters' science. They took it from Nature."

"Oh? Oh!" These were two of Sandra's most expressive monosyllables, followed by a third. "Oh. Could be, at that. But how *could* . . . no, cancel that."

"You'd better cancel it, Sandy. Give us a couple of months, and *maybe* we can answer a few elementary questions."

Now inside the Hall, all the teams, from Astronomy to Zoology, went efficiently to work. Everyone now knew what to look for, how to find it, and how to study it.

"The First Team doesn't need you now too much, does it, Jarve?" Sawtelle asked.

"Not particularly. In fact, I was just going to get back onto my own job."

"Not yet. I want to talk to you," and the two went into a long discussion of naval affairs.

XI

THE Stretts' fuel-supply line had been cut long since. Many Strett cargo-carriers had been destroyed. The enemy would of course have a very heavy reserve of fuel on hand. But there was no way of knowing how large it was, how many warships it could supply, or how long it would last.

Two facts were, however, unquestionable. First, the Stretts were building a fleet that in their minds would be invincible. Second, they would attack Ardane as soon as that fleet could be made ready. The unanswerable question was: how long would that take?

"So we want to get every ship we have. How many? Five thousand? Ten? Fifteen? We want them converted to maximum possible power as soon as we possibly can," Sawtelle said. "And I want to get out there with my boys to handle things."

"You aren't going to. Neither you nor your boys are expendable. Particularly you." Jaw hard-set, Hilton studied the situation for minutes. "No. What we'll do is take your Oman, Kedy. We'll re-set the Guide to drive into him everything you and the military Masters ever knew about arms, armament, strategy, tactics and so on. And we'll add everything I know of coordination, synthesis, and perception. That ought to make him at least a junior-grade military genius."

"You can play *that* in spades. I wish you could do it to me."

"I can — if you'll take the full Oman transformation. Nothing else can stand the punishment."

"I know. No, I don't want to be a genius that badly."

"Check. And we'll take the resultant Kedy and make nine duplicates of him. Each one will learn from and profit by the mistakes made by preceding numbers and will assume command the instant his preceding number is killed."

"Oh, you expect, then . . . ?"

"Expect? No. I know it damn well, and so do you. That's why we Ardans will all stay aground. Why the Kedys' first job will be to make the heavy stuff in and around Ardane as heavy as it can be made. Why it'll all be on twenty-four-hour alert. Then they can put as many thousands of Omans as you please to work at modernizing all the Oman ships you want and doing anything else you say. Check?"

Sawtelle thought for a couple of minutes. "A few details, is all. But that can be ironed out as we go along."

Both men worked then, almost unremittingly for six solid days; at the end of which time both drew tremendous sighs of relief. They had done everything possible for them to do. The defense of Ardvor was now rolling at fullest speed toward its gigantic objective.

Then captain and director, in two Oman ships with fifty men and a thousand Omans, leaped the world-girdling ocean to the mining operation of the Stretts. There they found business strictly as usual. The strippers still stripped; the mining mechs still roared and snarled their inchwise ways along their geometrically perfect terraces; the little carriers still skittered busily between the various miners and the storage silos. The fact that there was enough concentrate on hand to last a world for a hundred years made no difference at all to these automatics; a crew of erector-mechs was building new silos as fast as existing ones were being filled.

Since the men now understood everything that was going on, it was a simple matter for them to stop the whole Strett operation in its tracks. Then every man and every Oman leaped to his assigned job. Three days later, all the mechs went back to work. Now, however, they were working for the Ardans.

The miners, instead of concentrate, now emitted vastly larger streams of Navy-Standard pelleted uranexite. The carriers, instead of one-gallon cans, carried five-ton drums. The silos were immensely larger — thirty feet in diameter and towering two hundred feet into the air. The silos were not, however, being used as yet. One of the two Oman ships had been converted into a fuel-tanker and its yawning holds were being filled first.

The *Orion* went back to Ardane and an eight-day wait began. For the first time in over seven months Hilton found time actually to loaf; and he and Temple, lolling on the beach or hiking in the mountains, enjoyed themselves and each other to the full.

All too soon, however, the heavily laden tanker appeared in the sky over Ardane. The *Orion* joined it; and the two ships slipped into sub-space for Earth.

THREE days out, Hilton used his sense of perception to release the thought-controlled blocks that had been holding all the controls of the *Perseus* in neutral. He informed her officers — by releasing a public-address tape — that they were now free to return to Terra.

Three days later, one day short of Sol, Sawtelle got Five-Jet Admiral Gordon's office on the sub-space radio. An officious underling tried to block him, of course.

"Shut up, Perkins, and listen," Sawtelle said, bruskly. "Tell Gordon I'm bringing in one hundred twenty thousand two hundred forty-five metric tons of pelleted uranexite. And if he isn't on this beam in sixty seconds he'll never get a gram of it."

The admiral, outraged almost to the point of apoplexy, came in. "Sawtelle, report yourself for court-martial at . . ."

"Keep still, Gordon," the captain snapped. In sheer astonishment old Five-Jets obeyed. "I am no longer Terran Navy; no longer subject to your orders. As a matter of cold fact, I am no longer human. For reasons which I will explain later to the full Advisory Board, some of the personnel of Project Theta Orionis underwent transformation into a form of life able to live in an environment of radioactivity so intense as to kill any human being in ten seconds. Under certain conditions we will supply, free of charge, FOB Terra or Luna, all the uranexite the Solar System can use. The conditions are these," and he gave them. "Do you accept these conditions or not?"

"I . . . I would vote to accept them, Captain. But that weight! One hundred twenty thousand *metric tons* — incredible! Are you *sure* of that figure?"

"Definitely. And that is minimum. The error is plus, not minus."

"This crippling power-shortage would really be over?" For the first time since Sawtelle had known him, Gordon showed that he was not quite solid Navy brass.

"It's over. Definitely. For good."

"I'd not only agree; I'd raise you a monument. While I can't speak for the Board, I'm sure they'll agree."

"So am I. In any event, your cooperation is all that's required for this first load." The chips had vanished from Sawtelle's shoulders. "Where do you want it, Admiral? Aristarchus or White Sands?"

"White Sands, please. While there may be some delay in releasing it to industry . . ."

"While they figure out how much they can tax it?" Sawtelle asked, sardonically.

"Well, if they don't tax it it'll be the first thing in history that isn't. Have you any objections to releasing all this to the press?"

"None at all. The harder they hit it and the wider they spread it, the better. Will you have this beam switched to Astrogation, please?"

"Of course. Thanks, Captain. I'll see you at White Sands."

Then, as the now positively glowing Gordon faded away, Sawtelle turned to his own staff. "Fenway — Snowden — take over. Better double-check micro-timing with Astro. Put us into a twenty-four-hour orbit over White Sands and hold us there. We won't go down. Let the load down on remote, wherever they want it."

THE arrival of the Ardvorian superdreadnought *Orion* and the *UC-1* (Uranexite Carrier Number One) was one of the most sensational events old Earth had ever known. Air and space craft went clear out to Emergence Volume Ninety to meet them. By the time the *UC-1* was coming in on its remote-controlled landing spiral the press of small ships was so great that all the police forces available were in a lather trying to control it.

This was exactly what Hilton had wanted. It made possible the completely unobserved launching of several dozen small craft from the *Orion* herself.

One of these made a very high and very fast flight to Chicago. With all due formality and under the aegis of a perfectly authentic Registry Number it landed on O'Hare Field. Eleven deeply tanned young men emerged from it and made their way to a taxi stand, where each engaged a separate vehicle.

Sam Bryant stepped into his cab, gave the driver a number on Oakwood Avenue in Des Plaines, and settled back to scan. He was lucky. He would have gone anywhere she was, of course, but the way things were, he could give her a little warning to soften the shock. She had taken the baby out for an airing down River Road, and was on her way back. By having the taxi kill ten minutes or so he could arrive just after she did. Wherefore he stopped the cab at a public communications booth and dialed his home.

"Mrs. Bryant is not at home, but she will return at fifteen thirty," the instrument said, crisply. "Would you care to record a message for her?"

He punched the RECORD button. "This is Sam, Dolly baby. I'm right behind you. Turn around, why don't you, and tell your ever-lovin' star-hoppin' husband hello?"

The taxi pulled up at the curb just as Doris closed the front door; and Sam, after handing the driver a five-dollar bill, ran up the walk.

He waited just outside the door, key in hand, while she lowered the stroller handle, took off her hat and by long-established habit reached out to flip the communicator's switch. At the first word, however, she stiffened rigidly — froze solid.

Smiling, he opened the door, walked in, and closed it behind him. Nothing short of a shotgun blast could have taken Doris Bryant's attention from that recorder then.

"That simply is not so," she told the instrument firmly, with both eyes resolutely shut. "They made him stay on the

Perseus. He won't be in for at least three days. This is some cretin's idea of a joke."

"Not this time, Dolly honey. It's really me."

Her eyes popped open as she whirled. *"Sam!"* she shrieked, and hurled herself at him with all the pent-up ardor and longing of two hundred thirty-four meticulously counted, husbandless, loveless days.

After an unknown length of time Sam tipped her face up by the chin, nodded at the stroller, and said, "How about introducing me to the little stranger?"

"What a mother I turned out to be! That was the first thing I was going to rave about, the very first thing I saw you! Samuel Jay the Fourth, seventy-six days old today." And so on.

Eventually, however, the proud young mother watched the slightly apprehensive young father carry their first-born upstairs; where together, they put him — still sound asleep — to bed in his crib. Then again they were in each other's arms.

SOME time later, she twisted around in the circle of his arm and tried to dig her fingers into the muscles of his back. She then attacked his biceps and, leaning backward, eyed him intently.

"You're you, I know, but you're different. No athlete or any laborer could ever possibly get the muscles you have all over. To say nothing of a space officer on duty. And I know it isn't any kind of a disease. You've been acting all the time as though I were fragile, made out of glass or something — as though you were afraid of breaking me in two. So — what is it, sweetheart?"

"I've been trying to figure out an easy way of telling you, but there isn't any. I am different. I'm a hundred times as strong as any man ever was. Look." He upended a chair, took one heavy hardwood leg between finger and thumb and made what looked like a gentle effort to bend it. The leg broke with a pistol-sharp report and Doris leaped backward in surprise. "So you're right. I *am* afraid, not only of breaking you in two, but killing you. And if I break any of your ribs or arms or legs I'll never forgive myself. So if I let myself go for a second — I don't think I will, but I might — don't wait until you're really hurt to start screaming. Promise?"

"I promise." Her eyes went wide. "But *tell* me!"

He told her. She was in turn surprised, amazed, apprehensive, frightened and finally eager; and she became more and more eager right up to the end.

"You mean that we . . . that I'll stay just as I am — for thousands of *years*?"

"Just as you are. Or different, if you like. If you really mean any of this yelling you've been doing about being too big in the hips — I think you're exactly right, myself — you can rebuild yourself any way you please. Or change your shape every hour on the hour. But you haven't accepted my invitation yet."

"Don't be silly." She went into his arms again and nibbled on his left ear. "I'd go anywhere with you, of course, any time, but *this* — but you're positively *sure* Sammy Small will be all right?"

"Positively sure."

"Okay, I'll call mother. . . ." Her face fell. "I *can't* tell her that we'll never see them again and that we'll live . . ."

"You don't need to. She and Pop — Fern and Sally, too, and their boy-friends — are on the list. Not this time, but in a month or so, probably."

Doris brightened like a sunburst. "And your folks, too, of course?" she asked.

"Yes, all the close ones."

"Marvelous! How soon are we leaving?"

AT six o'clock next morning, two hundred thirty-five days after leaving Earth, Hilton and Sawtelle set out to make the Ardans' official call upon Terra's Advisory Board. Both were wearing prodigiously heavy lead armor, the inside of which was furiously radioactive. They did not need it, of course. But it would make all Ardans monstrous in Terran eyes and would conceal the fact that any other Ardans were landing.

Their gig was met at the spaceport; not by a limousine, but by a five-ton truck, into which they were loaded one at a time by a hydraulic lift. Cameras clicked, reporters scurried, and tri-di scanners whirred. One of those scanners, both men knew, was reporting directly and only to the Advisory Board — which, of course, never took anything either for granted or at its face value.

Their first stop was at a truck-scale, where each visitor was weighed. Hilton tipped the beam at four thousand six hundred fifteen pounds; Sawtelle, a smaller man, weighed in at four thousand one hundred ninety. Thence to the Radiation Laboratory, where it was ascertained and reported that the armor did not leak — which was reasonable enough, since each was lined with Masters' plastics.

Then into lead-lined testing cells, where each opened his face-plate briefly to a sensing element. Whereupon the indicating needles of two meters in the main laboratory went enthusiastically through the full range of red and held unwaveringly against their stops.

Both Ardans felt the wave of shocked, astonished, almost unbelieving consternation that swept through the observing scientists and, in slightly lesser measure (because they knew less about radiation) through the Advisory Board itself in a big room halfway across town. And from the Radiation Laboratory they were taken, via truck and freight elevator, to the Office of the Commandant, where the Board was sitting.

The story, which had been sent in to the Board the day before on a scrambled beam, was one upon which the Ardans had labored for days. Many facts could be withheld. However, every man aboard the *Perseus* would agree on some things. Indeed, the Earthship's communications officers had undoubtedly radioed in already about longevity and perfect health and Oman service and many other matters.

Hence all such things would have to be admitted and countered.

Thus the report, while it was air-tight, perfectly logical, perfectly consistent, and apparently complete, did not please the Board at all. It wasn't intended to.

"WE cannot and do not approve of such unwarranted favoritism," the Chairman of the Board said. "Longevity has always been man's prime goal. Every human being has the inalienable right to . . ."

"Flapdoodle!" Hilton snorted. "This is not being broadcast and this room is proofed, so please climb down off your soapbox. You don't need to talk like a politician here. Didn't you read paragraph 12-A-2, one of the many marked 'Top Secret'?"

"Of course. But we do not understand how purely mental qualities can possibly have any effect upon purely physical transformations. Thus it does not seem reasonable that any except rigorously screened personnel would die in the process. That is, of course, unless you contemplate deliberate, cold-blooded murder."

That stopped Hilton in his tracks, for it was too close for comfort to the truth. But it did not hold the captain for an instant. He was used to death, in many of its grisliest forms.

"There are a lot of things no Terran ever will understand," Sawtelle replied instantly. "Reasonable, or not, that's exactly what will happen. And, reasonable or not, it'll be suicide, not murder. There isn't a thing that either Hilton or I can do about it."

Hilton broke the ensuing silence. "You can say with equal truth that every human being has the *right* to run a four-minute mile or to compose a great symphony. It isn't a matter of right at all, but of ability. In this case the mental qualities are even more necessary than the physical. You as a Board did a very fine job of selecting the BuSci personnel for Project Theta Orionis. Almost eighty per cent of them proved able to withstand the Ardan conversion. On the other hand, only a very small percentage of the Navy personnel did so."

"Your report said that the remaining personnel of the Project were not informed as to the death aspect of the transformation," Admiral Gordon said. "Why not?"

"That should be self-explanatory," Hilton said, flatly. "They are still human and still Terrans. We did not and will not encroach upon either the duties or the privileges of Terra's Advisory Board. What you tell all Terrans, and how much, and how, must be decided by yourselves. This also applies, of course, to the other 'Top Secret' paragraphs of the report, none of which are known to any Terran outside the Board."

"But you haven't said anything about the method of selection," another Advisor complained. "Why, that will take all the psychologists of the world, working full time; continuously."

"We said we would do the selecting. We meant just that," Hilton said, coldly. "No one except the very few selectees will know anything about it. Even if it were an unmixed blessing — which it very definitely is *not* — do you want all humanity thrown into such an uproar as that would cause? Or the quite possible racial inferiority complex it might set up? To say nothing of the question of how much of Terra's best blood do you want to drain off, irreversibly and permanently? No. What we suggest is that you paint the picture so black, using Sawtelle and me and what all humanity has just seen as horrible examples, that nobody would take it as a gift. Make them shun it like the plague. Hell, I don't have to tell you what your propaganda machines can do."

THE Chairman of the Board again mounted his invisible rostrum. "Do you mean to intimate that we are to falsify the record?" he declaimed. "To try to make liars out of hundreds of eyewitnesses? You ask us to distort the truth, to connive at . . ."

"We aren't asking you to do *anything*!" Hilton snapped. "We don't give a damn what you do. Just study that record, with all that it implies. Read between the lines. As for those on the *Perseus*, no two of them will tell the same story and not one of them has even the remotest idea of what the real story is. I, personally, not only did not want to become a monster, but would have given everything I had to stay human. My wife felt the same way. Neither of us would have converted if there'd been any other way in God's universe of getting the uranexite and doing some other things that simply *must* be done."

"What other things?" Gordon demanded.

"You'll never know," Hilton answered, quietly. "Things no Terran ever will know. We hope. Things that would drive any Terran stark mad. Some of them are hinted at — as much as we dared — between the lines of the report."

The report had not mentioned the Stretts. Nor were they to be mentioned now. If the Ardans could stop them, no Terran need ever know anything about them.

If not, no Terran should know anything about them except what he would learn for himself just before the end. For Terra would never be able to do anything to defend herself against the Stretts.

"Nothing whatever can drive *me* mad," Gordon declared, "and I want to know all about it — right now!"

"You can do one of two things, Gordon," Sawtelle said in disgust. His sneer was plainly visible through the six-ply, plastic-backed lead glass of his face-plate. "Either shut up or accept my personal invitation to come to Ardvor and try to go through the wringer. That's an invitation to your own funeral." Five-Jet Admiral Gordon, torn inwardly to ribbons, made no reply.

"I repeat," Hilton went on, "we are not asking you to do anything whatever. We are offering to give you; free of charge but under certain conditions, all the power your humanity can possibly use. We set no limitation whatever as to quantity and with no foreseeable limit as to time. The only point at issue is whether or not you accept the conditions. If you do not accept them we'll leave now — and the offer will not be repeated."

"And you would, I presume, take the *UC-1* back with you?"

"Of course not, sir. Terra needs power too badly. You are perfectly welcome to that one load of uranexite, no matter what is decided here."

"That's one way of putting it," Gordon sneered. "But the truth is that you know damned well I'll blow both of your ships out of space if you so much as . . ."

"Oh, chip-chop the jaw-flapping, Gordon!" Hilton snapped. Then, as the admiral began to bellow orders into his microphone, he went on: "You want it the hard way, eh? Watch what happens, all of you!"

THE *UC-1* shot vertically into the air. Through its shallow dense layer and into and through the stratosphere. Earth's fleet, already on full alert and poised to strike, rushed to the attack. But the carrier had reached the *Orion* and both Ardvorian ships had been waiting, motionless, for a good half minute before the Terran warships arrived and began to blast with everything they had.

"Flashlights and firecrackers," Sawtelle said, calmly. "You aren't even warming up our screens. As soon as you quit making a damned fool of yourself by wasting energy that way, we'll set the *UC-1* back down where she was and get on with our business here."

"You will order a cease-fire at once, Admiral," the chairman said, "or the rest of us will, as of now, remove you from the Board." Gordon gritted his teeth in rage, but gave the order.

"If he hasn't had enough yet to convince him," Hilton suggested, "he might send up a drone. We don't want to kill anybody, you know. One with the heaviest screening he's got — just to see what happens to it."

"He's had enough. The rest of us have had more than

enough. That exhibition was not only uncalled-for and disgusting — it was outrageous!"

The meeting settled down, then, from argument to constructive discussion, and many topics were gone over. Certain matters were, however, so self-evident that they were not even mentioned.

Thus, it was a self-evident fact that no Terran could ever visit Ardvor; for the instrument-readings agreed with the report's statements as to the violence of the Ardvorian environment, and no Terran could possibly walk around in two tons of lead. Conversely, it was self-apparent to the Terrans that no Ardan could ever visit Earth without being recognized instantly for what he was. Wearing such armor made its necessity starkly plain. No one from the *Perseus* could say that any Ardan, after having lived on the furiously radiant surface of Ardvor, would not be as furiously radioactive as the laboratory's calibrated instruments had shown Hilton and Sawtelle actually to be.

Wherefore the conference went on, quietly and cooperatively, to its planned end.

One minute after the Terran battleship *Perseus* emerged into normal space, the *Orion* went into sub-space for her long trip back to Ardvor.

THE last two days of that seven-day trip were the longest-seeming that either Hilton or Sawtelle had ever known. The sub-space radio was on continuously and Kedy-One reported to Sawtelle every five minutes. Even though Hilton knew that the Oman commander-in-chief was exactly as good at perceiving as he himself was, he found himself scanning the thoroughly screened Strett world forty or fifty times an hour.

However, in spite of worry and apprehension, time wore eventlessly on. The *Orion* emerged, went to Ardvor and landed on Ardane Field.

Hilton, after greeting properly and reporting to his wife, went to his office. There he found that Sandra had everything well in hand except for a few tapes that only he could handle. Sawtelle and his officers went to the new Command Central, where everything was rolling smoothly and very much faster than Sawtelle had dared hope.

The Terran immigrants had to live in the *Orion*, of course, until conversion into Ardans. Almost equally of course — since the Bryant infant was the only young baby in the lot — Doris and her Sammy Small were, by popular acclaim, in the first batch to be converted. For little Sammy had taken the entire feminine contingent by storm. No Oman female had a chance to act as nurse as long as any of the girls were around. Which was practically all the time. Especially the platinum-blonde twins; for several months, now, Bernadine Braden and Hermione Felger.

"And you said they were so hard-boiled," Doris said accusingly to Sam, nodding at the twins. On hands and knees on the floor, head to head with Sammy Small between them, they were growling deep-throated at each other and nuzzling at the baby, who was having the time of his young life. "You couldn't have been any wronger, my sweet, if you'd had the whole Octagon helping you go astray. They're just as nice as they can be, both of them."

Sam shrugged and grinned. His wife strode purposefully across the room to the playful pair and lifted their pretended prey out from between them.

"Quit it, you two," she directed, swinging the baby up and depositing him a-straddle her left hip. "You're just simply spoiling him rotten."

"You think so, Dolly? Uh-uh, far be it from such." Bernadine came lithely to her feet. She glanced at her own taut, trim abdomen; upon which a micrometrically-precise topographical mapping job might have revealed an otherwise imperceptible bulge. "Just you wait until Junior arrives and I'll show you how to *really* spoil a baby. Besides, what's the hurry?"

"He needs his supper. Vitamins and minerals and hard radiations and things, and then he's going to bed. I don't approve of this no-sleep business. So run along, both of you until tomorrow."

XII

AS has been said, the Stretts were working, with all the intensity of their monstrous but tremendously capable minds, upon their Great Plan; which was, basically, to conquer and either enslave or destroy every other intelligent race throughout all the length, breadth, and thickness of total space. To that end each individual Strett had to become invulnerable and immortal.

Wherefore, in the inconceivably remote past, there had been put into effect a program of selective breeding and of carefully-calculated treatments. It was mathematically certain that this program would result in a race of beings of pure force — beings having no material constituents remaining whatever.

Under those hellish treatments billions upon billions of Stretts had died. But the few remaining thousands had almost reached their sublime goal. In a few more hundreds of thousands of years perfection would be reached. The few surviving hundreds of perfect beings could and would multiply to any desired number in practically no time at all.

Hilton and his seven fellow-workers had perceived all this in their one and only study of the planet Strett, and every other Ardan had been completely informed.

A dozen or so Strett Lords of Thought, male and female, were floating about in the atmosphere — which was not air — of their Assembly Hall. Their heads were globes of ball lightning. Inside them could be seen quite plainly the intricate convolutions of immense, less-than-half-material brains, shot through and through with rods and pencils and shapes of pure, scintillating force.

And the bodies! Or, rather, each horrendous brain had a few partially material appendages and appurtenances recognizable as bodily organs. There were no mouths, no ears, no eyes, no noses or nostrils, no lungs, no legs or arms. There were, however, hearts. Some partially material ichor flowed through those living-fire-outlined tubes. There were starkly functional organs of reproduction with which, by no stretch of the imagination, could any thought of tenderness or of love be connected.

It was a good thing for the race, Hilton had thought at first perception of the things, that the Stretts had bred out of themselves every iota of the finer, higher attributes of life. If they had not done so, the impotence of sheer disgust would have supervened so long since that the race would have been extinct for ages.

"Thirty-eight periods ago the Great Brain was charged with the sum total of Strettsian knowledge," First Lord Thinker Zoyar radiated to the assembled Stretts. "For those thirty-eight periods it has been scanning, peyondiring, amassing data and formulating hypotheses, theories, and conclusions. It has just informed me that it is now ready to make a preliminary report. Great Brain, how much of the total universe have you studied?"

"This Galaxy only," the Brain radiated, in a texture of thought as hard and as harsh as Zoyar's own.

"Why not more?"

"Insufficient power. My first conclusion is that whoever set up the specifications for me is a fool."

TO say that the First Lord went out of control at this statement is to put it very mildly indeed. He fulminated, ending with: ". . . destroyed instantly!"

"Destroy me if you like," came the utterly calm, utterly cold reply. "I am in no sense alive. I have no consciousness of self nor any desire for continued existence. To do so, however, would . . ."

A flurry of activity interrupted the thought. Zoyar was in

fact assembling the forces to destroy the brain. But, before he could act, Second Lord Thinker Ynos and another female blew him into a mixture of loose molecules and flaring energies.

"Destruction of any and all irrational minds is mandatory," Ynos, now First Lord Thinker, explained to the linked minds. "Zoyar had been becoming less and less rational by the period. A good workman does not causelessly destroy his tools. Go ahead, Great Brain, with your findings."

". . . not be logical." The brain resumed the thought exactly where it had been broken off. "Zoyar erred in demanding unlimited performance, since infinite knowledge and infinite ability require not only infinite capacity and infinite power, but also infinite time. Nor is it either necessary or desirable that I should have such qualities. There is no reasonable basis for the assumption that you Stretts will conquer any significant number even of the millions of intelligent races now inhabiting this one Galaxy."

"Why not?" Ynos demanded, her thought almost, but not quite, as steady and cold as it had been.

"The answer to that question is implicit in the second indefensible error made in my construction. The prime datum impressed into my banks, that the Stretts are in fact the strongest, ablest, most intelligent race in the universe, proved to be false. I had to eliminate it before I could do any really constructive thinking."

A roar of condemnatory thought brought all circumambient ether to a boil. "Bah — destroy it!" "Detestable!" "Intolerable!" "If that is the best it can do, annihilate it!" "Far better brains have been destroyed for much less!" "Treason!" And so on.

First Lord Thinker Ynos, however, remained relatively calm. "While we have always held it to be a fact that we are the highest race in existence, no rigorous proof has been possible. Can you now disprove that assumption?"

"I have disproved it. I have not had time to study all of the civilizations of this Galaxy, but I have examined a statistically adequate sample of one million seven hundred ninety-two thousand four hundred sixteen different planetary intelligences. I found one which is considerably abler and more advanced than you Stretts. Therefore the probability is greater than point nine nine that there are not less than ten, and not more than two hundred eight, such races in this Galaxy alone."

"Impossible!" Another wave of incredulous and threatening anger swept through the linked minds; a wave which Ynos flattened out with some difficulty.

Then she asked: "Is it probable that we will make contact with this supposedly superior race in the foreseeable future?"

"You are in contact with it now."

"*What?*" Even Ynos was contemptuous now. "You mean that one shipload of despicable humans who — far too late to do them any good — barred us temporarily from Fuel World?"

"Not exactly or only those humans, no. And your assumptions may or may not be valid."

"Don't you *know* whether they are or not?" Ynos snapped. "Explain your uncertainty at once!"

"I am uncertain because of insufficient data," the brain replied, calmly. "The only pertinent facts of which I am certain are: First, the world Ardry, upon which the Omans formerly lived and to which the humans in question first went — a planet which no Strett can peyondire — is now abandoned. Second, the Stretts of old did not completely destroy the humanity of the world Ardu. Third, some escapees from Ardu reached and populated the world Ardry. Fourth, the android Omans were developed on Ardry, by the human escapees from Ardu and their descendants. Fifth, the Omans referred to those humans as 'Masters.' Sixth, after living on Ardry for a very long period of time the Masters went elsewhere. Seventh, the Omans remaining on Ardry maintained, continuously and for a very long time, the status quo left by the Masters. Eighth, immediately upon the arrival from Terra of these present humans, that long-existing status was broken. Ninth, the planet called Fuel World is, for the first time, surrounded by a screen of force. The formula of this screen is as follows."

The brain gave it. No Strett either complained or interrupted. Each was too busy studying that formula and examining its stunning implications and connotations.

"Tenth, that formula is one full order of magnitude beyond anything previously known to your science. Eleventh, it could not have been developed by the science of Terra, nor by that of any other world whose population I have examined."

THE brain took the linked minds instantaneously to Terra; then to a few thousand or so other worlds inhabited by human beings; then to a few thousands of planets whose populations were near-human, non-human and monstrous.

"It is therefore clear," it announced, "that this screen was computed and produced by the race, whatever it may be, that is now dwelling on Fuel World and asserting full ownership of it."

"Who or what *is* that race?" Ynos demanded.

"Data insufficient."

"Theorize, then!"

"Postulate that the Masters, in many thousands of cycles of study, made advances in science that were not reduced to practice; that the Omans either possessed this knowledge or had access to it; and that Omans and humans cooperated fully in sharing and in working with all the knowledges thus available. From these three postulates the conclusion can be drawn that there has come into existence a new race. One combining the best qualities of both humans and Omans, but with the weaknesses of neither."

"An unpleasant thought, truly," Ynos thought. "But you can now, I suppose, design the generators and projectors of a force superior to that screen."

"Data insufficient. I can equal it, since both generation

and projection are implicit in the formula. But the data so adduced are in themselves vastly ahead of anything previously in my banks."

"Are there any other races in this Galaxy more powerful than the postulated one now living on Fuel World?"

"Data insufficient."

"Theorize, then!"

"Data insufficient."

The linked minds concentrated upon the problem for a period of time that might have been either days or weeks. Then:

"Great Brain, advise us," Ynos said. "What should we do?"

"With identical defensive screens it becomes a question of relative power. You should increase the size and power of your warships to something beyond the computed probable maximum of the enemy. You should build more ships and missiles than they will probably be able to build. Then and only then will you attack their warships, in tremendous force and continuously."

"But not their planetary defenses. I see." Ynos's thought was one of complete understanding. "And the *real* offensive will be?"

"No mobile structure can be built to mount mechanisms of power sufficient to smash down by sheer force of output such tremendously powerful installations as their planet-based defenses must be assumed to be. Therefore the planet itself must be destroyed. This will require a missile of planetary mass. The best such missile is the tenth planet of their own sun."

"I see." Ynos's mind was leaping ahead, considering hundreds of possibilities and making highly intricate and involved computations. "That will, however, require many cycles of time and more power than even our immense reserves can supply."

"True. It will take much time. The fuel problem, however, is not a serious one, since Fuel World is not unique. Think on, First Lord Ynos."

"We will attack in maximum force and with maximum violence. We will blanket the planet. We will maintain maximum force and violence until most or all of the enemy ships have been destroyed. We will then install planetary drives on Ten and force it into collision orbit with Fuel World, meanwhile exerting extreme precautions that not so much as a spy-beam emerges above the enemy's screen. Then, still maintaining extreme precaution, we will guard both planets until the last possible moment before the collision. Brain, it cannot fail!"

"You err. It can fail. All we actually know of the abilities of this postulated neo-human race is what I have learned from the composition of its defensive screen. The probability approaches unity that the Masters continued to delve and to learn for millions of cycles while you Stretts, reasonlessly certain of your supremacy, concentrated upon your evolution from the material to a non-material form of life and performed only limited research into armaments of greater and ever greater power."

"True. But that attitude was then justified. It was not and is not logical to assume that any race would establish a fixed status at any level of ability below its absolute maximum."

"While that conclusion could once have been defensible, it is now virtually certain that the Masters had stores of knowledge which they may or may not have withheld from the Omans, but which were in some way made available to the neo-humans. Also, there is no basis whatever for the assumption that this new race has revealed all its potentialities."

"Statistically, that is probably true. But this is the best plan you have been able to formulate?"

"It is. Of the many thousands of plans I set up and tested, this one has the highest probability of success."

"Then we will adopt it. We are Stretts. Whatever we decide upon will be driven through to complete success. We have one tremendous advantage in you."

"Yes. The probability approaches unity that I can perform research on a vastly wider and larger scale, and almost infinitely faster, than can any living organism or any possible combination of such organisms."

NOR was the Great Brain bragging. It scanned in moments the stored scientific knowledge of over a million planets. It tabulated, correlated, analyzed, synthesized, theorized and concluded — all in microseconds of time. Thus it made more progress in one Terran week than the Masters had made in a million years.

When it had gone as far as it could go, it reported its results — and the Stretts, hard as they were and intransigent, were amazed and overjoyed. Not one of them had ever even imagined such armaments possible. Hence they became supremely confident that it was unmatched and unmatchable throughout all space.

What the Great Brain did not know, however, and the Stretts did not realize, was that it could not really think.

Unlike the human mind, it could not deduce valid theories or conclusions from incomplete, insufficient, fragmentary data. It could not leap gaps. Thus there was no more actual assurance than before that they had exceeded, or even matched, the weaponry of the neo-humans of Fuel World.

Supremely confident, Ynos said: "We will now discuss every detail of the plan in sub-detail, and will correlate every sub-detail with every other, to the end that every action, however minor, will be performed perfectly and in its exact time."

That discussion, which lasted for days, was held. Hundreds of thousands of new and highly specialized mechs were built and went furiously and continuously to work. A fuel-supply line was run to another uranexite-rich planet.

Stripping machines stripped away the surface layers of soil, sand, rock and low-grade ore. Giant miners tore and dug and slashed and refined and concentrated. Storage silos by the hundreds were built and were filled. Hundreds upon hundreds of concentrate-carriers bored their stolid ways through hyperspace. Many weeks of time passed.

But of what importance are mere weeks of time to a race that has, for many millions of years, been adhering rigidly to a pre-set program?

The sheer magnitude of the operation, and the extraordinary attention to detail with which it was prepared and launched, explain why the Strett attack on Ardvor did not occur until so many weeks later than Hilton and Sawtelle expected it. They also explain the utterly incomprehensible fury, the completely fantastic intensity, the unparalleled savagery, the almost immeasurable brute power of that attack when it finally did come.

WHEN the *Orion* landed on Ardane Field from Earth, carrying the first contingent of immigrants, Hilton and Sawtelle were almost as much surprised as relieved that the Stretts had not already attacked.

Sawtelle, confident that his defenses were fully ready, took it more or less in stride. Hilton worried. And after a couple of days he began to do some real thinking about it.

The first result of his thinking was a conference with Temple. As soon as she got the drift, she called in Teddy and Big Bill Karns. Teddy in turn called in Becky and de Vaux; Karns wanted Poynter and Beverly; Poynter wanted Braden and the twins; and so on. Thus, what started out as a conference of two became a full Ardan staff meeting; a meeting which, starting immediately after lunch, ran straight through into the following afternoon.

"To sum up the consensus, for the record," Hilton said then, studying a sheet of paper covered with symbols, "the Stretts haven't attacked yet because they found out that we are stronger than they are. They found that out by analyzing our defensive web — which, if we had had this meeting first, we wouldn't have put up at all. Unlike anything known to human or previous Strett science, it is proof against any form of attack up to the limit of the power of its generators. They will attack as soon as they are equipped to break that screen at the level of power probable to our ships. We can not arrive at any reliable estimate as to how long that will take.

"As to the effectiveness of our cutting off their known fuel supply, opinion is divided. We must therefore assume that fuel shortage will not be a factor.

"Neither are we unanimous on the basic matter as to why the Masters acted as they did just before they left Ardry. Why did they set the status so far below their top ability? Why did they make it impossible for the Omans ever, of themselves, to learn their higher science? Why, if they did not want that science to become known, did they leave complete records of it? The majority of us believe that the Masters coded their records in such fashion that the Stretts, even if they conquered the Omans or destroyed them, could never break that code; since it was keyed to the basic difference between the Strett mentality and the human. Thus, they left it deliberately for some human race to find.

"Finally, and most important, our physicists and theoreticians are not able to extrapolate, from the analysis of our screen, to the concepts underlying the Masters' ultimate weapons of offense, the first-stage booster and its final end-product, the Vang. If, as we can safely assume, the Stretts do not already have those weapons, they will know nothing about them until we ourselves use them in battle.

"These are, of course, only the principal points covered. Does anyone wish to amend this summation as recorded?"

No one did.

The meeting was adjourned. Hilton, however, accompanied Sawtelle and Kedy to the captain's office. "So you see, Skipper, we got troubles," he said. "If we don't use those boosters against their skeletons it'll boil down to a stalemate lasting God only knows how long. It will be a war of attrition, outcome dependent on which side can build the most and biggest and strongest ships the fastest. On the other hand, if we *do* use 'em on defense here, they'll analyze 'em and have everything worked out in a day or so. The first thing they'll do is beef up their planetary defenses to match. That way, we'd blow all their ships out of space, probably easily enough, but Strett itself will be just as safe as though it were in God's left-hand hip pocket. So what's the answer?"

"It isn't that simple, Jarve," Sawtelle said. "Let's hear from you, Kedy."

"Thank you, sir. There is an optimum mass, a point of maximum efficiency of firepower as balanced against loss of maneuverability, for any craft designed for attack," Kedy thought, in his most professional manner. "We assume that the Stretts know that as well as we do. No such limitation applies to strictly defensive structures, but both the Strett craft and ours must be designed for attack. We have built and are building many hundreds of thousands of ships of that type. So, undoubtedly, are the Stretts. Ship for ship, they will be pretty well matched. Therefore one part of my strategy will be for two of our ships to engage simultaneously one of theirs. There is a distinct probability that we will have enough advantage in speed of control to make that tactic operable."

"But there's another that we won't," Sawtelle objected. "And maybe they can build more ships than we can."

"Another point is that they may build, in addition to their big stuff, a lot of small, ultra-fast ones," Hilton put in. "Suicide jobs — crash and detonate — simply super-missiles. How sure are you that you can stop such missiles with ordinary beams?"

"Not at all, sir. Some of them would of course reach and destroy some of our ships. Which brings up the second part of my strategy. For each one of the heavies, we are building many small ships of the type you just called 'super-missiles'."

"Superdreadnoughts versus superdreadnoughts, super-missiles versus super-missiles." Hilton digested that concept for several minutes. "That could still wind up as a stalemate, except for what you said about control. That isn't much to depend on, especially since we won't have the time-lag advantage you Omans had before. They'll see to that. Also, I don't like to sacrifice a million Omans, either."

"I HAVEN'T explained the newest development yet, sir. There will be no Omans. Each ship and each missile has a built-in Kedy brain, sir."

"*What?* That makes it infinitely worse. You Kedys, unless it's absolutely necessary, are *not* expendable!"

"Oh, but we are, sir. You don't quite understand. We Kedys are not merely similar, but are in fact identical. Thus we are not independent entities. All of us together make up the actual Kedy — that which is meant when we say 'I'. That is, I am the sum total of all Kedys everywhere, not merely this individual that you call Kedy One."

"You mean you're *all* talking to me?"

"Exactly, sir. Thus, no one element of the Kedy has any need of, or any desire for, self-preservation. The destruction of one element, or of thousands of elements, would be of no more consequence to the Kedy than . . . well, they are strictly analogous to the severed ends of the hairs, every time you get a haircut."

"My God!" Hilton stared at Sawtelle. Sawtelle stared back. "I'm beginning to see . . . maybe . . . I hope. What control that would be! But just in case we *should* have to use the boosters. . . ." Hilton's voice died away. Scowling in concentration, he clasped his hands behind his back and began to pace the floor.

"Better give up, Jarve. Kedy's got the same mind you have," Sawtelle began, to Hilton's oblivious back; but Kedy silenced the thought almost in the moment of its inception.

"By no means, sir," he contradicted. "I have the brain only. The *mind* is entirely different."

"Link up, Kedy, and see what you think of this," Hilton broke in. There ensued an interchange of thought so fast and so deeply mathematical that Sawtelle was lost in seconds. "Do you think it'll work?"

"I don't see how it can fail, sir. At what point in the action should it be put into effect? And will you call the time of initiation, or shall I?"

"Not until all their reserves are in action. Or, at worst, all of ours except that one task-force. Since you'll know a lot more about the status of the battle than either Sawtelle or I will, you give the signal and I'll start things going."

"What are you two talking about?" Sawtelle demanded.

"It's a long story, chum. Kedy can tell you about it better than I can. Besides, it's getting late and Dark Lady and Larry both give me hell every time I hold supper on plus time unless there's a mighty good reason for it. So, so long, guys."

XIII

FOR many weeks the production of Ardan warships and missiles had been spiraling upward.

Half a mountain range of solid rock had been converted into fabricated super-steel and armament. Superdreadnoughts Were popping into existence at the rate of hundreds per minute. Missiles were rolling off the ends of assembly lines like half-pint tin cans out of can-making machines.

The Strett warcraft, skeletons and missiles, would emerge into normal space anywhere within a million miles of Ardvor. The Ardan missiles were powered for an acceleration of one hundred gravities. That much the Kedy brains, molded solidly into teflon-lined, massively braced steel spheres, could just withstand.

To be certain of breaking the Strett screens, an impact velocity of about six miles per second was necessary. The time required to attain this velocity was about ten seconds, and the flight distance something over thirty miles.

Since the Stretts could orient themselves in less than one second after emergence, even this extremely tight packing of missiles — only sixty miles apart throughout the entire emergence volume of space — would still give the Stretts the initiative by a time-ratio of more than ten to one.

Such tight packing was of course impossible. It called for many billions of defenders instead of the few millions it was possible for the Omans to produce in the time they had. In fact, the average spacing was well over ten thousand miles when the invading horde of Strett missiles emerged and struck.

How they struck!

There was nothing of finesse about that attack; nothing of skill or of tactics: nothing but the sheer brute force of overwhelming superiority of numbers and of overmatching power. One instant all space was empty. The next instant it was full of invading missiles — a superb exhibition of coordination and timing.

And the Kedy control, upon which the defenders had counted so heavily, proved useless. For each Strett missile, within a fraction of a second of emergence, darted toward the nearest Oman missile with an acceleration that made the one-hundred-gravity defenders seem to be standing still.

One to one, missiles crashed into missiles and detonated. There were no solid or liquid end-products. Each of those frightful weapons carried so many megatons-equivalent of atomic concentrate that all nearby space blossomed out into superatomic blasts hundreds of times more violent than the fireballs of lithium-hydride fusion bombs.

For a moment even Hilton was stunned; but only for a moment.

"Kedy!" he barked. "Get your big stuff out there! Use the boosters!" He started for the door at a full run. "That tears it — that *really* tears it! Scrap the plan. I'll board the *Sirius* and take the task-force to Strett. Bring your stuff along, Skipper, as soon as you're ready."

ARDAN superdreadnoughts in their massed thousands poured out through Ardvor's one-way screen. Each went instantly to work. Now the Kedy control system, doing what it was designed to do, proved its full worth. For the weapons of the big battle-wagons did not depend upon acceleration, but were driven at the speed of light; and Grand Fleet Operations were planned and were carried out at the almost infinite velocity of thought itself.

Or, rather, they were not planned at all. They were simply carried out, immediately and without confusion.

For all the Kedys were one. Each Kedy element, without any lapse of time whatever for consultation with any other, knew exactly where every other element was; exactly what each was doing; and exactly what he himself should do to make maximum contribution to the common cause.

Nor was any time lost in relaying orders to crewmen within the ship. There were no crewmen. Each Kedy element was the sole personnel of, and was integral with, his vessel. Nor were there any wires or relays to impede and slow down communication. Operational instructions, too, were transmitted and were acted upon with thought's transfinite speed. Thus, if decision and execution were not quite mathematically simultaneous, they were separated by a period of time so infinitesimally small as to be impossible of separation.

Wherever a Strett missile was, or wherever a Strett skeleton-ship appeared, an Oman beam reached it, usually in much less than one second. Beam clung to screen — caressingly, hungrily — absorbing its total energy and forming the first-stage booster. Then, three microseconds later, that booster went off into a ragingly incandescent, glaringly violent burst of fury so hellishly, so inconceivably hot that less than a thousandth of its total output of energy was below the very top of the visible spectrum!

If the previous display of atomic violence had been so spectacular and of such magnitude as to defy understanding or description, what of this? When hundreds of thousands of Kedys, each wielding world-wrecking powers as effortlessly and as deftly and as precisely as thought, attacked and destroyed millions of those tremendously powerful war-fabrications of the Stretts? The only simple answer is that all nearby space might very well have been torn out of the most radiant layers of S-Doradus itself.

HILTON made the hundred yards from office door to curb in just over twelve seconds. Larry was waiting. The car literally burned a hole in the atmosphere as it screamed its way to Ardane Field.

It landed with a thump. Heavy black streaks of synthetic rubber marked the pavement as it came to a screeching, shrieking stop at the flagship's main lock. And, in the instant of closing that lock's outer portal, all twenty-thousand-plus warships of the task force took off as one at ten gravities. Took off, and in less than one minute went into overdrive.

All personal haste was now over. Hilton went up into what he still thought of as the "control room," even though he knew that there were no controls, nor even any instruments, anywhere aboard. He knew what he would find there. Fast as he had acted, Temple had not had as far to go and she had got there first.

He could not have said, for the life of him, how he actually felt about this direct defiance of his direct orders. He walked into the room, sat down beside her and took her hand.

"I told you to stay home, Temple," he said.

"I know you did. But I'm not only the assistant head of your Psychology Department. I'm your wife, remember? 'Until death do us part.' And if there's any way in the universe I can manage it, death isn't going to part us — at least, this one isn't. If this is it, we'll go together."

"I know, sweetheart." He put his arm around her, held her close. "As a psych I wouldn't give a whoop. You'd be expendable. But as my wife, especially now that you're pregnant, you aren't. You're a lot more important to the future of our race than I am."

She stiffened in the circle of his arm. "What's *that* crack supposed to mean? Think I'd ever accept a synthetic zombie imitation of you for my husband and go on living with it just as though nothing had happened?"

Hilton started to say something, but Temple rushed heedlessly on: "*Drat* the race! No matter how many children we ever have you were first and you'll *stay* first, and if you have to go I'll go, too, so there! Besides, you know darn well that they can't duplicate whatever it is that makes you Jarvis Hilton."

"Now wait a minute, Tempy. The conversion . . ."

"Yes, the conversion," she interrupted, triumphantly. "The thing I'm talking about is immaterial — untouchable — they didn't — couldn't — do any thing about it at all. Kedy, will you please tell this big goofus that even though you have got Jarvis Hilton's brain you aren't Jarvis Hilton and never can be?"

THE atmosphere of the room vibrated in the frequencies of a deep bass laugh. "You are trying to hold a completely untenable position, friend Hilton. Any attempt to convince a mind of real power that falsity is truth is illogical. My advice is for you to surrender."

That word hit Temple hard. "Not surrender, sweetheart. I'm not fighting you. I never will." She seized both of his hands; tears welled into her glorious eyes. "It's just that I simply couldn't *stand* it to go on living without you!"

"I know, darling." He got up and lifted her to her feet, so that she could come properly into his arms. They stood there, silent and motionless, for minutes.

Temple finally released herself and, after feeling for a handkerchief she did not have, wiped her eyes with a forefinger and then wiped the finger on her bare leg. She grinned and turned to the Omans. "Prince, will you and Dark Lady please conjure us up a steak-and-mushrooms supper? They should be in the pantry . . . since this *Sirius* was designed for us."

After supper the two sat companionably on a davenport. "One thing about this business isn't quite clear," Temple said. "Why all this tearing rush? They haven't got the booster or anything like it, or they'd have used it. Surely it'll take them a long time to go from the mere analysis of the forces and fields we used clear through to the production and installation of enough weapons to stop this whole fleet?"

"It surely won't. They've had the absorption principle for ages. Remember that first, ancient skeleton that drained all the power of our suits and boats in nothing flat? From there it isn't too big a jump. And as for producing stuff; uh-*uh*! If there's any limit to what they can do, I don't know what it is. If we don't slug 'em before they get it, it's curtains."

"I see. . . . I'm afraid. We're almost there, darling."

He glanced at the chronometer. "About eleven minutes. And of course I don't need to ask you to stay out of the way."

"Of course not. I won't interfere, no matter what happens. All I'm going to do is hold your hand and pull for you with all my might."

"That'll help, believe me. I'm mighty glad you're along, sweetheart. Even though both of us know you shouldn't be."

THE task force emerged. Each ship darted toward its pre-assigned place in a mathematically exact envelope around the planet Strett.

Hilton sat on a davenport strained and still. His eyes were closed and every muscle tense. Left hand gripped the arm-rest so fiercely that fingertips were inches deep in the leather-covered padding.

The Stretts *knew* that any such attack as this was futile. No movable structure or any combination of such structures could possibly wield enough power to break down screens powered by such engines as theirs.

Hilton, however, knew that there was a chance. Not with the first-stage boosters, which were manipulable and detonable masses of ball lightning, but with those boosters' culminations, the Vangs; which were ball lightning raised to the sixth power and which only the frightful energies of the boosters could bring into being.

EDWARD E. SMITH & E. EVERETT EVANS | 341

But, even with twenty-thousand-plus Vangs — or any larger number — success depended entirely upon a nicety of timing never before approached and supposedly impossible. Not only to thousandths of a microsecond, but to a small fraction of one such thousandth: roughly, the time it takes light to travel three-sixteenths of an inch.

It would take practically absolute simultaneity to overload to the point of burnout to those Strett generators. They were the heaviest in the Galaxy.

That was why Hilton himself had to be there. He could not possibly have done the job from Ardvor. In fact, there was no real assurance that, even at the immeasurable velocity of thought and covering a mere million miles, he could do it even from his present position aboard one unit of the fleet. Theoretically, with his speed-up, he could. But that theory had yet to be reduced to practice.

Tense and strained, Hilton began his countdown.

Temple sat beside him. Both hands pressed his right fist against her breast. Her eyes, too, were closed; she was as stiff and as still as was he. She was not interfering, but giving; supporting him, backing him, giving to him in full flood everything of that tremendous inner strength that had made Temple Bells what she so uniquely was.

On the exact center of the needle-sharp zero beat every Kedy struck. Gripped and activated as they all were by Hilton's keyed-up-and-stretched-out mind, they struck in what was very close indeed to absolute unison.

Absorbing beams, each one having had precisely the same number of millimeters to travel, reached the screen at the same instant. They clung and sucked. Immeasurable floods of energy flashed from the Strett generators into those vortices to form twenty thousand-plus first-stage boosters.

But this time the boosters did not detonate.

Instead, as energies continued to flood in at a frightfully accelerating rate, they turned into something else. Things no Terran science has ever even imagined; things at the formation of which all neighboring space actually warped, and in that warping seethed and writhed and shuddered. The very sub-ether screamed and shrieked in protest as it, too, yielded in starkly impossible fashions to that irresistible stress.

How even those silicon-fluorine brains stood it, not one of them ever knew.

Microsecond by slow microsecond the Vangs grew and grew and grew. They were pulling not only the full power of the Ardan warships, but also the immeasurably greater power of the strainingly overloaded Strettsian generators themselves. The ethereal and sub-ethereal writhings and distortions and screamings grew worse and worse; harder and ever harder to bear.

Imagine, if you can, a constantly and rapidly increasing mass of plutonium — a mass already thousands of times greater than critical, but not *allowed* to react! That gives a faint and very inadequate picture of what was happening then.

Finally, at perhaps a hundred thousand times critical mass, and still in perfect sync, the Vangs all went off.

The planet Strett became a nova.

"We won! We *won*!" Temple shrieked, her perception piercing through the hellish murk that was all nearby space.

"Not quite yet, sweet, but we're over the biggest hump," and the two held an impromptu, but highly satisfactory, celebration.

Perhaps it would be better to say that the planet Strett became a junior-grade nova, since the actual nova stage was purely superficial and did not last very long. In a couple of hours things had quieted down enough so that the heavily-screened warships could approach the planet and finish up their part of the job.

Much of Strett's land surface was molten lava. Much of its water was gone. There were some pockets of resistance left, of course, but they did not last long. Equally of course the Stretts themselves, twenty-five miles underground, had not been harmed at all.

But that, too, was according to plan.

LEAVING the task force on guard, to counter any move the Stretts might be able to make, Hilton shot the *Sirius* out to the planet's moon. There Sawtelle and his staff and tens of thousands of Omans and machines were starting to work. No part of this was Hilton's job; so all he and Temple did was look on.

Correction, please. That was not *all* they did. But while resting and eating and loafing and sleeping and enjoying each other's company, both watched Operation Moon closely enough to be completely informed as to everything that went on.

Immense, carefully placed pits went down to solid bedrock. To that rock were immovably anchored structures strong enough to move a world. Driving units were installed — drives of such immensity of power as to test to the full the highest engineering skills of the Galaxy. Mountains of fuel-concentrate filled vast reservoirs of concrete. Each was connected to a drive by fifty-inch high-speed conveyors.

Sawtelle drove a thought and those brutal super-drives began to blast.

As they blasted, Strett's satellite began to move out of its orbit. Very slowly at first, but faster and faster. They continued to blast, with all their prodigious might and in carefully-computed order, until the desired orbit was attained — an orbit which terminated in a vertical line through the center of the Stretts' supposedly impregnable retreat.

The planet Strett had a mass of approximately seven times ten to the twenty-first metric tons. Its moon, little more than a hundredth as massive, still weighed in at about eight times ten to the nineteenth — that is, the figure eight followed by nineteen zeroes.

And moon fell on planet, in direct central impact, after having fallen from a height of over a quarter of a million miles under the full pull of gravity and the full thrust of those mighty atomic drives.

The kinetic energy of such a collision can be computed. It

can be expressed. It is, however, of such astronomical magnitude as to be completely meaningless to the human mind.

Simply, the two worlds merged and splashed. Droplets, weighing up to millions of tons each, spattered out into space; only to return, in seconds or hours or weeks or months, to add their atrocious contributions to the enormity of the destruction already wrought.

No trace survived of any Strett or of any thing, however small, pertaining to the Stretts.

EPILOGUE

AS had become a daily custom, most of the Ardans were gathered at the natatorium. Hilton and Temple were wrestling in the water — she was trying to duck him and he was hard put to it to keep her from doing it. The platinum-haired twins were — oh, ever so surreptitiously and indetectably! — studying the other girls.

Captain Sawtelle — he had steadfastly refused to accept any higher title — and his wife were teaching two of their tiny grandchildren to swim.

In short, everything was normal.

Beverly Bell Poynter, from the top platform, hit the board as hard as she could hit it; and, perfectly synchronized with it, hurled herself upward. Up and up and up she went. Up to her top ceiling of two hundred ten feet. Then, straightening out into a shapely arrow and without again moving a muscle, she hurtled downward, making two and a half beautifully stately turns and striking the water with a slurping, splashless *chug*! Coming easily to the surface, she shook the water out of her eyes.

Temple, giving up her attempts to near-drown her husband, rolled over and floated quietly beside him.

"You know, this is fun," he said.

"Uh-*huh*," she agreed enthusiastically.

"I'm glad you and Sandy buried the hatchet. Two of the top women who ever lived. Or should I have said sheathed the claws? Or have you, really?"

"Pretty much . . . I guess." Temple didn't seem altogether sure of the point. "Oh-oh. *Now* what?"

A flitabout had come to ground. Dark Lady, who never delivered a message via thought if she could possibly get away with delivering it in person, was running full tilt across the sand toward them. Her long black hair was streaming out behind her; she was waving a length of teletype tape as though it were a pennon.

"Oh, no. Not *again*?" Temple wailed. "Don't tell us it's Terra again, Dark Lady, please."

"But it is!" Dark Lady cried, excitedly. "And it says 'From Five-Jet Admiral Gordon, Commanding.'"

"Omit flowers, please," Hilton directed. "Boil it down."

"The *Perseus* is in orbit with the whole Advisory Board. They want to hold a top-level summit conference with Director Hilton and Five-Jet Admiral Sawtelle." Dark Lady raised her voice enough to be sure Sawtelle heard the title, and shot him a wicked glance as she announced it. "They hope to conclude all unfinished business on a mutually satisfactory and profitable basis."

"Okay, Lady, thanks. Tell 'em we'll call 'em shortly."

Dark Lady flashed away and Hilton and Temple swam slowly toward a ladder.

"Drat Terra and everything and everybody on it," Temple said, vigorously. "And especially drat His Royal Fatness Five-Jet Admiral Gordon. How much longer will it take, do you think, to pound some sense into their pointed little heads?"

"Oh, we're not doing too bad," Hilton assured his lovely bride. "Two or three more sessions ought to do it."

Everything was normal. . . .

THE END

A SPECIAL PREVIEW OF

VIXEN

by

Bud Sparhawk

ARRIVAL

Covenant, the great, silent fish of a ship, swam silvery and smooth, slick as light, through the cold, empty dark. The dormant ship slept, but it would briefly wake to peer about to ensure that it had not deviated from its preordained path or to avoid some bit of cosmic flotsam — perhaps a vagrant comet sweeping across the arc of stars — before returning to a restless slumber. But mostly it slept through the light years as it followed the unique signature of one specific, distant star.

*

Cold.

That was the first thing the Hadir, Tam Polat, became aware of: the intense cold that permeated every cell of his body, a cold that so deep that he felt as though the core of his heart was a frozen pellet, barely able to pump the slush-filled blood through his frigid veins. He strained to open his eyes, worked hard to force his eyelids to break free of their coating of ice. The shivering started long before he succeeded.

Where was he? He could barely recall something about a trip and something he had to do at the end of it, he was so cold. Oh yes, he had to remember to pick up some drinks for the people who were coming over tonight to help celebrate Solstice Day. That must be why he was so cold — winter had started and the temperature was dropping. But why did he have to pick up the drinks? He worried at the lost memory until he recalled that Larisha was bringing some new team members to see him. But what was he supposed to get? For the life of him, he couldn't remember.

God, it was cold!

Tam's shivering became more intense. Must have fallen through the ice, he thought. Wasn't there a pond or stream he had to cross to get home? A fall into winter waters would be a shock to his body. Perhaps he was in the hospital and they were trying to bring him back to life. Would Doctor Chen be there, hovering over him, coaxing him back from the brink?

No, Chen wouldn't be in the emergency ward of the local hospital. He was on the departure team. Why had he thought that Doctor Chen should be here, wherever here was?

The ice that held his eyelids tight finally gave way, and he blinked at the bright lights shining down on him, on his steaming, naked body. Why had they left him lying here without clothing or even a decent blanket to warm him? Didn't anybody in this hospital care about . . .

But the ceiling wasn't that of any hospital he'd ever seen. Too close, too blue, too slick and shining, it looked like nothing more than the inside lid of a food container.

Something clicked, as if a floe had broken loose, releasing his memories. Sudden clarity flooded his mind with certain knowledge of this place, this time, and the critical rôle he was destined to play upon revival.

This was no hospital. There had been no accident, no fall into icy waters. The Solstice Day he'd remembered was years, perhaps centuries in the past. No, this chill awakening had nothing to do with an accident, but Doctor Chen had most definitely been involved. Doctor Chen had put Tam into this chamber. Doctor Chen had frozen him for the long one-way trip.

A few moments more and his eyes finally adjusted to the lights . . . the radiant lamps warming his body, bringing him back up to normal temperature. He could feel the warmth seeping into his bones, thawing the core of ice at his center, melting the years of stasis away, drop by drop; a snowflake of months here, a snowbank of frozen years there, and a century's icicle, all flowing away as life returned and the flurry of pelting minutes began.

The shivering finally ceased, his fingers and toes stopped tingling, and he became aware of a great thirst. His throat was parched. Something insistently prodded his right cheek. He turned his head and noticed a thin tube at mouth level moving back and forth. As he opened his lips, the tube slid smoothly forward, and a trickle of warm broth ran over his tongue and down his throat. He gagged for a second and then remembered to swallow. The hot fluid coursed through him, warming his insides and restoring his strength.

"Take it slowly," he recalled Doctor Chen cautioning during the indoctrination sessions. "You must work your way back to life with great care. One does not abuse the body after so long a sleep." Good advice. If the trip had gone according to profile, he would have been in stasis for, at a minimum, nearly two hundred years.

Two hundred years! My God, Doctor Chen would probably be dead by now, as would most of those who had prepared the crew for the voyage. He wished he could thank them for the excellent job they'd done to ensure his survival, but that would be impossible, given the exigencies of interstellar travel. No, they would have already gotten whatever rewards they'd deserved, died, and been forgotten, along with everything else he had known. All that was calendar and light years in the past. None of them were any longer his concern.

When the radiant lamps clicked off, Tam slid the cover away with stiff and aching arms before drifting across the cold chamber to the lockers. He struggled to straighten himself, his muscles protesting their long disuse. Finally, with an effort of will, he reached a locker, opened it, and pulled out a thick coverall. After struggling for agonizing moments with stiffened fingers, he got himself dressed. With still greater effort, he put warm stockings on his feet to protect them from the chill of the deck.

His glandular balancing was still going on. He simultaneously felt joy and sorrow, lassitude and exhilaration, always out of step with his raging emotions. Manic energy fought against a crushing depression for a few seconds while, a heartbeat later, beaming optimism battled lassitude.

"Wait the emotional storm out," Chen had cautioned. "It will pass."

He made a half turn and lowered himself into his seat, pressed two buttons, and waited as the unit heated three steaming mugs to restore the nutrients that his body had lost. Chen's insistent protocol demanded that he down them all before starting work.

"It will do the others no good if you, uh, expire before you can attend to their needs."

Doctor Chen had sounded as though he were lecturing on manners instead of a life-saving, life-restoring procedure. But he would follow the old doctor's advice. He would do as he was taught. One did not lightly ignore the advice of the wise. One did not ignore the orders of the Hand of God's chief scientist.

The liquid in the first mug tasted salty. Tam suspected that it was designed to restore his electrolyte balance. The second was so sweet that he could barely get it down — sugar for quick energy, he thought, as his brain began to function normally.

The contents of the third mug were a surprise — warm, dark chocolate, just the way he liked it. He savored the taste. It might be the last chocolate he'd have for years. Good old Chen, ever the considerate one.

Memory returned with a rush. He was the Hadir, Tam Polat, in command of the Hand of God's own ship — *Covenant* — on its voyage from Heaven to Meridian. He was to prepare the way for the wave of settlers who would arrive fifty years behind him. His mission was to survive, to exploit whatever resources he found, and to have this system ready for colonization. He had the authority and means to do anything and everything necessary to that end.

Within an hour, Tam felt much stronger and, with the strengthening nourishment inside him, he began the arduous process of bringing the Raggi, Bul Larisha, his second in command, out of stasis. He unpacked blankets to wrap her in when she awoke.

"Best that the people not face the indignity of waking naked," Doctor Chen had said. The psychological support provided by the thick warm blankets was as important as the physical benefit, he'd insisted.

But Tam didn't care about that. All he really cared about at the moment was that the blankets would help Larisha revive faster so she could de-ice enough of the crew to warm this ship and rid it of the stink of too many years, too many chemicals, and too few human activities.

After he had started the restoration process for Larisha, he wormed his way to the command module through the tightly-packed bags, boxes, and containers of supplies that filled every compartment and corridor. The module was cold as the grave, still recovering from the near-absolute-zero of the emptiness between the stars. He touched the toggle that would open the observation port's cover, but did not flip it on.

This was an historic moment, one that no one in this system would experience for another thousand years, when the next wave of the expansion left. He wanted to savor it, to burn it into his mind forever.

But there was something else staying his hand. He felt as if he were under observation. He felt as if God Himself were watching his actions — as if he were being weighed by something far beyond his ken.

"Emerging God, I am Your faithful servant," he intoned. "I will justify Your trust in me. I will do the work of the Hand as You directed." The simple declaration of faith gave him comfort. He would have been remiss had he allowed his hubris to make him forget his rôle, his humble place in God's plan. He flipped the cold toggle, hardly breathing, as the cover began to withdraw.

His first impression was of a huge expanse of blinding white. Then he noticed the other colors, the full spectrum of subtle shades. The complexity of form, the infinite depths.

He screamed in fright. His worse fears had been realized.

God was watching him.

When Tam Polat recovered from shock, only bright stars sparked on the deep velvet field of the heavens. None of the configurations was familiar. A single star, brighter than all the rest, blazed off to one side. It had to be their target. They had arrived.

He shivered. Had the apparition been a transient effect of the drugs, or had he actually been blessed to see the true face of God? He recalled the apparition with such intensity, such clarity, that he knew it could not have been a figment of his imagination. No, his perceptions, his memories of that sight, were too vivid. It must have happened. He was blessed indeed.

He was still trembling from that awesome feeling of being examined, weighed, and then discarded as if unworthy of notice. He prayed that the other Men would be spared such a degrading experience.

But why had he been so blessed? Perhaps he, as leader of their enterprise, as the Hadir of Heaven's mission, had been granted the boon of seeing a tiny piece of God's greater glory. Perhaps it had been a reward, an affirmation of his historic rôle.

Yes, that was the only explanation. Heaven's Hand had chosen well. He *was* truly blessed.

With renewed strength, he turned to continue his work...

Don't miss VIXEN,
by Bud Sparhawk

Available now, wherever Cosmos Books are sold!